LUNARMANCER

JAKE BENNETT

Contents

Year Key

BEB:
Before End of Budúcnosť

AEB:
After End of Budúcnosť

Chapter 1

Carthage

688 A.E.B

There is a continent, a large one, made up of several islands spanning many miles and separate from the mainland. One of those islands was Carthage. Carthage had a number of pleasant little villages, but there was one in particular, the village of Reme in the southern hills where the neighbours knew each other well, and a friendly atmosphere pervaded, with very little conflict to see and hear. However, Reme was one of the few to house animals with anthropomorphic features as well as sapience. They were well known by many as metazoans. Each metazoan had a dwelling to call their own, and one, whose name was Marcarius—though everyone knew him as Mark— was resting in his house. He was a husky with silvery white fur on his body, though his shoulders, part of his back, and the top of his head and his ears were black. He wore a blue coat with a red outer garment, which were relatively clean and fur free despite his propensity to moult and sandals a little worn from countless mileage. A fire was burning while Mark slept, filling the room with heat. His desk, had a few pieces of paper and a feather quill placed upright in a jar, waiting to be used again.

Suddenly, Mark's ears pricked up as he heard a knock at the door, a gentle and firm knock at that. Mark, not wanting to leave the couch at the present time, groaned. "Ugh... Hello, what is it?" He kept his eyes shut.

"Marcarius," an elderly voice called. "Are you in? I must talk with you." Mark hoped the voice would go away.

"Door's open, feel free to come in."

The door of Mark's house opened and a large rabbit with floppy ears entered the room. His ears were covered in brown fur, while his body was an off-cream colour. The toast-coloured fur on his hands almost resembled gloves. His figure was rotund, though not fat. He held a cane in his hand. Shutting the door behind him, the rabbit, known as Chip, turned to see Mark lying on his back on his couch.

"Wake up!" Chip yelled. Without warning, Chip lifted his cane in the air, bringing it down onto Mark's nose. The husky howled in pain and immediately rose to his feet, nursing the edge of his snout.

"You didn't need to do that, Chip," Mark said, almost shocked. Chip bared his teeth for a moment.

"Stand up when your elders come into the room, boy! You have bad etiquette," the rabbit said in a frustrated tone. "I have information that might be of interest to you, so kindly lend me your ear." Mark was still nursing his snout, the pain receding.

Finally, he responded, "I'll prepare a cup of tea for you, One sugar or two?" "Make it one sugar please and with milk," Chip replied. Mark quietly
thought. *The tea will be sugary water if he is not wary.*

The two then sat down at the table after the drinks were prepared. He then felt compelled to ask why the old rabbit had paid him a visit, wondering if he was infringing any laws. His fears finally subsided as he took a sip of his tea. "What brings you here Chip?" Chip silently sipped his tea again, then promptly and gently put his teacup down.

"I found a human in the Carthagian woods," he said. Mark looked at Chip. "A human? Is that all you have to say? You came all this way to tell me about a human?" Mark said, not concealing his disappointment. "They don't usually tread into our grounds that often. Other villages they do, though not this one. They don't visit the citadel unless they are on business."

"Yes, true they do not visit often. I found her in the woods all alone," Chip said. Mark looked at Chip with a puzzled look on his face.

"Forgive me for the stupid question. But I assume you found her as a baby?" Chip nodded.

"Correct. It was on a morning stroll that I was taking. I could smell her scent a little while away. I kept my distance and saw the baby lying on the ground. She was wrapped in cloth, a little dirty although that could be dealt with. I was surprised that a baby could be left for so long without being stolen away by bandits or killed." Mark couldn't believe what he was hearing, a human baby found in the woods? *What were the odds of that?* He decided to enquire further as to where the baby was now. Chip replied she was at the citadel.

"It's safe there for now, though, if possible, I want you to raise her as your own," Chip said.

Mark didn't know what to think. He and his wife, Andrea, already had a young puppy named Tristan; it would be weird, Mark thought, to raise a human as a daughter. Mark fell silent for a few moments, wondering if he was ready to raise this baby. He turned to Chip and silently nodded. A few days later, the baby was presented to him and his wife. The child had warm beige skin and brown eyes. She attempted to reach for Mark's fur under his chin. Mark didn't hesitate in allowing the baby to touch his face and smiled at her. Their son Tristan entered the room, a small fellow with lighter fur than his father. He eyed this creature suspiciously. "That's a human?" He asked. His parents nodded, showing the odd addition to the family. Tristan tilted his head to the side.

~

706 A.E.B

The girl grew into a slender young woman. She was named Reika because Chip compared her to a flower. When Reika turned twelve, she was given to the citadel as a servant to the King Tertullian, a wise and masterful ruler. He was a gorilla, with grey fur on his body and silvery fur on his back. He too, like Chip, was a rotund beast, which was to be expected considering what he was. Reika's duties centred around the king's kitchen, serving the tables mostly, as well as general tasks, including cleaning the palace. Her respite was minimal.

She was allowed little time off, and was busy throughout her days, her only downtime in the evenings and even then, she was often required for a particular task. Not that she minded the work, she was endlessly enthusiastic at best, neutral at worst, not wanting to renounce the work until the job was done to the best reasonable standard, seeing laziness as reprehensible. For six years she continued to serve in the palace, being a great asset to the king.

Her clothes were relatively simple. She had a modest purple vest, and her pants were simple in design too. The crotch of the pants rested slightly below her knees; the legging sections of her pants were slightly lower, with yellow bands that gently clamped around her shins as well as a yellow stretching waistband holding the pants up. Her hair was black and long, coming down to the front of her shoulders as well as behind her back, resting on the higher half of her shoulder blades.

When working at the palace, she would wear her hair in a straight ponytail midway between the top and the back of her head while retaining the front bangs, removing it once the day was done or when she had time off, which on this day was the case. Her complexion was a healthy, warm beige one, with rich brown eyes that reminded one of dark autumn leaves. Beautiful, not glamorous. Nothing about her came across as ostentatious.

She was heading to Reme where she was raised by Mark, travelling along the dusty highway. Reika didn't have to go too far on foot. She had a carriage take her ten miles. When the village was close, she continued along the road alone. Reme was composed of houses made of stone that resembled gold, almost immaculate, which gave the false impression the village had only been built recently. The small houses were roughly twenty feet wide on each side, with a height of eighteen feet. Most of them were crowded to the east of the shops, except for Mark's house, which resided near the marketplace. The width of his house was greater than the others.

One of the metazoans from Reme approached her. A red squirrel, who matched the young woman's height. He had been minding a stall of his with fresh fruit and vegetables before he spotted her. "What brings you here?" He asked.

"I am here to visit my father," Reika replied.

If the squirrel thought it was unusual that a human had a father in a metazoan village, he said nothing. "Anything you would like from my stall?"

"I won't be here long, and I am meeting my friends here. But I'll get some food to have along the way for the three of us."

The squirrel handed Reika a small wheat-coloured bag containing three apples, bananas and oranges each. She paid the squirrel five small silver coins, each with an image of Tertullian on them. The squirrel was incredibly happy. "You take care of yourself," he said. Reika smiled at the squirrel as she walked away towards Mark's house.

She arrived outside and knocked on the door. Mark opened it immediately and greeted her in. As he welcomed her inside, he proceeded to walk back to his fireplace, readjusting the coals with a golden pole. The black sections of his fur had lighter shades than when he first saw Reika. "Nice to see you again," Mark said with a light smile on his face.

"How are you, Father?" Reika asked.

"Fine." He moved away from the fire back to his desk, sipping

5

the tea that he had made for himself prior to Reika's arrival. Reika's eyes scoured the room. "Where's Mother?"

"She's out back." Mark looked back at Reika as she stood in the hallway. "How is the king doing?"

"Busy," Reika said. "As always. What of Tristan?"

"He was fine last I heard. He moved in with his wife, Vita, a very polite husky. They live in one of the villages in the north. As for you, what are you planning on next today, Reika?"

"Oh, just going to spend time with Melito and Tabitha for a while and unwind."

Mark smiled back at Reika. "Well, that's good to hear."

"It's in the usual place, the Carthagian forest," Reika said. She glanced at a woodland painting resting on the mantlepiece.

"Is there any part that you haven't been to I wonder?" He said with a chuckle, knowing Reika often liked visiting the forest, even as a child.

There was a warm feeling that was in Reika's chest whenever she visited Mark. As a young girl, she had been apprehensive about serving in the palace, wondering why the two huskies left her to stay there. She had needed a few days to readjust to palace life, but that was all. She never cursed Mark or Andrea for leaving her at the palace, as it led to her meeting new friends.

Andrea walked into the house. "Sweetheart!" The two gave each other a hug. Dogs themselves did not hug, as it was uncomfortable, and they felt they could not escape. Mark and Andrea made an exception for they wanted to look after Reika and care for her.

"The king has treated you well, little one. I hope you have been eating and sleeping enough, my dear?" Andrea said as she patted Reika on the head. "I have, thanks."

"Keep at your work while you are there, Reika," Mark said. "As long as you don't slouch, I'm satisfied." He reached for a quill, dipped it in the inkpot, and began to write on a small piece of paper.

"Is there anything you need before I head off, Mark?"

"I wouldn't worry for now, just enjoy yourself with your

friends." "Thank you. Lovely to see you but I had better get going," Reika said.

"Have a good day, sweetie!" Andrea said. Mark gave Reika a hug, bidding her farewell. As Reika left the house, she spotted her friends Melito and Tabitha in the distance. Melito was a marmoset, the hair on his head was sharp and curly, with grey skin clothed in black fur and yellow eyes. He had a strange maroon birthmark on his right palm that resembled a jagged arch, while Tabitha was a tamarin, with brown eyes with dark orange skin and bright fur like a tangerine. Their height was just below Reika's eyeline. Both were wearing green trousers along with grey shoes. They also wore armoured plating on their chests.

They were royal guards for King Tertullian and had been friends with Reika ever since childhood. When Reika first arrived at the palace, Melito had taken curious interest in her. Melito had found something familiar about Reika and that familiarity had caused him to befriend this human, bringing Tabitha along.

The three exchanged their hellos, then left Reme, gently walking toward the forest in the north, back in the direction of the citadel that Reika came from. After a mile, they were taken away by the carriage who dropped Reika off at the village previously.

The three made it to the forest in good time, the sun gently beating down on their heads, and the wind singing through the trees, akin to a skilled bard. They walked beside the stream, heading west, and following it. Maple leaves were abundant, not yet on the verge of falling, instead fresh and crisp with the grass having a soft texture, one that would be a mercy to the most sensitive of feet. Reika looked at her two friends walking in front of her.

"So... what are you going to show me?" She asked. Melito looked back at her.

"Reika, it's a surprise, you'll see!" He replied. Reika outwardly looked composed. Inside, she could barely contain her excitement, going as far as saying, "Are we there yet?"

To which Tabitha replied, "Not yet. I think you are going to love this particular view."

They finally reached the end of the stream, hearing a rushing waterfall only a few feet away. Melito and Tabitha turned around. Melito raised his hand and pointed to the cliff. "Let us know what you think, Reika."

Reika walked towards the cliff, eager to behold what lay below it. She looked in awe of the sight of a large lake, so blue, majestic, almost inviting. Plenty of trees surrounded the lake with room to walk around its edge. A secondary stream also lay on the farthest side of the lake, proceeding through the forest all the way to the sea.

"This is a lovely view," Reika said, a small smile on her face. Reika moved closer to the cliff-edge while Melito and Tabitha watched from a distance.

Suddenly, the bushes to Melito's left rustled with movement. Melito swiftly glanced in the direction of the noise. A lion leapt from the shadows, catching the two metazoans by surprise.

The lion swung around and with his paw, grabbed Melito by the neck and started choking him. "You cannot stand up to me, you little fool," he growled in triumph at the monkey who was firmly in his grasp. "I'll take care of you and your friends."

The lion was Darius, tall, at least double Melito's size, with golden fur and a brown scruffy mane. He wore grey trousers coupled with thick boots, a cuff on top of each foot. Tabitha was scared, her friend trying to gasp for air desperately. "Tabs!" said Melito hoarsely. "Get... away... Take Reika... and get away from here." Darius snorted and threw Melito across the stream. Melito collided with a tree, knocking him out cold. Tabitha backed away from Darius, but another attacker clasped her in a tight grip, a black leopard named Vera, wearing similar trousers to Darius while sporting armour in the same manner as the king's guard. Vera had piercing yellow eyes with navy blue fur. Tabitha instantly recognised the leopard.

"You traitor! You dare show your face around here? Get off!" It was no use Tabitha struggling, Vera merely smirked.

Reika heard the commotion and backed off, but she was close to the cliff- face, with a foreboding drop below her. *Dead end, how am I going to get out of this?* she thought. She could hear fast, thundering footsteps pressing towards her and she saw a rhino charging. The rhino was Barzillai, sporting the same trousers as Darius, with a larger muscle tone and structure than his two comrades and only slightly taller than Darius.

Reika had no time to dodge and could only cross her arms in front of her, as futile as that defence would be. When the rhino's fist collided with her arms there was a discharge of energy. The small explosion dizzied her. Reika felt her consciousness fading, the last words she heard being, "Nowhere to go little one!" as she plummeted over the edge into the lake below. A strange looking barrier that resembled a purple, stained-glass structure surrounded her as she fell. Both were completely engulfed upon impact with the water.

"Rot in your watery grave!" Barzillai uttered as he turned from the cliff.

On the bed of the lake, the barrier dissipated, and water rushed in at her. Reika sluggishly regained consciousness. She had no idea where she was but could feel a significant weight pushing against her. She tried to take a breath, which she soon realised was a mistake. Reika felt for the bed of the lake for a moment, then promptly pushed herself off the ground. She swam up to the surface of the water, the light of the sun growing in intensity the closer she got to the surface.

When she breached out of the water, she took a massive gulp of air. She steadied herself, allowing her arms to lie on the water with her legs keeping her afloat. *I should have been dead from that fall, and if not, I should have drowned.* Reika thought. *How do I get up the cliff?* She began wonder if Melito and Tabitha were ok. Thinking of the possibility of herself getting caught, Reika went under the surface of the water and swam to the shore as fast as she could. She climbed out of the water and found the path of the stream then walked alongside it.

After about an hour, Reika's clothes had dried in the sun, though the smell of the lake, while not terrible, stuck to her like sap. She thought about Vera, who she knew as the former captain of Tertullian's royal guard. Her successor, Ignatius, had taken over after Vera had sided with a diminutive caiman terrorist by the name of Magnus. The armour Vera wore was a means to spite Ignatius, as well as a means of bringing disgrace to the royal guard.

Reika hesitated, wondering whether to go back the lake. Part of her wanted to help her friends, but on the other hand, she knew if she went up against the three thugs that had attacked them, she would not stand a chance. She had never faced battle before. She thought about finding her way back to the citadel to warn the king; time was a problem and by the time she would get back, her friends would be dead.

A strange white light moved at a brisk pace, edging its way down the stream in the direction Reika had come from. Reika stared at the light in astonishment.

"What is that light? Where is it going?" As fast she could run, Reika raced after the light back towards the lake, where she found it had stopped at the shoreline, completely static but glowing all the same. "What does it want?" Reika wondered.

The light moved towards Reika like a person beginning a run up to an obstacle, much to her horror. The light collided with Reika, phasing into her. A blue aura surrounded her, holding her just a foot above the ground with her body completely frozen in place. Reika tried to move in vain; her body would not respond to her commands, robbing her of even the ability to even speak, almost like a form of sleep paralysis only worse. As Reika looked at her body, terrified by what was taking place, her body slowly begin to disintegrate in front of her eyes, the lake finally fading from view.

~

Reika could still feel the environment around her despite what was happening, though she couldn't fathom where she was about to end up. Her body was atomised as she was being whisked away.

Her consciousness returned even though she remained formless. She saw a grey castle floating on what appeared to be a rock that had been pulled presumably from somewhere in the world. Reika phased through the castle door and felt her body reconstitute inside the castle itself. Reika was still unable to move, but she could see the hall itself, constructed from a light blue stone with majestic white pillars greatly placed leading to a door at the end of the hall. *Where... am I? How did I get dragged here? Who even lives in a place like this?* The blue aura faded completely, with Reika dropping to the floor like a stone.

It hurt, but at least she could move again. She rubbed her hip. As she ventured through the corridor, Reika grew more concerned. "I have a bad feeling about this." She stopped in front of the door. Confusion was beginning to turn to anger. "I'd like to give the one who brought me here a piece of my mind," she said to herself, clenching her fist tightly. The door then opened of itself, revealing a dark room, which Reika entered with some trepidation, nervously clasping her left hand on her chest. "Hello, is there anyone in?" She called. No response was given. "HELLO!"

The door closed behind Reika, leaving her in darkness.

"Young one, we finally meet face to face," a voice called. Reika was surprised to hear any voice at all but didn't know where it was coming from. "Where are you? Tell me who you are."

Reika looked closely in front of her, spotting two unlit torches at the back of the room from which fire started to sprout, like a flower budding. The flames began to form snake trails, coalescing into a singular fireball which lit up the room. The torches still burned but the large fireball was gradually forming a human shape, the fire weaving together as tightly knitted cloth.

The fire began to die down on the human-like form, revealing an elderly man underneath with long grey hair and a beard, brown eyes, and a pale complexion. He wore black boots, a dark navy blue shirt with navy trousers, and a red coat with orange on the sleeves. Armoured plating gleamed underneath his coat, and he wore a cummerbund, holding the robe tightly to him. Reika looked in amazement. Then her expression grew sour. She stormed over to the man, furious with him. She began her tirade with her arms on her hips in disapproval, not caring for the dazzling display she saw.

"Alright, what is this trickery? Did you use that magic light to bring me here? Why did you feel the need to kidnap me and whisk me away like that? My friends are being attacked and I need to go back and help them. They could be dying any minute and you don't even care. You have no right to drag me here against my will. How dare you do that, what do you have to say for yourself?"

The man was not pleased, his expression also turning sour, mirroring hers. Reika's anger subsided beneath his glare. "Accusing me of kidnapping you is a very serious charge. Such bad form," he said sternly. "Your tirade against me isn't going to keep your friends safe. Be patient. There is power residing in you. I intend to awaken it fully."

Reika just stared at the man in amazement. "Power?" She said, "What are you talking about?" The man didn't respond, he placed his hand on Reika's forehead and without warning, she felt an energy surge within her for a few brief moments before finally subsiding.

"It is done," the man said. "You will know when I return you to the lake. We will meet again soon, Reika."

The blue aura surrounded Reika once again; this time she wasn't afraid at all and able to speak. "Wait, I don't even know your name. Can't you tell me who you are before you send me back?"

The man nodded. "My name is Antonius. Now, go back to your friends, I will bring you back here soon, we'll talk more."

As Reika's form again disintegrated, she responded, "Ok... I guess."

Reika's form reappeared at the very spot she was taken from. The castle's stone walls transformed into trees and water, like metal bars shifting into a molten state. The aura vanished as before, with Reika gently being placed on her feet, much to her relief. She stood there with her arms crossed, pondering what possible powers Antonius had awoken. *I hope my friends are ok. Climbing may take too long, it's not as if I can...* A thought without warning flashed into Reika's mind. *Fly... Wait a second, Maybe I can?* Reika closed her eyes; she could feel the grass peel away from her feet. She then opened them, looking down, her eyes widened immediately.

Did her eyes deceive her? Was she really hovering above the floor? A smile slowly appeared on Reika's face. *No way! It actually worked. This is weird; I had no idea I could do this.* Reika then lowered herself back to the ground again, staring at her hands. *What else am I able to do? Don't have much time, I need to get to my friends fast.* She didn't have any more time to think, as she could hear the voices of the thugs who had attacked her coming from the left. Without a moment's hesitation, Reika hid herself in the bushes behind her, using a small gap in the leaves to peer through and see what was going on.

Barzillai, the rhino who had attacked Reika and her friends, was carrying Melito over his shoulder. Darius was doing the same thing with Tabitha.

"Get ready to drown these Carthagian fools. Let these guards die like the human," Vera commanded. Darius put Tabitha down, with Barzillai following suit with Melito. Darius licked his teeth, holding his belt and strutting around the unconscious guards.

"You and your friend are on a one-way ticket to a watery grave; I hope you enjoy it." Reika seethed in anger. *Lowlife fiends. You three will all pay for this.*

Barzillai picked up Melito by the throat, sneering and pointing his finger at the marmoset's unconscious face. "Not sure whether to be pleased or sorry in granting you a quick death," Barzillai said in casual tone. Melito did not respond.

"Pretty quiet fella. Are you scared?" asked Barzillai. Darius rolled his eyes at Barzillai's stupidity, shaking his head and turning. In that moment, Reika suddenly caught his eye.

"You!" Darius roared.

Reika stood near the stream, crossing her arms, staring at the three thugs with a glare of indignation.

"Leave my friends alone. Only thugs would hit someone unarmed. You all make me sick." Barzillai and Darius took Melito and Tabitha and discarded them, with Melito thrown in the lake and Tabitha left by the shore with her head in the water to drown. Barzillai banged his fists together getting ready to charge. Vera stood back, a smirk of satisfaction on her face as she looked on.

"Don't worry, you can die like your friends you furless maggot!"

Barzillai charged toward Reika, but before he could collide, Reika leapt into the air performing a perfect split before landing on the ground again. Barzillai skidded along the ground, trying to slow himself down, before hitting into a tree. Darius took his spear and threw it hard and fast at Reika. She held out her hands to stop the spear in its tracks, pausing it in mid-air. It spun around into her hand, and she commandeered it as her own. Undaunted by her abilities, Darius charged in for an attack, hoisting a second spear.

Reika struggled to block his strikes, attempting to dodge wherever possible, countering to try to push Darius back, but to no avail. The two were at a standstill. Reika was out of breath. Fighting was not her strong suit, she was merely a servant, not prepared for this kind of work. Darius swiped at her again. This time, he shattered the spear she held on impact. Reika thrust her palm forward, inadvertently pushing Darius back without so much as even touching him. Barzillai, having recovered, looked shocked by all he saw. He threw a punch at Reika which stopped dead in its tracks once she had turned round, holding her hand out.

The young woman was astounded herself, however, she didn't have time to think what was going on, she was buckling under the strain. Darius beat his chest with his right hand, his guttural roar was like a warrior chant. He made his advance and pounced like the feline he was. Reika bounced into the air again, causing Darius to pounce on Barzillai by mistake. Reika hovered above the stream, witnessing the two animals trying to get to their feet. They saw Reika drawing her hands together swiftly and without warning, their two heads collided and both creatures slumped on the floor unconscious but alive.

Vera stared in awe as Reika's feet once again contacted solid ground. She couldn't bring herself to say anything. *This girl is dangerous. This was a fight we shouldn't have started. We need to regroup.* Vera felt deeper fear when Reika turned to stare at her. "Get out of my sight right now," Reika said, firmly. "Take your friends away too. You made a huge mistake."

Unfortunately for the leopard, she had no choice to agree. She glanced at Reika in anger. "Make no mistake you little brat, we will return and kill you all." Vera spat on the ground a small pellet housed in her mouth, causing smoke to appear. When it dissipated, she and her comrades were nowhere to be seen.

Reika was relieved that she would live another day, though she remembered Tabitha and Melito. She pulled Tabitha from the lake, leaving her on the grass, then swam across the water to pull Melito back to shore. She placed the two monkeys on their backs and tried her best to revive both of them, pressing their chests and breathing into their mouths. Nothing happened even, after a dozen tries. Despairing, Reika wondered if she was too late to rescue them. Without a moment to take in the possibility, or to accept the fact the monkeys had perished, they instantly sat up violently gasping for air, startling Reika.

"Ugh, took you long enough, Reika," Tabitha spluttered, water leaking from her mouth and nose. Reika's face lit up instantly.

"You're both alright! Do not scare me like that!" She put one arm around each of the monkeys, hugging them both to their confusion. Melito surveyed the landscape cautiously so as not to miss a repeat of what happened to him.

"What happened? Where are those thugs?" He asked.

Tabitha's confusion remained. "Did you defeat them? Also, how did you survive going over the waterfall?"

Reika was silent, not really knowing how to explain the situation. "Well... It is kind of an odd story really," Reika said awkwardly "I am not even sure how I survived, I just found myself awake underwater. I swam away. When they came down here. I fought them. I knocked two of the goons out and Vera escaped."

Melito raised an eyebrow. "How? You are a little scrawny, we didn't have a chance either." But he dropped the question without bothering to continue his enquiry. "Anyway, what matters is you are safe and so are we. We might as well get going."

"Hmm, you can go on ahead of me, I'll head home later. I want to stay for a while."

Melito squinted his eyes. "You want to stay a little longer? If you want to that's fine."

"Thanks. I'll catch up later." Melito and Tabitha made their way toward the cliff-face that the thugs had walked down with them, while Reika sat down with her legs crossed, leaning back against a tree. She closed her eyes and drifted off to sleep. *So nice, you wouldn't even think a fight had taken place here in the first place.*

About an hour later, Reika awoke. She felt that she had stayed at the lake long enough, wanting to go home. She didn't mind making her own way back. The forest itself had been safe most of her life. She rose to her feet, glancing at the lake in front of her, stepping toward it. "Haven't properly tested what I can do. At least I will not have Vera and her goons interrupting. Here goes nothing."

Reika began once again to levitate off the ground above the grass. She leaned her body forward while slowly moving across the lake without so much as touching it. She then placed her hand in the water to make a rippled trail, distorting her reflection on the water. Just as she tried to edge her way up, she began to wobble. Reika shook her arms to try to steady herself with a slight drop occurring. She nearly touched the water and stopped just short. Despite this, Reika could absolutely confirm she was not dreaming, this was really happening. A boost in her confidence soared just as she did high above the lake into the sky. She was thinking to herself with an open smile. *I can't believe this; I am flying. I feel just like a bird. The wind in my hair and between my fingers and toes feels so nice. This is an amazing view. I could stay up here for hours.* For a brief time, Reika just hovered there awestruck at the view she was getting. She turned her gaze towards the stream at the top of the water. *Time to go home now.*

I had better meet up with the others, was what entered her mind, and homeward she went.

Melito and Tabitha discussed Reika, the thugs, and what had taken place as they walked by the stream. "I wonder how Reika beat them. I wish I didn't interrupt her," Melito wondered.

"She'll tell us later," answered Tabitha. "So, I wouldn't even worry about it.

It would be intriguing to learn more." "I agree, Tabs."

"I wonder why she wanted to stay. She won't catch up to us at this rate."

Suddenly, they heard a "YAHOO!" in the distance, the source of the noise behind the monkeys. "Hey Melito, did you hear that?"

"Yeah, it sounds like Reika... How it's her I am not sure. She cannot have caught up with us this quickly?"

"But where is she now?" Tabitha asked.

"Up here!" an excited voice called. To their astonishment, after looking up, the two apes saw Reika flying in the air, circling them like a hawk. "Hey!" Reika yelled in a playful manner. "I thought you said you were going to get home before me."

"Um... Does not look like it now," Tabitha muttered. Melito scratched his head. "Today has just gotten weird."

At last, Reika's altitude diminished, and she hovered above the ground in front of her friends. Melito just stared at Reika for a moment, unable to fully articulate or phrase his question. "Reika, how in the world are you doing that? Is that what you used to defeat Vera's goons?"

Reika began her explanation. "Well, there was this man named Antonius, He used a spell to whisk me away and brought me to his home. He awakened some magical power within me, then sent me back. Behold the result." At once, her hovering ended. Reika hunched over with her hands on her knees, slightly out of breath, after which she straightened herself.

"Was it a challenge? Looks like it takes a lot out of you," Melito asked.

"It was pretty easy to knock them out, even if the confrontation was brief." "You said Antonius," said Tabitha. "The sorcerer?"

"Yep, that very man, Tabitha." Reika's smile immediately disappeared. She remembered her ungracious and ill-mannered confrontation with Antonius. "I wish I wasn't so rude. When he wants to speak to me again, I am not sure. Certainly, a strange day." Melito did not have too much to say. "Let's head home, I have had enough action for one day," he said.

Reika was rubbing the back of her head. "Yeah, I have got an aching head right now. I do need to rest... I... Ow, it's getting worse."

Tabitha looked worried.

"Reika? What's wrong?" Tabitha didn't receive a response quickly. Reika was still clutching her head, reeling from a pain that felt like her skull was being ripped in two. "My head... The pain... make it stop."

It gradually receded. Melito helped then Reika to her feet. She hadn't even been aware she collapsed.

"You ok?" He asked. "You really should take a rest."

"I should be," replied Reika. "I'm fine, we really need to get going. Do not worry about me too much, I should be fuuugh..." As Reika was speaking, she fainted and collapsed. Melito grabbed her just in time. Tabitha could only look at her friend with concern. "Reika, what's going on with you?"

Melito slung the unconscious human over his shoulder. "Right, let's get Reika back to the citadel."

Little did they realise, the moon was visible.

Chapter 2

Lunar Path's Aperture

I t was a tiring endeavour to bring Reika back to the citadel, and even more so to carry her up the stairs. The citadel where Reika had lived as a servant for the past six years had been constructed of orange stone, including the walls surrounding the main castle courtyard. The courtyard had fountains, four on each side spread neatly apart with the stone of the courtyard being a dull beige. There was barely a crack in sight, as the guards maintained the citadel regularly at the request of Captain Ignatius. The throne room was composed of beautiful white stone and the throne itself was varying degrees of orange stone. The king was not anywhere in sight at the present time, as he had previously retired to his bedroom to sleep. The guards, who had the same armour and trousers as that of Melito and Tabitha, all wore golden helmets disguising their faces. Melito and Tabitha signalled for the doors to be opened. Melito was still carrying Reika across the courtyard; he had not taken a break the entire journey, worry driving him on. Both he and Tabitha pressed on to the inside of the citadel, the guards allowing them safe passage through.

They journeyed up the stairs to their left and they went through many a corridor upstairs and past the main entertainment room. This room housed a piano along with various games such as chess. Other metazoan guards included the sand cat, Cyprian, the cobra, Vipsania, the elephant, Augustine, and the pig, Firmillian. Cyprian had light milky fur with brown patches of fur on his forehead that resembled tribal tattoos. His massive, light green irises almost hid the whites of his eyes, leaving the slit pupils showing. He was the smallest guard in the room. Vipsania or Vips as she was known was not your standard cobra: she had arms and legs like her fellow metazoans. Her build was medium-sized in comparison to the other two in the room. Her scales were moss green, and the inside of her hood was chartreuse.

Augustine himself had a very light ochry brown hide. He was the tallest and the most muscular in the room. Firmillian was the oldest and was small in stature, in between that of Cyprian and Vips. His flesh was a rather dark pink, light rose hybrid colour and his armour, as opposed to the gold armour of the guard, was striped black and white alternately. Firmillian was present at the gold-plated terebinth piano, playing a soft melody, a relaxing one you might hear at a social gathering. Cyprian and Vips were playing chess together, the cat with white pieces and the cobra with black. Augustine was admiring the paintings on the walls.

The two monkeys didn't stop to chat. Instead, they entered the southern corridor and opened the door to Reika's bedroom. There was a soft bed, a chest of drawers, a painting of the citadel, and a decent sized window with a view of the courtyard, complete with the surrounding forest and the road to Reme in the distance. Another road made a sharp bend to the west and then to the north.

Melito laid Reika gently on her bed, leaving her there for a few moments. "What is even wrong with her? What could be causing her to be like this?" Tabitha enquired. Melito just shook his head.

"I don't know," he replied. "I wish I had answers."

At last Reika woke up. She sat up, still a little weak from what had transpired in the forest. Confused at where she was, Reika asked. "What happened? Did I just fall unconscious?"

"You did," Melito responded. "You were clutching your head in pain, then collapsed." Reika looked to her left out of the window.

"I feel ok, but I'll keep an eye on my health. I would like to know what caused that headache."

"What matters is that you are alive," Melito said. "But I agree, I would still keep an eye on your health all the same. If we hadn't been there, you would have been unconscious in the woods, then who knows what could have happened? Especially if Vera and her goons had decided to come back."

"Melito has a point. You had us worried for a while," Tabitha added. The two monkeys turned to leave Reika alone. "We're going get some sleep, take care Reika."

"Thanks for the concern, both of you. I appreciate it. Good night."

The door shut, but Reika did not go to sleep quickly, she was perplexed about her present condition. Did Antonius do something terrible to her? Answers reeled in her head, lacking any plausible choice. Prior to her encounter with Antonius, telekinesis was not something Reika had ever attempted or even considered before. Was she simply not used to it? Was there benign or malignant power at play here? She did not dwell too much on the question any longer, as she desired sleep.

Melito and Tabitha left the room quietly and headed to the entertainment room.

"A busy day?" Augustine enquired as he continued staring at the paintings. "I'll say," Melito replied. "We were attacked by Vera in the woods." Cyprian turned his head toward the conversation, though kept one eye on

Vips. "You're sure that Ignatius doesn't need to know what went on in the forest? Sounds like important information."

Melito snorted. "I was on my way now, Cyprian. Reika fainted and I had to carry her here. I am not a multitasker."

Cyprian was satisfied with the response, turning back to his game. Firmillian finished the melody that he was playing, leaving the seat to face Melito.

"You hurt, boy?"

"My back aches. I was thrown against a tree. I'll probably feel it a lot worse in the morning."

Vips looked up. "Go and see the nurse then, she'll fix you up. How serious is it?"

"Well, I haven't broken my back, it just feels very bruised. If I hit the tree harder, I would have been in trouble."

"Yet you managed to carry Reika all the way here back to her bedroom?" Augustine asked.

"With a bit of difficulty, yes," Melito replied. "One of the trials of being a royal guard: grinning and bearing the pain."

❧

After hearing Melito's story, Captain Ignatius placed a cougar named Basil on watch. Basil had beige and white fur, with the white resembling gloves on his hands. Brown markings on his face that glistened in the moonlight.

As peaceful and serene as the night was, Basil was bored. Despite being a large cat, he detested the night shifts that he was given. The pace of his evening was about to change, however. He detected a smell that didn't match the rest of the air. *What is that smell? Whatever it is, it is not good.* His suspicions would turn out correct, as Barzillai, the hulking rhinoceros, brazenly strode up to the gateway.

Two royal guards who were positioned at the gate raised their swords, preparing to slice Barzillai in two. Barzillai paused, looking up at the large gate, then turned his attention to the guards. "Alright, where's that little brat? I know she is here. My friends and I will show you a world of pain!" The guard on Barzillai's left pointed his sword at the rhino, dangerously close to the horns on his face.

"You can't be here, get out!"

Barzillai merely sneered, kicking the guard onto the floor. The other leapt forward to attack but suffered the same fate. Basil saw, from a distance, the citadel gates were flung open and without hesitation, using the wall's structure as his ancestors would use a mountain face, climbed his way down speedily.

Bazillai eventually came to meet him.

"Get out!" Basil yelled. "The likes of you don't belong here."

Barzillai grinned once again. "Tough luck, I am here to stay. Haven't you got a ball of yarn to play with or catnip to smell?" He said mockingly.

Basil bared his teeth. A guard in one of the windows behind him threw down a spear, which Basil caught. "Mock me or any of my brethren and you die. The same goes if you mock my peers here too! You'll have your head stuck on a pike!"

Basil rushed into combat with Barzillai, hitting the rhino hard on his horns with the blunt section of the spear. Barzillai recoiled briefly, countering by swiftly knocking Basil to the ground and leaping in the air to crush the big cat. Basil rolled quickly out the way, managing to clip Barzillai on the leg with the spear. When the guard tried to lunge at the rhino again, Barzillai stole the spear from him and broke it in half. Using the two halves of the spear, Barzillai proceeded to beat Basil repeatedly, making the cat shriek.

Reika awoke, hearing the commotion, walking to the window slightly delirious from only being asleep for a few hours. "What is going on? I am trying to sleep. Seriously some people can be..." Immediately, Reika's eyes widened when saw Barzillai down below, clubbing Basil.

Reika leapt from her bedroom window, landing in the courtyard safely, her telekinesis allowing her to slow her descent. She stumbled a little when she landed, trying to get her footing. Raising her hand, she shoved Barzillai with a telekinetic projectile. Basil scrambled to his feet. His armour had protected him somewhat, but he was still worse for wear. He ran to Reika quickly, bewildered, and grateful.

Reika was surprised herself. She had never made such a rash

decision in her life. Leaping out of a high window? Plunging herself into a fight she no ounce of experience in? She heard her name called by Basil.

"You jumped out of the window? Are you mad?" Reika looked at the cougar. "It doesn't matter right now." Barzillai eventually got up to his knees, only briefly fazed by what happened. Smirking, he knew that he had found the target he is looking for. "Well, well, if it isn't the one who dodged death," he said.

Reika looked at the rhino.

"If it's me you want, it's me you'll get. But I won't go down easy!" Reika shouted.

"Barzillai is my name, kid. I haven't forgotten what you did to me and Darius and now, we are going to crush you. Your name?"

"Reika, and I won't let you kill me." Laughing off Reika's threats as idle, Barzillai goaded her.

"Come at me then, you little brat." Reika lifted herself off the ground and before anyone knew what had happened, she had decked Barzillai. The punch which sent him flying back. Reika was stunned; how did she hit him so hard? *Is there anything else I can do?* Reika thought.

Basil couldn't believe what he was seeing. Magic. When did she learn to do that?

Reika flew back to where Basil was standing. "Basil, more of these thugs may show up," Basil nodded his head in agreement. "They will not get to the king."

Two guards then appeared. "Thanks for the assist," Reika said. "There are more coming."

Out of nowhere, others appeared on the wall. Vera and Darius, accompanied by two more. One was a tiger named Felix with blue eyes. His back and the area around his eyes had orange fur with black stripes. His chest and face were white. The other was a brown bear named Marcion. Both sported the same boots and trousers as their comrades.

But nothing could have prepared Reika for the final member of their gang.

Magnus revealed himself. He was the smallest of the group, a diminutive caiman, covered in two shades of green armoured scales. He sported the same boots and trousers as his underlings, but he also wore a double blue sash, which left his arms and the left side of his chest exposed. The creature examined Reika from a distance.

"So, you are the witch who gave my comrades trouble eh?" He said with mild amusement in his voice. "Younger than I had initially thought. We could use someone like you. So, here is what I offer to you. Turn yourself over to me and I will spare your friends. Now what do you say little one?"

Reika's face showed her disgust. She felt physically ill. "Forget it, I will never help someone like you. I am not interested in hurting others. You are wasting your time."

"That's a shame. We would have made a great team," Magnus said, with a look of genuine disappointment on his face. He stood behind his team, a spectator to the battle that was sure to take place. "Kill her!" he shouted.

The expression on Reika's face soon changed to one of trepidation. What had she gotten herself into? The two guards drew their swords, at the ready to defend the keep. The thugs all charged; weapons drawn. Vera revealed her deadly elbow blades, while Marcion and Felix drew swords.

The weapons of the two groups clashed. The guards did well, parrying the attacks of Felix and Marcion. Reika thrust Vera away with a telekinetic push. Darius was right behind her, ready to stab whoever came in his path. Reika dodged the attack just in time, only to find Felix drawing his blade to strike Reika down. Vera got to her feet and backed off, turned her attention to the guards, easier prey. Felix swiftly brought his own blade down upon Reika.

Reika caught the sword in her hands. Every moment it seemed she was finding new ways to channel this awesome power within her. She flung Felix back, pushing the sword away from her, then jumped into the air, using Darius as a launch pad. She rocketed towards Felix, knocking him flat onto the floor unconscious.

"This is the end!" Marcion shouted, swinging his sword at Reika. He soon realised his mistake as she spun around immediately and raised her left arm. A barrier appeared, surrounding it. She felt no pain from the blow, though the kinetic force travelled through her arm and body. Reika partially recoiled from it.

Vera was too busy fighting the guards to engage Reika herself, secretly relieved she was not fighting her. At the same time, the guards fighting her were putting up a valiant effort. *Ignatius trained them well,* Vera thought. *That girl, however, has no training, yet has power. Why?* Magnus could only watch in stunned silence. *There is no way she should be this powerful at her age,* he thought. He had assumed Vera's story to be exaggerated, but it appeared she had told the truth about the girl's powers. The look on his face turned to anger. *I'll have to retreat for now, we cannot win.*

The thugs pressed their attacks on Reika and the two guards, but to no avail.

Their frustration intensified. Reika backed away quickly, still hovering. "Guards, take cover!" She called. Reika then brought her arms together

forming an X shape with them. Blue energy began to emanate from her arms, saturating her with light resembling glowing water. The sound that emitted from the energy was electrical.

"What is she doing?" Felix whispered. The energy soon escalated. Reika began to speak.

"Begone!" As Reika yelled, she formed a star shape with her body, unleashing a blue, glowing shockwave from her. Magnus covered his eyes due to the intensity of the light. Vera was a safe distance away and had time to jump onto the wall to avoid the blast. The two guards were outside the blast radius, near the door.

Melito and Tabitha were running through the corridors back to the throne room. Just then, they heard the explosion and hurried to the door to investigate.

"What was that?" Tabitha asked.

"An explosion, I hope Reika's alright, and we are not too late," Melito replied.

The two opened it enough to peer outside. Melito was surprised. The thugs were unconscious on the ground, with Reika standing in the middle of the courtyard, clearly tired, though glad to be alive. Magnus could only watch from the side-lines, seething with anger at what this young human had done.

That brat... how dare she humiliate my henchmen; she'll pay for this dearly.

The guards rallied around Reika, still in awe of what they saw. "We'll get help from inside," they said.

Just as the guards were ready to head away, Reika started to feel a sharp pain in her head like she did in the forest, only the pain felt much worse. She slumped to the floor, kneeling, still holding her head. "Urgh! Make it stop."

Magnus looked in confusion, trying to piece together what was happening. He looked up at the moon, noticing it was at its fullest. Something clicked. He started to tremble like a fearful child.

He was still watching Reika clasping her head in absolute agony, her voice changing from painful moans to snarls of rage. A ghastly jet-black and purple aura was emerging. It burst forth from Reika, a dark flame raging around her. It enveloped her completely. At last, it vanished, all were staring at where Reika was standing.

Her body was black as her hair, apart from the chest which retained her warm beige skin tone. Scales had formed all over. Her fingers had fused together to make two fingers and one thumb on each hand. Likewise, her toes fused together to make three toes. They had changed into something more claw like. Wings had sprouted from Reika's back and her mouth and nose had become a long snout. Reika's clothes had disappeared in the transformation and the eyes were reptilian, while the hair on her head had morphed into a mane. She was only slightly larger than normal, a small stature, though imposing. She resembled a black dragon.

The guards, terrified, ran inside the citadel.

~

Magnus' crew were indeed surprised by what had taken place. Vera was terrified inside, doing her best to try to hide it. *A weredragon living here? We are in big trouble.*

The group were discussing amongst themselves the strange event that had transpired.

"An interesting turn of events," remarked Darius. "What a fell beast," said Marcion.

Barzillai didn't care, smacking his fists together. "Same brat, different coat.

I say we kill this beast and be done with it."

Reika looked towards Barzillai, snarling at him. "Er... It's staring at us," Darius said.

Marcion merely scoffed at the creature. "Oh, come on, this puny dragon won't be able to hurt us. It's laughably tiny. We could easily take that thing on." Reika looked again, baring her teeth and squinting her eyes in anger, then finally let out a loud, ear-piercing roar. "Oh, I wish I hadn't said that," Marcion said.

Vera couldn't stand what was happening any longer. A rare feeling of terror seized her. "Get away from her, that's an order!"

The others did not heed her warning, beginning to attack the weredragon head on. Reika stood her ground, hissing in anticipation. The strikes from the thugs themselves didn't even make contact with Reika, hitting only the air around her. Bazillai finally managed to strike Reika in the face, bashing her away into the air. Reika crashed and scuffed along the floor, then swiftly returned to her feet. She stamped her right foot on the ground, spread her arms out and roared.

Magnus stepped back, not wanting to get caught in the cross-fire. Reika flew swiftly towards the thugs, uppercutting Barzillai in the chin, kicking Marcion in the chest, tripping up Darius with a kick to the back of the legs, followed by thrusting an elbow into his stomach. The thugs got to their feet, retreating toward the front gate Barzillai had battered down. Reika turned around, opening her mouth, a giant fireball shooting at Vera who was standing on the wall. Vera leapt from the wall just in time, rolling forwards down the hill. She made it to the bottom of the hill, proceeding to escape.

Reika turned her attention to Magnus, striding up to him boldly, looking down at the diminutive caiman. "Easy girl, don't hurt me... I'm just a tiny caiman," Magnus said with a nervous smile on his face. Reika didn't respond at first, letting out a shriek few seconds later, as if to say, "Get out!"

"I'm gone!" Magnus ran full pelt out of the citadel as fast as he could.

Felix awoke, and as soon as he did, he high tailed it out of there when he saw the dark dragon in the courtyard. "Wait for me!" He called out to his comrades as he rushed out of the citadel.

After Magnus ran away, Reika looked on into the distance, standing in place. Melito and Tabitha exchanged glances, confused. The two of them approached Reika slowly. The weredragon turned its head round, glancing back to see who was behind it.

"Reika?" Melito asked. Reika didn't say anything, she just continued to look back at him.

"Reika?" He said again.

Reika spun around, aggressively hissing at Melito. She charged at him but stopped short at striking him, as if something were trying to hold her back. Melito gently stepped back a few feet, holding two small tomahawks in his hand. He observed the beast in front of him. It made no attempt to go for him again, instead clutching its head. Then, without warning, Reika fled from the palace, using her wings to fly from the citadel, making a turn to the north.

"We've got to go after her," Tabitha stated.

"Agreed," Melito said. Then the two ran down the stairs, leaving the citadel, turning to the right after they reached the bottom of the hill.

~

For a few hours they moved through the forest. All the while they kept the dragon in their sights. They got close to Mt Carthage, a tall mountain located in the north of the island, its size incredible despite its lone nature. A stone stair structure led to the very top. The two apes climbed the stairs. It took a fair amount of time, but they made it to the top of the mountain. They saw a cave to their left, its entrance facing east.

They entered the cave. A pool of deep water lay within. "It's very quiet, would Reika be hiding here?" Melito wondered. Tabitha scanned the cave.

"Reika!" She called, her voice echoing.

Melito turned to Tabitha with a sneer, putting his finger on his mouth. "Shh, do you want her to hear?"

They didn't have time to think as the water began to shift, Reika emerged from the pool, jumping out onto dry land. The water trickled down the scales of the beast as she stared at them, teeth slightly bared. "Oh rats, my fault," Tabitha said.

Reika didn't bother moving from where she was standing at all; she stared at them the same way as before. Tabitha walked towards Reika with trepidation, Melito looking on in shock.

"Tabs, what are you doing?" "I want to know if she is ok."

"Don't be a fool and get killed, get back here."

Reika finally moved, standing next to Tabitha. She leaned over, smelling Tabitha's fur, investigating it. Reika then growled at Tabitha, circling the tamarin, as she stood there desperately trying her best to compose herself. "Maybe this was a bad idea," Tabitha whimpered.

"Maybe?" Melito responded, raising his eyebrow. "You may be next on the menu."

Despite his words, Melito walked over, his tomahawks in each hand at the ready just in case Reika turned on them.

Reika stepped away from Tabitha, letting out a roar. The sound of the roar bounced from every side of the cave, finally echoing across the forest outside.

"Reika, back off!" Melito yelled.

Reika directed her attention to Melito, and strangely she obeyed. She squinted, staring at Melito intently, opening her jaws.

"Tabs? Melito?" She finally uttered, her voice somewhat deeper in tone, sounding like she had aged a number of years. It was a little sluggish in delivery too, as if Reika was re-training herself to talk.

"Wha... You can talk? Reika? You can understand us?" Tabitha asked. The change in Reika's face seemed to indicate that she was collecting her thoughts, the primitive bestial mind regaining higher function.

"Somehow, yes. What are you doing here?" Reika asked, now her speech sped up a bit, almost matching her original pace of speech.

The weredragon then looked up, examining the cave with a bewildered expression. Reika met Melito's eyes once again, "What... happened?"

"We were looking for you. You took off after the battle with Magnus' goons."

"Where are they? And how did I end up here?"

"You don't remember what happened? Magnus's thugs invaded the castle and you fought them off."

Reika placed her hand under her snout, beginning to scratch it as she pondered what had taken place. "I do remember fighting them, but then my mind blanked. Part of me was semi-conscious when you both showed up."

"You restrained yourself, didn't you?" Tabitha said. "You hissed at us, tried to attack Melito and flew off."

"It just about worked," Reika said. "Thus you are still alive. Then I lapsed into unconsciousness again."

Reika stopped for a moment, walking back to the pool of water. She could make out the vague figure of her monstrous form reflected in the dull, stagnant water. "I don't know what's happening to me, I can't go back like this."

Melito approached Reika. "You can't stay here forever. Sooner or later, you will have to leave."

Reika spun round, looking at Melito with mournful eyes,

holding back her tears as best she could. "Melito... Look at me. I am a monster."

Tabitha shook her head as she moved toward Reika, placing her hands on Reika's cold, scaly shoulders in a sisterly manner. "Reika, that doesn't matter, you are still you underneath."

"Stay here or come with us, it's your choice," Melito added. Reika looked away for split second.

"Alright, we'll leave in the morning," she finally said.

Five days after the incident, Magnus had arrived at another island called Zeitreisen. He went to a southern town close the sea. As he departed from the ship, an elf was sitting by the local inn. His name was Lief. He had short black hair, brown eyes, and white skin, wearing a smart white vest and black trousers with brown boots—altogether an ordinary looking fellow. He observed the caiman leaving the boat, furrowing his eyebrows. The creature looked miserable. Lief left the seat he was on and made his way over to the dock. "You look annoyed, little caiman," he said, as he barred the exit. Magnus just jumped off the dock onto the land, bypassing Lief altogether. "Whoa, hold on, what's up?

Perhaps I can help?"

"What is it you want in return?" Magnus said abruptly, his green scales almost turning red.

"Nothing, just wondering is going on. You simply seemed to have a pretty rough time."

"If you can go to Carthage to stop a weredragon for me, then be my guest. Get it out of my sight." Lief pulled Magnus on his shoulder and knelt to his level. "You saw a weredragon in Carthage? Who was the individual in question?"

He asked curiously.

"A human woman. Black hair, warm beige skin, large brown eyes, and small stature. Taller than me by a fair bit however."

The elf stared back. "Where is she now?"

Magnus felt calmer talking to the elf. His instinct had been to run away from Reika in the hopes that he would never have to face her as that monster again, but now he saw other possibilities. He scratched his chin. "I do not know. I and my comrades escaped."

The elf stood up and placed his hand under his chin, standing there in deep contemplation.

"Hmm, I do have a means of taking that weredragon off your hands. In fact, my master has a use for them. I do not expect you to find them, not that you are incapable or anything, but I will save you the trouble. I will search for the girl myself. Your conversation has been most helpful."

Lief left for the town. Magnus smirked. "Maybe I'll go find her first. Either way, it gets her out of the way."

While Magnus had begun his escape from Carthage, Reika woke up the next morning refreshed. The light of sun made contact with the contours of the cave wall, exposing the stagnant pool's bed, laden with calcium and algae which, as one looked deeper into the pool, became murkier, making it harder to discern what was down there.

Reika got to her feet, yawning loudly. She swiftly shut her mouth, restraining the noise she made with her vocal cords. It was going to take some getting used to. In the sunlight she could conduct a proper examination of her bestial form, looking down at the weird shape of her toes and hands. Turning her attention to the cave entrance, Reika wondered where her friends had gone. She walked out of the cave. She could hear a faint voice in her head calling her name. She didn't think much of the voice and dismissed it right away.

"Reika? Can you hear me?" Reika was startled as the voice was now loud and clear. The way the voice sounded didn't sound like it came from the cave at all. "We must speak at once. There is a temple north of the Carthagian Citadel. Use it to come to me."

Reika then ascertained it was Antonius communicating with her telepathically. Reika didn't say anything, she nodded her head in response. She then went on her way.

Melito and Tabitha were looking out into the distance just outside the cave.

They spotted Reika leaving.

"Morning sleepyhead," said Melito.

Tabitha chuckled to herself. "We could hear you snoring away there."

Reika turned around with a look of annoyance on her face. It didn't last long after she started to fix her gaze on the sunrise, observing all around her, smiling. *I have to admit, this is a very beautiful morning.* Reika being to feel a weird sensation within her body, as though darkness was beginning to envelope her, not in a threatening way, however. It covered Reika completely then faded promptly away, revealing her human form once again, her clothes restored along with the rest of her body. She stared at her hands in surprise and heard her normal voice had been restored.

Tabitha grinned, "Hey, you're human again."

"Yeah, I guess I am?" Reika said, her smile was faint and short-lived. "But... What am I really?"

Reika remained silent for a moment with her friends just staring at her. "I have to go."

"You want to leave now? Come back with us."

"There are answers I need, Melito. I want to know why I turned into that beast. Go back to the castle and tell everyone I am fine. I promise I will return." Melito just looked at Reika in silence, closing his eyes to think. He reopened them to give his answer.

"Fine, we'll meet you there. Be back soon."

Reika started to hover in the air, ready for her departure. "See you later." She turned and flew away, performing a half U-turn as she flew off the mountain into the forest below. Her friends made their way to the stairs, down the mountain, back to the citadel.

Reika continued making her way north, traversing the forest. She finally stuck her head through a hedgerow and caught a

36

glimpse of a grey temple layered with ancient square bricks, surrounded by a moat.

Reika left the hedgerow and sauntered across the open ground. As she approached the door, it opened as if it were ready to receive her. She gazed down the shadowy staircase beyond. "Will this temple take me to see Antonius? One way to find out."

Reika walked down the stairs. As she went deeper, she eyed the inside of the temple: flaming torches shone, stationed on the wall and equally positioned between the floor and roof. She observed the interior around her, seeing an arcane stone on the floor, bearing the shape of a powerful dragon. This stone was pure white marble in comparison to the grey dull bricks that composed the temple's outer structure.

She wandered over to the marble in the middle of the room. Gently she placed her feet on the dragon icon. Since Reika barely wore shoes, the roughness of the stone was inconsequential.

She stood waiting for something to occur, postulating how the stone would take her to Antonius' Castle. Without warning, the stone below her started to glow yellow. Lightning shot out quickly from the marble, colliding with Reika instantly. If anyone had been watching, they would have seen a young girl vapourised in front of their eyes. However, Reika found herself back at Antonius' Castle, at least once the hazy smoke around her had cleared. No burn marks were present on Reika's skin. She was a little alarmed, despite no harm befalling her. Seeing the doors of the castle, she hurried as fast as her legs could carry her, hoping to find the answers she sought.

Mark was summoned to the castle by Ignatius. Ignatius was a Rottweiler with brown eyes and fur. He had brown fur on his face, too, aside from his mouth, nose, and ears, which sported orange fur. His armour was like that of the rest of the guards with a few distinguishing badges. The news that he had to bear was not good.

"You want to send Reika away? Why?" Mark said.

"What I heard transpire last night was a terrible sight. It was a full moon; the guards alerted me and told me she had transformed into a weredragon."

"That's absolutely ridiculous," Mark replied. "Reika has been out under the full moon before. How could she be one of them?"

"I don't know but it's still the case," Ignatius told the husky. "I punish soldiers who withhold important information, it's a good way to make sure they tell me the truth."

"And you are going to send her away? The king will have much to say..." Ignatius held his hand out to silence Mark. "King Tertullian is not here now.

He was taken through the tunnels to a secret place." Ignatius pointed to a grey block door with a sculptured mural embedded in it. "He left me in charge, and I say she leaves. I am under strict orders to protect the king's people." Mark bared his teeth in anger, he couldn't stand what was being said to him anymore.

"If I were ruling the throne, I would not send her away like this, I'd find another means of protecting everyone else. If what you say about Reika is false, you are sending my daughter away to die! But if it is true, then countless others will be at risk, and you'll be held responsible. That would reflect badly on you, wouldn't it?"

"Not if I send royal guards to accompany her. Also, it will not be a permanent exile for her. If there is a means to cure her, they must find it."

"And if there is no cure?" Mark asked.

Ignatius paused for a moment. "Then she may never return," he replied in a stoic tone. "Now... Leave this chamber and do not question my judgement on this subject again."

Mark headed out the small room in disgust. He said nothing more and didn't even growl at Ignatius. At the door he turned, and spoke once more, this time it was in a calm manner. "Any idea where she might be right now?"

"That I cannot answer, but I'll let you know if we find her."

Mark nodded his head and said no more as he exited the throne room. Ignatius looked at Mark's retreating form, wondering if he was doing the right thing. But deep down he knew the people had to be put first.

Melito and Tabitha entered the throne room quickly, almost out of breath.

They stopped to recover for a moment, then finally approached Ignatius. "Melito, Tabitha, where have you been?" Ignatius asked, looking at them with anger in his eyes.

"We went to find Reika. She had left the citadel," Melito said. Ignatius gave the same explanation he had given to Mark to both the monkeys standing in his presence. The two of them were deeply upset.

"You realise we cannot have a weredragon here? Who knows what sort of damage she might do?"

Melito tried to be as careful as possible with his next response, so as to not cause Ignatius to lose his temper. "Sir, with due respect, I am merely a humble servant of the king, but this is our friend we are talking about."

"I understand you have been friends for a long time." Ignatius looked at Melito with something approaching kindness. "But we cannot afford any casualties, even if we move her to another room." He looked away from the duo toward the throne. "Until she is cured, Reika cannot live here."

Melito and Tabitha both gasped.

"You can't be serious?" Tabitha shouted.

"Of course, I am," Ignatius barked back. "Do I detect you defying me?"

"I don't know what you want us to do. Sir, is there any way you'll allow her back in?" Melito asked.

Ignatius paused for a moment before giving his answer. "There is one way. Go find the Anodyne Stone. An artefact that will be able to undo the horror inflicted on Reika."

"Both of us?"

"Yes, you and Tabitha, you will accompany Reika. There is an individual in Caledonia who wields a legendary sword, The Draco

Ferrum. He will go with you as well."

Tabitha's face lit up. "Sure, why not? If it means allowing Reika back, we'll go."

"Good. Lastly, take the teleporter in the catacombs back to Reme. Then sail straight to Caledonia."

"There's a snag, Reika won't be back for a while. She has gone to see Antonius," Melito said. "How long she'll be I don't know. Something tells me it's going to be a while. Maybe it wasn't her plan to be away for so long?"

Ignatius paused for a while. "She's gone to see him? How strange. What does he want with a servant girl?" He pondered. Then he addressed the two monkeys. "Hold your search, let her return here. She'll be brought up to speed on her return. You are dismissed. I'll require both of you in the coming days." With that, Ignatius marched out of the room. The two monkeys could only stand there in silence, trying to process it all. They would lose their friend to exile if they failed.

Reika entered the hallway and saw Antonius standing in the same place where he met her for the first time. She made her way towards him but this time with a calm demeanour. "Ah, you have returned," he said. Reika was a little nervous, as she had previously insulted Antonius with her outburst.

"Firstly, I apologise for my behaviour toward you, I was so rude, I had no right to be angry with you."

Antonius smiled. "Dwell not on it young one, I know you were in distress." He cleared his throat and put his hands behind his back, eager to listen. "Now, I want to speak with you. Start from the beginning and keep it brief."

"I met up with my friends after Vera and her gang disappeared. I fell unconscious and after those thugs came to the citadel last night. I fought with them, but a sharp pain came into my head and coursed through my body. I felt like I was dying horribly. The next thing I know, I wake up fully cognisant and I see Melito and Tabitha, and I found out I had the body of a dragon. When it was daytime, my body returned to normal." Antonius nodded his head as Reika spoke. Then she turned away, clasping her arms. "I'm scared, what is going on?"

"Reika, what you turned into was a weredragon," Antonius replied.

Reika's eyes widened, with a puzzled expression on her face. "A weredragon?"

"It's a foul curse. By day, human, or whatever species you are. By night, well, that you already know."

Reika looked into Antonius' eyes, like a child seeking reassurance from a parent after they had heard something terrible. Antonius knew there was no easy way to answer her.

"Do you know how to cure it?" Reika asked.

Antonius shook his head. "It's too powerful even for me to dissipate." "Will I become that thing every night? I can't show myself to people like that when night falls. Who knows what I could potentially do…"

Antonius pointed at Reika, "Stay out of the moon's rays and you will remain human. However, the transformation will not be complete unless there is a full moon."

"So, I could go out at night as long as the moon is obscured?" asked Reika. "Possibly," said Antonius. "I wouldn't chance it, it's not worth the risk. It's

something you do at your own peril." He then spread out his right arm as if he was giving a tour. "In the meantime, stay here for a while," Antonius said. "Feel free to explore and use the training area."

Reika headed back outside into the courtyard after Antonius had finished speaking. She ran quickly to the edge of the yard to take a closer look at what lay below. She looked carefully and saw a lone rock just floating in place in the air. Now she got a proper look of the sight that had passed her by when she was brought to the castle for the first time. She saw the ocean below, as well as a large view of her homeland. *We are so high up,* Reika thought. *He was here all this time?*

Stepping back away from the cliff, Reika decided to take a run and try to land on the smaller rock that was floating below. Like a lightning bolt she dashed toward the edge and leapt as far as her feet would push her. For a few seconds she let herself fall down through the sky. Before touchdown, Reika used her magic to slow her descent, landing safely, although clumsily. "Still have to work on that."

To her surprise, Antonius followed suit, landing right next to Reika, firmly planting his feet on the ground. The slow descent was clearly easy for him. "Now, time for you to learn how to fight properly. A mere handful of lowly criminals don't compare to that of a sorcerer or sorceress." Reika nodded her head.

Antonius continued. "The prophetess, Lady Ysellian requested to come here from the Dragelve Consortium and will arrive once you're properly trained. Any questions?"

"Consortium?" Reika asked. Antonius scratched his beard with a cough. "A formal alliance of dragons and elves. It was founded over six thousand years ago. They keep to themselves, but their rulers will send help to others if needed. The Dragelve Sorcerer's Guild, of which I am a member, are protectors of this world. Now, to business, young one."

Antonius then raised his right hand, snapping his fingers, which caused a ball of fire the size of a wooden barrel. It vanished from view to reveal a red ornate chest. Reika went over to the chest and opened it up. Lying on a purple cushion was a purple sword. It had a single edge, the tip of the blade curving back rather than at a point in the middle. Reika picked the handle of the blade in her right hand, examining it. The handle was a very dark blue. The sword's metal looked faded, not by time, rather, it was designed that way. "It's beautiful," she said.

"It is a well-crafted blade," Antonius said. "Now, it's yours." "It's mine?"

"Use it well. It is a magic blade."

Reika tilted her right hand so that the blade was lightly lying on her left palm. "Err... I don't have a sheath to put this in," Reika said, awkwardly chuckling. Antonius pinched the bridge of his nose with his eyes shut, shaking his head in dismay. "The wielder can de-summon and re-summon it at any time they choose." Reika unclasped her hand, and the blade vanished into vapour. She turned back to the sorcerer.

"What else about me has changed?"

"Your physical strength. Because of our magic, most of us are stronger than we look. Do not assume, however, that makes you invincible. You need a bit of toning up as well to really take advantage of it." Reika stared at her right arm for a moment. *It's strange, those animals should have torn me to shreds but couldn't. But there must be others more dangerous than they.* She thought.

She then got into a defensive pose, with the sword reappearing in her hands. "Does this blade have a name?"

"Luniram, that's what it is called."

Reika then stood her ground, as Antonius did the same, both ready to strike.

Back at the citadel, Tabitha was firing arrows at targets around the courtyard, but the challenge was not just trying to get a bullseye but also to dodge Vips. The speed of a cobra was dangerous to the untrained and here, Vips was one of the guards well versed in agility training. It was difficult for Tabitha to fire a perfect bullseye. She had no time to check if she had fired correctly nor time to really line her shot up. No matter what, she had to stay on the move, especially with Vips trying to slash her. Vips eventually grabbed Tabitha's arms, hissing at the tamarin. Tabitha gave a kick to the abdomen to get Vips off her. The cobra recoiled, holding her right hand on the place where the tamarin had hit her.

"Isn't that a bit cheap?" Vips asked.

"Cheap?" Tabitha replied. "When is a battle ever fair?" Vips shook her head. "Never mind."

Tabitha looked at the arrows on the targets. She noticed that some of the arrows hit the inner rings, others the outer rings. One or two had snapped after hitting the wall. One arrow had hit the bullseye precisely. It was just to the left of the centre of the eastern wall.

"Only one, great," Tabitha groaned.

"You have plenty of chances here, not so much out there, so if you want to get good, let's keep going," Vips said.

Meanwhile, Melito was training in the castle courtyard. He was doing press ups on the floor, and they were not the easiest in the world, as he had placed five kilos of sand on his back, one kilo each in a small bag. "Come on, boy, push harder!" Firmillian called as he stood there watching the marmoset. Melito's face was drenched in sweat as he continued with the exercise. Firmilian added another sandbag. Melito still kept going, regardless of how many were placed on him.

Eventually he dropped to the floor on his front, breathing heavily. Firmillian picked the sandbags off the marmoset, who then rolled onto his back, lying there. The pig gave him water to drink from a pouch. Melito felt much better though he remained on the ground, his arms aching.

"Quick rest I'm afraid, we'll be moving onto combat shortly."

Melito picked himself up from the floor. He was handed his tomahawks by Firmillian, who in turn held up two small round wooden shields with bullseyes in the middle of each of them. "Hit them as hard as you can and knock them both out of my hands."

Melito twirled the tomahawks. He began to smash the shields aggressively. Firmillian sometimes responded with a backhanded knock-back with the shield to push Melito and throw him off. Melito threw one of the tomahawks at one of the shields, something Firmillian didn't expect. It remained stuck in the shield until Melito dislodged it. A large crack was left in the shield. Melito kicked the shield from below, breaking it in two.

Firmillian still had one shield left, holding it tightly in front of him. Melito kicked the shield, shoving Firmillian backwards a few steps. He continued to hold the shield nervously, weathering the assault. Melito tossed a tomahawk once again, leaving it embedded in the shield. He approached Firmillian and tore the tomahawk away, ripping the shield apart.

"I think you'll need better shields. Those ones were awfully made." "Certainly do, boy," Firmillain said. "But now the real fight begins."

A hedgehog of dark green and brown hues, with big eyes and wearing trousers like those of the other guards, came over to Firmillian after he had spoken with Tabitha and Vips. The hedgehog was a diminutive fellow, his head just below Firmillian's shoulder. He handed a bronze shield and sword to Firmillian. "Thank you very much, Clement," the pig said.

As Clement backed off, Firmillian charged, trying to slash the marmoset. Melito leapt out of the way and swung his tomahawks around at Firmillian, who raised his shield in his left to block the attack. He lunged at Melito. The point of the sword settled just a few inches from Melito's chest. "I needn't tell you how careless you were just there. Now try again. Hit my armour at least once." Melito backed off, somewhat frustrated. He swung his tomahawks twice; the shield blocked them again. Firmillian moved forward while he made a few stabs with his sword. This caused Melito to shift away from the pig, taking great care to avoid the sharp points of the blade.

Melito halted, he launched a mighty kick planted squarely into the centre of the shield, knocking Firmillian off-balance. The pig stumbled over, landing on his posterior with his sword wielding arm as a support. He raised his shield high as Melito brought both the tomahawks down. Melito brought them down several times, over and over again like a thug beating his target to a pulp. Firmillian thrust the shield forward as Melito hit, using it to mitigate the strength of the strikes while also causing the marmoset to be thrown off-balance.

Melito recovered, though it was in the nick of the time. He just managed to avoid another slash from Firmillian. Without hesitation, Melito brought both tomahawks crashing against Firmillian's armour, touching the chest and back. He did not penetrate the armour, though it suffered some scratches. Firmillian was impressed. "You attacked without reservation, very good. But you are too aggressive, you need finesse, or you waste your attacks." Melito handed the tomahawks back to Clement, and Firmillian returned the sword and shield.

Firmillian called to Tabitha and Vips. "That's enough training, time for a rest." Tabitha handed her bow to Clement, who let the bow hang on his arm. The tamarin proceeded to retrieve the arrows off the ground and targets, the others helping, except Clement who was already taking the equipment over to a cart so he could haul them away.

"Where's Reika anyway?" Clement asked. "She usually gives me a hand putting these away and helping in the nursery."

"She has gone to see Antonius," Melito said. "Didn't you get the message from the captain?" Melito then grabbed one handle of the cart while Clement grabbed the other.

"Magic training, eh?" He said with a curious smile.

"Perhaps, she does know a few tricks. Unfortunately, we have discovered she is cursed. She becomes a weredragon when the full moon appears," Melito replied.

Clement's face transitioned from beaming smile to visible shock. "A weredragon? Here?"

"Yes... Reika will return here to speak with Ignatius. He..." Melito bit his bottom lip gently to hold back any sign of sadness. "He is sending her away until she has been cured."

"My apologies, Melito, what a shame. Any idea why she turns into that beast?"

"None." Melito opened the throne room door. Clement continued to pull on the cart right after Melito. "In the meantime, I and Tabitha need to train."

"Well, I wish you all the best then, Melito, all three of you. I think the rest of the servants are going to miss Reika."

"No doubt."

They finally got to the end of the throne room and moved into the narrow hickory stone corridor that was, if one were to face the throne, to the left. They went into a spacious room where various weapons were placed on shiny racks of gold, not a visible sign of dust to be seen. They set to work, putting the weapons back in their proper place.

Chapter 3

The Ferrum Champion

709 A.E.B

For three years Reika had been training, and it was tough. Her arms and legs were now well defined with slender muscle. Antonius didn't let up for a second when she faced him. Every spell she fired he would counter with precision, deflecting it back at her.

The old man started channelling fire through his fists, causing Reika to fall back and stay on the defensive. "Come on, you're better than this," Antonius said. Reika was panting heavily. She had no trouble with the thugs that attacked Carthage. They were nowhere in the same league as Antonius; she couldn't match him at all. This wasn't a surprise to Reika; the old man was far more experienced than she was. Antonius concentrated the fire into his fingertips, firing small fiery bullets in rapid succession. Reika saw the attack coming, pulling up a barrier, wincing as the fiery bullets hammered into the defensive spell.

Despite their miniature size, they had a powerful knock-back to them. Antonius changed tack and fired one huge fiery blast at Reika. She summoned a barrier which enveloped her left forearm and hand and smacked the fireball away. She summoned Luniram in her right hand after the barrier disappeared, just as Antonius summoned a broadsword of his own. He flew towards her, stopping suddenly in front to throw her off-balance. Her heart skipped a beat.

Reika tried to swipe her sword at Antonius, who swiftly dodged her cuts twice with instant speed that made him look as if he was fading in and out of existence. Reika slashed again and the edge of Luniram nearly cut the bridge of Antonius' nose.

Antonius straightened, somewhat impressed. He swung his blade in a downward strike with his right arm. Reika blocked it, holding her sword in her right hand, pressing her left palm against the flat of the blade. She strained to hold the elderly man back, a man seemingly past his prime but with enough strength to keep pushing with inhuman force. He was holding his left arm behind his back and the leverage in his right arm wasn't even his full strength. He kept his eyes locked with hers. Secretly, however, he was staring at the crescent moon in the distance behind her. *Strong as she is now, this strength is not her own today. She's not in full control.*

Antonius summoned a cloud behind Reika, covering the moon. Reika felt her strength falter. For a while she kept pushing back but no headway was made. Eventually she backed away from Antonius. Reika couldn't understand, but there was no time for her to process the change as Antonius forced her back with a telekinetic projectile. She regained her footing in time before Antonius could deliver a sword-blow, barely rolling out of the way.

The old man cast his sword away into a blazing flame.

Reika was breathing heavily. Her sword disappeared and she fell on her posterior, completely exhausted. "Very well done. That's enough for today," Antonius said. He handed Reika a small water bottle, letting her have a swig.

"Master, three years on, you have been harder and harder to defeat, and you still weren't fighting all out, were you?"

"No, if I had fought at full strength, you'd be dead." Antonius then sat down on the stone floor as well. "I think you and I deserve a long rest."

Reika pressed with another question. "Is there anyone you require me to meet?"

"As a matter of fact, there are: two of the elder dragons, Zermanion and Thorodan. You'll meet with Lady Ysellian as I have said before." Although aware of the dragons' existence, Reika had never seen one before. She didn't like the prospect of meeting a terrifying looking beast.

"Aren't they dangerous?" She asked apprehensively.

"Dangerous, yes. But kind as well. You'll meet the three eventually." The two finished up for the day, with Reika heading to bed after a decent sized meal. Reika awoke the next morning after a long sleep in the bedroom that had been given to her. It was a small room which didn't have much in the way of possessions or decoration, though the room was relaxing enough that one could be content with lying there, just contemplating. She got up from the bed, moving over to the small chest of drawers. Reika inspected the small objects on the top of the drawers. A small pottery fragment attracted her attention. She'd known it was there for a while, although she'd never really examined it as her training often left her drained at the end of the day. It was an incomplete image. A woman with her right arm raised in the air, though only her top half of her body could be seen. The rest was missing. Reika focused intently on it. *Who... is on this?* she wondered.

She heard Antonius telepathically calling her name, and the young woman replaced the pottery fragment gently on the drawers, headed out of her room and went to the main hall. She hurried to the middle of the room after she couldn't find Antonius, wondering where he could possibly be.

"Master? Where are you?"

Antonius appeared in the incredible display that he had shown the first time he and Reika met.

"Made you jump, didn't I? Sorry," Antonius said, trying his best not to chuckle.

"Admittedly, you did," Reika responded. "You said we were to meet the dragon elders. Where are they?"

"They shall be arriving shortly. Patience." Flashes of sharp red, blue, and yellow bolts crackled and snapped, revealing three figures. The elemental flashes dissipated, leaving the elders in question visible to the eye. Reika stared at them for a moment, squinting intently. They didn't look like tall strong beasts but ordinary humans. Each of them was clad in hooded white robes with golden cummerbunds. Two of them removed their hoods. They were both male. Zermanion with grey hair and Thorodan bald with a large black beard. One feature that did catch Reika's attention was their eyes, both blue, a hybridisation of reptilian and human, like a cat's eye.

"You're human?" Reika said, in surprise.

"Humanoid in structure we are, though sometimes we transform into our true forms. But it is easier to have a conversation with us while we are this way," Thorodan said. The female figure, named Ysellian, removed her hood, revealing a very beautiful olive-skinned woman with brown eyes and long black hair combed back.

"Hold still for a moment, I need to bring your weredragon form out," she said with a stern yet also gentle voice.

"I can't transform at will. Even if I could, I might hurt you."

"You won't, child. Hold still."

Ysellian raised her hand as bright grey energy flowed from her fingertips. She brought her hand down. The energy coiled around Reika, starting to cover

her, and once it dissolved from under her feet, it started to reveal her as a weredragon. Reika was not pleased at all.

"Why... Why did you do that?" She asked. Ysellian frowned at Reika. "Hold your tongue."

Reika apologised quickly. She noticed her mind was clear. The bestial nature of the transformation wasn't present, much to Reika's relief.

"I feel fine. What has happened to me?" She asked again.

"I simply summoned the light of the moon and channelled it into your body," Ysellian replied.

"Can I turn back?"

"Once I release my spell, you will return to normal. Like this, for instance." Ysellian snapped her fingers and the grey energy left Reika. As the energy disappeared, the young woman was restored back to her human form. Reika stared at her hands, amazed at what the prophetess in front of her was capable of. "Wow, is this a cure?"

"We cannot remove the curse I'm afraid. There is a stone of great power that banishes malediction. The problem is, it was stolen away centuries ago, and we have never been able to retrieve it," Zermanion said.

Reika's face fell. "I see, so... if the stone is found, would that help remove my curse?"

"The key word is *if*. I am sure one like you would not go at it alone. It may be a perilous journey for you. Your physical and magical prowess, though enhanced thanks to your training, doesn't mean that you cannot be beaten."

Reika nodded. "Even the Master was holding back in my training. I... I need my friends' help, I need allies. What should I do for now?"

"Go to Ignatius in the fortress you once called home," Ysellian said. "He will send you on your way."

Standing in her place, Reika didn't know what to think at all, something in her made her hesitant to return to the castle. Deep down she knew she had to. "Back to Ignatius? Wait a minute, he'll not be pleased if he finds out I am a weredragon." Antonius looked at Reika then placed his hands on her shoulders. "Just go there and await his instructions." Reika looked up at Antonius, nodded her head, and moved toward the room behind her master.

Reika stopped and looked back. "Lady Ysellian, there was a piece of pottery I was looking at in my quarters, can you tell me of its story? All I could see was a woman with her right hand raised up." Antonius kept his composure, as did Ysellian. She closed her eyes. Reika stared at her, baffled. Ysellian opened them a few moments later. "An event to take place. Nothing to concern you at this time. Focus on your journey. Until we meet again, Reika." She and her companions disappeared the same way they arrived.

Reika placed her question about the pottery within her mind as one would place cutlery in a drawer. She moved on, wondering if she could fly to the citadel. However, uncertainty crept into her mind. She needed to verify this point.

"I assume flying everywhere is out of the question, Master?"

"Levitation is not for traversing the entire world, let alone the continent. Only a short distance. It's used mostly for battle. Keep that power to a minimum as you travel and use it only when necessary; it's taxing as you know doubt have experienced."

"Understood, thank you."

Antonius led her to another room. Here, she observed the stonework had the same properties as the stone that had brought her to the castle three years ago.

She turned back to her master, uncertain. This had been her new home, a place away from the dangers of the world, especially if others discovered her curse. She didn't want to depart. Antonius silently nodded toward the magical stone. She stepped onto it, and this time fire instantly engulfed Reika. Antonius crossed his arms. She called out to him, "Master, what is the story of that pottery?"

But it was too late.

The fire receded, the smoke fading. Reika now stood in a corridor to the west of the citadel's throne room, the same place that she had been unaware that Ignatius and Mark were talking about her. *Safe landing, that's a relief.* It was strange to be back after such a long time, and to have reached it so easily. The question about the pottery was there but for now, she would have to get that answer another time.

Reika entered the room. Ignatius stood in front of the small chair and some of the guards were standing in a line on both sides, wearing armour. Ignatius saw Reika come in, but he didn't say anything, as he was too busy addressing the two familiar monkeys standing in front of him.

Melito and Tabitha's bodies had changed during her absence. Melito was more muscular than his once skinny frame, and Tabitha also had a decent muscle tone on her.

Ignatius directed his attention to Reika. Melito and Tabitha both looked upset. Reika was a little puzzled. She wondered what was wrong, before she began to fear the worst, that they would execute her for being what she was.

Ignatius approached her, placing his arms behind his back. "It came to my attention a triennial ago that you transformed into a weredragon. I am afraid that you must depart from this place, I cannot risk the safety of the people. King Tertullian also agreed. You understand that?"

Reika was deeply troubled by what she heard. "Yes," Reika said with a lump in her throat.

"The elders sent you to me for the journey you must soon face. Find the Anodyne Stone, the destroyer of curses, and I will allow you to return. Melito and Tabitha will go with you. With them, you are going to find the wielder of the Draco Ferrum, Junayd. You're dismissed."

Ignatius left of the room promptly. The guards prepared themselves to leave and follow suit. Reika didn't say anything, she just stood in place, not even sure how to respond. Melito led Reika away with Tabitha following them. One of the soldiers opened the wall, revealing a hidden staircase to a dark passage below. The three made their way down into the passage and the wall closed behind them. They found themselves in a small room.

"Very rarely do we ever venture down here except in emergencies," Melito said. "There is a teleporter that will take us to Reme and one the other side that brings us here."

Tabitha was relieved. "It will save us a long trek back to the village, that's for sure."

"And it's a way of keeping us hidden. The actual maze is designed to trick invaders into thinking anyone who escapes from them goes down here. They are sealed and lost forever. But not us, thanks to this." Melito pressed his palm against a grey stone brick and the floor glowed, brightening at a snail's pace. Lightning swirled from the floor, engulfing all three of them. When the lightning vanished, the room they were in resembled the previous one, only something was off... It was a mirrored image!

They exited the room into another corridor. Reika noticed a large boulder that partially obscured a staircase on her left. She followed her friends up another staircase in front of her, each step brighter than the last. Eventually they were at the top, back in Reme, safe and sound. As soon as they were in the open air, Reika ran towards Mark's house at full speed and knocked on the door. Mark opened it. Immediately he hugged Reika.

"It's been a long time since I have seen you." "I missed you, Father!"

Andrea stepped out, giving Reika a hug too. Mark then noticed her semi- muscular arms. "Antonius took care of you alright too, I see."

"Yes." Reika gulped. "I'm sorry, I can't stay."

"I know. Ignatius told me. No matter what happens... You'll always be our daughter." Reika shut her eyes, holding Mark, a disconsolate expression on her face.

Melito and Tabitha only watched. "Be careful out there," Mark said. "Is there anything you need?"

"Can we use your motorboat?" Reika asked.

"Sadly, it's being fixed, and it won't be ready for a while. There is a speed boat I have that you can use."

The trio arrived at the dock and there they found a small, but a decent-sized speed boat tied to the side, with a four-foot propeller. Reika walked over to the boat and leapt from the dock onto it. "Hop on," Reika called. Both the monkeys followed and leapt onto the boat.

"To the west we go," Tabitha cheered. Without a moment's hesitation, they pushed the boat away from the dock. Melito started the engine and the propeller whirred, pushing the boat along. It was steered by a wheel and rudder.

Sometime later, Melito was starting to get rather impatient. "This is taking forever. If only Mark's motorboat was fixed." Tabitha looked at Melito. "There wasn't anything that could be done," she replied. Silence fell for a few seconds.

"How long till we get there?" Melito asked.

"We've been on the ocean for an hour and a half and at the current speed we are moving, we have another half hour to go," Tabitha replied. Melito then laid back on the raft, letting out a big yawn.

"Brilliant, simply brilliant."

Reika wasn't talkative throughout the journey. Melito observed the look on her face. She was looking over the horizon with a smile on her face. "What are you so cheerful about?" Melito asked.

"Chip and I used to sail a lot when I was a child. It was lovely, just being out here brings all those memories back. Haven't been on the sea for a while so it's nice to return to it after all these years." Melito was content with the answer. "When you put it that way, maybe traversing the sea for this long isn't that bad." "All the same," Reika said, her tone lower spirited. "I am going to be miss

Mark and Andrea as well as the other guards of the castle." "I'm sure we'll see them again Reika... For now, let's..."

Just as Melito was speaking, he saw a large object approaching them fast. "Hey, what is that?"

"Rats, a ship, we have to move right now," Tabitha said, panicking. Reika looked in horror. "It's coming for us!"

Melito called to his friends to jump, and they did, the speed boat destroyed as the ship collided with it. A piece of the speed boat spun away, hitting Reika in the head, knocking her unconscious.

Reika was sluggish in waking up. She felt awful, groaning as she awoke. *Where am I, what happened to me?* Her eyes focused quickly, and Reika realised where she was. *A ship, how did I get here? I need to get off right now. But first, where are Melito and Tabitha?*

Reika used the mast to pull herself to her feet, making her way quietly toward the door of the cabin that she could see in the distance. She eyed the large door in front of her, knocking with some hesitation. The door opened and Vera stepped out. Reika quickly backed away from the door. "Vera?"

"Hehe, you again. I have been waiting to hurt you." Vera grabbed Reika by the neck and pulled her back near the door, dropping the human on the floor with a thud. "I'd better give my friends a proper introduction to you," Vera said to Reika, grinning in anticipation.

The other thugs appeared in a rectangular formation around Reika. "Friends, what do you propose we should do with her?" Marcion enquired.

"There is one idea that comes to mind, Marcion. Roast her over an open fire!" Darius said.

Felix put his hand on Darius' shoulder. "Not now, we'll let Magnus take care of her."

Vera stepped away from Reika to join the formation, making room for Magnus, who emerged from his quarters, smiling. "Welcome to the *Tetraspis*, young one," he said. "I believe it is time for a little interrogation."

Reika raised her eyebrows as she stood up, somewhat perplexed, especially after the "greeting" she was given. "Is that all? That's hardly threatening. I was expecting something much worse," Reika said, brushing her hair with her hand casually. "It's not really any of your concern where we are going. You rammed into us and destroyed the boat we were on."

With a flick of her wrists, she could unleash destructive magical power.

Magnus seemed to read her thoughts.

"I would give some serious thought about fighting us right now if I were you. We have your friends. Anything happens to me or my crew, and they suffer." She gritted her teeth. It was the one leverage he had, and he had used it expertly. Magnus strutted about on the deck, encircling Reika. "You're not going anywhere. You and your friends are my prisoners," Magnus sneered.

"We caught you; we keep you, it's as simple as that. I wouldn't try flying your way out of here. I have a set of cannons here that would shoot you down in no time."

Reika had an idea. "If that's the case, then there is one thing that I request. We'll fight. If I win, you'll let my friends and I go," Magnus smirked. It occurred to Reika she had never seen Magnus fight. She had no idea how strong he really was. "You want to perish? So be it." He faced Reika.

Reika pointed towards Magnus' sheath. "My sword Luniram. You stole it from me."

The sword reappeared in Reika's hand, much to Magnus' surprise. "Fine.

Use it. I don't care, you'll be the first human to mount on my wall."

He drew what seemed to be a dagger from underneath his vest. Before Reika's eyes, the blade took shape and expanded, growing to two feet long at least.

The other thugs watched, expectant.

Reika held her sword level. *Let's see how powerful I am.* Magnus made the first move, charging. Reika followed suit. They collided, both trying to cut each

other, blocking each other's attacks with precise movements. Reika fought with elegance, switching between two and one-handed forms.

Magnus fought with broader, sweeping strokes, which caused Reika to dodge and back off. She parried a block from Magnus. He wasn't surprised. He knew Reika's strength all too well from how she had defeated his crew. He was also aware that she was more powerful than when they'd last met, the moon not even boosting her strength this time. Reika was aware of this too. A few years ago, she would have struggled in a physical altercation and now she could confirm that Antonius was correct, her strength had indeed been enhanced. With one final upward strike, she knocked the caiman back.

Once Magnus steadied himself, he strafed further back, raising his hand in the air. To Reika's astonishment, the sea formed a pillar-like structure near the ship. Magnus thrust his hand forward, causing the pillar to crash into Reika at high velocity, pushing her against the side of the ship wall, and drenching the decks.

She struggled against the current, spluttering. The water came back for a second attack with Reika promptly summoning a fiery barrier to protect herself, evaporating the sea even as it washed over her, which impressed Magnus considerably. Reika concentrated the fire around her right arm, which she raised, firing a blast at him. The caiman drew the sea towards him, away from Reika, using the water as a shield to block the flaming bolt. Splashes of superheated water burned some of the scales on his left shoulder.

Magnus, in anger, charged again at Reika, seeking to cut her down swiftly while she recovered from their magical exchange. The young human rolling to the side quickly. Using her magic, Reika threw herself to the other side of the ship away from Magnus, landing carefully balanced on the railing.

Magnus chuckled to himself. "You're a strong one, I'll give you that. Whoever trained you taught you well."

Reika stepped off the wall onto the ship, already tiring from the fight. "I don't get it. You are not even breaking a sweat."

"My stamina is practically limitless. Something you lack," Magnus replied.

Reika's eyes widened. Perhaps she had taken on a foe she could not best?

The two walked in a semi-circle looking at each other. Without warning, Reika pushed her hand through the air, causing Magnus to drop his sword and fly across the ship, smacking into the deck above the cabin door. He fell to the ground with a thud but picked himself up quickly. "You will not embarrass me any further. I will have my trophy." Reika raised her hand and shot a telekinetic projectile at the deck of the ship, opening a large, cracked hole, promptly jumping down into it.

She found herself in a hold, where she saw Melito and Tabitha tied to a pillar.

There was a knife on a table. She took it, cutting the monkeys free.

"Find a boat. I'll meet you on it." Reika flew back through the hole onto the upper deck. Magnus waited for her.

As she ran, Reika charged blue energy along her arm, swiping it in the air, causing a massive blue shockwave which knocked the crew to the deck, Magnus found himself knocked back through the cabin door, which came off its hinges.

Reika fled.

Both Melito and Tabitha found a dinghy at the stern of the ship on some rails. Melito looked this way and that. Eventually, he saw a lever to the right in front of him and he pulled on it. A hatch leading to the sea opened, high enough to prevent the water from entering the ship. A ramp also slid out, just about touching the water. They both struggled to push the dinghy.

Reika bolted across the deck taking a magic leap through the air. "Come on, where are you?" She said wondering where her friends were.

The two monkeys called to her. She looked over the railings and saw them floating off in a tiny dinghy. She grinned. She leapt down, controlling her descent with magic, the touch down proving more graceful than her previous efforts.

"Any ideas, Reika?"

"Only one." Reika held out her hand, a flame emanated from her, winding down her arm faster and faster until it reached her palm. The flame with a mighty shove propelled the dinghy away from the *Tetraspis*.

~

The trio finally made it to Caledonia's dock, like the dock in Carthage but with less people. Melito climbed out of the boat, Tabitha and Reika following suit. Reika nearly fell over as she stood upright, and her two friends supported her. She had kept the magical fire burning for a long time. Melito was concerned.

"Are you alright?" He asked.

"Yeah," she replied. "Phew," she added, forcing some levity into her voice.

They all left the port, heading towards a set of towering brown mountains in the distance.

It was a long journey across barren plains and sparse copses of greenery. Any of the trees that they did pass along the way were dry and parched. They finally found themselves inside a cave with brown craggy rocks on the walls and ceilings.

Melito scouted ahead, heading further into the cave. Exiting an archway, Melito found himself in a larger cavern. He was amazed by what he saw: rail tracks both on the ground and suspended over gigantic chasms, the tracks held up by long poles of scaffolding. Unfortunately, some the tracks were missing. The structure holding the tracks was still intact for the most part. Tabitha and Reika followed Melito into the larger cavern, also awed by the old mine-cart rails.

"Stay here, allow me to test this," Melito said. He stepped onto the track, checking with unease to see if the rails were able to support his weight. "Come on, it's safe!" He called. Just to be certain, Melito proceeded to climb down the wooden sleepers sloping diagonally into the next section of the cavern. Tabitha gently placed her feet on the rails, starting to walk with trepidation across the sleepers. She edged her way down, down the sloping rail and Reika did the same. They were then side by side with Melito, on the ground, in a narrow passage that still allowed a small party to traverse safely beside the rails. Soon, they departed from the narrow passage, leaving what resembled an outward cone into another cavern.

This one had five rails side by side over a narrow chasm. Unfortunately, many of these rails had gaps in them where the rails had spilt and fallen down. The trio walked down the rails, avoiding the holes, making their way to the next section of the cave. Melito stepped on a sleeper that gave away under his right foot. He toppled forward.

"Whoa!" Reika and Tabitha reached for him, holding him by his arms in place as he yelped. His echo began to die down. He stared at the chasm below. The other two pulled him back to safety. "That was close," Tabitha said.

"Yes, Thanks to both of you for stopping me fall! I would have been a goner," Melito replied. "Let's use the rails if we can."

They continued along the rails, ensuring that they didn't step on the sleepers, and after what felt like an arduous trip, the three passed into another cavern. The rails here were in much better condition. Pools spread below them. Some railways divided where they reached small crevices in the stone, and others were missing sleepers; presumably someone was going to repair them. The trio made their way along the rails, pondering on whether or not the mines were still being worked on, heading to another cavern, turning left to find two more small pools. These, they would have to cross. They took a run and jumped across them.

The next cavern took them right and out the caves. Melito looked to the west, spotting another cave leading into the mountains to the northwest. Two buildings in the distance hugged the coast.

"Onward," Reika said.

~

On the *Tetraspis,* Magnus sat in his cabin. He was in a foul mood after his defeat, talking to himself incessantly. "Hmph, this is only a setback, I shall have my vengeance on that filthy skinbag. She and her friends won't be celebrating for long, I will find those fools in time and make them writhe. They shall not elude me again." The others were sleeping silently in the lower decks of the ship, recovering from the wounds they'd suffered from Reika's shockwave. Magnus made his way down into the lower decks and stared at the empty compartment where the dinghy once sat. He knew it needed to be replaced.

Then he was struck by an idea and grinned.

The building that Reika, Melito, and Tabitha arrived at was an inn. It had a sign above the door that read in huge wooden letters *Costa Enano.* A beach hut was situated only a few feet away. In stark contrast to the barren desert around them, the structures of the buildings were made of robust ironwood with a lighter shade of the same material used for the roofs. Dwarves bustled about, some gathering crops, one drawing water from a stone well. Their metal armour shone in the sun. Very seldom did the three see dwarves and when they did, the small people had business to conduct, usually bringing small gems as tribute to Tertullian.

Alongside the buildings were four tents of large cream colour. At one of them, a middle-aged strong man with an olive-skinned complexion stood, his face sporting a rough black beard. A purple cummerbund held his light tan trousers up and he had a small tan turban that covered the top of his head, with a tan shirt and a beige vest. He was conversing with one of the dwarves. He appeared to be on his lunch break. The dwarf, with a long brown beard and shiny armour, was laughing. Clearly the two men were having some friendly banter.

The three approached the man. "My, my... How did you get here?" He said, startled by their appearance and approach.

"Through the mines," Reika replied. The man nearly choked on the drink he held in his hand.

"Oh really? A little dangerous if you ask me... I think my friends should have closed that mine off. It's still under repairs."

He put his drink down and shook the hands of the three in turn. "Avi is the name, I'm a merchant. Anything I can give to you at this juncture?"

"Not at the moment," Melito answered. "We just need a place for us to stay.

The inn over there perhaps?"

"Yes," said Avi. "You can stay there. I'll alert the dwarves if you decide to go through the mines a second time, there is another set of caves to the north."

"Thanks."

"Anything else you need, young monkey..." "Melito."

"Melito. Need something, I can help you get it." Melito wiped the sweat from his forehead.

"Water would be nice." Avi gestured towards the stone well by the inn. "Over there is where you'll find the water, you look like you need it, especially with all that fur on you and your tamarin compatriot here..."

"Tabitha. My friends call me Tabs." "No problem, Tabs."

There was a small queue to the well for Melito, four dwarves in front of him, each with different hair colours: brown, blonde, ginger, and white. Melito figured they needed it more than him, as they worked down in the mines.

"'Bout time we got some wa'er 'ere," said the ginger dwarf.

"Wait your turn! Some of us 'ere be needing a swig of it," the blonde dwarf said.

The brown-haired dwarf took his fair share, stepping out of the way so the others could collect their water. The ginger dwarf was next, drinking his water till his thirst was quenched.

"Smashing, especially in this part of the world," he remarked.

The blonde dwarf looked behind him after his drink, seeing Melito waiting patiently for the line to move along.

"You'll like this wa'er mate, 'ave a swig."

Melito filled his drink flask and brought it to his mouth. "So clean, I needed that. My head doesn't hurt anymore."

Melito and Tabitha made their way inside the inn after the marmoset was refreshed by the well. Reika stopped for a moment before she followed her friends, turning her head to the left. There, standing twenty feet away, was a mysterious figure. He wore black armour with gold trimming. A beige scarf was wrapped around his face, revealing only a golden visor. "Who is that?" Reika asked herself.

The figure held his hand to signal to Reika that he wanted to talk. Cautiously, she approached him.

"You must be the new pupil of Antonius," the armoured stranger said. "Yes, I am."

"So far from what I have seen, you seem to be doing ok but you... need to improve. Especially with what lies ahead."

Reika scratched the back of her head. "You have a point there. I am still a learner." The man removed his scarf to reveal a mask underneath. Joints could be seen in the helmet. His short to mid-length black hair was exposed. Reika couldn't see into the eyeholes. The stranger's vision, however, did not seem to be impaired.

"How do I know your intentions are good if I can't see your face? I cannot trust a man in a mask."

"I have to be this way for the time being. The mask blocks out mental powers, mind reading essentially, just in case someone may be watching. They cannot know who I am, let me just say... I am a friend."

"What about a name?"

"Call me... Visiert."

"All right... Visiert. I hope I can trust you."

"Hmph, hold me to that. You certainly can..." Visiert stopped in his train of thought. "Wait a second," he said. "You have never heard of me?"

"I am afraid not," Reika replied.

"It's no trouble at all. Anyway, be careful on your journey, I have much work to do myself. Farewell." Visiert made his way to the east back along the dusty highway, putting back on his scarf and raising his hood again. Sand clouds swirled behind him, leaving the road completely empty. Reika entered the inn. She did not say a word about the masked man to her friends.

After a long night, the trio left the mining town behind and arrived at the second cavern. This time, no rails were present to carry them across, nor was the distance small enough for them to leap across. Melito moved to the edge with Tabitha, peering down the chasm. "It's a long way down," he said. "How are we going get across?"

Reika walked over to Melito with a smile on her face. "Easy," she said. "The same way I caught up with you in the forest."

Melito stared at Reika, his eyes swiftly widening. "Fly across?"

Reika just nodded. "Give me a while though. I haven't lifted anyone else.

Only myself." Melito's face dropped.

Facing the large crevice, Reika just walked casually off the edge, looking as though she were walking on invisible glass. She stopped in place. "Ready!" She called. Tabitha also looked at Reika with a little apprehension.

"Be careful Reika, don't drop us!" Tabitha called.

Reika raised her arms. The two monkeys felt the ground peel away. At a leisurely pace, they hovered across the chasm, suspended above the large drop. Tabitha was staring intently at Reika as they were drawn closer to her. Reika

turned herself round to face away from the entrance of the cave. "Here's the tough part," Reika said.

"Wait, what are you doing?" asked Melito.

His question was not answered as Reika swiftly flew to the other side of the cavern, landing feet first, trying her best to ensure that her friends landed safely alongside her. Melito stood there in shock. "That was a bit rushed," he remarked. Reika breathed out a huge sigh of relief, promptly straightening herself. She smiled back at Melito, this time very awkwardly. "I'll be more careful next time." Luckily for the trio, these caverns were drastically smaller, as the mines were incomplete. They pressed on, finding less railways and pools. They at last came to one final tunnel, which housed some evenly placed stalagmites near the exit. The trio didn't stop for too long and moved past the structures, leaving the caves behind. They saw a small town up north in the distance, proceeding there without stopping for repast, following the dusty highway that lay in front of them.

Entering the village of Bahaduro from the western fence, the trio looked in awe at the village. It was bigger than Reme. The buildings were made of smooth brown stones with artistic cracks and wooden roofs, all of which were in surprisingly good condition considering they were in a desert. Even the stones beneath Reika's feet were surprisingly cool, never burning her feet at all.

"It's different from ours. This village has a proper market. We don't even have that," Reika said, thinking of the lone fruit selling merchant who had once sold her three of a kind in Reme. In front of them were a line of tents that had much fruit and vegetables lying in open crates.

"Want to take a look around?" Melito asked.

"It's worth it," Tabitha replied. Melito went in one direction north while Tabitha went south.

Tabitha looked at the tents in the south. One that was closest to the path had a collection of stone vases, tablets, and other pots. One of the big vases showed a man with a sword fighting a monstrous dragon. The dragon's hand brandished a dark blade.

"What is this? Something that happened in the past?" Tabitha asked.

"An ancient prophecy my dear," said the old woman who resided at the tent. She had an olive complexion, mid-length wavy white hair, and wore ecru robes. Despite her evident age, she had few wrinkles. "A dragon of pure evil to be slain by a hero. It has yet to happen."

Tabitha was intrigued. "Prophecy, eh? Don't really hear that these days. Any idea who is the man fighting the dragon?"

"I believe that..." said the old woman. "It's the wielder of the Draco Ferrum.

He is the one to carry out this most sacred task. I only wish it is true." "What of the vase itself? It looks relatively new."

"It's a copy, young simian. My late husband was a potter. He left the painting to me. Nowadays, my son and daughter have taken the business over. I still watch over the tent here for them. They are currently teaching some of the little ones to make these."

Melito explored the tents in the north, coming to a bend in the path and speaking to a young man and woman there. They were making pottery themselves. Some small children were getting involved, attempting to make pottery of their own out of muddy clay. Many were laughing amongst themselves, having a good time crafting the small pots. Melito smiled.

That takes me back to my childhood, making my own pots, He thought. *I should get back to this in my spare time. It has been a long time.* He looked at the crude creations the children were making. *They'll get better.* He looked at a complete tablet that was near him. *These are dragons,* he thought. *Monstrous ones, not like the ones with which I am familiar.* The dark creatures in the image were all ravenous, ready to go after something.

"What are the beasts in this image?" Melito asked.

The man stopped what he was doing and walked over to Melito. "Weredragons. They disappeared long ago according to many stories. I don't believe that. Some people claim there have been sightings of them over the years, though they always vanish without a trace. Others completely deny they exist. This piece shows an invasion by them, ready to wreak havoc upon this world."

Melito did his best to hide his shock, knowing Reika transformed into one of those creatures. "What can be done to stop them?"

"The Anodyne Stone is a possibility but good luck finding the thing, it's been gone for so long, its existence is doubted by many of us outside the Dragelve Consortium. Even Lady Ysellian's visions of this have been called into question."

"Thanks for the information," Melito said.

Reika meanwhile walked through the marketplace. She looked at the food in the stalls, uncertain what she wanted to buy. As she walked down, Reika halted when a dragonfruit caught her eye. "This actually looks rather delicious." Before she could complete her transaction, two large gorillas walked towards her, one white and one black. Their names were Charlton and Heston.

"Well, well, what's a human like you doing in a place like this?" Charlton asked. Reika looked at the two gorillas nervously. She didn't like where this was going.

"Taking a look around here, why?"

"I suggest you get out of the way before you get hurt," Heston said in a threatening tone.

"Hey, just leave me alone," Reika said, now slightly worried. She started to feel quite powerless, discovering that when tried to use her magic, she couldn't. Little did she know that Heston had a rune hanging from his belt, a rune that had the word "NIL" written on it. Heston grabbed Reika. "Get away from me!" Reika cried out, slapping Heston on the face, he let her go afterwards. It did little but aggravate the gorilla even more.

"HEY! PICK ON SOMEONE ELSE!" A voice shouted.

The apes turned around to hear where the voice had come from. Reika then caught sight of a young man leaping down from the roof of a nearby building. He leapt off one of the houses, landing in front of Reika. The young man had a dark olive complexion with brown eyes and unkempt black hair. His upper body was bare, with a healthy muscular physique. He wore a purple cummerbund that held up his beige trousers; the legs of the trousers were large though the ends left his feet exposed. The man also carried a large blue sword that was almost as tall as him. It was strange, especially in comparison to Reika's blade. The sword was partially flat at the tail end but had a sharp edge suitable for cutting. Though it looked as thick as a paddle, the young man seemed able to hold the blade easily.

He held his sword in a defensive stance. "Begone! Have you nothing better to do?"

"You little fool, get out of the way!" Charlton growled.

"You want the girl? You have to go through me," the young man said.

Reika looked at the man in front of her. *Brave man,* she thought. The two apes charged at him, but the young warrior swung the sword, pushing them back. They both threw punches at him but then the man planted the blade in the ground, and caught their fists easily. He pushed them back, punching Charlton in the left cheek and kicking Heston in the chest. Grabbing the hilt of the sword, and then using the flat side like a boat paddle, the man bashed the two apes to the floor. Victorious, the young man ripped the rune from Heston's belt and crushed it to dust in his hand. Reika felt her power return.

The two gorillas got up off the floor, still recovering from the attack. "We won't forget this!" Charlton snarled. With that, the apes fled away from the market further into the town.

Both Melito and Tabitha arrived on the scene quickly, surprised that Reika was ok. "Thanks for the help," Reika said, looking at the young man with awe on her face. He looked at her in return.

"You're welcome. Stay away from those guys. They are trouble," he said. "I didn't know that, I'm new here."

"Who are you?"

"Reika."

"I'm Junayd."

Reika's eyes widened. This was the man they had been looking for.

As her friends approached, Reika did a sideways thumbs up towards them, indicating all was well.

"My two friends and I, we are searching for the one who wields the Draco Ferrum and..." She left the question hanging.

Junayd looked down at the sword, then held it up high in the air. "Oh this?

Yeah, this is it."

"You are younger than I imagined," Reika remarked.

Melito finally drew up beside Reika. Junayd looked at Melito in the eyes, his face rather serious.

"You're Reika's friends, right?"

"Yep."

"You really shouldn't leave your friend alone in Bahaduro. She nearly got hurt." Junayd pointed at Melito's armour. "And judging by your clothes, I'd say you were royal guards... soldiers. Very careless."

Melito's face swiftly seethed with anger. "Now wait a minute, how dare you..."

Junayd pointed his sword at Melito, who promptly backed away, holding his hands in the air.

"How dare I what? Care to finish that sentence? You were sent with her right? So... do your job. Understand?"

Melito started to sweat and was silent for a moment. "No problem."

Junayd pulled the blade away from Melito, embedding it into the sand with a smile on his face. "I'm Junayd, your names?"

"Melito, the girl behind me is Tabitha."

"A marmoset and a tamarin. We don't get many metazoans around here.

Usually, they stay at the inn while on business or time away," Junayd said. "Do you know a good place to stay?" Tabitha asked.

Junayd lifted his right arm and pointed with his thumb behind him. "To my house we go."

"How do we know you are not going to hurt us? How do we know you really are who you say you are?" Melito asked.

"You don't trust me?"

"Prove you are genuine. There are shady people who lure the innocent into their traps."

"Alright. Here's proof." Junayd pointed with his finger at the blade. The sword began to disintegrate into shards of light, disappearing completely.

"The Draco Ferrum," Melito whispered.

"Ignatius sent you to find me, did he not?" Junayd said.

"I am so sorry, forgive me for my questions," Melito said. Junayd merely chuckled. "Hey, no worries."

He turned. "We'll talk at my place. Tongues wag you see. My house has a blue and ecru striped tent by it. You can't miss it." And with that, Junayd hopped from building to building, the same way he arrived.

Tabitha could only watch in amazement. "That guy has serious skills. Puts our tree climbing to shame." All three then ventured to the tall blue and ecru striped tent he had pointed out to them, located on the eastern side of the town.

Little did they know Lief was watching from the top of the inn. "I finally found you," the elf said. "Exactly as described by Magnus."

The three rested inside Junayd's tent—not his house recovering after the long trip, enjoying a sizeable meal with fruit. They found great satisfaction in eating the fruit, including the dragonfruit that Reika had eventually purchased.

The tent itself had various items within it. A maroon carpet lay on the floor of the tent. Two mats with russet-coloured covers on them covered the ground. A map of the world lay next to a steel blue teapot on a table. Two teacups rested on another table to the right, and on the left were books, as well as a large sack.

Reika then turned her attention to Junayd who sat opposite her. "Nice tent you have. Don't you have a house next to it?"

"The tent has a little bit more room. The house is being used for storage right now. Very seldom do I even sleep in it. Unfortunately, I was only informed of your arrival this morning, otherwise I would have prepared beds for you there. The inn will have to do."

Reika took a quick sip of the wine from the cup in front of her, putting it down gently. "How powerful is the Ferrum?" She finally asked.

"Quite... or rather I say, sort of... It's not at full power." "You seemed pretty strong to me you know."

Junayd chuckled. "Yes, I can defeat those goons easily with it, but someone more powerful, not so much. I need to power it up at forges built around the continent. The forges were created by warrior monks who later became the Order of the Ferrum. Once I have travelled to all the forges, the blade will be at full strength."

"Oh..." Reika cut straight to her next point. "Can you still help us?"

"Yes, it's what I am here for. Where do you need to go, anyway?"

"We are looking for the Anodyne Stone."

Junayd raised his right eyebrow. "The elders haven't retrieved it; they are still searching for it. And you are trying to get it?"

"Junayd, finding the stone is urgent. I cannot continue to live with the weredragon's curse. Please help us out," Reika begged.

The young man started to think for a moment, holding his chin in his hand. He then let go of it. "Alright, I'll give you a hand." He stood up. "It's going to be dangerous; I'll tell you that." Reika nodded and agreed.

"Certainly, it will be dangerous, but we are prepared." She then snapped her fingers and a small current of fire snaked up her arm, coalescing onto a gentle looking flame floating above her palm. Junayd reeled backwards, taken aback by what he saw.

"Magic!" He exclaimed. "Are you a pupil of Antonius by any chance?" "For these past three years, yes. I still have much to learn." Reika clasped her hand around the flame, extinguishing it. "You seem surprised?"

"Guess I am not the only one with magic powers," Junayd replied. "This is getting very interesting."

Late that afternoon they all made their way to the inn to rest for the next day with Reika and Junayd immediately settling into their bedrooms and falling asleep. The bedrooms had remarkably comfortable beds. Simple chests of drawers were present outside the separate rooms along with small counters and sinks made of fine oak. A few hours passed with Melito and Tabitha guarding the rooms. Tabitha walked over to Melito down the corridor.

"Tough night staying up guarding the both of them," Tabitha said. Melito nodded. "Well, they need someone to sound the alarm. In the cave there wasn't a problem, but Reika was attacked earlier today, and Junayd caused a commotion. Someone might come after them."

"It's nothing they can't handle, same with us." "True there."

Melito leaned back on the table. He looked at a torn image hanging on the wall: it showed a man with a sword, fighting a monstrous dragon; the bottom half of their bodies were missing. "I hope that beast isn't real," he said.

Tabitha looked at the image. "You reckon the figure might be Junayd? The one fighting that monster?" Melito raised his eyebrows.

"Junayd?"

"Yes, an old woman told me this figure in the picture is the wielder of the Draco Ferrum. I don't think there are any other wielders of his sacred blade."

Meanwhile, Reika awoke to voices, a little delirious at first due to deep sleep. "Hmm? What's that?" Getting up from her bed, Reika left her room.

"Reika? Where are you going?" Melito asked.

"I can hear people talking downstairs, I'll be back in a moment."

Reika swiftly kept going down the stairs. She crouched and hid near the stairs to the basement to make sure she avoided detection, listening in on the conversation. Reika peered down the stairs and saw Charlton and Heston, standing in front of a portal of black and purple flames which had the visage of a woman in the middle. She wore grey armour with blue leg plates, breast plates and pauldrons. She brandished a blue armoured helmet on her head which only exposed her mouth and neck. Ears also poked through the sides of the helmet.

Reika looked at the woman in surprise, noticing her pointy ears. This woman was an elf. Unbeknownst to Reika, this woman's servant Lief had previously spoken with Magnus about what the caiman saw.

Lief himself was present at the inn, though Reika didn't know his name, standing next to the two monkeys. For the first time in her life, Reika had seen elves.

"You both are useless! You allowed this young whelp to beat you? That rune is lost. It took us years to find it and yet you allowed it to be destroyed?" the elf woman said in a stern voice.

"We are sorry!" Charlton said. The elf merely held her palm in the air, not interested in hearing the excuse.

"Be grateful you haven't been slain by me or my master. I am very disappointed." Afterwards, the portal turned dark and thinned like a vapour, leaving Charlton and Heston relieved and upset. Lief stayed where he was, shaking his head in dismay.

At the top of the stairs, Reika's composure was beginning to dissolve. *I need to speak with Junayd.* She headed back up the stairs quickly, trying not to make a sound as she went. Reika entered Junayd's bedroom. Melito and Tabitha didn't even get a chance to speak. Reika started to shake Junayd to wake him up. Junayd was somewhat confused.

"Ugh... Wha...?" He said. "Oh, Reika, what are you doing up?"

"I could hear some people talking," Reika said. "The two thugs that attacked me in town, they were speaking with an elvish woman in the basement."

Junayd lowered himself back onto the bed. "Eh, there are people always talking and..." His eyes without warning widened and he leapt from his bed onto his feet. "What did you say?"

"An elvish woman." Junayd was silent for a few seconds, wondering who Reika saw. "Know her?"

"What did she look like?"

Reika placed her index finger on her chin, staring at the floor thinking. "She was wearing armour. Her face was obscured by a helmet, but her ears were not. She wasn't physically there; she was communicating with them through a portal. There was an elf man too. He was just in a plain vest and trousers, black hair on his head."

Junayd placed his right hand behind his head scratching it. He had an inkling of who the elf woman was but couldn't quite think who. "Whoever she is, I have a feeling this won't be the last time she shows up, in person or otherwise. Not sure about the elf man though."

Junayd made his way back to the bed, lying on it and facing the wall, looking away from Reika. "Get some rest, Reika." As Junayd fell asleep, Reika headed back to her bed and lay down.

Lief left the basement and went upstairs. He peeked his head into the corridor outside the bedrooms. He could see Tabitha and Melito guarding one of the rooms. The elf man grinned. Their presence told him which one Reika was in. "Time to let you run loose for a while."

Lief raised his hand up with the bright energy emanating from his fingertips, much like Ysellian in Antonius' Castle, lowering his hand afterwards. The energy snaked along the floor without Melito and Tabitha noticing it, slipping underneath the bedroom door. Its final stop was into Reika's head. She was sound asleep until pain forced her awake. Once again, she was groggy. The pain was one she recognised, and Reika started to panic. The pain in her head intensified, as if someone was trying to rip her head open. She then began to yell at the top of her voice as darkness enveloped her, transforming her into the weredragon once again. His work done, Lief exited from the inn swiftly through the back window. He hid away behind a house to the left of the inn waiting to see what would happen next.

Tabitha and Melito backed away from the room. Before they could think of what to do, Junayd awoke suddenly, leaping to his feet and rushing to Reika's room. He stared at Reika with his eyes widening in shock. Reika, now draconic in form, snapped her head towards Junayd, her feet stomping on the floor, advancing. She grabbed him by the neck and tossed him out the window. Junayd recovered quickly in the air, landing on his feet.

He summoned his sword as Reika leapt out of the window after him. She charged. Junayd dodged quickly, holding his sword to keep up his defence. *So, she is one of them.* Reika roared at Junayd in anger, trying to slash at him with black claws. Junayd blocked every strike with his sword.

Both Melito and Tabitha rushed outside, surprised to see what was going on. "We kept her in the shade, away from the moon, who did this to her?" Melito asked.

Junayd kicked Reika to the floor. The villagers awoke to the noise of Reika's roar and were terrified. Most stayed where they were in their beds. Reika had no interest in them at all, she was fixated on Junayd, as if she had a specific goal in mind. Tabitha was concerned. *Don't kill her,* she thought. Junayd swung his blade, forcing the weredragon to step back. The weredragon started to look worried by the deadly blade. She backed off, gazing at the Draco Ferrum. Junayd stepped closer, stabbing his sword down into the ground. Reika's expression changed from worry to fury once again.

Lief watched. He was about to jump in to stop Junayd when suddenly he fell through a sangria-coloured portal that opened below him; he dropped onto the sand hard. His surroundings told him he had just travelled a mile to the west of the village. He looked to his right and there stood Visiert. Visiert's hair had inverted in colour, a silvery sheen as opposed to his usual black hair. It was also straighter than it had been previously. The elf backed away.

"You! You stop me from getting my quarry?"

"The girl is not yours to take. Stand down right now."

Lief immediately charged at Visiert with a small blade in his hand. Visiert dodged and struck Lief on the face, causing the assailant to drop his blade on the floor. Lief was sent flying, scuffing along the sand. He got to his feet, barely blocking the next attack from the armoured man. He swung his right fist at Visiert. The armoured figure's dodge was casual yet efficient. He grabbed the elf man, holding him in a grapple.

"How are you this strong for a human?" Lief spat.

"No need for you to know elf. Now tell me, who are you working for?" Lief growled. "I am not telling you anything."

"Alright, have it your way." Visiert released the elf from his grip, then blasted him in the chest. It knocked the elf unconscious, though spared him from death. *If it's true what the Consortium say about Reika being cursed, this is going to make the endgame difficult.* Visiert's hair returned to its original state. He hauled Lief onto his back and, holding a rune in his hand with the image of a person entering a ring with flames around it, he disappeared into another portal.

Meanwhile, a little boy with dark hair stepped out of his tent, his mother calling his name, Jaser, telling back to him back inside. Reika turned to stare at the boy. She stepped towards him. His frightened expression gazed back at her. She raised her arm in the air, pausing for a time. A conflict was arising within the creature. Finally, Reika backed away from Jaser, clutching her head in pain. The boy looked back over his shoulder at the creature as he heeded his mother's call.

Leaping at Reika while she was distracted, Junayd grabbed her and wrestled her to the ground, pinning her there. Her jaws snapped at him. Junayd punched Reika in the cheek, knocking her unconscious.

Slowly, Junayd got to his feet. He witnessed the darkness enve-lope Reika, the weredragon form fading away from her, revealing her human form, fully clothed, once again. The cheek Junayd had punched showed no sign of damage, indicating either a swift healing or that whatever was done to her in weredragon form did not carry over; it was almost as if she had two entirely separate bodies.

"Interesting," he said again.

Her two friends ran towards Junayd. They looked down at Reika, rather disturbed. "Is she hurt?" Tabitha asked.

Junayd looked at Tabitha. "If you knock a weredragon out cold, their host turns back to normal. Let us bring her back inside the inn." He picked Reika up to take her back to her room. The villagers could only stand there with their eyes on Junayd. He nodded his head to indicate the people should go back to their tents and houses.

While Reika was asleep on her bed in the inn, Junayd sat down with Melito and Tabitha around the table. The atmosphere was not a pleasant one. For some time, they sat there thinking about what had transpired. What caused Reika to transform? Both monkeys were careful to put Reika in a room where the moon's rays would not affect her.

Junayd had his fingers intertwined, covering his mouth and leaning over with a stern expression, pondering what could be done. "We can't risk taking Reika with us if the full moon is out. We have to move during the day or when the night is cloudy. Right now, it's safe, but not forever," he finally said.

Melito shook his head in amazement. "There's no guarantee the weather will be consistent. Clouds can vanish at a moment's notice; they won't stop the moon for long."

"I don't have any other ideas," Junayd said. "If other people were to discover what she is, they'll try to either attack her, or make use of her powers for evil. Considering the people of Bahaduro know what she is, The Sultan could have her executed if he wished."

"That sword of yours can defeat her again," Tabitha blurted out.

"But do you really want me to?" Junayd asked. Tabitha couldn't answer, she just looked towards Melito for reassurance. The bedroom door opened, and Reika stepped out. The other three turned to see her.

"It happened again, didn't it? Is everyone ok?" Reika asked.

"Yes. So are the villagers," Junayd replied.

Heaving a deep sigh of relief, Reika clutched her head. "We were inside, how did I...?" The young woman's eyes widened when a thought crossed her mind. "The elf woman! She must have cast a spell or got that elf man to turn me into that monster."

Junayd arose from his chair. "How do you know?"

"Lady Ysellian could do it as well. She transformed me by transferring the moon's light into me. Except, I couldn't control myself this time, I was enslaved."

"In that case, we need to vigilant, just in case the mysterious elf man returns," Junayd said. "Tomorrow morning, we leave." Junayd sat silently in the chair, thinking again. "I should have known the moment I crushed that rune that something was up with the twins when they went after you."

"Rune? That thing on Heston's belt? The two apes were berated for letting it be destroyed. What did it do?"

"It cancels out magic, it has no effect on the Ferrum. They are scarce and many have been lost over the years. Heston wore it on his belt. Why would he have been given such a thing?"

Junayd said no more for that night, retiring to his bedroom to sleep, leaving Reika alone with her own thoughts.

They left the inn the next morning, walking through the town. The villagers were all outside, staring at Reika, some mothers pushing their children gently away, including Jaser, others clutching their children tight. Reika eyed them with a sad look on her face, ashamed by what had transpired.

The group walked out of the village itself and turned to the north, making their way along a desert path. No one spoke during the walk. It was a long trek, with the desert sun beating down on their heads, drawing the sweat from their bodies without ceasing. Luckily, they had some water jugs with them to keep them refreshed and cool. Reika knew it would be quicker to fly across the desert, but it wouldn't be worth the risk of exhaustion, considering the heat. All she could do was try to conjure ice into the air to cool herself, although the heat made it hard to sustain, as the ice would melt and evaporate as quickly as she could conjure it. Eventually she gave up and had to endure the terrible heat.

Melito and Tabitha continued wiping the sweat from their head, throwing it to the desert ground, where it evaporated. Junayd was of course used to the heat; it didn't bother him too much. To him, it was just a day like any other. Junayd had changed into robes just before their departure that matched the colour of his trousers. He wore walking boots that came up to his shins. The robes were a simple beige colour. A small hood hung loosely behind Junayd's head, attached to the robes. The same purple cummerbund held the robes tightly.

Junayd paused for a moment as he beheld a tall structure in the distance near a broad mountain range. They made their way towards the structure.

Reika was amazed at the size of the building. It was a tall tower with open windows, derelict, with cracks in the bricks of the wall. No door could be found at the entrance of the tower itself; it was open for all to see. They all stood in place, staring at the impressively high structure before them.

"So, what is this tower anyway?" Reika asked.

"It was used by soldiers as a base of operations. It was abandoned a hundred years ago," Junayd replied. "The soldiers themselves felt there was no need to stay at the tower and even

Caledonia's Sultan at the time agreed. They didn't bother with destroying the tower, so they left it there."

Reika shrugged.

"Or that's what the people were told..." Junayd added. "There are stories that something more sinister drove them away."

Melito was already by the door, glancing back at Reika and Junayd, interrupting them. "Hey, are you two going to keep us waiting?" He called.

"Relax, we'll get to the boat. Stop fretting," Junayd said, "Besides, there is nothing wrong with a history lesson. Especially giving one to a cute and curious girl."

Reika giggled and smiled back at Junayd. "Aww you..." Reika found her gaze drawn back to the tower. "What was the evil thing that drove the guards away?"

"They say there is a crystal up there. Some of the retired guards, those who are still alive, said that the crystal was there to bind the dead and that was what sent the guards running. For what reason that artefact ended up there I cannot fathom. Get rid of it, and the dead will be able to go to the afterlife."

Tabitha's knees were shaking as she scanned the surroundings for danger.

She hurried over to Junayd. "Are there ghosts in the tower, then?" She asked. "Yes... Why? You scared?" Junayd enquired.

"Why deny it? There is no point," said Tabitha. She was glancing back at the mountains behind them.

"When the crystal up there is gone, you won't have to worry. Get rid of it now and we will be fine," Junayd said.

"Ok, we'll go in," Tabitha said in a quiet voice. Melito walked back to Tabitha to speak with her.

"Tabs, what happened to the brave girl I know?"

"Ghosts are horrible. Cut me some slack," Tabitha snapped.

Junayd took Reika aside to speak in private. "You're not considering flying up, are you?"

"No, why do you ask? The objective is to destroy the artefact up there."

"True, but I should warn you, there are enchanted cannons that shoot any object that flies near them."

For a few seconds, Reika just stared at Junayd before devolving into laughter. "As if a trap is going to work after a hundred years," she said, barely trying to contain herself.

"I'm serious." Junayd caught sight of a small rock next to him. He picked it up and threw it at one of the windows. A flash of light burst forth from the tower, vaporising the rock. Reika felt very humbled.

"Err... Thanks for letting me know," she said sheepishly. The two of them joined Melito and Junayd to enter the tower itself.

Lief awoke inside a prison cell. He grimaced, still feeling pain in his chest where Visiert's attack had struck. He was tied down onto a chair with magical binds around his limbs. Visiert towered over him in the cell.

"I would have done far worse to you if my superiors demanded it," he said stoically.

Lief smirked. "You can do your worst now..." Lief's voice was hoarse due to his aching chest. "I see no reason why I should tell you anything."

"You'll find you don't have a choice in the matter," Visiert said as he pulled a chair towards him and sat down on it. "Your superiors. Tell me who you are working for now."

Lief stared at Visiert smugly. "Why hide behind a mask human? Are you so cowardly that you will not address me without that ridiculous mask?"

Visiert backhanded the elf. "Just tell me who called upon you to do this dirty deed." Visiert's tone had become a little more irritated. Lief stared back at Visiert.

"Why bother wasting your time with an underling like me? What are you going to do if I told you outright? Or should I just give you a hint to figure it out on your own? Why don't I instead say whatever comes into my head and waste your time? What say you?"

"This is a dangerous game you are playing, elf. Do not test my patience."

Lief remained composed. "Isn't it obvious to you human? The weredragons are needed by my master for conquest. Surely you know who he is Visiert?"

The masked man had a think. "I have a gut feeling." He rose to leave. "Enjoy the comfort that this cell has to offer."

Chapter 4

Tether of Life and Death

The stone walls of the tower were cracked considerably, it was like a miniature maze and Junayd led the others on their way through the corridors. They made it to a staircase which took them to a room filled with black ooze. There were stone platforms sitting in the ooze, too far for an ordinary person to jump across. The ooze did not move like ordinary water; waves rose into sharp points that folded in on each other. Tabitha walked over to the pooling liquid. A giant spirit reared its head from the ooze. Tabitha recoiled in shock, letting out a brief screech. The spirit clamped its mouth shut and promptly disappeared.

The poor tamarin was shaking. "I can't do this; I want to go back."

Melito went over to her and looked her in the eye. "They aren't going to hurt you," he said calmly to her. "That one didn't, we will be fine."

Melito inspected the ooze. "I don't like the look of this, what is this vile stuff? No horrid smell is coming from it."

"A deadly liquid called Taksaph," Junayd answered. "Stick a limb in there and it will be disintegrated. It was used in ancient times as a punishment for the vilest criminals."

"What about those planks over there?" Reika asked, pointing to the planks resting against the wall. "A bit damaged, but I think they will do."

Junayd went to pick them up. They were a little heavy, but he was able to lift them on his own—only just. He thought cooperation would be better than throwing his back out, even with his magically enhanced strength. "Melito, please give me a hand with these."

Melito complied and platform by platform they placed the planks over the Taksaph to ensure that they could cross safely. As Junayd placed the last one, Melito crossed after him. He looked to his comrades on the other side.

"Right, Come on Tabitha, it's perfectly safe." Tabitha placed her feet gently on the plank. "Don't look down" looped over and over in her mind, her confidence returning gradually as she walked over the boards. Unpleasant thoughts of she and the others being dissolved by the vile substance entered her mind. The last plank creaked below her as she moved, causing her to step back off it.

"Tabs, it's fine, trust me," Melito said, reassuringly. Tabitha nodded. She pelted across the plank, relieved at once that she'd made it to the other side. Reika stood there watching, then followed suit, casually but not carelessly. She made it to her comrades on the other side.

"Onwards and upwards," Junayd said. They all headed for the staircase opposite the one they'd left behind, on the other side of the Taksaph.

In the next room, they found two pools on either side of a platform. This time, the waters were algae-ridden. Melito stared at the water in disgust. They wasted no time heading to the other side quickly.

In the third room, the platforms floated in the air in front of them. The drop was high indeed, a false move would leave a broken body on the ground.

"Melito, Tabitha, make your way slowly around the edge," Junayd said. "What about you and Reika? Can you fly too?"

"Yes, though I tend not to do that often."

Junayd ran to the edge and with a few mighty leaps he made it to the other side. Reika herself stepped away from the edge. She ran full pelt and leapt. There wasn't much going through her mind until she made it to the other side of the chamber, it was like she didn't even know she had leapt more than once. *I'm getting the knack of this! Exhilarating!* she thought.

Despite cracks, the narrow strip of floor running around the edge of the hall was stable enough to hold Melito and Tabitha's weight. They held the wall tightly.

"What if we fall?" Tabitha asked.

"It's alright," Junayd called. "We'll catch you if you do, just keep going."

The monkeys made it halfway, when another malicious looking spirit poked itself through the wall, making Tabitha jump and nearly fall off. Melito grabbed her hand just in time.

"Hold on!" He called, but soon the indent in the wall he had been holding onto crumbled and the two began to fall, screaming as they went.

Reika held out both her hands, slowing their descent, then levitating them back up. She strained with the effort and couldn't hold them much longer.

"Reika, need a hand here?" Junayd held out his hands too, alleviating the strain on Reika.

"Thank you," she said.

Together they lifted the monkeys back onto the platform, letting the pair steady themselves before they let go. The two young humans were tired.

"I think we'd better float you the rest of the way," Junayd said.

Melito shook his head. "Don't. We'll make it, Junayd; you need to recover." The two monkeys continued on their way, and more ghosts gradually emerged from below. This time, Tabitha was prepared, and soldiered on despite their more aggressive flight pattern.

"That's it Tabs, keep going!" Reika called.

Eventually the two monkeys caught up after a long struggle and the group was reunited. The ghosts all disappeared, leaving the chamber once again vacant. One final staircase lay before them and lo and behold, they found themselves at the top of the tower.

Tabitha focused on the horizon, seeing the village in the south far away. She turned to the east and finally to the north. Mountains surrounded the tower and more could be found behind a vibrant set of trees in the distance. The trees were not clustered together as they were in Carthage. Here, they were more spread out, so calling it a forest did not do it justice. Most of them were palm trees no taller than the average human, with a few baobab trees that towered above them. A dusty road wove past the trees, continuing to the north.

"Desert trees?" Tabitha asked in a bewildering tone.

"Oh yes," Junayd replied. "Magnificent fruit the baobab trees have to offer when they are ripe for the season. The oil of the tree does wonders for cracked skin."

Reika spotted a dark purple crystal that was floating near the middle of the tower roof behind her. All its edges glowed in the bright sunlight as it turned.

"Is that the crystal, Junayd?" Reika enquired. "Yes, time to get rid of it."

Junayd approached the crystal, summoning the Draco Ferrum on the way. He swung the blade from his left and it collided with a barrier, causing lavender- coloured lightning bolts to coil around the Ferrum. Junayd stepped away. The barrier was left cracked and shattered like glass. He tried again. The Ferrum collided with the crystal, recoiling. The force knocked the Ferrum out of Junayd's hands.

"The Ferrum is too weak, there has to be another way to destroy it," he said.

"The cannons. Why don't we bring one of them up and that will blast it to oblivion?" Melito asked.

"A good idea. Help me."

Junayd and Melito headed down the stairs back to the previous room. Junayd opened a small brick door, which revealed one of the cannons that was used to defend the tower. The cannon was an ornately decorated weapon with a metre and a half bronze barrel, strong twelve-inch wheels of cast iron, and the frame was made of the same material. Melito examined the cannon, tapping the breach.

"Won't it fire upon us like it did the rock?"

"No Melito, not like this. We can control it manually, or it must be magically linked to the other cannons to work. While it's away from that section in the wall, it's perfectly safe, unless it were to be dropped from a large height. It's just going to be a chore lifting it upstairs."

Junayd pulled the cannon out of the hole in the wall and away to the stairs. He grabbed the barrel, allowing Melito to hold the breach end. With leaden steps, they hauled the cannon back up the stairs.

Reika and Tabitha waited. Tabitha then crossed her arms, tapping her right foot impatiently. Reika stood there with her hands on hips. At last Junayd and Melito arrived with the cannon. They wheeled it over to the east side of the tower, pointing it directly at the crystal.

"Stand back!" Junayd called. The young man placed his right hand on an ornate panel that glowed a fiery hot red. A blast shot from the barrel, colliding with the crystal. Instantly on contact, the crystal was vapourised with no chance to shatter. All the ghosts shot from the tower, vanishing into the sky as the dark energy from the crystal consumed them. Many of the ghosts screeched. The energy coalesced into the sky into a shrinking ball, floating high into the clouds and finally culminating in a massive explosion. The ghosts were wiped out in a flash, the explosion reduced to noth-ingness.

The cannon's recoil was powerful.

During this time, Junayd held his hand out, as did Reika, to stop the cannon from rolling into the wall and off the edge of the tower. Their power caused the cannon to come to a gradual halt, stopping just in time.

"Junayd, what would have happened if that cannon fell to the ground?" Reika asked in an uneasy manner.

"A chain reaction that would bring this tower down. Its explosion would detonate the others," Junayd replied candidly. He pulled the cannon back to the stairs. He gestured, indicating to Melito he wanted to take the cannon back down.

"All the way down again?"

"Yes, back to where we got it from." Melito shook his head, but still helped Junayd lug the heavy cannon back down the staircase.

"Who do you think left the crystal here? Anyone we know Reika?" Tabitha asked.

"No one I know. Did we set them free or banish them?" Reika stared back at where the explosion had been in the sky, not sure how to feel.

The journey to the desert forest was just as tiring as it had been to reach the abandoned tower. Melito held his drinking bottle in his hand, tipping it on the floor. A single droplet fell from the spout from the bottle.

"Is there a water hole around here?"

Junayd pointed in the distance along the pathway. "Yes, right at the end." "I am not tarrying here. Let's move." Melito dashed for the lake without a hitch, followed by Tabitha.

"I would say you both are glad you don't have fur. I am almost envious!" Tabitha called out as she chased after Melito. Junayd chuckled, getting ready to run. As soon he did, Reika sprinted off.

Junayd made it to the oasis and Reika finished a few seconds after him. The two of them had to stop for a breather. Melito and Tabitha stood by the lake. It was a relatively small one that could still be used for a dip in. It was an imperfect round shape with a small number of healthy palm trees perfectly placed around the water's edge.

"Amazing! It's real! The water is real!" Melito said with a child-like excitement. He had no hesitation diving into the water, swimming under the surface, which closed up and rippled for a time. A few seconds later, he leapt from the water with an amazing bound, landing onto the sand.

"REFRESHMENT!" he shouted, shaking himself dry, much to Tabitha's disgust when she was splashed by Melito.

"Watch it!"

Both Junayd and Reika laughed. Melito gestured to the water with his thumbs. "The water is fine. Drink up."

The group were soon asleep under the cool shade of the trees. Reika woke up first. She looked around. The desert was beautiful, even at night, the full moon's light reflecting off the lake. Parts of the light of the moon shone onto the trees with a gentle white illumination. Reika, despite being tired walked over to the edge of the trees, careful to remain in their shadow and not to allow herself to enter the light of the moon.

"Lovely night. So cool here as well," she remarked to herself. The beauty was offset by her dread she would turn into the beast; that dread did not go away even in the shadow of the trees.

Junayd himself had awakened. He looked up at the sky and groaned silently. "Urgh, still a young night." He then noticed Reika sitting by the edge of the trees. He walked over and sat gently beside her. "There is a possibility that it is still out cold."

Reika turned round in confusion. "Out cold?"

"Many throughout the history of this world have been afflicted and have been overtaken by the curse. Normal by day but increasingly bestial during the night. You have a strong will, however, eventually you will lose."

Reika was quiet for a moment, clutching her arms. "I want to be free from it."

"Indeed. The villagers, you saw the horror on their faces. You don't want to see them like that again," Junayd said, this time in a soft tone. "Just make sure you stay out of the moon's light." He averted his sight from Reika to the sky. "The clouds should be veiling it right now."

It happened as Junayd spoke, and Reika stepped out into the open by the lake. "I used to look at the moon on some nights when I was younger. Pity I can't do that as much now. Thanks to this... vile curse..." Junayd stood up and held Reika's right hand, with no resistance from her. A part of her felt open to continue talking. "This curse has taken away any chance of living in my own village," she continued. "I was a servant in the citadel for six years and now... A beast is what I am. What may happen if I become it again? The look on the

faces of the mothers and their children. *I* did that to them. It took everything to stop myself from killing a boy."

Junayd placed his hand on her shoulder. Her sullen expression made a quick transition to surprise. A faint smile followed. "I will help you. The Anodyne Stone is the cure for your affliction. Give the citizens time, we mustn't return to Bahaduro until you are normal again."

He paused for a few moments; an awkward silence fell. He placed his hands on his hips with a cough to break the silence.

"What weapon do you have, Reika?" "Oh, this." She summoned her sword. "Where did you get it?"

"Antonius gave it to me." "May I take a look?"

Reika handed Junayd her sword. He flipped it in the air, catching it in his right hand. "Hmm, It's not bad at all, not too shabby."

"Are you familiar with it?"

"Only tangentially. It was given to a mighty household from the southern archipelago, it's their heirloom. Adequate, though I do have to be honest here, a little antiquated." The blade vanished from Junayd's sight. "Hey!"

Reika sniggered. "Isn't the sword you carry old?" "That's a point."

The two sat down by the lake, continuing their conversation, not really feeling too sleepy at all. A question jumped into Reika's mind.

"The spell was used on me to trigger the transformation—on the two separate occasions—the first I was in full control of myself, the second I wasn't. Why the difference?"

"Simple: the emphasis is placed by the one using the spell," Junayd said. "The weredragon has its own consciousness. You can either suppress the mind of the host or the weredragon itself. What can't be done is suppress either completely. The mind of one or the other will only be suppressed either by the spell or if one is knocked unconscious."

"So, I could be seen as an aggressive human if the weredragon's mind took my place?"

"Just as your mind, Reika, can be in the *weredragon's* place. I'm thinking it is possible to transform at will. Unfortunately, that may allow the weredragon to claim control if given time."

Reika nervously pinched her hands, causing Junayd to place his over hers to discourage her from making her hands sore. Nothing about Junayd felt creepy to Reika. If anything, she felt she was safe near him. "As long as you are not in the moon's light, it cannot awaken while you are asleep."

Junayd then enquired about Reika's parentage. "Your parents... are they?" "I don't know what happened to them," Reika replied. "I'd ask the ones who adopted me, Mark and Andrea about them but they never answered me." "Oh... I see." He paused for a few seconds. "Anyway, what was it you did in the citadel?"

"Serving tables, kitchen duty, general servitude to the king really." "Must be tiring though."

Reika began to smile. "Yeah... but worth it. I've been a servant since I was twelve. Laidback as Mark is, he told me not to slouch at home, it's something I have carried with me since then."

Just talking to Reika was fascinating for Junayd. He was

amazed by what he heard regarding the work ethic of the young woman speaking to him. He knew his parents wouldn't allow him to slack off. He was allowed time to unwind and relax. Nevertheless, he was often told to make sure he had finished his work.

"What about your parents?" Reika asked.

"They're alive... They're currently out of town. That's why you didn't see them. They leave me in charge of the home and to make a little extra money. You will usually see my mother Naomi tending to the field. My father Avi is a merchant. He conducts his business at a mining town, although he has done work elsewhere."

"I passed through that town on the way here. There was a man wearing garb similar to yours. He looked like you, only with a turban and beard."

"That's him! The miners love trading gold with him in exchange for new equipment. No dissatisfaction on either side."

Reika kept her eyes on the lake. "How do you know so much about the curse?"

"So much? You give me too much credit. Meeting with the dragons provided me with *some* knowledge on it. But in truth they only told me what they thought I needed to know."

Junayd propped himself to his feet, both walking back under the trees where they had lain previously. "Rest up," he said. "We leave here at dawn."

As she lay down beneath the trees, Reika laid her hand on her chest. "Why... Why am I cursed to turn into that beast? I have to find out the truth."

The next day, the group found themselves at a magnificent castle, leaving the Desert Woods behind. The grey blue stone was very different to the Carthagian Citadel. It was highly maintained, the bricks neatly arranged, held together by strong clay. They crossed a bridge across a large moat, unusual due to the stone walls with wooden flooring. They approached the guards who were stationed outside a small wooden door that led the castle interior.

"State your business," one of the guards said.

"Just passing through, no harm to befall you," Junayd said.

"Don't try anything," said the other guard. He then recognised Junayd. "My apologies, young sir, go through, but please do explain to the Sultan why you are going through here."

The door opened and the group entered a large hall. Pools of water lay both sides of the hall. The stonework was as neat and immaculate as the exterior. The Sultan was sitting on a throne like that of Tertullian's. He had an olive complexion, with grey hair on his head and no crown. His robes were regal purple and crimson colours that blended intricately together.

"Your majesty," Junayd called.

"Good morning, young Junayd. Is there a reason you have come here?" "Yes...I'll explain..."

The Sultan, named Fadil, listened to him. At several points Fadil asked questions and was answered to his satisfaction.

"I see, where do you plan to go?" Fadil asked.

"I don't know exactly," Junayd said. "We are trying to find the Anodyne Stone that can heal Reika here. I could find some more allies in Zeitreisen to help us. I have one in mind."

"Hmm. Well, there is a favour that I ask of you Junayd, there is a beast who is in one of our storerooms, it needs to be destroyed. Kill it and you may pass to the docks."

"Very well, sire." Junayd and the others proceeded through the room into the upper sections of the castle. As they did, Fadil eyed Reika suspiciously.

He raised a hand, stopping her in her tracks. She faced towards his throne, bowed, and awaited his words. "I would never hurt your subjects. It was my intention to stay out of the moon in Bahaduro."

"Thankfully you didn't lay a single finger—or claw I should say —upon them," the Sultan said. "Junayd's words have been confirmed by the guards who spoke with the villagers. You also somehow managed to stay your hand from slaying a young boy.

That doesn't change the fact that you are a threat to my kingdom. I will allow you through here, but I have my eyes on you as long as you bear that curse. I will not hesitate to have you executed should you even think about turning into that... beast or harm my subjects again. Am I clear?"

Reika was silent, only nodding her head. "Your friends are waiting."

The soldiers were all in their quarters, each room housing a bed, with small spaces for shelving and food supplies. Weaponry and armour of many types were housed in crates in a storage room next to their quarters.

The storage room itself was open. Here, men could practice and fight to the best of their ability, making sure that they were prepared for times of war.

"They are sending a bunch of young'uns to do the job of a soldier, amazing what this world has come to," one remarked, as the group passed them by.

"One of which wields the Draco Ferrum, I think we are in safe and capable hands," his colleague retorted.

"I don't trust that woman. Innocent face, but there is something dark under it. The villagers claim she transformed into a terrible beast."

"No fear of that, it's still daytime, I wouldn't give it a moment's thought."

Junayd signalled to the others to stay put with his hand, advancing down the stairs to see what kind of beast the Caledonian soldiers were having trouble with.

Cautiously, he approached the doorway. The room's shelves were empty, and there was a foul smell coming from somewhere deeper in.

He then caught sight of a large creature. It had no legs or arms to speak of. It was hard to ascertain what the creature even was. It loosely resembled a large caterpillar, its upper body housing six large claws, with mandibles around where a mouth should be.

As Junayd watched, it awoke, its two large eyes as black as the deepest abyss. It saw Junayd and lunged at him immediately. Junayd barely dodged out of the way. The creature's ear-piercing screech echoed within the confines of the defiled room.

"What is that?" Reika said, from the top of the stairs.

"It's a foul beast, an eupithecia!" Junayd replied. "It's undoubtedly the beast the Sultan referred to. Stay back, I'll take care of it."

He summoned the Draco Ferrum with the snap of his fingers. The beast lunged at Junayd, clutching the sword with its mandibles, straining to push against him as Junayd tried to hold his ground. Junayd heard the rough stone scrapping beneath his boots. He let go of the Draco Ferrum and ran to the right of the eupithecia. It swallowed up the blade quite easily.

Moments later, it then screeched with pain as the blade burst from its chest, zooming back into Junayd's hand. He sneered at the beast in triumph, though not for long. Green clouds of energy had started to form around the eupithecia, closing the gaping wound shut. The beast glared at Junayd, then went to slice him with its claws, breaking the rock of the floor as he once again rolled out of the way of its grip. It hissed in frustration.

"Why resist my grasp, boy? I have eaten soldiers who didn't squirm this much!" it said, in a whispering harsh voice.

Junayd stopped for a moment, composing himself.

"The foul beast has speech... I have no intention of letting you devour me.

Now tell me, who sent you?"

The beast smiled through his mandibles. "Wouldn't you like to know human? Thanks to the one who brought me here, you cannot kill me, as you have so witnessed."

"In battle there is always a road to victory, a green skinned log like you is no exception to that rule."

"Such foolishness, young wretch. What part of you should I devour first?

The arms and the legs definitely sound good to me."

The eupithecia charged towards Junayd again. This time, the

creature managed to pin Junayd against the wall to the right of the door. Its face pushed close to Junayd, attempting to gnaw the young human's head with his mandibles. Its claws acted like a cage, preventing the young man from going left or right. Junayd summoned fire into his hands, forcing the eupithecia to back off, recoiling in pain as the claws showed signs of terrible burns, though they healed quickly with the same green clouds.

Junayd had caught sight of a small emerald amulet embedded in one of the creature's claws, the top right hand one. *Where did he get that amulet? Maybe if I cut it from him, I might be able to kill him?* Junayd thought. He took a few brief seconds to recover before making his way back towards the eupithecia. He charged his blade with light blue energy, firing a sword-shaped blast from it at the enchanted claw, which in turn caused the creature to recoil in pain once again. The claw regenerated as the last of the energy flowed from the amulet, before the amulet itself fell to the ground, freed from its moorings.

Unaware of its vulnerability, the eupithecia made one final charge but Junayd, using the blade charged with energy, cut the creature in half.

The sight wasn't too gory, as the creature's body where the cut had been made started to turn to energy which overtook the creature's body. As the creature's head collapsed to the ground, the blue energy consumed it, transforming into smoke. Junayd desummoned his blade, holding the amulet in his hand. He felt its healing powers working on him. The amulet at last lost its green shine, becoming black as night.

Reika came down the stairs to investigate. "Where did it get it from?"

"My guess, it could have been the elf woman you spoke of. This amulet was given to him and embedded his claw. But why post such a creature here? We cannot let this fall into anyone's hands."

With that, Junayd and the rest of the group headed back to the throne room.

As they walked, Reika had more questions.

"Is there someone here who knows where the amulet comes from?"

"There is one person I know who might. His name is Irenaeus, one of the scholars who resides here. He may be able to point us in the right direction. You go back to the throne room; I'll talk with you later about the amulet."

Traversing back the way they came, the group stopped outside a small library. Reika, Melito, and Tabitha went on to the throne room to inform the Sultan that the creature was slain. Junayd lingered.

Tall bookshelves practically covered the wall opposite the entrance, with one small section allowing room for a desk. There, a dark-skinned man sat in similar but less regal robes than Fadil's. Instead, they were the robes of a scholar. A quill and inkpot sat upon his desk, with which he was quietly writing.

"Excuse me!" Junayd called.

The man turned round to see Junayd. "Ah hello my boy. What can I do for you?"

"Irenaeus, I have an artefact I've just recovered from the eupithecia downstairs. It was embedded in its claw. Any idea where it came from?"

Junayd handed the amulet to Irenaeus, who examined the stone carefully, seemingly impressed with the structure of the amulet.

"This amulet, I thought it was lost for eternity! It was believed to have been stolen from a temple, a home for golems. It's their most revered artefact. On mineral and organic life alike, it has a regenerative factor, no doubt you already have witnessed it. The vigour of the user is enhanced. The creature must have been hard to take down."

Irenaeus scratched his chin, closing his old eyes. "I think, it's worth paying a visit to Zeitreisen, if you are going there. The Temporal Knight will assist in returning this gem to its proper place. I believe he retired back to his normal life after his previous journey, but I think he'll be willing to give you a hand."

Junayd nodded. "Does the temple still exist?"

The old man tapped the table with his right hand. "To this very day. It does make me wonder if the amulet is there."

Junayd's face showed visible confusion. "I'm sorry, it's there? What's this, then? I thought it was stolen?"

Irenaeus looked sternly at Junayd in the eyes. "That is why you must find the Temporal Knight, go back in time, and return it there, to ensure that the evil deed remains undone. Confusing, yes, but you'll get it eventually."

Junayd didn't know what to say. Had the old scholar lost his mind? Junayd just scratched the back of his head. "I'll go to him then; I have just never really thought about... time travel until now."

"Naturally Junayd. Only a time traveller would be aware of *changes* in the timeline. Unless we are partakers of the journey, we wouldn't even notice the difference. A strange thought to ponder."

"You have been a great help, Irenaeus, thanks for your assistance." With that, Junayd departed and left Irenaeus to attend to his work.

Fadil addressed Junayd upon his return to the throne room. "Well done, my boy! Thank you very much for taking out the beast. Lo and behold, the secret staircase over there has been opened to you. Feel free to leave, or, if you like, rest here a little longer."

"Thank you sire."

Taking the hidden path, they found themselves in a room with walls like the fortress, with light tan-coloured stone. There was a large, neat pool of water with a dragon statue found on a walkway. Not a crack was present in sight.

"It's a dragon forge, I can power my sword here!" Junayd said. He approached the statue and held out his sword in front of him. The statue's eyes started to glow with a bright light, which quickly shot forth, colliding with the Draco Ferrum. Junayd fell to the floor. Reika made her way to Junayd and knelt by him.

"Can you stand up?" Reika asked. "That looked dangerous."

Junayd picked himself up. He felt okay, but certainly different.

"I'm fine, you were right to be concerned. Although, the power coursing through the Ferrum is tremendous."

Leaving the fortress, the group made their way to the port. Junayd explained on the way to Reika, Melito, and Tabitha the history of the amulet given to him by Irenaeus. He also told them who the Temporal Knight was, a time travelling hero who had saved the world three years ago. The rumours claimed that he journeyed through time to stop history from being altered by a similar warrior who hailed from another realm, a mirror of their world. Together they all wondered whether it was possible for history to be changed. How would anyone know if it had been altered?

The conclusion that the group settled on was that even if it was true, and history had been changed, they would never even realise it. If the Temporal Knight had altered events, or gone back and undone damage, they would be none the wiser. Whatever the truth was, they all felt certain he could help them in this endeavour. However, Junayd had no clue as to the knight's true identity.

Chapter 5

Zeitreisen

They arrived at the port safe and sound. Some Caledonian guards were present in their shining red armour. Junayd told the others to wait outside while he got the tickets for the boat that would take them to another sub-continent, that of Zeitreisen. As Junayd was getting the tickets, Reika caught a glimpse of another man in shiny grey armour. She went over to speak with him. "Hi there!" The man turned around. He sported black hair and a beard, both rather curly, and blue eyes and warm ivory skin. He was in his mid-thirties. "Good day! Looks like we'll be on the same ship," he said.

"Yes, my friend is inside buying the tickets for himself, I and two others, they too are my friends."

The armoured man pointed at Melito and Tabitha. "The two monkeys in armour over there? The guards?"

"Yes sir." Reika stared at man's grey armour. "You're a knight, aren't you?"

The knight smiled back at Reika and nodded. "I am indeed. Delighted to meet you. I'm Lord Berinon. Your name?"

"Reika. You heading to Zeitreisen too, then?"

Berinon nodded. "Yes, I'm returning home. I was sent here to

Caledonia to work for a while. Now I'm heading home to Aevumshire. I spent a bit of time at the fortress. They have nice whisky—outside my work of course! Can't drink on duty."

"Hmm. Anyway, I wish you a safe journey home," Reika finally said.

"I'm sure we'll probably meet again soon, young lady. Till then, I bid you farewell. A pleasure to meet one as well-mannered as you, the gesture is most appreciated."

Berinon left for the ship, walking down the long pier. Reika could only watch him go.

Junayd was inside the harbour warehouse, where a guard was serving other customers their tickets. He observed the various customers in his presence. The customer at the very front of the queue was an elvish man with short black hair wearing armour. The armour housed a dark hue of purple on the breast plating and the abdominal area, along with shoulder guards and tassets on the top of his legs down to his knees. He wore a metal headband around his head which had alternating grey and mauve coloured sections. His ears were exposed, with his black hair tucked behind them. He had a handsome middle-aged face, along with dark brown eyes and a pale complexion. He presented his coins for his ticket, the guard handing it straight to him. He walked alongside the queue for the exit. Junayd kept the elf locked in his line of vision, concerned.

A bounty hunter, here? Need to watch out for him. The armour he recognised as belonging to a guild comprised of dangerous hunters from many races. He was wondering if the man was going to be on the same ship, quick to remember some of the elves lived in Zeitreisen themselves. He also considered the fact that the elves' homeland Elvenheim was on the mainland.

He had heard stories of an elvish bounty hunter who had fought against the Temporal Knight. The man had fought the knight for reasons not known to the general public and was bested in the fight by the knight, presumed dead. Junayd wondered if the elvish man was the same individual from that story. He knew elves were stronger than humans, despite their fair appearance. Before he could think any more on the matter, an ochre, humanoid golem, who looked like an armoured knight of crystalline structure with red eyes being the only visible feature on his face—the rest obscured by the shadow of his helmet—nudged Junayd.

"Your turn boy, we haven't got all day," he said, in a deep booming voice.

Junayd went to the counter. "What deals do you offer?" He asked.

"Here's my recommendation," the guard replied. "Get the special pass and you'll be able to have you and a maximum of seven others with you on that ticket. Just pay me two hundred reptibloons and I will give you this pass." Junayd took two coins from his pocket, two grand-looking coins roughly thirty-five millimetres in diameter, each with a value of one hundred reptibloons as indicated by the number on the face. This was a currency issued from the dragons that was widely used. Other races used their own currency, mainly in their villages, but all had the option to use reptibloons if they wished. The guard was impressed and gave Junayd a red card printed with the words "One Year Pass" in bold, gold writing.

Junayd was pleased with the purchase and left the office to showcase the ticket to the rest of the group. "It was the ticket seller's recommendation, so I took him up on his offer. We'd better get going."

The group left for the ship in order to set sail for Zeitreisen.

The ship known as the SS *Hikari* was rather grand, magnificent and was four hundred and twenty feet long. Not a single part of the deck bore signs of dust or rot. It glided along the ocean, which lapped the sides of the boat gently. The wooden decks were polished. The dining room featured twenty oak tables, ten on each side in rows, along with open windows, allowing the ocean breeze to permeate the ship. The group were situated on the starboard side on one of the two middle tables, tucking into the fruit that was being given to them.

Various servants were waiting on the tables, one of whom was an agile macaque, holding the dinner plates with incredible ease as he wound between other guests and fellow servants, managing to place the dishes on the tables with elegant precision. Another was an elf chef with shortened black hair, blue eyes, and fair skin.

"I wonder what Zeitreisen is like. Any nice places?" Reika asked. Junayd put down the pomegranate in his right hand on the table.

"It's not bad overall, the tundra in the north is barren, not quite so with the rest of the island: breath-taking hills, a neat little village known as Aevumshire, you name it, it's got it."

"If the Temporal Knight can be found in the village that would save us time." Tabitha threw a grape into the air, catching it in her mouth. "How much longer till we get to the island, Junayd?"

"Two weeks at best if we have good weather, so we need to enjoy the boat trip."

Melito smiled as he placed an orange slice in his mouth. "No rush there, this fruit is tremendous."

Unbeknownst to the passengers on the *Hikari*, the *Tetraspis* was pursuing the ship from the northwest. Magnus watched through his gold-plated binoculars. "Grand, hopefully the sweet gold and possessions on board will be worth it." Vera directed her gaze over the starboard of the *Tertaspis*. She grinned as she looked through her own telescope. "A mere passenger boat, easy pickings for us."

A Caledonian sailor, a young man with brown eyes, dark skin, and a short, thick beard that aged him considerably, got his telescope out when he spotted a ship in the distance that was steadily approaching. To his horror, he saw the *Tetraspis* on their tail. He pelted to the captain's cabin at the end of the boat.

"*Tetraspis!* Between the port and stern sides. Sound the alarm!" He said to the captain when he burst through the door. The metazoan captain, Manius, was a grey warthog. Despite his slightly round figure, his uniform fit him perfectly. He sounded off to the rest of his crew.

"Full steam ahead, pirates are on us, non-combatant passengers await instructions, combatant members prepare the cannons."

"I thought this was a passenger vessel?" Reika said as she departed with Junayd from the table.

"It is, but in this part of the ocean, they need to defend themselves from pirates," Junayd responded. He headed for the deck, along with Reika, Melito, and Tabitha.

Manius was heading down below when Junayd and the others arrived. "Pirates, Captain?" Junayd asked.

"I'm afraid so. What are you doing here? You should be ready to evacuate on our command."

Junayd summoned the Draco Ferrum. Manius was stunned. "We can fight, sir," Junayd said.

"Oh, good, and what of the others?"

Reika summoned her sword, Melito pulled out his axes, and Tabitha her bow.

The captain looked at them each in turn.

"Do any of you happen to recognise the name *Tetraspis?*"

Reika stared at the captain in alarm. "Yes, I and my two companions from Carthage were captured by that ship. Fortunately, we managed to escape."

"Then you know our enemy. I want you to protect the non-combatants while we get our cannons ready to attack."

～

Magnus lowered his binoculars, rubbed his eyes, then placed the binoculars back over his eyes. Reika was in his sights. "So, the hairless skinbag is on that ship, eh? She has brought a boyfriend with her, I see. The Ferrum Champion. Not that it will do her any good..."

～

Junayd squeezed his hands shut. "Reika, can you summon a barrier large enough to cover the ship?"

The young woman gaped at him. "That big? I have never used the barrier like that, only human sized."

"Well, it looks like we need to test it. I'll help you out."

Junayd and Reika went to opposite ends of the *Hikari*, Junayd to the bow and Reika to the stern.

Meanwhile, Magnus signalled to his crew to activate the cannons housed within the hull in the ship. These cannons were magical, charmed to fire or cease fire on a verbal command. They had a shiny chrome finish, and large wheels settled in rails on the ship to move them into position, allowing for a decent recoil.

"Fire!" Magnus yelled. Blasts of light emanated from the *Tetraspis* cannons, whizzing above the water at top speed.

The two humans on the *Hikari* raised their hands into the air, then slammed them onto the deck. The purple stained-glass barrier covered the boat as quickly as a knight might shut the visor on his helmet. The cannon blasts collided with the barrier, causing small cracks to appear. *Rather in our barrier than in the ship's hull*, Reika thought. Magnus was furious. "Direct hit but no damage. Aim for the two humans defending it."

The cannons fired their blasts of light once again. Junayd could see the lights aiming for him and knew he was in trouble.

"He's smart, I'll give him that," Junayd said. He temporarily pulled some of the barrier away from the ship's hull, shielding himself with a prism of magical glass. Reika responded in the same way, but to her horror, more cannon blasts were already coming towards the ship. She removed the barrier from her quickly to protect the port-side of the ship. She and Junayd could feel the strain on their power as impacts detonated across the barrier. They finally dropped the barrier, weak from the struggle.

Junayd pushed himself to his feet using the Draco Ferrum. "This is getting really annoying." He had to think fast. Reika went over to Junayd. "Those cannons are the same type as the ones you warned me about at the tower. Is there a way to stop the *Tetraspis* from firing or to destroy them?"

"Not from here, we are going to have to get closer."

Captain Manius chimed in. "What's going on with your barriers? They'll fire again." As if on cue, the *Tetraspis'* cannons fired. Junayd and Reika summoned a dome shape around the ship in the nick of time. They couldn't sustain it for long, but luckily for the duo, the energy blasts from the cannons were stopped by the barrier just before it vanished.

Manius squinted at the ship then towards Junayd. "Any ideas, boy?"

"One, and it's going to be risky. Reika, come with me. Captain, turn the ship towards the *Tetraspis*. Save your ammunition until we get close enough."

Manius was struck by a thought. "We cannot let those cannons fire upon this ship again, we'll chase the *Tetraspis* off, they will not expect us to pursue them. If we are to fire, what weak points do you know about?"

"I believe the cannons are, you destroy one of them, the *Tetraspis* will be taken down."

Manius nodded. He hurried away from Junayd and Reika. He arrived in his cabin. "Full steam ahead!" He bellowed in a speaking tube. He turned to the pilot; a weasel next to him. "Move the *Hikari* towards the *Tetraspis*. On my command, steer away in order to get alongside it." The pilot nodded and complied.

Junayd and Reika ran to the front of the *Hikari*, the ship turning away from the east towards the *Tetraspis*.

"Junayd, what now?" Reika enquired. Junayd grinned back.

"We'll form a magical barrier. We'll trick the *Tetraspis* into thinking we are charging into them and once we get alongside it, we blow the cannons on the ship to smithereens."

"What shape shall we make?"

"Doesn't matter, but this time, we'll envelop the bow." Reika was a little apprehensive. "I hope this works." "It will."

The two humans each began to form a shield of magic of equal measure, connecting the two to create an axe shape. The barrier was a foot thick, covering the bow of the *Hikari* effectively.

Magnus was somewhat puzzled at first. His confusion transitioned to concern, moulding into outright fear. "They are not stopping. Move out, move out!" The *Tetraspis* began its course to the east, moving away from the *Hikari*, which now pursued the pirate ship.

"Give it more steam, lads!" Manius cried. *We might make it Zeitreisen on time AND destroy a pirate boat,* he thought happily.

Magnus rushed down below deck. He called to his crew members. They had managed to build a new boat to replace the dinghy Reika and the others stole to get away. Only, this one was different, it had an unusual quality not often seen. It was a submersible craft built with strange technology. It was also bigger than the previous lifeboat, allowing Magnus and the rest of his crew to climb inside.

Magnus kicked the lever down. The door of the ship opened and as soon as he and the others got in the boat, it began to turn invisible and slide down the rails. The rails rattled and then a *boom* as they hit the water. Magnus and his comrades had escaped from the *Tetraspis*. The submersible wound round to their port-side. Though a ripple on the water was present, Magnus was counting on the *Hikari* crew not noticing it. He wanted to attack. He wanted to use the same water magic to strike that skinbag, Reika. But any attempt to use the same water spell would have given away his location.

The submersible was quick and silent enough that the two humans could not see it; they were too busy trying to make sure their barrier could hold. Little did Magnus know what would happen next.

Just as the submersible dived, the SS *Hikari* got within range of the pirate ship on the starboard side, at least five hundred metres. The barrier shifted from the stern to enveloping the starboard, leaving only the gunports exposed. Manius stared at the ship, he didn't say a word for what felt like an eternity.

"Fire!"

A thunderous boom echoed from the cannons as they fired upon the *Tetraspis*. Some of the cannon shots exposed the ones inside the *Tetrapis*. A direct hit from a cannonball, which had flown from middle of the *Hikari* crashed into one of the cannons and within an instant, The *Tetrapsis* was blown to pieces in a fiery blaze. Charred planks of wood were scattered on the water. There was little left of the cannons to speak of except for fleeting boiling sea water where the *Tetraspis* was. The magical barrier finally faded away. The *Hikari* was safe.

The passengers all cheered. Reika and Junayd were triumphant but exhausted.

"Well done for holding in there, Reika." "Thanks, you did well too."

The captain came up to them both. "Impressive plan, we showed those pirates a thing or two. For your efforts in this endeavour, feel free to dine at the captain's table. Oh, and bring your two monkey friends along."

While all were celebrating, Reika could not shake the feeling that this wasn't the last time she would see Magnus despite his ship's destruction. It would only be a matter of time before he and his crew would resurface again.

Berinon sat alone in his room after the dinner. He was thinking about Junayd and Reika's protection of the ship with the barriers they created. "I did not expect such power from these youths. Who are they?" He wondered.

Though he was willing to spring into action, if need be, he was called to assist with firing one of the cannons as one the gunners had been knocked unconscious in the fray and he obliged. Berinon was the one who pulled the final shot and he had also sat at the table near Manius, though he didn't converse with Reika and the others. He did give a friendly nod to her, and she replied in kind. Junayd didn't notice as he was conversing with the elf chef in front of him. Berinon didn't mind, though he wondered if he would see them again after they arrived.

Two weeks passed, and the SS *Hikari* finally made port in Zeitreisen. After emerging from the boat and the captain warmly thanking them one last time for their heroic efforts, the group found themselves facing a snowy landscape which connected to a multitude of large hills, stretching for miles. The snowy wasteland had a forest in the distance, though the leaves were not an inviting green colour. Instead, they were bitter blue leaves of varying shades. A large dome of lapis lazuli stone, with large spires surrounding it, could be seen in the centre of this forest. *What is that?* Reika thought. *It's a magnificent building for an odd- looking forest.* She heard Junayd calling her name. Without a word, the group made their way to the south, away from the forest.

After leaving the snow behind, the group travelled further south. They discovered a sandy path on the way, almost straight. It wove over and around the hills.

The air was cool, and the sun was going down; they had to find shelter soon. Thankfully, a lone farmhouse with a barn could be seen in the distance. When they were finally alongside the farm-house the group sat down, off the path, on the grass, exhausted from the journey.

The farmhouse was built from immaculate white stone, framed by dark oak with an oak porch. The barn next to the house was like it but lacked a porch and had a roof made of straw, skil-fully bound together with an oily tar. A young man exited the barn. He had rather curly brown hair, with a beard framing his mouth, and brown eyes. His shirt had rolled up sleeves and gripped his upper body tightly. He wore brown boots with grey soles that had straps around the ankle section of the boots, and black trousers.

He spotted the group, but instead of sending them away, he came over with a warm smile on his face. "Hello there! Good day, young travellers."

Junayd stood, feeling a little better after his short rest. The others followed suit.

"Hello, are you the man in charge of the farm here?"

"Sort of, it is my family farm, but my guardian is the owner." The farmer extended his hand, shaking Junayd's. "I am Quinn. Your names?"

"Junayd. The girl next to me is Reika and the two monkeys to her right are Melito and Tabitha."

Quinn gave his attention to the two monkeys. "I see. Judging by your clothing, you must be Carthagian guards?"

"We are," Tabitha said.

"They have been accompanying me on a journey," Reika said. "Junayd joined up a little later."

"Is that a fact?" Quinn asked. He pulled out a pipe from his pocket, lighting it and beginning to smoke. "Well, they seem to have done a decent job so far. Why don't I provide you some accommo-dation for the night? I don't recommend travelling on from here right now."

Reika's countenance contracted a smile. "Thank you, much appreciated."

Quinn placed the pipe back in his mouth. "Excellent! Come inside. Meet the others."

The group followed Quinn into the house. The interior was quaint, a lovely wooden chair stationed on top of a large green rug with gold decorated trimming. A large shelf, with various utensils stacked on it, stood next to the kitchen sideboard and sink, where a man and a woman were working.

The man in front of the cutting board, Zane, in a way like Quinn, wore the exact same clothes, only he was slightly shorter, his hair was straighter and longer, and he lacked a beard. He had the same brown eyes as his brother.

The woman next to him was small in stature. She wore a long dress and scruffy, long black hair fell from her head. Her complexion was darker than the others, though she had the same brown eyes. The young woman left her task, with Zane saying "Thanks," and she came over to greet the newcomers, introducing herself as Kayleigh. She sat down in another chair next to Quinn.

"We hope you enjoy your stay. You'll find some beds upstairs." The group expressed their thanks.

"Zane, can you be a good man and get the beds prepared?" Quinn asked. Zane, who had been cutting vegetables, turned round. "No problem."

Before Zane went up the stairs, a young white woman, only slightly shorter than Zane, came down in clothes matching those of Kayleigh. Her brown hair was long and wavy, reaching down to her shoulder blades. She also possessed jade-coloured eyes. The two kissed each other on the lips lightly.

"I'll take over, Zane," she said.

"Thanks Emeline," Zane said. "But you do enough for me." "The baby is asleep. I'll handle the dinner."

Zane went upstairs to prepare the rooms, while Emeline continued to prepare their evening meal. No meat was present, though not because the household was vegetarian. Quinn, Zane, and their manager, Arthur, who was away on business at this time, would sometimes sit around a fire outside their house eating steak on long sticks. They didn't have any meat to speak of at the time but that was a good thing as far as they were concerned, eating meat they reasoned would have been insensitive to the metazoans in their presence, who mostly ate fruit and vegetables.

Some populations still imported non-sapient meat from Zeitreisen or from Caledonia, but it was costly. Melito and Tabitha didn't mind, it made no odds to them whether non-sapient meat was eaten but they said nothing and let their hosts continue.

Humans in Carthage were exempt from meat abstinence, that included Reika, though they were required to consume it on segregated grounds so as not to offend their metazoan friends who did abstain. Mark and Andrea spoke with many humans to assist in raising Reika, asking her about what they should feed her, considering a diverse diet of meat, vegetables, and fruit to feed her properly.

The food presented to the group smelled incredible and caused their mouths to water. After they had eaten, they all sat down in the living room.

Junayd was a little restless throughout the meal. Reika looked at him, trying to figure out what was wrong. While Quinn was speaking with Melito and Tabitha, he whispered, "I want to ask him where the Temporal Knight is."

"Right now, just unwind. It's too early to ask him. What are you so antsy about?"

Junayd pointed to the window with his thumb, in the hopes Quinn wouldn't notice. "Just between you and me, I can't stand the smell of the stable."

Reika gave Junayd a funny look. "I didn't even notice it."

"If you were me right now, you would know how awful it smells." "It's a farm, of course it's going to smell a little bit."

"A bit? I feel like I am going to throw up. I don't like dung smell. Sorry, I grew up in a desert, not in the land of a country yokel."

Quinn sharply turned to Junayd. "I heard that. Just watch it." "Sorry."

"You are forgiven."

Reika turned her attention to Kayleign next to Quinn. "I hope you don't see me as rude but, how did a lady like you end up here?"

"The Temporal Knight brought me here after I helped him out." Reika felt her heart skip a beat. "He offered me a place as a friend. Right now, I am here to earn money and pay off the people I stole from."

Reika was puzzled at first, but a smile followed afterwards. "That's admirable of you."

"Thanks, it's been difficult but worth it."

"She's a hard worker, alright," Quinn added. "Does wonders in the kitchen with the food. Has a talent for keeping animals under control as well."

Kayleigh eyed Reika for a moment. "No offence err..." "Reika."

"Reika... Don't want to offend you but, you dress funny." Reika looked down at her vest and pants. She beamed at Kayleign.

Reika woke up in the dark. She was slow to get up. "Ugh, midnight awakening. I am glad the moon isn't out tonight." She heard footsteps coming up the stairs. Quietly she left her bedroom, headed to her right and made her way to the landing. She stopped short of the stairs. All Reika did was look away for a brief second, before facing the stairs once again. She saw Zane and gasped in shock, trying to make sure she didn't wake up the rest of the house.

Zane smiled back. "Crossing the stairs is not the best idea."

Reika held her chest, her heart thudding. "What are you doing? Trying to give me a heart attack?"

Zane scratched his head in confusion. "Sorry, that wasn't my intention." Reika stepped back to allow Zane to make his way across the landing.

"You're a weredragon aren't you?" He asked. "How do you know that?"

"I was told to await your arrival. You desire to be rid of the curse." Reika clutched her arms, looking down at the floor in shame. She could only nod her head in acknowledgement.

There was, however, a question that was burning in her soul and Reika knew she had to ask it; the question pertained to the building she had seen in the forest. "There was a lapis lazuli dome I saw in the distance when we arrived, it was a sight to behold. Can you tell me what it is?"

"That is the Time Gate, one of many places in the world where time travel is possible, a gateway for the Temporal Knight, to aid him in his journey three years ago. An alteration in the timeline had to be undone. The one responsible enabled a vicious tyrant to have a hold over this continent. Of course, you wouldn't know that. To you, nothing has changed at all."

"That doesn't sound easy," Reika said.

"Oh, it isn't. Life is not always easy, and this is no exception."
"Who is the knight?"

Zane walked away from Reika, chuckling to himself.

"Zane?" He turned around with his arms spread out and a smile on his face. "You are looking at him."

Reika stood in place with her jaw hanging open. "You... You are the Temporal Knight? But you are so young."

Zane grinned back. "I've had other people react in that way."

Reika collected her thoughts together. "Junayd told me about you. You saved the world once, didn't you?"

"As I had mentioned before, yes. But I had Kayleign, whom you met earlier, and Berinon, who is currently not here now, assist me in my journey."

Reika then remembered the knight she met back in Caledonia, before getting on the ship.

"Berinon? I met a knight called Berinon once, near a boat in Caledonia." "Oh, so you do know him?"

"Sort off... We only met briefly."

"Knowing him, he probably has gone back to Aevumshire which is south of here. It's where he resides. He loves whiskey, the finest batches in Zeitreisen are made there."

Zane turned away. It seemed the conversation was over. Reika was about to head back to sleep when a thought had crossed her mind. "Before I forget, there is an amulet that we have and we were told to return it to the temple, to the *place and time* it was taken from." Reika swiftly strode back to the guest room and rummaged in her bag, pulling out the amulet. "Junayd asked me to give it to you."

Zane's eyes widened. "I know what you are referring to now. A temple that belongs to golems. May I examine the amulet?"

Reika handed the amulet to Zane. "Who last had this?"

"A eupithecia, the amulet healed its wounds. It's out of power. We need to get rid of it."

"Yes. This shouldn't be here. Irenaeus, I assume, already told you what happened? It was stolen centuries ago from a temple. It cannot fall into evil hands again." Zane looked sombre. "When we are travelling to another period in history, I or one the elves who use time travel, are in charge. Do you understand?"

"Perfectly."

Zane backed off and headed toward the staircase. "In that case, I'll see you in the morning. Get a good night's rest." With that, Zane went down the stairs. *Hard to believe, the man we've been looking for is here, and he is just a farm boy, what are the odds?*

She then heard the cry of a baby in the room downstairs. She went down to see what was going on. Emeline was holding the tiny boy. The baby's complexion matched Zane's.

"Aww, he's so cute," Reika said. Emeline looked back at Reika, placing the baby gently down.

"Thank you," she said. Emeline let her eyes rest on Reika for a while. "Have we met?"

Reika thought for a few moments. "I think we have."

"I remember you. You're the servant girl from Carthage. You served my father and I at the table we sat at. So polite too."

"Oh really? That... That was a while ago," Reika said, struggling to get the words out. "Who was your father, Emeline? I have forgotten."

"A king. He rules over a province on the mainland, a boat trip to the southwest from here."

"So... how come you are not there? Didn't you want the throne?"

"No, my older sister was next in line. I think she'll handle it better than I. Zane visited the city I dwelt in once. I looked at him, he saw me. We had a chat with each other, worked together in the field. He eventually proposed to me."

"And what of your father, what did he say?"

"My father said he would give his blessing only if Zane could see the value in his farming work, something he lacked at the time. Afterwards, he and I married. Sometime later, this adorable little chap arrives."

"What's the baby's name?" Reika asked.

"Peyton, want to hold him?" She handed Peyton to Reika, who held the child in her arms, smiling back at him. Peyton reached for Reika's cheek, which Reika allowed the child to touch.

"He's so tiny. To think we start like this," Reika said softly.

She handed Peyton back Emeline gently, after which Peyton was laid down to rest.

"He certainly likes you, Reika. Is there a nursery in the citadel?"

"Yes, though when I did help out it was tough keeping the little ones in line. They try your patience. In the end, though, I have to remind myself what I was like as a little one. It's worth it helping them grow."

"It's not easy being a parent. You'll learn that and more when you have a family."

Reika beamed back at Emeline. "I'm sure I will. Even the ones who raised me had their fair share of trouble. Eventually they managed to get me to behave."

Reika began to depart for her bedroom. "I'll leave you to it, Emeline. See you the morning."

"Have a good night, Reika." Emeline then turned and left the room, as Reika headed back upstairs to her bedroom for a long sleep.

The group, including Zane, were waiting outside when Reika finally woke up. She left the house at long last rubbing her head.

"Took you long enough to get up. Tired?" Junayd teased.

"Just a bit, ugh..." Reika said, her eyelids drooping rather low.

"Nice morning, I have to admit," Melito said. "So peaceful and quiet here too."

"I can agree with that," Tabitha added.

Quinn smiled at the group. "I wish you well on your journey. Zane, I'll be closing the farm for a little while here."

"Why don't I send a hired hand to the farm? That way you won't have to close down."

Quinn nodded. Zane then addressed Reika and others. "We'll head to the Time Gate now. Kayleign, you'll look after the farm. Help Quinn and Emeline out anyway you can."

"You get back from this journey safely, ok?" She replied.

Zane said farewell to each of them in turn. Then, he went with the others.

With each passing step, the air started to get colder, the warm breeze transitioning into a biting chill. Only a small amount of snow was falling but that didn't change the fact the snow showed no signs of melting. Reika used a flame to warm herself and the others. Melito didn't mind the cold, having fur. Tabitha's fur likewise kept her warm. The chill of the air was only felt around the metazoans' face and hands.

Despite the flame, it wasn't enough to completely keep the cold away, as the wind kept thwarting Reika's efforts to sustain it. The cold didn't affect Zane in the slightest, as he was wearing a hooded black cloak. Despite the snow clinging to it, Zane pressed on.

They finally made it to the forest after a long day's trek. Junayd pulled the hood of his robes up to protect his face from the cold. Reika had no choice but to extinguish the flame to avoid burning the forest down. The cold now felt worse and her cheeks began to go red. "F-f...f-f... Freezing!" She blurted out.

"You really should have brought a coat, Reika," Junayd said. He seemed to become sympathetic. "I'm really not used to this kind of temperature, either. These robes do a fine job protecting me from sunburn but they're useless here."

For a moment, Junayd had a think. "If the Time Gate is a place to warm us up, I'll gladly trek through the forest to get to it."

Reika walked up slowly next to Junayd. It was a struggle for her. "We need to get moving, Junayd, we can't stay here anymore." A shiver made her voice tremble. "Especially if we want to stay warm."

Following the path deeper into the forest wasn't hard, though the freezing air certainly didn't make the journey easy. The ground was mostly flat, though Reika's feet had started to feel numb.

Junayd kept looking in different directions, watching out for possible predators who could pick them off one by one. The only sound that could be heard was a wind passing through the trees, rattling the leaves as it went.

They managed to reach a clear opening in the trees, the gargantuan dome looming in front of them. The lapis lazuli stone was an amazing sight to behold. The imperfections in the rock complimented the perfection of the dome shape.

A small paving to the party's left caught Melito's attention near the entrance of the temple. He made his way over to the paving, brushing away the snow as he crouched down to investigate.

"A teleporter? It hasn't got any power running through it."

"Don't worry about that, it only responds to my command," Zane replied.

As Zane approached the large double doors, they opened sluggishly with a loud, deep creaking on both sides. All the group stared into the interior of the temple. The hallway was incredible in scope. A large staircase in the middle of the room led to a small double door. A few corridors led elsewhere in the temple structure.

They all ventured up the stairs, following Zane through the double doors. They found themselves in a downsized version of the larger hall, with a weird machine hanging above a marble panel. Junayd scanned the room. Stepping on the marble panel, he crouched to inspect them closer, then directed his gaze to the machine above.

Zane moved a large stone dial that was on the wall. Giving it five revolutions, the machine above the heads of the rest of the group sparked with energy, leaping from one section of the impressive structure to another in rapid succession. The metal itself began to glow intensely like a miniature sun.

"Try to stay within the confines of the marble," Zane said. "I don't want any limbs flying all over this place." Zane threw his cloak into the corner of the room. He stood alongside the rest of the group.

Chapter 6

No Stranger of Time

209 A.E.B

A large beam shot out of the metal, creating what looked like a dome around the group. For a moment, the sound of a small explosion could be heard outside the dome, which itself evaporated shortly after.

"We have reached our destination," Zane said. "Five hundred years into the past, to be precise. If you'll step off the platform and exit the room, we can proceed." Zane sounded casual. The others could only stare at him as he exited the room.

"That was quite a ride," Tabitha said.

They all left the temple, arriving in the same cold forest once again. Not much had changed except the arrangement of the trees, with some being smaller than back in their time.

"I think to save time I'll teleport us all there with the panel," Zane said. "As I said, the panel near the entrance responds to my mind if I desire to use it from afar."

"How far will it take us from here?" Junayd asked.

"In the case of the Time Gate we used, it's within the boundaries of Zeitreisen Island. It's not a machine capable of sending you to any location in the world. Each of the Time Gate's teleporters have a limited radius." Zane activated the panel with a wave of his hand. "All with one accord, let us traverse. I go first, then you will go through."

As each of the group stepped on the panel one by one, they witnessed the world in front of them change. Their vision was clouded by an icy mist which then dissipated to reveal mountains. A large crater could be seen in the ground. Junayd peered over the side of the crater for a closer look. As he gazed at the centre of the crater, the rock looked as though it merged with the light blue glistening crystals at the bottom.

Zane leapt off the edge, sliding down the crater's side, dodging lumps of rock protruding out of the sides of the crater until he reached the crystalline bottom. Using the last ounce of his momentum, Zane leapt onto one of the crystals. He strolled over to a sharp dome that was the height of his shin. Junayd also found his way down, leaping from the protruding rocky platforms, finding himself at the bottom of the crater with Zane.

"Crazy, aren't you?" Junayd said.

"Maybe. No crazier than you, leaping from ledge to ledge, Junayd." The young man was slightly annoyed by Zane's comment.

"I have leapt off buildings, but the worst thing that could happen is a bad fall. You were sliding down and could have impaled yourself on the crystals here."

"Maybe," Zane replied. "But I knew that wouldn't happen." "Foresight?"

"Yes, though I don't use it often. It provides glimpses of the future to me in short bursts when on the move. If I am standing still, however, the accuracy and length of time I can gaze into the future is greater. The downside is that it's incredibly taxing."

"How far can you see?"

"Just enough to get by in a fight. Don't expect visions of the far future from me."

Zane tapped one of the crystals on the dome. A small chime echoed from it. The crystals were beginning to shift away from the mound, revealing a passage of evenly built crystal wall that had a checkered pattern of blue and purple tiles, clear enough that one could see through the tiles themselves. Reika had made her way down, a little tired after climbing. Both Melito and Tabitha were following behind. Junayd looked back.

"You took your sweet time getting down," he said.

"I did. Not a fan of sliding down a sheer rockface. I prefer climbing down gently. I may have rough feet but not that rough."

Reika saw the passageway that Zane stood near, edging her way towards it.

Zane placed his arm as a barrier in front of her.

"Easy. It's not a place you would want to get stuck in."

"I only wanted to look at what was down there. What is inside that passage?"

"The very temple where that amulet is from," Zane said.

Zane then jumped straight down the hole. A slant in it could be seen a few feet below, allowing him to slide down into a chamber made of the same structure as the entrance. He reached the bottom of the chute, sliding on the floor, at last screeching to a stop. He got to his feet, shifting into the now horizontal passage.

"It's safe!" his voice echoed back up the passageway. "You can come down." Reika peered into the hole, wondering what she was thinking. She had been insane enough to leap out of her bedroom window, but this felt different. She reasoned that it wasn't that high, then backed away. "You first or me?" She said.

"I'll go, you follow," Junayd said. "The others can jump down after you." Junayd went to the hole, leaping like Zane had. Reika went after him.

She and Junayd arrived in the chamber, sliding on the floor, with Junayd rolling himself out of the way as she barrelled along the ground and halted a few feet away from Zane.

Eventually Tabitha and Melito arrived, straightening themselves after the descent.

"Ooh, you can make a lot of money with this stuff, we'd be richer than the Caledonian Sultan!" Tabitha remarked, her eyes beholding the glowing chamber. Melito spied another passageway, with a ladder on it. "That slide was the way in, and that ladder takes us up again, but how do we get out of here and into the heart of the temple?"

"That way," Zane responded as he pointed towards a structure above his head. "Right, follow me and stay close."

Eventually, the group found themselves in a small maze comprised of solid crystal tiles, just like the previous chamber. It didn't take too long for them to head farther into the temple itself. The tiles felt very cold on Reika's feet.

"Where's the welcoming party?" Melito asked. "I don't like it."
"They'll be here," Zane answered.

The group followed the maze to the lower level.

Behind them, a golem formed out of the wall, his colour shifted to a mandarin orange. He followed the group from a close distance, keeping his steps silent.

"Where do you think you're going young ones?" He asked.

Despite the strong voice, his address was polite. The group all looked at the golem itself, stopping where they were. The golem had red eyes staring out of his helmet, just like the golem that Junayd had encountered at Caledonia Harbour.

"There is something you carry with you isn't there? An amulet? Hand it over please." Junayd held out the amulet, with the golem's expression turning to one of horror at its lack of colour. "It's been away for a long time then?" the golem asked.

Junayd moved towards to the golem.

"Yes, it has, but it was stolen recently in this time was it not?

We came from the future and are simply here to return it. Your name?"

"Ray Citrine. And I am pleased you are here to return it. It *was* stolen recently; mercenaries took it from us. One of our own kind, He went into hiding after he and his team stole the amulet, selling it to the highest bidder. The bidder had already hidden it away by the time my troops got to him. We lost hope when we were informed it was misplaced at sea."

"I and my companions found it embedded in the claw of an eupithecia. It was terrorising the Caledonian Palace. It refused to confess where it came from. I wish I had more information to go on, sir."

"Understandable, young man, I am just astounded that such a creature had it in its possession. Still, I am grateful for its return. If you follow me downstairs, we need to seal it away in our lowest chamber. And a test of skill for one of our most recently appointed guards who had to replace the previous one, slain by the merc leader himself. Follow me."

They all followed Ray to a lower level. There was no maze this time, but a larger room leading to a small chasm, as well as a stair-case north of it surrounded by a rectangular trench of water, algae-less and pristine. Ray ran to the chasm, leaping over it to the other side. He didn't leave the crouching position that he landed in. A crystalline bridge began to form, tiles appearing one after another eventually reaching the other side where the group were standing.

Reika, Melito, and Tabitha were impressed by what had just occurred. They all passed over the bridge with Junayd and Zane heading along the bridge too. They passed the wall near the chasm to the trench, jumping over the small gap to reach the staircase, heading downstairs into a chamber below, an open room that led into another chasm, vast and deep. A large circular platform could be found at least thirty feet down. On the same level as the group, weightless platforms floated, perfectly still.

Ray stood on a tile to their right, heading downwards to the circular platform, which had a smaller, white golem on it. The platform promptly returned after Ray stepped off it. All three humans stepped on the platform, and it brought them down to the level where the golems stood. Ray was addressing the young golem. His name was Bruce Diamond. Tabitha and Melito stood there watching what was going on.

Ray noticed the three humans leaving the platforms. "The one who is the Temporal Knight, you are the one to undergo this challenge. Best Bruce in combat. I want to test yours and his strengths before you return our amulet and entrust it to his care. Please step forward."

Zane stepped forward alone.

"Win or lose, he must prove his worth to us," Ray said.

Bruce drew a sword from his chest, a crystalline sword which matched his own appearance.

"Show me your strength, Temporal Knight."

Zane called on his sword which appeared at first with a sharp light that formed, before fading to reveal its material and ordinary form. He was ready to engage in the fight with Bruce.

"Begin!" Ray yelled.

Bruce and Zane threw their first strikes and locked their blades, constantly trying to cut each other. Every strike one made was blocked instantly by the other. Zane pulled back, firing a hefty fireball at Bruce, causing the young golem to stagger for a moment until he called ice around him to douse the flames. Once the flames dissipated, he formed the ice into a boulder shape, kicking it with incredible velocity towards Zane. As the boulder reached him it shrank and vanished into fine hot vapour.

Little did Bruce realise that Zane had used his chrono-magic to slow time around him and managed to melt the boulder considerably with the heat of his sword coated in flames, de-summoning the flames before time resumed its natural course. *Can't keep using that too much, it's exhausting using chrono- magic this way. I need to take him down.* Zane thought. He changed the sword in a blinding flash into a bludgeon, swiftly charging toward Bruce. A successful sweeping strike knocked the golem to the floor. Bruce touched the crystal floor under him, creating what looked like a sheet of ice. It slunk towards Zane like a snake in the grass.

Zane backed off, encasing the bludgeon in flames, melting the ice instantly. The fire was extinguished, and Zane replaced it with bright lightning bolts that slithered rapidly towards Bruce. The golem stood there undeterred as the lightning zipped under him, vanishing from view. Zane reformed the bludgeon into a sword.

Spikes fired from the wall, deadly enough to impale him. The young man used a repelling barrier to knock these spikes away and press his attack upon the golem, who also made his advance.

Environmental advantage. That won't work outside here. Zane thought. The two smashed their blades together, locking not only their weapons but their eyes. Zane continued to push against Bruce, straining to force the golem back. The golem looked impassive. Bruce knew he didn't even have to struggle against the flesh of man, the rock and crystal were on his side.

Zane had to think fast. He couldn't afford to alter the flow of time for himself too much due to the toll it took on him, but he could slow it just enough to get the edge. He slowed time down for a brief second, so he had a chance to get away from Bruce, then slashed at him with all his might, hitting the right side of the golem. Time resumed its normal pace for Zane as Bruce yelped and slumped to the floor, dropping his sword.

Junayd and the others cheered, ecstatic with Zane's victory. The young golem scraped part of the floor, taking a small chunk of it and crushed it into a fine powder which he rubbed on his wound. It closed rapidly, leaving no sign of damage. The pain receded from the wound like a passing thought, and Bruce lifted himself to his feet.

"Admirable contest," Ray said. "I am most pleased with your efforts, both of you. The pedestal should be appearing right now."

As Ray ceased speaking, a pedestal grew in the same manner as a plant bursting from the ground. A bowl shape formed once it had reached hip height, roughly three feet tall. Ray made his way over to the pedestal with the amulet in his hands. He placed it gently on the pedestal and from it a noise reminiscent of a gently tapped gong could be heard. The pedestal itself began to liquefy, allowing the amulet to sink into the bowl shape and then into the floor with the pedestal dissolving. A glow like a bright green wave spread through the crystal chamber floors and walls. The section of the floor from which Bruce had removed a small chunk repaired itself. It was like watching glass cracking in full reverse. The strength and durability of the temple was restored.

"We appreciate your efforts, Temporal Knight. All of you, thank you for bringing the amulet back to us once again."

"Happy to assist," Zane replied. "If it wasn't for my companions here bringing the amulet to me, it wouldn't have gotten back here safe and sound. We'll be leaving now, so make sure that amulet is well protected." Ray nodded his head, then turned his attention to Bruce, who moved over to where his elder was standing, looking at him.

Ray began to address Bruce. "Do not let that amulet be stolen." Bruce nodded back. Zane shook Bruce's hand.

"Not bad for a young human such as yourself," Bruce said. With that, Zane departed on the floating platform, leaving Reika and Junayd to follow behind when it returned.

Junayd was thinking about Zane's unique weapon. "That weapon you carry, it's Verwandeln. It is able to transform into a wide array of weapons that you see fit," he said.

"Oh yes," Zane said. "A magic sword crafted by the elves, very handy in many situations. It's limited to hand-to-hand weapons, so it isn't possible to turn into a huge cannon."

They, along with Melito, Reika, and Tabitha, exited the temple, leaving the crystal dome entrance to seal itself back up. Junayd remembered what Irenaeus had said regarding the temple being in good condition back in their present.

"The temple would have been in ruins Zane, wouldn't it? Back in our time, assuming we didn't return?" Junayd asked.

Zane smiled back. "I wouldn't worry, the temple should be fine now since we have restored the amulet to it. Call it a major disaster averted."

Melito overheard the conversation between the two men. No word left his lips. *Disaster? Changed? I wonder if he can do the same for...* Tabitha interrupted Melito's train of thought, causing him to forget what he dwelt upon. "You heading up the crater? I wouldn't daydream if I were you, one false move and we are back down here again." She clambered her way up the crater.

Reika moved past Melito. He stayed where he was for a few seconds, alone in his thoughts. He made his way up the crater shortly after.

～

709 A.E.B

The group finally made it back to their own time.

They arrived at the village of Aevumshire, though just after noon the next day. The buildings were made of beautiful brown oak with thatched hay roofs. A dragon statue could be found in the west of the town, surrounded by a pool of water. The streets had beautiful cobblestones and not a weed in sight. To their right, after entering from the north side of the village, was an inn, which was slightly larger than the other houses and shops. Zane headed inside the inn, finding a shiny wooden floor with similar oak and stone framing to the type found at the farm. Several chairs and tables were evenly spaced throughout the pub, with two barmaids serving drinks along with waiters bringing various dishes out.

Zane went upstairs to find Berinon sitting at a table with a pint glass in his hand, almost empty. The look in his eyes indicated heavy contemplation. Of what, Zane did not know.

Berinon swivelled around on his chair, promptly downing the small vestige of his pint down his throat. "Afternoon, Zane. You caught me at a good time, I am currently on leave."

"Nice. Say, my new comrades are on a journey. They have brought me along.

What say you?"

Berinon squinted at Zane curiously. "Oh, have they? By any chance is it a boy, a girl, and two monkeys? I met a young woman at the dock not long ago. She had a friend, a young man with a very distinctive sword from what I heard. They were accompanied by two guards from Carthage, which you don't see every day."

"Yes, that's right. Reika claimed she met you before she got on the boat." "The former two managed to save the S.S. *Hikari* from some reprobate pirates. Huge barriers all around the ship... Then I took the final shot and blew the *Tetraspis* away," Berinon went on, he then took another swig of the new beer a barmaid set down on his table. "I will accompany you. However, if there's no rush, why not stay for a drink?"

Junayd felt powerful energy in the air. He turned, making his way past the shops and houses. Reika followed him. She knew what Junayd was going towards: a forge.

Junayd headed down the stairs, finding himself in a room that was exactly like the secret one they'd found in Caledonia. Like before, he approached the statue with the Draco Ferrum. As the light from the statue fed the sword, Junayd could feel his strength increasing. Finally, the light vanished, phasing into the blade. Junayd de-summoned the blade, new strength coursing through his body. He exited back up the stairs where Reika was standing and the two of them hurried as quickly as possible back to Melito and Tabitha before Zane returned.

Berinon placed three small coins on the table, which the barman counted quickly and efficiently, nodding his head, indicating that the right amount had been paid. Berinon got up from his chair, following Zane to the ground floor.

Berinon met with the others outside, he knew Reika already.

"I wanted to ask you in Caledonia, but I never got the chance—would you like to come with us?" Reika asked.

"I shall gladly oblige," Berinon responded. "I think our next stop should be Entella. We will just be passing through there, but the settlement should provide us with some supplies."

Melito was silent, concealing his unhappiness.

They all then headed to the path by which they had entered the village but then a voice shouted, "Hold it right there!"

Junayd saw the same elvish man whom he'd seen in Caledonia coming towards them. The elf had a scowl on his face, staring at Zane intently. Zane stepped in front of his friends and his group. The villagers backed away from the fray.

"Rian? What are you doing here?" Zane called.

"There's a price on your head. I was offered fifty thousand in reptibloons to kill you," he said, his voice commanding.

"You're still thirsty for my blood?" Zane said in anger.

"I'm a bounty hunter. I work for those who have the necessary funds. I haven't forgotten what you did to me in our last fight."

"Bounty Hunter? Zane, you know this man?" Reika said in surprise.

"Oh, I do. He works for a guild. If the price is right, they are willing to help anyone, even the enemies," Zane said in response.

Rian smirked, "True there. Now, time for me to collect my payment."

Zane stepped forward, followed by Berinon. Zane summoned Verwandeln once again. Berinon summoned a lance out of thin air.

"Sorry, but we're going deny you getting your payment," Zane said. "Get out of our way."

Rian pulled out a gun from behind him; a small blade was attached to the bottom. He cocked the gun. "Time to die farm boy."

Rian pulled the trigger. Zane raised his hands quickly. From his perspective, time had slowed to a crawl, even his ally Berinon. Taking his sword, Zane casually walked over to the bullets, cutting each one into pieces one by one. Every bullet he cut and cut until they were reduced to harmless specks of ash before regaining normal speed. The friction of his cuts caused the small fragments to glow red hot. The ash cloud blew over Zane and Berinon harmlessly.

The magic was taxing but Zane was still able to counter a quick strike from Rian who, seeing his bullets were ineffectual, had swiftly switched to holding his gun like a sword, and tried to slash Zane with the small blade. Zane didn't even bother turning round, instead holding his sword behind his back, keeping Rian's strike from landing, then swiftly pushing him away. From Reika, Melito, and Tabitha's perspectives, Zane moved incredibly fast. After pushing Rian away, he resumed his regular speed.

Berinon chimed in, trying to strike Rian with the lance, the elf barely managing to dodge the attack, with a small piece of his hair nicked by the blade. Berinon jabbed Rian in the stomach with the butt of the weapon while he was distracted by the cut and Rian staggered, trying to draw up his gun for another shot. But before he could, Rian found a cord of rope around his throat, its colour suspiciously like Verwandeln's.

Zane had the upper hand.

Junayd was very impressed. *Verwandeln, an adaptable weapon, versatile,* he thought.

"You have gotten sloppy," Zane said. "Haven't you forgotten as the Temporal Knight I change the flow of time around my body? I can predict your every move." His breathing was slightly heavy from the magical exertion. Rian was silent for a moment.

"But every time you use it, you tire yourself out," the elf said. "I can weaken you through that. Anyone can." The elf grinned.

Zane was not impressed. "Drop it! Drop your gun now!"

Rian complied. Zane then pulled the cord away from his neck. "Urgh... You're lucky it's my break now, otherwise I would keep trying to kill you." Rian picked up his gun and walked away straight into the inn, leaving the group in shock. The villagers didn't know how to react, Rian never gave them any look, it indicated to some that Rian wasn't going to harm them, others kept their distance.

Junayd couldn't even believe what had just happened. "Wow, cantankerous scum, isn't he?" He blurted out.

"Yep, he is foul tempered," Zane replied. "However, if we want his help, we may have to pay him."

Melito was furious. "Pay him? Work with scoundrels like him?"

"Yes and No. If a bounty hunter engages in illegal activity, they can be arrested," Zane explained. "It's ultimately up to you, but I have a feeling it won't be the last time we see him." Zane directed his attention away from the inn to a shop on the northern end of the town. "But if you'll excuse me, I need to get a farmhand."

Junayd stepped forward. "I could talk to him."

Zane raised an eyebrow. "You want to? This is a bounty hunter you are dealing with here."

Junayd nodded his head. "Yes, someone who is willing to plunge into sewage in order to get a job done."

Junayd headed up the stairs. He saw Rian at the bar drinking. Gently he approached him. "Hey there."

Rian immediately produced a knife from the gauntlet from his sleeve. "WHOA! Put that knife down, I'm not here to fight, I just want to talk..."

Junayd held his palms to the side.

Rian glared. "Fine, I'll put it down. What is it?"

Junayd regained composure; his confidence returned. "You and Zane had quite a history, it seems..."

"Not really your concern. What is it you are asking?" Junayd reached into the pocket of his robes and placed a beige cotton bag tied with a string on the table. He then sat down next to Rian, who didn't move from where he was, nor make a move towards Junayd. "You haven't received your payment yet, so I am offering you a job.

Whoever hired you, their type of money is chicken feed, absolute chicken feed."

"Heh, right... And what are you going to offer to change my mind?" Rian asked, smirking at the young man who, to an elf, was merely a little boy.

"One hundred thousand reptibloons. That's my offer, Rian." "Two hundred thousand."

Junayd was not impressed. "Unreasonable." He said as he tried his best to contain his anger. "One hundred and fifty thousand, how does that sound? I am not going higher than that."

The elf nodded. "Done." Junayd handed the bag over to Rian. *Absolute extortion,* Junayd thought as he went down the stairs. He had to restrain himself. A look of happiness was on his face by the time he exited the inn. Berinon could see that Junayd's smile was feigned. Reika noticed it as well.

The shop Zane needed was one of many in town and had all kinds of accoutrements: tools for building, pans for cooking, and many other miscellaneous things. The goblin behind the counter was a stout fellow with seaweed green skin. The sclera of his eyes was that of a faded yellow, a yellow from leaving a white object in the sun for many hours. It wasn't a sign of ill health among his people, just a common trait they had. His clothes were relatively simple, though fashionable: a burgundy waistcoat with goldenrod rims.

His trousers were raisin black, almost regal. He had set aside a pair of overalls that he wore for various jobs while running his shop.

Zane strolled in. "Borin, good to see to you."

"Zane, my boy," the goblin greeted Zane, shaking his hand. "What brings you here? Pull up a chair."

Zane explained the situation to Borin: about Reika, The Draco Ferrum, and the weredragon's curse. "So... I was wondering if it was possible for you to oversee the operation of the farm until my return?"

Borin was quiet. "That is going to be very difficult, the shop must be managed, and I am one goblin. My hands are tied here." He tapped the table with his fingers for a moment. "I'll send my two best employees to assist Quinn, Emeline, and Kayleigh. It's the least I can do for you saving my business. Family to feed, roof over my head, and customer service to provide and all that."

Zane was glad. "I appreciate that, they will be grateful. I don't like leaving them alone to work the farm. My role as the Temporal Knight does require me to leave in order to lend my help to those who need it. Been a while since my last journey. It would be nice to have a change of pace for a while." Borin poured out some tea for himself and Zane. The young human happily accepted the drink.

"The only thing that's changed about you is your love of your work. Still, you're the boy who had a heart for adventure. But you have a wife to keep you in check." The two shared a laugh.

"How very true," Zane replied. "I didn't appreciate the beauty of it. I get to be a man who brings bountiful harvests to those who need it the most. I have Emeline to thank for that." He downed the rest of his tea, placing the mug on the counter. Borin placed the mug he was drinking from next to Zane's.

"Expect my employees to be round tomorrow. They'll see to it the farm remains in good working order. Go in peace, my friend." They shook hands again and with that, Zane left.

The group journeyed via sea to Entella, a place of lush, green open grasslands. They arrived eventually in the coastal settlement of Costa Primado with wooden huts of gorgeous timber. Unlike previous villages, the abodes were not placed smartly in a line; the spots seemed random yet were organised. They all were beautiful. Some pecan coloured; others tortilla coloured. All had straw roofs held together by tar of a chocolate hue. The sand of the shore was close to the plains themselves, the sea gently lapping against the coast.

Reika was on the port side of the ship, admiring the view of the settlement as they were docking. Melito stood alongside her. "I never knew of this place. This settlement is a good sight, worth stopping here for the night, don't you think?"

"Yes, I wouldn't mind a little dip in the sea."

"I think I'll be getting coconuts from the palm trees you see over there." Melito pointed to the palm trees dotting in the settlement's east side. The two made their way off the ship, joining up with the rest the group and the other passengers.

Berinon took a deep breath in and then out. "The ocean breeze! This place would be a fine place to retire. For now, a lovely place for me to have a vacation should our journey be successful."

"We don't get trees quite like this except in the north of Caledonia, not even the beaches themselves compare to the magnificence of the ones here," Junayd said.

"I wouldn't quite say that myself, Junayd. They are nothing to scoff at." "Oh, I didn't say they were bad. There is an inn by the sea, along with a beach house and an inn called Costa Enano. Both located in the south of my country. You should take a trip one time."

"I thank you for the recommendation, Junayd. Sounds like a lovely place. Now..." Berinon clapped and rubbed his hands together. "It's about time we get some grub. I have heard from travellers there are some fantastic steaks in this place. Care to join me?"

"Much obliged, I haven't had any steak for a while."

Reika was dipping her toes in the sea, with Tabitha also removing her shoes and rolling up her trousers. "Ever do this as a child, Reika?"

"I remember Mark and Andrea walking alongside each other on the beach, they stayed close to ensure Tristan and I didn't get swept away by the tide. This does bring back some good memories."

Tabitha gave a brief shriek, making Reika jump. Something crept around the tamarin's leg. She lifted her leg from the sea, her breathing slowing down to a crawl. It was a piece of green seaweed that wrapped around her feet. The two both shared a laugh, dumping the seaweed back into the sea.

Melito climbed the palm trees and picked three coconuts. He took them to Reika and Tabitha near the sea and he cracked them in half, giving them over to his friends. The marmoset did his best to smile. He kept his thoughts to himself. Tabitha could see her friend staring at the coconut shell.

"Melito? What's wrong?"

"I'd rather not talk right now about it. Let's bask in the moment." Melito took a sip of the milk from the coconut. Reika and Tabitha did so likewise.

"If you want to talk later, Melito, we can," Reika said.

"I appreciate that... We are not far from where I used to live. The castle that is northeast of this town." He clenched his lips shut. "I'm sorry, I have to go." And go he did, walking down the coast before turning into the town. The other two could only watch with sadness.

Zane came up to them. "I have booked a few rooms for us. We'll need to rest here for the night then set out in the morning."

Reika faced Zane, slightly irritated, hastily forcing her face return to a neutral expression. "Thanks."

Zane squinted at her. "Am I interrupting something?"

"Melito just walked off. I wish we could cheer him up. Something has set him off here."

"His home, the Castle of Entella, destroyed many years ago. I think it will be worth going there to pay our respects. Melito deserves that much." Then Zane left them alone.

Rian was watching from afar back on the ship. All he did was glare at Zane.

Is he planning what I think he is? Nothing ever changes.

The next morning, they set out from the settlement. It was relatively easy, the grass was cool on those with bare feet. After a few hours, the group found themselves at the castle near the eastern coast but by the time they got there, it was raining heavily. They circled the outside to find the entrance until at last, they found an opening on the eastern wall where they could take shelter.

Melito fixed his gaze on the large castle. He didn't say anything, just kept looking at it with a mournful expression. He shed no tears. There was only a feeling of resentment, a difficult feeling to hold back.

The group found a pair of large ironwood doors which had collapsed, rotting away due to lack of maintenance on their rusted metal frames. Weeds, vines, and all sorts of flowers were growing in the wood as well as the paving inside the castle grounds and the flower beds.

They saw a large structure within the walls, a lone gigantic tower. The flags present had been subject to the claws of time, ravaged by the elements, and torn. Melito felt physically sick, seeing his old home in such a horrible state. He had only been a toddler when taken away by his mother, but it still hurt.

"How long has it been like this?" Reika asked.

"Twenty-four years. It was attacked by Welk Seha, A nasty piece of work. He rules an island not too far from here," Zane said. Reika merely stared the castle.

"That vile beast," she said. "I can't bear to look at this place. Why would he do something like this?"

Junayd turned to Reika. "You don't have to go in if you don't want to," he said.

Tabitha also chimed in. "Junayd's right, you know." She turned to Melito. "I would be devastated if this happened to my home."

Melito edged his way into the castle grounds alongside his friends. He also clutched his fist tightly in anger at what he saw. "Should we ever go to Welk Seha's fortress, we'll kill him. He will pay for what he has done to my people. He drove my family away from here, the royal family of Entella."

Junayd gasped. "Wait? You were a prince?"

Melito turned to Junayd. "I would have been if my family had stayed. My father ruled this place. He was merciful yet stern. He and my mother took me away when I was a boy, Welk Seha showed up and destroyed the citadel, many were scattered. I ended up in Carthage with both my parents. They stayed in Reme for a while but sent me to the citadel where I would be safe. I have not seen them since."

Melito smiled weakly. "They wanted me to train in Carthage, so one day, I could be strong enough to fight Welk Seha with the power of our greatest weapon, Entella's Bane."

"We have your back, Melito," Tabitha said. "We all have each other's back, right?"

"I guess we do," Melito responded.

Zane went inside to investigate the interior of the castle. The courtroom pillars of stone housed large cracks. Broad banquet tables were overturned, piles of rubble lying on the floor in gigantic clumps, randomly scattered around. Some of the tables rested on their sides as if they had been used as a barrier. Any trace of a carpet had rotted and been eaten away, leaving behind a stone floor with cracks on it. A similar set of doors to the wall entrance lay on the stone floor, splintered, ruined and rotten.

"What are you looking for, Zane?" Berinon enquired quietly, to ensure that no one was hearing him.

"Bodies..." Zane said. "I want to be sure if there are any. So far, the hall is clear." He halted in place. "If there were any attackers, their bodies could have been retrieved later. No civilian ones around, at least not in here. We need to check some of the other chambers. In the meantime, get the others inside."

Melito had already entered before Zane could stop him. The marmoset was quiet, approaching the ruined throne. He took no notice of Zane, who had gone deeper into the castle. Melito got closer to the throne, beholding it as a shell of its former self. The soft cushion had been eaten away and the gold scratched; it was almost ready to collapse. He turned away from the throne, sitting in front of it. There was no escaping his morose disposition.

I wouldn't mind undoing this. Will Zane agree to it? He sat there for several minutes, staring at the entrance of the throne room. Torrential rain poured outside. A powerful wind pushed the rain to the south, so much so that if one stood close to the entrance, they could see the water droplets move along the ground. The only noise they could hear was the sound of the droplets crashing onto the broken paving. At last, Zane returned to the throne room.

"We must talk, Melito—away from the others."

The rain was enough to hide their voices from a distance. Tabitha glanced in their direction but no more than that, tears ran down her cheeks. Rian also looked on, thinking what Zane could be saying to Melito. *I knew it, he is going to help him.*

"Can we stop the assault on my home or is it going to happen no matter what we do?" Melito asked.

Zane was silent, part of him was hesitant to answer. "It *is* possible to change the past, of that I am certain, the problem is the risk is far too high, even for us." Melito was a little disappointed.

"I see... I wish I could change it myself."

"However," Zane said. "I spoke with an old orangutan by the name of Juste. He claimed to be the old weaponsmith of this castle. On the day I met him on my travels, he told me that an evacuation of the citizens happened both before and when Welk arrived to attack. Beforehand, the king of Entella had prepared his soldiers for three days to ensure a fighting chance. The soldiers did have help. I think this will be a time to step in ourselves."

Melito was intrigued. "How will we go back in time? There is no time machine here."

"If you are looking for one, there is one to the north not too far from here. One of a few that exist. It's closed off to all but me and anyone else who comes with me."

"Then what are we waiting for?" Melito said.

"Relax..." Zane said. "Time travel, remember? We can go shortly but right now we need to rest here and it's pelting down outside. We needn't get wet again."

"Allow me one more question. You said they had three days of preparation?

You sure that's enough time?"

Zane grinned, "Trust me, I know what I am doing."

Chapter 7

Entella: Siege of 687

I t wasn't easy to get a good night's sleep within the destroyed castle for Melito. He tried his best to do so, but a deep sleep was out of his grasp.

Coming here to rest was a mistake. The sooner we go back in time and try to help my people out the better.

He began to think carefully about what Zane had said. He was going to step in and assist his own people in their escape. A strange endeavour, yet one that brought him some comfort: his people may be alright. He lay himself down comfortably next to the wall, allowing himself to drift off into sleep.

Morning came very quickly for Melito. He wondered if he had really slept for a few hours or a few minutes. They departed shortly after breakfast. As they encircled the walls, they passed by a group of small mounds on the northern side about fifty feet away, Melito did wonder what they were, he then realised they were tumuli, burial mounds. How old they were he couldn't guess; they were not new, but they certainly didn't exist for many years. Melito just moved on with a heavy heart, no one dared to ask him what they were.

The group pressed on for a mile and as Zane had said, sure

enough, there was a time machine to the north. It resided alone in the field north of the Entellan Citadel. It was like the Time Gate in Zeitreisen, colour and all. The main difference was it small in scope in comparison to the original but nevertheless would serve its purpose to the group. Its door matched the rest of the lapis lazuli coloured stone. It opened by itself when Zane approached.

Before it had even opened all the way, Melito barged his way through the door, down the passageway, the torches illuminating both sides while he journeyed towards the Time Gate's main mechanism. He was fortunate that he didn't bash into Zane on the way through. Zane became very irritated.

Melito disappeared from view.

"Will you wait for us please?" Zane said in a vexed manner as he rushed down the stairs. The others made haste after them. They all found themselves inside a time chamber laid out the same way as the gate found in Zeitereisen, the difference being the type of stone used to construct the interior. Zane saw Melito messing around with the time dial. "What are you doing, Melito?"

"Zane, how do I get this machine to work? We need to go back!" Melito tried to turn the dial quickly, but Zane yanked him on the shoulders away from it. He started pointing at the marmoset angrily.

"Will you stop and slow down?" Zane said, with his teeth bared. "It's a time machine, we can go to any period of history. We have plenty of time to go back."

"I apologise, I panicked," Melito said awkwardly.

Zane pointed to the panel silently, indicating all to step onto the panel ready to travel through time. He turned the dial on the wall two revolutions, indicating at least a twenty-four-year jump, as this dial had numbers that resembled a clock. "The time we are going to is three days before the attack. We'll have enough time to warn them, prepare the soldiers for battle, and civilians to leave in safety."

Just then, Zane quickly ran onto the panel to be whisked to the past with his own comrades in the same flashing light as before.

~

687 A.E.B

The group then found themselves in the same room. Melito went upstairs with Zane rushing after him. Melito halted in place.

"Strange, it's almost as if we haven't left at all," Melito said.

"Oh, believe me, we have indeed gone back in time. Onwards to your home." Melito got a chance to see the castle in full glory. As they entered the courtyard, they all admired the scenery, the flowerbeds that had been subject to weed growth in the present did not have this problem, nor did the rest of the beautiful stone of the castle walls have cracks, and the full flags on the walls of the castle flew proudly. The doors also had not suffered damage, both the courtyard entrance and the main tower. Once near the courtyard entrance, they were stopped by guards who wore the same armour as found in Carthage and Caledonia, only green. They held their spears to Melito's face. "Halt where you are," they said sharply. Melito backed away.

Reika drew close to Junayd. "I didn't expect this," she said. "Hands behind your head."

Reika and the others complied.

"Who are you?" One of the guards uttered in anger.

Reika gulped. "We don't want trouble. We just came through the time machine with the Temporal Knight." She looked at Zane. "I..."

The guard smacked Reika in the face with the back of his hand. Reika recoiled from the pain.

"Don't lie, or we will kill you!" the guard shouted.

"STOP!" Melito shouted. One of the guards spun around pointing the spear at his throat.

"You dare presume to command us boy?" "Boy? I am twenty-six."

"We'll place you under arrest, King Julius will have much to ask and..." The guard stopped and looked at Melito's hand, noticing the strange birth mark on his right palm. "Just a moment, your hand, what is that?"

"It's a birthmark, what's that to you?" The guards lowered their spears quickly. "Forgive us, is this all of you?"

"Yes, now let us inside the castle. The young farm boy you see there is the one who brought us here, we are from the future."

"Future?"

"Why ask such silly questions? You have a Time Gate not far from here. Only the Temporal Knight and others who accompany him are authorised to use it."

One of the guards removed his helmet to reveal his face. He was a golden- haired gibbon with grey skin. "Oh yes. Such a place is off-limits to guards like us. We are a bit jittery; I confess."

All of them made their way through the courtyard into the throne room. The carpet was pristine. The many tables were laid out for casual socialising, with very comfortable stools at their feet. Not a crack in the pillars was in sight.

The king of the castle was sitting on his throne and the group were presented to him by the guards. The king stepped from his throne and down the grey polished stone. His face was much like Melito's, only rather aged, with grey hair starting to show on the sides of his face. He wore armour plating, pauldrons, and gauntlets resembling the guard's armour with a shinier polish.

"Let me see your hand," the king said. Melito held up his hand with the birthmark so the king could examine it carefully. "This marking could only belong to my son, yet you stand before me with this mark?"

Melito then recognised his own father. He held back his emotions tightly, not wanting to break down in front of his friends.

"I am your son."

The king's eyes widened. For a moment, all held their breath. Many of the guards wondering if Melito would be accused of magical deception, or whether the king would simply refuse to accept this as the truth, but then before their eyes he opened his arms, and drew Melito into an embrace.

"I've come from the future. There is a warning we bring," Melito said, as they parted. His eyes shone with restrained tears.

The king, Julius, then stopped him. "We shall discuss it later, for now, make yourselves our honoured guests."

Around lunch, the banquet tables were filled to the brim with many of the king's subjects, all of whom were metazoan, mostly primates. Reika offered to give assistance to the servants. They were positively surprised by her request and Julius allowed it. *Just like the old days,* she thought, as she tied her hair back. She was summoned by the king.

The others sat down at the tables, engaging in conversations with the subjects of the palace. Julius spoke with Melito in private in the courtyard, the two walking around it. "My boy, it is good to see you, even under these strange circumstances. In all my years, no one has ever come through the Time Gate," Julius said, he gave his son a one-armed hug.

"Same here," Melito responded.

"Now then let's cut to the chase, my son, what is going to transpire here?" "Father, King Welk Seha is on his way to attack. He will tear down this place.

You need to get your subjects out of here to safety."

Julius could only look at Melito in shock. "When? When will he attack?" "Three days from now."

"Many dead?"

"I am uncertain," Melito said nervously, unsure how to answer. "We need the people to leave here right now. They cannot stay here; it might be too late. With the help of the Temporal Knight and others, I can defeat Welk."

Julius contemplated the matter for a moment. "We will not speak to the subjects now. Let me tell them when the celebration is over. I will speak with the royal guard in secret first, it is important that they start training to be ready to fight against the vile fiend who is plotting our destruction."

"Very good, better safe than sorry."

"I will ensure that your mother, and you, will leave on the boats with the soldiers."

Melito frowned.

King Julius smiled knowingly. "I do not fully understand the mysteries of time travel, but if I do not send you and your mother away, you will cease to exist here, no? Then we will be unprepared for the attack. Any rupture in the timeline could be catastrophic."

Melito felt himself choking up. He desired to fix the past, so that he could remain with his parents in Entella rather than be forced to flee, but if he changed things too much, he would unmake his own reality; the cycle had to be repeated. A small marmoset ran across the courtyard and over to his father. Melito stared at the child but didn't say anything. It was him as a toddler. He kept his mouth tightly shut. "My dear son," Julius said to the boy, giving him a hug. "What's wrong Father?" The boy asked.

"Nothing son, nothing at all. I think it will be alright."

Melito remained silent. The younger version then looked at him. "Who are you?" He enquired.

Melito was caught off-guard by the question. "I'm just here to assist your father. You'll understand in time." Melito kept his right hand by his side and stayed deliberately vague, not wanting to say who he was to the young lad.

"Come along son, it's time to eat," Julius said. Rian was watching from the shadows, listening to what was going on. He furrowed his brows and squinted his eyes in rage.

That hypocrite, he thought. *How sickening.* He then stormed away but composed himself before entering the throne room. Melito saw a shadow leaving the courtyard, but he didn't think any further about it and moved on.

Zane was leaning on the wall to the left side of Rian. "You better not plan anything that will impede our goal here," he said firmly, as Rian re-emerged.

Rian didn't look at Zane, merely stood there clenching his fist.

"It still amazes me how you are so hypocritical, that you refuse to rescue one person from a personal plight of theirs and yet are willing to help a fallen prince save what would have been his future subjects."

Zane shook his head, baring his teeth in frustration. "Under no circumstances can I change the time-stream for one individual's personal reasons. History may have to take its course. There are, however, certain times where I need to step in if it brings forth a greater good. If I so much as tweak the past based on someone's own desires, who knows what catastrophe could be caused? Even the ones among our group have the potential to be ruthless tyrants."

"Yet..." Rian interjected, "There was one tyrant you could never thwart. Others had to take her down. Furthermore, the were-dragon's curse was allowed to flourish. One of whom who bears the curse is in our midst!" The elf pointed to where Reika was busying about the palace throne room. "She is serving tables, who knows what could be changed even by her doing that."

"She is trying to get rid of the curse, Rian. That's what we are doing on this journey. The curse itself was prophesied years prior to this time. Also, who is to say Reika wasn't meant to come here and serve tables?"

Rian was utterly exasperated. "I could kill you right now, farm boy. Perhaps even call Welk Seha here..."

Zane stepped away from the wall.

"Don't you dare! I faced you in battle before and I can defeat you again if you step out of line. And I can have Junayd terminate our contract, taking your precious pay from you by force. I may not know who hired you to kill me, but should I divulge the fact you've double-crossed your previous employer who wanted me gone to anyone here, you would become an easy target for them for putting this place at risk. Even one such as you would find difficulty in taking on so many opponents. Stick to your end of the deal. Welk will be on his way anyway."

Rian just stared at Zane. "You know deep down you are a selfish recreant.

Your family was saved from destruction."

"Janshai did me a favour when I rescued him from that evil spirit that took hold of him. He was the one who offered to rescue them. The elves *never* punished me for that. They allowed it. I wasn't using the time travel for *my* personal gain; it was so he could return his favour. I could not rescue them myself because of the potential damage that could be done to the timeline."

"Any agreement that I made can be broken if a higher wage is offered," Rian said, sniggering at Zane. "It's only a matter of time."

"Only as a possibility," Zane said. "No way do I see you betraying us now, you know you are better than that and so did she."

Rian's composure then instantly snapped.

"Don't... mention her... ever!" He snarled, trying his best not to let anyone hear his voice. Zane wasn't fazed by Rian's outburst in the slightest.

"I will mention her... Stay in line... Or our deal is off, Rian."

The elf walked slowly back into the throne room, glancing back at Zane one last time. "I wonder how a so-called messiah like you is able to keep a clear conscience."

With that, Rian moved back to the tables to eat, taking a glass of wine from one of the servants and downing it fast, the servant staring at him in amazement.

Zane crossed his arms. *You have no idea what I must live with,* he thought.

Reika was also looking from a distance, her eyes glued to Rian as he sat at one of the far tables near the throne. She wondered what was wrong with the elf, why he hated Zane so much, and why Zane looked upset. But she didn't wonder for long as someone called from behind, asking for a refill of his glass of wine. Reika went back to her work without a word.

King Julius and Melito re-entered the hall. The king went to his table, silently signalling to the guests to continue. "Reika, you have been a great asset this afternoon, but I think you deserve a long break. Feel free to dine with the guests."

Reika bowed her head.

Melito went to her. "May I speak with you in private?"

"Sure." Melito took Reika aside into the corridor. Tabitha saw them after finishing her meal and went after them. The chatter was loud enough from the denizens of the citadel to drown out their conversation. "Are you ok, Melito?"

The young marmoset sat on the wooden seats next to the door. Reika sat to the metazoan's right while Tabitha sat next to Reika. "Sometimes, there is a memory that flashes back to me whenever I look at you," Melito said. He crossed his arms. "I remember the day that Entella was attacked. My mother was carrying me. I could see a woman defending one of the boats. She stared at me for a few moments. She was one the first humans I had ever seen. There was another person, a man brandishing a *blue sword*..."

Tabitha was astonished.

Reika was struck by a thought.

"Junayd and I were there?"

"Must have been. We're not really changing anything. It's a *loop*. I never said anything to you until now. Even when you came to the citadel for the first time, I knew something about you was familiar, I couldn't quite put my finger on it. I befriended you, as did Tabitha. Passing through Entella made me wonder if we were fated to meet." Melito stopped. "You must think I have been using you."

Reika smiled. "Melito, it is alright. If your memory is right and it was Junayd and I protecting you, what makes you think you were using me when you met me at the citadel? You were just a boy; you didn't manipulate or use me at all. You, Tabitha, and I became firm friends, and you have stood up for me."

"Reika is right, you would never take advantage of anyone," Tabitha added. Melito smiled back at the two of them. "Thanks, I needed that."

Melito and Tabitha headed back to the hall for the banquet.

Reika was about to follow them when Junayd entered the hallway. "Is he alright?" the swordsman asked.

"Yes. He was worried our friendship was not genuine." She told him everything that was told to her.

"He's worrying too much; how could he conceive of such an idea? He was a boy." Junayd leaned against the stone. "But if he is correct, then it looks like fate has funny way of bringing us together, if fate is even a thing." He placed his head in his hand. "This is making my head hurt."

Junayd then looked at Reika again and smiled at her. "What is it?"

"I noticed you tie your hair while you were serving the tables. You should wear it like that more often, it suits you."

Reika cheerily placed the back of her left hand under the pony-tail, lifting it slightly, then did a flick push back, bringing her arm down to her side again. "Heh, it's more of a work hairstyle, it's not a beauty kind of thing for me." Reika pulled the hair-tie out, letting her hair fall back into its usual place. "Let us go to the banquet."

Within a shadowy fortress, far away to the east of Entella, an island could be found where Welk Seha dwelt. The island itself was formed from volcanic flow. The southern part of the island had much in the way of open plains, a small, lush forest, and winding hills. The northern section of the island was quite different. If one continued north across the border, much of the rich greenery became coated by barren ash and burned away. The skies blackened with fire thanks to the active volcano. There was a castle in the distance, northwest of the volcano, constructed from hardened obsidian.

It had been left alone for years, until metazoans had journeyed to the island. Specifically, Scorpions, many of whom had heavily armoured exoskeletons that made up their limbs. The ones who colonised this island had black exoskeletons matching that of the island's basalt rock, with completely red eyes. Their mouths were almost human but lacked anything resembling lips as well as having rather pronounced canine fangs. Their feet lacked posable toes, instead having what looked like a large bone sting on each foot.

Welk Seha was no exception, except he was larger than the others, towering over an average human by three feet. He wore a blood red spiked crown on his head, with a scarf of the same colour concealing his mouth. The strange blade he held in his hand was a large cylindrical paddle with a stinger on the end with a long handle. Part of the handle had a guard.

One of the smaller scorpions approached Welk Seha, taking a bow at the steps. "The troops are ready at your command, sir. They only need your word to go on their way."

Though none could see what lay under the scarf, it was clear from the chuckle that emerged from behind it that the king was pleased. He rose to his full height from his throne and moved down the stairs, the servant backing away to make way. "Time to pay the primates a visit."

He left the stairs, placing his sword into a sash wrapped around his right shoulder and left side of his chest. He made his way to the towering wooden doors of his castle which opened to him. As he marched out of the throne room, countless soldiers made their way out, following behind him to the docks, all loading themselves onto the boats for the journey to Entella. Others watched and waited, closing the doors of their fortress behind their king.

For three days, the soldiers of Entella prepared themselves for the battle to come. Many practiced shooting their arrows at straw targets, some sharpened their swords, axes, and maces, and others struck sand-filled cushions to test their strength. Unfortunately, there was a problem with the civilians. While some departed from the citadel, others were afraid. They were terrified about what would happen if they left.

Julius allowed them time to compose themselves to leave when they are ready. A warning was given that all were to leave by the third day. Some refused. Julius was particularly frustrated with a group of bonobos. They didn't learn this lesson.

"Why have you not left? An invasion is going to happen. You will likely lose your lives!"

"There is no invasion... We have had many years of peace, why would that change?" They replied.

Julius was enraged. "I have been patient and tried to be fair here, but you cannot be stiff-necked forever. If one is complacent, bad things occur. We should be vigilant. Get on the boats and leave this place. Hide away safely or stay and die. Is that clear?" The group were silent, grumbling as they went on the boat. "And stop your whining too!" Julius added.

There were more to get onto the boat, but Julius had enough. In the end, he went inside the castle, asking a strong baboon guard to escort any stragglers onto the boat.

"Right, you lot," the baboon growled. "Onto the boat and no complaints!"

The king went into a corridor linking back to the castle where his wife Laria was waiting. She was a female marmoset in a royal dress of scarlet. They hugged each other. "They'll be here soon, my love. We must get Melito onto one of the boats." The marmoset made her way back through the corridor, her husband alongside her as she went.

"Some are still afraid of leaving Julius, they are worried they'll never be coming back."

"Unfortunately, I can't say for certain if we are going to come back. It is a terrible thing, but I want my people to survive. We cannot delay leaving any longer."

"I couldn't leave without you..."

"Fear not dearest. It's for the best we go together for our son's sake."

~

Melito watched what was going on in contemplative silence. He had previously filled his hours with practice in the training room, awaiting the inevitable. Tabitha trained with him, allowing him space, but also showing she was there for him.

An orangutan in armoured garb made his way to the young marmoset. Melito turned. "Juste, I presume?"

"Yes indeed, young man." The two shook hands. Juste produced out a weapon, a large double axe with a long handle. The shaft was wooden and the double axe head was remarkably refined and sharp. Melito didn't dare touch the axe head lest he cut his skin. "I think you'll appreciate this axe we are giving you. Fine craftsmanship, no slip, incredibly durable, and what's more with this one, the weapon has been designed to pierce armour, including that of Welk Seha. Try it out on this iron bar."

Melito took hold of the weapon. He swung the axe at the iron bar. The axe split the bar without any significant damage done to the head, much to the amazement of Melito. "Very well put together, this will come very handy in the fight ahead."

"It enhances the strength of the wielder as long as you hold it. It can be summoned so that you don't have to carry it around. Should come in handy against Welk. It is the weapon of our king. Entella's Bane."

Melito smiled. "Consider me impressed."

"Your companion uses a bow with arrows, yes? I have something for her too."

Juste handed Tabitha a beautiful bow, about the third the size of Tabitha. Tabitha plucked the bowstring; it made a satisfying *twang*. She was also impressed by the arrows Juste gave her, which housed small, green and red feathers on the ends of them. "Neatly crafted, love to see what they can do," she said.

"Thanks. Like the axe, they can penetrate armour. They are also magical and can be summoned by your own command. Highly recommended, ma'am."

Tabitha began to smile.

An alarm sounded upstairs. Melito, Tabitha, and the other

soldiers present in the training room all rushed upstairs to the throne room.

"Hurry, sire, hurry!" called a guard from outside.

"Let me through!" Melito called. "I must know what it is."

He made his way up the stony stairs of a watchtower on the south-east side, ensuring that he didn't trip—it was a long way down.

The watchman, a gorilla, called to Melito.

Melito froze. He recognised the gorilla. It was King Tertullian in his younger years, bearing the armour of the Entellan guard, long before he'd taken over Carthage. Melito didn't say anything.

"Find something?" Melito asked.

"Over there, I see ships," Tertullian responded. He handed his telescope over to Melito who put it to his right eye and looked through it, seeing the menacing warships closing toward them in the distance from the east.

"Send word to the king," Melito said. "Get the remaining citizens out of here as fast as you can. Make sure to get Laria to leave with her son, that is of utmost importance."

Tertullian looked at Melito in amazement, then realised what he had to do. "Very well, Master Melito, I will need some help from your comrades to ensure an easy escape for the civilians."

"They should be able to take care of it. Find your best commander to lead one half of the army, the other half shall escort the civilians to the boats and sail with them for protection." Tertullian nodded his head in agreement, climbing down the side of the tower to find his officer. Melito followed suit, heading back inside the throne room to see what was going on.

Welk Seha watched from the boat, smiling to himself. *The fools can try but they will not succeed, I'll make certain of that,* he thought.

"We should be arriving in about fifteen minutes, sir," one of the servants on the ship said. "Fifteen?" Welk Seha said. "We have to be moving quicker than that, we cannot afford to let them get away."

~

Junayd and Reika found themselves taking the last group of women and children and less able-bodied men to the boats down the corridors of the castle. Reika tried to hurry them down the corridors as speedily as possible, although this was difficult, as the stone corridors were rather narrow, making rushing down it with a large crowd next to impossible.

They finally made it to the docks outside which were south of the castle, where two large ships were docked, both armed, to escort the fleet of smaller ships. "Get on the boats quickly. Soldiers, cover the civilians every way you can!" Junayd bellowed.

Reika edged her way to the shoreline near the dock, trying to see what was going on. She spotted the large ships in the distance approaching fast.

"Junayd!" She called to him. "We're almost out of time, Welk is getting closer."

Junayd rushed over to Reika to take a look for himself. "This isn't good. I thought we had more time. Reika, stay with the boats and get the civilians on. I need to warn Zane and the others."

Reika nodded her head with her hand on her chest. "Be careful," she said.

Junayd smiled and dashed back down the corridor. Reika noticed three worried children and turned her attention to them. Two soldiers appeared, a lemur and a siamang.

"Get on the boat quickly little ones, the soldiers will protect you," Reika said calmly to them. Two of the children complied, making their way to the ships as fast as their little legs could carry them, the siamang staying with them. The lemur soldier, whom Reika realised was the third child's father, remained. The young lemur was a little frightened and didn't want to move.

"Climb on, you'll be fine," Reika said as she held her hand out.

The little lemur climbed onto Reika's back. "I'll take you to the boat, don't be afraid. Your father is here too."

He nodded as he and Reika rushed along the promenade, taking the child over to the boat. Reika handed the child over to the lemur soldier once they reached the gangplank.

"Thanks for helping my son. Cyril is a nervous little chap," he said.

Just then, one of Welk's ships launched a huge fiery metal ball at them, sizeable enough to make a human sized hole in the ship. Reika gazed at the speeding metal ball in horror. Swiftly she flew onto one of the boats, landing on the deck and stretching out her hands. The metal ball was frozen in place, many of the children looking in awe and cheering, as did many of the soldiers. Reika strained to hold the ball telekinetically in place and with all her might, shoved the ball fast right back at the very ship that had fired upon them, smashing a hole in the side of the hull, causing it to sink.

Many of the scorpion soldiers on the boat tried to escape from the ship in their lifeboats, making their way to the shore.

Reika started to sweat, already very tired from the ordeal. "Hope they don't try that again, the cowards." She then spotted Queen Laria, clutching her son tightly. Reika briefly looked at the child, realising it was Melito, as a toddler. She wanted to say something but stayed silent as the tiny marmoset was carried into the boat. The young toddler looked at Reika for a moment, wondering what she was thinking and why this woman was looking at him. "What is that, Mother?" He asked. "There was another passing through with a blue blade."

"A human," she said. "She and the others are helping us to leave."

The doors of the ship finally closed. Reika turned her attention back to the ships that were approaching.

Two more ships broke off from the main fleet, making their way towards Entella, but Reika didn't notice as more metal spheres hurtled their way from another. Some she stopped in their tracks and threw away. Others she used as a means of knocking subsequent projectiles off course. In a moment of reprieve, Reika stared at the ships carefully. No weapons could be seen but she did see some of the crew on the ship dressed in robes. *Sorcerers. They're conjuring the metal spheres. They mustn't be allowed to get to the shore.*

The assault had begun.

~

Junayd had found his way back in the throne room where Zane, Berinon, Tabitha, Rian and the other soldiers were present. Julius was wearing his battle armour, holding an axe of his own, matching the very one Melito had been given.

"Father, you're here?" Melito said.

"Yes. I'm staying. Tertullian was told to get the best commander was he not?"

Melito was perturbed. What would this mean? Hadn't his father fled with his mother in his own timeline?

"Welk's not too far from here," Junayd said.

"Let him come," Julius replied. "We'll be ready for him."

The enemy ships drew up, some making their way to the docks, while others used metal-clad prows as siege-weapons, crashing through the seaside keep's walls.

"ATTACK!" Welk Seha cried, as his soldiers swarmed in. While some crawled into the windows of the throne room, A small squad hiding in a metal- clad testudo advanced towards the main doors, a foul and crude battering ram they carried with a metallic skull in the likeness of their people. Thrice the scorpions smashed the doors and with one final crash, the doors were rent asunder, crashing to the floor.

Julius commanded all to fight even as the first scorpions squirmed their way into the throne room.

Tabitha kept her distance, firing arrows rapidly one by one. Berinon jumped right into the fray, using his lance to cut into some of the soldiers while also jabbing and smashing the others with the wooden pole of the lance. Rian took out his gun, shooting the soldiers while cutting them down if they got too close with his bayonet. Junayd also cut through a few of the soldiers. He caught sight of the other half of the scorpion troop heading to the docks away from the door of the citadel.

He had to run through the crowd, slicing and dicing through the enemy to get back to Reika, knowing that she was in danger. He followed the platoon of scorpion soldiers who were running to the docks but finally overtook them, leaping out in front. They all stopped in their tracks.

"You want to get to the boats, go through me!" He shouted. Junayd beat his chest, then signalled them with his hand to come at him. The soldiers all ran towards him but though they were many, they struggled to hold him down. Junayd knocked each one of them to the ground with ease.

Reika waited for another volley of metal spheres, watching the sorcerers intently. They raised their hands high and electrical bands coiled around their arms, the energy collided above them, creating the spheres. Once they were large enough, they hurled them through the air. Reika held them once again, straining a bit, she could tell she was getting weak. She only had one chance to fling them back.

Reika hoped for the best and sent the spheres back towards the ships. The sorcerers saw the spheres return though didn't count on being the targets. The spheres hit the decks of the ships and crashed into the ships. A few of the sorcerers were crushed and the ships were set ablaze. The ones still alive panicked, desperately trying put the fires out. *I hope they don't send any more our way after that.*

Reika then caught sight of Junayd. She summoned a trail of flames that coiled around her hands, once again coalescing into fireballs, which she lobbed at the scorpions. She jumped off the ship onto the grassy plain. The scorpions felt the intense heat, writhing in pain. Reika drew her sword, running through the platoon, each scorpion that got too close she would swiftly slash across the chest. She leapt towards Junayd while he moved closer to her.

"Not too many now. You ok, Reika?" "I've been better."

The scorpions surrounded Junayd and Reika, ready to attack, raising their weapons to cut down the two of them.

"Reika, you may want fly from here, this will get messy," Junayd said. Reika manoeuvred herself away from the scorpion group onto a small ledge, just high enough to prevent the scorpions from getting her easily, shielding herself with a magical barrier. Junayd charged his sword with energy and stabbed it into the ground with great force. A burst of burning energy shot forth from the blade, sweeping over all the scorpions, each one knocked into the air by the blast. An electrical surge followed, vaporising the small group of scorpions that had surrounded Junayd. The energy flickered down to nothing, leaving Junayd holding the hilt of his blade, exhausted. Reika removed her barrier. She vacated the ledge and floated down to Junayd.

"That was incredible. Will you be able to recover?" Reika said.

"I'll be fine, I just need a rest, it's not an easy attack to use," Junayd responded. "I hope the others are doing well."

The fighting in the throne room was getting intense. The carpet floor had been shredded to ribbons and deep gouges were scored in the pillars. The scorpions began to overwhelm the soldiers; one smashed a knight into one of the banquet tables, collapsing it entirely. Other tables were also overturned and broken. Tabitha kept shooting the scorpions from a distance, ensuring to duck behind one of the tables that functioned like a shield wall for her. Berinon and Rian pressed their attacks too, Rian reloading his gun quickly, dealing out rapid shots, while Berinon knocked many scorpions to the floor, impaling some that got too close with his lance.

Welk stood near the ruined doors to survey the battle. He set his sights on Julius, who himself was fighting against the scorpions.

Welk eyed one of his troops and gave the command to fire an arrow at Julius. The trooper fired his arrow and it collided with Julius in his back. He let out a loud gasp. Melito spun around in dismay, seeing his father fall to the ground. Drawing his massive bludgeon of a sword, Welk made his way to Julius, ready to finish him off. Julius struggled away with the arrow firmly planted in his back. Welk drew near.

Welk raised his sword and brought the blade down onto his foe, but before it struck true, he felt sharp piercing pain in his back.

Melito had thrown a tomahawk right into it. A second one followed shortly after, Welk spun round and grabbed it.

"Zane! Get my father out of here now!" Melito called.

Welk eventually managed to dislodge the tomahawk from his back. Beforehand, Zane slowed down time around him and Julius, hauling the king away to the boat. Melito summoned his axe and strode towards his foe. The massive scorpion stood in place as his wounds begun to quickly knit themselves back together. It took some effort to close the wounds as the scorpion grimaced. "You'll pay for robbing me of my prize!" the beast shouted. Welk swung the blade at the small marmoset, who stepped back, swinging the axe in response, smashing it into the giant blade, pushing it away. The two both kept swinging broad strokes, their weapons recoiling with each clash, their arms feeling numb from the shockwaves.

Tabitha kept her distance, firing arrows at Welk Seha. Welk winced every time an arrow hit him on the back.

"Tabs! Don't stop and stay back!" Melito called.

Welk flew into a rage. "Don't interfere, fool." He signalled five of his remaining troops to charge Tabitha, but Berinon quickly rushed to her defence, Rian following close behind. Arrows flew towards Berinon but he swung his lance rapidly, every arrow bouncing off it. Rian fired five well-placed shots into the heads of the archers, removing the threat.

Zane carefully removed the arrow from Julius, then held him upright to stop him from slouching against the wall. The marmoset's breathing sounded very laboured. Zane opened his free hand, turning it at a leisurely pace. Julius could feel the pain getting worse, then a sharp pain was felt and afterwards, it disappeared entirely.

"I didn't think I would be saved in this way," he said. "Thank you boy."

With that, Zane closed his hand, removing the spell from Julius. He breathed a heavy sigh.

"Your son needs you your majesty," he said.

"My son? He's fighting Welk. You have to get me back!" Julius said.

"No, that's not what I meant," Zane said firmly, "His younger self, you have a responsibility to get him to safety, that's where you belong."

Julius looked at Zane hesitantly but knew deep down he was right. "I'll go to him."

Julius made his way to the boat where his wife and the younger Melito were waiting; they opened the door to let him on. "Sail on now. Get us away from this place." The boats hoisted their anchors, sailing away as fast as they could.

Welk's other boats, which were armed to the teeth, began their advance on the Entellan boats, ready to strike, but little did they know that the Entellans were already prepared to fight them off.

Zane managed to hide his fatigue and left the shore to head back to the others, running as fast as he could.

Melito continued his fight against Welk, smashing the creature with his axe with unbridled ferocity, eventually knocking the blade out of the creature's hands. Welk grabbed the haft of the axe, holding back Melito from striking the death blow. Welk had been pierced with many arrows, yet he was still strong.

"Certainly, more of a fighter than the old fool," he said mockingly.

"You wouldn't know, you have shown me you are nothing but a poltroon.

All you did was have your soldiers fire on him, how dishonourable."

Melito let go of the axe, much to Welk's confusion. The scorpion grinned. "How foolish, you handed your own weapon to me..." Melito didn't waste any time talking, he ran up one of the pillars away from Welk and jumped from

it, shooting through the air like a torpedo. He zoomed past Welk as the monstrous brute tried swing the axe at him, but instead of hitting the marmoset, he ended up lodging the axe in the pillar he was standing near. The axe was embedded deep into the stone, Welk attempted to pull the axe out but couldn't move it. Melito swiftly ran the other side of the pillar back to the pillar he jumped from, leaping again, but this time with a somersault in the air which culminated with a double-kick, slamming Welk's head into the pillar.

The beast collapsed, knocked out cold. As Melito hastily moved out of the way, the pillar collapsed onto the Scorpion King with a thud. Melito stood triumphantly over Welk's unconscious body. He observed his surroundings: the throne room was ruin, the banquet tables ruined, some of the pillars cracked, and the doors left lying on the floor, in the exact same position that he found them, the only difference being that there were dead bodies, Entellans on both sides, monkey and scorpion alike.

The others and the surviving soldiers cheered him.

Reika and Junayd arrived in the throne room to see what was going on. Melito looked at the two, smiling at them. Raising his axe high, he was about to cut the beast's head off when without warning, the rubble started to overturn. Welk's right arm lashed out, scratching Melito on the leg. He winced, toppling to the floor. Welk emerged from the rubble, severely weakened, and bruised, the arrow stems had broken off at various points, leaving the tips embedded in his back. He glared at Reika suspiciously.

Melito lay there clutching his leg, his breathing ragged. Welk held a grey ball in his hand, and he threw it onto the ground. An ashy cloud erupted violently, almost covering the entire throne room. The thickness of the smoke blinded the group, incapacitating not only their sight, but also making it hard to breathe, as if something had entered their lungs and lingered.

By the time the smoke cleared, and everyone in the room had recovered, it was too late. Welk had disappeared.

Zane entered the throne room. He saw Melito was injured and getting weaker. "What's happened to him?" Zane asked.

"He's been poisoned. Please help him!" Tabitha replied.

"Stay back for a moment." The young man knelt down and once again with the twist of his hand as before, small vestiges of cloudy fluid exited from Melito's leg. Once the final drips left, his wound closed like a tear repaired by a tailor. Melito heaved a deep sigh of relief. He saw that Zane had expended his stamina. "What was that?" Melito asked.

"Temporal Regeneration," Zane responded. "It allows me to reverse time in a small pocket, in your case, your wounds."

Melito steadily got to his feet. Welk had fled from the citadel. His countenance fell. "Father, I have failed you... I'm sorry." He removed the axe from the rubble, holding it for only a few moments before it vanished in front of his eyes. "Zane, thank you, I may have lost this kingdom, but at least I have not lost my parents or their subjects. Though too many guards here are dead."

Zane walked over to Melito gently placing his hand on his shoulder. "He would be proud of you," he said. "Entella may be lost, but its people will live on." Zane headed for the entrance.

Melito accompanied him. "Shouldn't we go after Welk?" He asked. "Melito, we're done here, your family is safe. Welk won't bother anyone for a while. News of this day will spread. If he rears his head, he can be defeated again. He will be stronger, however. For now, we go back to the future... I mean, our time." Zane beckoned the group to follow him.

"What are you standing around for?" Melito asked the soldiers.

"You need to leave. Stay safe on your travels and avoid contact with Welk. But first, we must clear the dead from here. Bury our own."

The soldiers who died were buried outside the citadel, the very same field that had been passed by Melito in his own time, the very burial mounds he beheld on his journey to the Time Gate. No one said anything for a while, just staring at the mounds in silence. As for the bodies of Welk's own soldiers they were heaped on each other and burned. Afterwards, the soldiers departed the castle, finding a boat of their own and promptly sailing in the direction the other Entellan ships had gone, hoping to catch up with them.

The throne room was quiet for its allotted time, left to deteriorate, until once again the group would tread its halls, taking shelter for the night.

A few days later, inside his castle, Welk Seha was resting in his bed; one of the servants was tending to his wounds. Unlike Welk's ordinary wounds, the

arrows had not healed instantly. The arrowheads were removed, and bandages were wrapped around his chest and back.

A strange thing happened to the arrows: each one mysteriously vanished upon their removal.

"That cursed ape from the future. If he isn't dead from that poison, I'll kill him for this. I need to find out where he has gone. No... If I kill his younger self, maybe that will undo my humiliating defeat? Where has he fled?" As he raised his voice, he winced in pain.

"Sire, you need to rest! You cannot move too much."

Welk glared back for a moment. He relented, letting his head rest on the navy pillow. He beckoned to one of the guards in the room. "Send my best troops out to find that little wretch. I want him dead."

"I'll see what I can do, sire." The guard was about depart from the room when something entered his mind. "Sire, there is a visitor who wants to see you." "Send them in, if they try anything, kill them." The guard beckoned to his right and then the visitor appeared. This woman was the very same elf who Reika had seen talking to Lief, Charlton, and Heston, though this had not yet occurred. She removed her helmet. The woman had ivory skin. Her hair and eye colour were like Reika's, and she wore a headband comparable to Rian's around her head. Her hair was pulled back into a ponytail. She had a single fringe which covered the left side of her forehead. "Who are you?" Welk asked.

The woman grinned back at the creature.

"Krea is my name. I have been sent here by my master. I understand you had a little trouble from some... pests from the future, is that so?"

Welk stared at the ceiling, sulking. "Yes, I really have."

Krea pulled on one of her gloves. "If you truly want to destroy that princeling, I have a few spells I could teach you, if you are keenly interested?"

Welk adjusted his head and looked at the elf in the eyes. She grinned back at him.

"I am listening, Krea."

The elf sat on a chair by Welk's bed, crossing her arms and her legs. "You'll be needing to add a little more to your repertoire. The problems they caused for your little invasion are just the beginning. If they truly are from the future, then there is no way to stop them from coming back from the future to stop you in this time is there? So much better to give them a taste of revenge. Preventing their victory in this time really doesn't have any savour."

Welk's demeanour changed. "You have my attention. You encountered the Temporal Knight did you not?"

Krea smirked. "When I was younger. He was a pain. I think he'll be just like an ant under a boot now. And so will the others. Any significant ones I should know about?"

Welk scratched his head with his right hand, wincing slightly. "Only a knight who was with him. I saw an elf bounty hunter with him too. A young man who held the Draco Ferrum, I don't recognise him. Future wielder maybe." Welk grunted with pain. "My servant here relayed to me that there was a human woman on one of the ships. She stopped the projectiles from my sorcerers from colliding with the ships at the dock and threw them back. Other ships were heavily damaged and some of the sorcerers killed." He remembered seeing Reika in the throne room. "Wait... Would her description be of use to you Krea?"

"Absolutely it will," Krea said. "Was there anything significant you saw?" "Well, you are here, your eyes and hair colour fit her description. Her skin was darker than yours. I know that's nothing to go on, there may be others like her. I did get a glimpse of her face back in the throne room and it was... familiar. I am reminded of a young sorceress I encountered once, a friend of hers too."

Krea's eyes widened in shock. She said nothing.

"You have my thanks. I'll keep in touch with you. Listen to your doctor while you're at it. You are no good if you don't let yourself heal properly. I think I should have brought an elixir along, it would have hastened your recovery."

Welk sighed. "Very well. I'll do what I can to assist you." He snapped his fingers. "Please escort Krea out, treat her with respect." Krea raised her hand to the servant. "No need, I'll see myself out." Krea began to vanish into dark vapour, frightening the guard and doctor a little.

Welk closed his eyes with a grin on his face. His pain, though still present, had little effect on his sleep. The guard left the room, as did the doctor, closing the door behind them.

Chapter 8

Trail of Three

709 A.E.B

Back in the present, the group left the citadel ruins behind. Melito couldn't help but wonder where his parents could have gone. He knew they had survived the attack thanks to Zane and the others, but beyond them escaping from the citadel to Carthage, with the Entellans scattering to other places to hide in safety and then taken to the Carthagian Citadel, he didn't know where they were, nor was he sure if they had lived after that.

"We need to fight him again," Melito said. The others all stopped to look at him.

"Excuse me?" Junayd said, with raised eyebrows. "We are exhausted, we need to rest up before even considering going after Welk. I just feel so tired. Using a powerful attack doesn't leave you with high stamina after usage. No, we need to rest now."

Melito fell silent. "Probably a good idea. What was I thinking? I need to calm down."

Hours later it had gotten dark. The vegetable stew Berinon cooked up was received with a generally favourable response, especially since Berinon asked for the ingredients to be put aside for him. He and Zane during the three days had brought some food to the Time Gate and sent it in time at least ten minutes after they had departed and would reclaim the food when they arrived back, waiting for the food to arrive. The sweet scent of the stew, which had thickly permeated the air, slowly faded as they settled in around the campfire, which was now burning away nicely.

They set up camp in an open field next to a giant hill of rock and grass overlooking the plains in the distance. There were a few trees nearby, not enough to make a forest, but thick enough to grant some protection from the rain. This

didn't matter as there was barely a cloud in the sky and thankfully the moon was absent. After the meal, Reika went to one of the trees and fell sound asleep under them.

Junayd sat a few feet away under another tree, contemplating everything that had happened, while at the same time making sure no one would come near Reika.

Zane, Berinon, Rian, Tabitha and Melito were all awake, sitting around the fire. Melito didn't say much, he merely sat there listening to the others. He complimented Berinon on his cooking but really didn't have much to say aside from that. Berinon could remember his previous journey with Zane vividly and talked about how they used to sit around their campfires, and the meals they'd eaten: a mixture of meat and vegetables as no metazoans had accompanied them. He also regaled them with stories of his own past conflicts as a youth, the fights he participated in, an incident that he was blamed for, which he talked about with shame, and his restoration to honour with great delight, all the while giving Zane the credit for helping him.

Tabitha just sat there in awe like a child. Melito finally spoke. "Is there a way to get to Welk Seha's island to avenge Entella?" Zane looked at him. "We need an airship."

Melito raised his eyebrow.

"What? I thought such things were stories. Do they really fly?" Zane nodded. "Yes."

"But how? How do we have such technology?"

"A golem civilisation known as Budúcnosť from seven hundred years ago was lost thanks to its sheer hubris, believing itself to be unassailable. Much of its knowledge was lost and over time, main-landers have been trying to recover what they could from some of the descendants of Budúcnosť. Not all golems hail from there, espe-cially the ones we have encountered. The ones that do moved to Perusia, specifically Triterrain, and recovered some of their tech-nology and allowed some of the human engineers to use the tech-nology as part of decommissioned seaships rather than dispose of them. One of them should be good enough to get us there."

"Why didn't you go back and save them from this destruction?" Melito asked.

"The elves told me not to," Zane replied. He sighed and his tone gradually became more glowering as he spoke. "It was a request from Budúcnosť's elders at the time. They wanted to learn from their ancestors' mistakes and never become an arrogant people again. Otherwise, I would have gone to help them. Maybe it would be the case they would have become very dangerous had the acci-dent never happened..."

Zane halted in his speech, leaving all but Berinon rather disqui-eted, as if the knight understood the pain within the young man. Zane promptly became tranquil, allowing himself to proceed onto another subject matter. "While Welk has many subjects under his rule, he is also working with others higher than he. Who they may be, I am not sure. Could he also be gathering the weredragons for someone? Though that is an assumption on my part."

"I think I may have an inkling who may be in charge," Junayd said coming over from the trees. "Reika spotted an elvish woman talking to two troublemakers through a portal in my hometown. She was wearing grey and blue armour. There was an elvish man there, in person, but we do not know where he is now."

Junayd then sat down by the fire with the others, opposite Zane, keeping Reika within his line of sight.

"We need to track the woman down," Zane said. "Three years ago, after I had repaired history, I was tasked with going back in time to 430 A.E.B. and I fought against a group of armoured elf warriors who attacked Elvenheim's capital of Valoa. They had single-handedly held the city hostage and as a new base of operations. Two of those were women and this one whom you refer to, she escaped my grasp. The other woman is dead, as are the male warriors. The one who fled was a tough fighter, but not the strongest. Janshai was. He was their leader of the group. He doesn't tangle with me now, however. Long story."

"Janshai saved Zane's family in return for saving him," Berinon added. "He was possessed by an evil spirit, a previous wielder of the Ferrum. He was granted amnesty for his past actions considering what had happened. The elf woman however, she disappeared. Valoa has had a slow but decent recovery ever since."

"Was Janshai working with someone?"

"He didn't know." Zane replied. "His memory was vague, it was a dragon who himself was banished for evil long ago, Janshai never told us who he was. His name I learnt was Destrian and he is still out there, and the elf woman is working for him."

Junayd was deep in thought. "The elf woman, what was her name? The one who escaped?"

Zane slouched forwards; hands clasped together as he leaned on them. Then he straightened himself. "Krea, that was her name. I think she is the same elf Reika saw, judging by the description that you have given me." He crossed his arms and closed his eyes.

"It was then about a month after I thwarted the rogue elves that I journeyed back through time and was tasked with taking a child to safety as Krea wanted her for a nefarious purpose. That was when I learnt that Krea was the same woman who attacked the capital years before. I hid the child successfully away and she was never found by the enemy."

"Where is the child now?" Junayd asked.

"Nowhere you need to know," Zane said. "If all goes well, she will be safe once this is all over." He sipped a small flask of water with a look of regret on his face. His disposition changed as a thought crossed his mind in a flash. "Welk's castle... Yes..."

Melito furrowed his eyebrows in bewilderment. "What's the matter?"

"The Anodyne Stone... Could Welk be in possession of it?" Junayd's eyes widened. "What makes you say that?"

Zane turned to Junayd. "It's not just *us* who are trying to find the stone, many have tried and failed. Some elven scouts have been following Welk's troops' dealings over the years. They saw a white golem, Falk Corundum, the same one whose team had helped him steal the golem's amulet. He had the Anodyne Stone briefly and handed it to Welk. Corundum won't be a problem; he has been missing for a while."

Zane smirked for a moment.

Melito stood up. "That airship, we need to make haste to get to it. Removing Welk is a step closer to stopping Krea and getting the Anodyne Stone."

"True, we require the airship now more than ever, but we can't just use it to waltz in, at least not yet," Zane said. "There is an artefact called the Kaleidogem on the island of Triterrain that we need in order to destroy the magical barrier surrounding the castle. Any airship will be destroyed if it collides with the barrier and teleporting inside would be nothing but suicide."

Zane took out a piece of parchment with a small quill and drew rather swiftly on it, at least that was how it appeared to the others. He held it up high for all of them to see. The stone itself was perfect, shaped like a gem the size of a fully grown human palm. The shading of the drawing seemed to indicate the gem would have had an array of colours inside like northern lights.

"This dark gem was crafted by dwarf sorcerers years ago as a means of conjuring large barriers and dissipating them. It exists in three separate pieces, each hidden in three villages of Triterrain. There are agents in those villages who keep watch over those stones to protect Welk and his forces from destruction and have done so since his defeat long ago...by us... Find those pieces, and we can enter the stronghold."

Zane threw the drawing onto the fire. "It is a question of finding the agents, it won't be easy."

"Surely the villagers would be punished for harbouring fugitives?" Junayd said.

"Not unless they are aiding and abetting those agents," Zane replied. "Most of the villagers do not know where the gem fragments are, they are well hidden. There may be some who do, so it is worth asking around. It has been a less than quarter of a century and the agents still haven't been found. The gems' energy is so great that trying to track the agents' movement is nigh on impossible. Anyone with foresight is disrupted by them to the point where they are effectively walking into a trap blindly."

"I wouldn't worry," Junayd said. "They are just as blind. Who would suspect that we are after the gem fragments? Complacency can cause someone to drop their guard, maybe these agents have had no opposition for so long, it will be too late for them to react."

"What about Welk Seha? There's a possibility he maybe on to us."

"Ha, he didn't even stop our full evacuation of Entella's civilians, there's no way he'll ever consider us going after the fragments, it's just absurd. Welk is an arrogant fool."

"Maybe Junayd... Maybe that could work. Debrief Reika tomorrow, we leave at dawn."

All went to sleep except Zane, who was looking at the horizon to the north, alone in his own thoughts for a few hours. He found himself walking a good fifty feet away from the camp, still deep in thought.

"All well with you Zane?" A voice said.

Zane looked to his left and saw Visiert approaching him. "What business do you have here, Visiert?" He asked.

"Keeping watch. Anyone who is coming after Reika must be stopped. Just need to be certain she will be safe." He shook Zane's hand.

"You've met her before, Visiert?"

"Back in Caledonia. She was staying at Costa Enano with her metazoan friends. What is *your* business here?"

Zane turned to the ocean. "Entella is to be rebuilt. I had to get the inhabitants of the island in the past away. The others fought valiantly to save them. Welk will not find the Entellans now." Zane then crossed his arms. "He may have the stone. The very stone that will destroy the weredragons."

Visiert lifted his head up more attentively. "You'll need the Kaleidogem, won't you?" He said.

"Yes. That will allow us to break through the barrier surrounding Welk's Castle, then we can sweep in and take the Anodyne Stone."

Visiert placed his right hand on his chin and his left on his hip. "Stay safe. He has grown far more dangerous than when you last faced him, even if he has been keeping a low profile." Visiert turned to walk away from Zane.

"Where are you headed, Visiert?"

"I'll be keeping an eye on the camp until tomorrow morning. It is going to be a long night for me, and I need my rest. You'll need it as well." The masked man stopped, as though wrestling with himself.

Finally, he said, "How is Reika anyway?"

Zane didn't reply at first, he just stared into the distance. "All things considered; she is alright on the surface. Not so much in her soul." He looked down to the ground in shame again before facing Visiert again.

"What are you vexed about?" the masked man asked. "Did I say something wrong?"

"No. I have a tough role. I already have Rian holding a grudge against me. Who's to say some of the rest here won't hate me as well? There are others who do already."

"You don't know that, Zane," Visiert said. "The child you saved all those years ago, she'll will be very forgiving."

Zane had a faint smile on his face. "Maybe." He rubbed the back of his head. "One way or the other, she is going to challenge me. Through my confession or through something she finds out on her own. Either way, she will find out the truth."

Visiert nodded in agreement. "Perhaps. For now, keep it to yourself, nobody needs to know."

"They do know of the child; they just don't know who it is. I have not told them. I said once this is over, she'll be safe."

"Then keep it that way. It's not relevant to the task, treat it as a mission completed. Anyone else you are concerned about?"

"Not really. I made it clear to Melito that though I could change the past, the risk was too high. I also told him that it had already been evacuated."

"His reaction?"

"He was disappointed, although he was more fixated on getting back to the past to stop Welk."

"He may enquire as to why you didn't stop Entella's destruction. If he does, just answer him honestly."

Zane smiled back, satisfied with the answer.

"So..." he said. "Junayd said Reika saw an elvish man who served an elvish woman. I am convinced that same woman was Krea: she wore blue and grey armour. Who was the man?"

Visiert didn't show his emotion as his mask obscured his face. He thought about it for a while.

"Lief... I stopped him in Caledonia. He was responsible for Reika attacking Junayd as a weredragon. I defeated him and took him into custody. He was in a chatty but rather irritating mood. Mocking others, even if there is a risk of being destroyed, seems to be his problem. He confessed that he was helping Krea. By extension that makes him in league with Destrian. Make sure to relay that information to the others."

"So, it *was* Krea that she saw?"

"Yes, it was. No further search needs to be done."

Visiert went to leave again. "I bid you farewell for now. We'll meet again."

Visiert opened a portal up and entered it, leaving Zane alone. Zane saw Visiert reappear far away on the hill nearby. He observed the masked man sit down near the hilltop, his eyes fixated on the camp, occasionally turning around to ensure no one was going to attack him or indeed the camp itself. Zane headed back to the trees, rubbing his eyes, snuggling down under the canopy, facing the west. As morning approached, and as Visiert watched, he witnessed Zane getting up to start the campfire. Melito also left the trees to talk to Zane. Visiert departed shortly afterwards.

When he woke up the next morning, Melito was still dwelling on what would have been his kingdom and his home had it not been for Welk Seha. A brief tear emerged from his left eye. He wiped it away with his arm. He sat up on thinking about what King Tertullian did for him. He remembered that since infancy, the king had raised him as his own, personally training him in combat and allowing Ignatius to push him harder than the others. His training with Firmillian was nothing by comparison.

Tabitha, he befriended when they were infants, and they'd treated each other as siblings, growing together as royal guards. He also remembered the first day Reika was brought to the citadel when she was twelve, how he and Tabitha made her feel right at home despite her perturbation at serving the king.

Melito left the tree he slept under to speak to Zane, who was up in the morning before everyone else in order to prepare breakfast: porridge with syrup, which was his contribution to the food that he and Berinon gathered.

"You had us save my people and for that I am grateful, but we couldn't stop Welk from destroying the kingdom. Is there a particular reason why we didn't go to stop the invasion?"

Zane looked sadly at him. "I believe I already told you why. Remember what I said about meeting Juste? The only thing I didn't say at the time was that we were the ones to help with the evacuation. Also, Welk would have attacked it again after licking his wounds. The golem's temple is inconsequential to him, and he wasn't the one who retrieved the amulet from there. Entella is different. He needs to believe your kingdom is gone. If your subjects are spread throughout Perusia, as are their descendants, he'll have failed his mission. Consider the fact that if we get rid of him in this time, our present time, you can regather your subjects and bring them back to Entella. It's to lull him into a false sense of security."

Melito looked surprised. "Bring them back? I can't do that; I don't even know where to start. Carthage has a king in Tertullian. I don't even know if my parents are still alive."

"You will find a way. Don't be disheartened. There is a path to victory and restoration, you just need to find it."

Melito stood there and nodded.

"Reika and Junayd, the memory of them was burned into me when I was a child. I saw Reika stopping the metal spheres. Junayd fought against Welk's soldiers. My mother had to cover my eyes. Reika was twelve when she came to the castle back in Carthage. Part of me recognised her. I became friends with her as Tabitha also did. What made us meet this human for the first time I will never know. Was it thankfulness? Was it the possibility of being brought to the Entellans to keep their descendants alive? Reika assured me I had no hand in manipulating her. I still feel uneasy."

"I don't think you did," Zane finally said. "Reika is correct. You were asking a question for yourself. Did you see her before? You got to know her; she became your friend. Consider any assistance you gleaned from her an after-thought. She is your friend, and you are hers. That has never changed. You were just a curious boy wondering who she was."

"Right. Thanks anyway, Zane, I appreciate the chat." Melito headed back to the trees, leaving Zane alone to tend to the break-fast. *Rian could certainly learn a lot from you Melito,* Zane thought.

Meanwhile Reika was being debriefed. She listened attentively to Junayd. Upon the mere mention of the Anodyne Stone being potentially found, her face lit up. She asked how they were going to get around faster. Junayd told Reika that they would be using an airship. She was staring at him blankly. "An airship?" "Yes. They were built recently. An old idea given new lease on life that could help us travel across the world. Just Perusia alone is a treat, and we may be the first customers to give this new generation of airships a whirl." Her expression was vacant. "Reika, Hello?" Junayd waved his hand in front of her face. "Sorry..." She finally said, "I am just thinking, an airship, that does sound

strange yet amazing."

Junayd smiled back at her. "I expect it will be a sight to behold. It will be my first experience for sure."

"What about Budúcnosť?"

"I'll speak with you about it later."

As soon as breakfast was finished, Zane continued to sit with the others around the campfire. "Last night, the agent of the dragons, Visiert, spoke to me. He managed to apprehend an elf who was in Caledonia. Sound familiar?"

"Yes. No wonder we didn't know where he was," Junayd replied. "Did Visiert find out anything?"

"The elf was working for Krea. It really is her. That's one less task to accomplish."

Reika remained silent. She had met Visiert in Caledonia and kept the interaction to herself, deeming it unimportant to say anything. She took the same route with the following statement, locking it in her mind: *I knew he would be a protector. He kept his word.*

"Is there a ship to go to Triterrain soon?" Junayd asked.

"Yes," replied Zane. "It's back at Costa Primado, the settlement we were at. We'll have to wait there until the boat has arrived. I think eleven a.m. We have three hours to get to the town."

"You're pushing things a little, aren't you Zane?"

"It's only an hour. Give it a half hour, one final bit of respite before we head off."

The ship arrived a day later in the sub-continent of Triterrain, a very strange one for a simple reason, it housed three different terrain patterns despite its position on the planet. One section at least an eighth of the large island was grassland that connected to a smaller island of grassland by a single wooden bridge, three eighths was desert, and one half was an icy tundra. The boat arrived at Triterrain safely, with the group making their way to the forest south of the dock. "My home is in the woods ahead," Rian said. "It's a little hamlet not too far from here. We'll find the first gem piece there."

Funny, I didn't think a bounty hunter would be welcome, Melito thought.

The forest was large, though relatively easy to traverse. The group finally stumbled up an open pathway, leading to a beautiful looking hamlet. The buildings were quaint, made of spruce wood, and with neatly arranged oak roofs. There was plenty of room to move between the houses themselves. The elves wore rather simple clothing, mostly green and brown peasant clothes, though they were surprisingly neat.

Junayd asked the villagers if they knew anything about the gem pieces. Most answered evasively, saying they didn't know anything, although they would let him know if they found it.

Reika went to a jeweller in the hamlet, who also claimed she did not know where the gem piece was. Berinon conversed with an elf couple who were cooking their breakfast. Unfortunately, this turned out to be fruitless. The man and the woman didn't know.

Rian was a little fed up with looking, deciding to have a drink instead. As he was about to draw water from the hamlet's stone well, he witnessed a glimmer brighter than that of a coin. *The gem piece,* he thought. *How simple. I need to retrieve it now.*

Rian lowered the bucket slowly into the water. His usage of magic was minimal as he wasn't accustomed to using magic as proficiently as his elven brethren. He used his magic to lift the gem piece into the basket. Pulling the bucket up successfully by his hands to avoid too much attention, Rian drank the water from it, retrieving the gem piece after his thirst had been quenched. He waited until the others were back in the inn before he made his way over to it.

"Say, that gem is not yours!"

Another elf, who had a complexion like Rian's, with blonde hair and a stature matching the bounty hunter, said pointedly. The elf's robes matched those of the rest of the villagers.

"I need this for a mission, it's very important that I take this with me. I am not asking your permission," Rian replied.

"Can't let you do that my friend," said the elf. "It is the most sacred item in our possession. So..."

"You don't care about it at all," Rian scoffed. "And it's not sacred. You are one of the agents guarding the gem pieces."

The elf pulled a knife from his pocket.

"You really want to fight here? Doesn't look good on you, does it?"

Rian just walked over to the elf and placed his hand on his chest, as if in consolation. A small knife slid from his wrist guard, stabbing the elf. The agent's eyes widened in shock. Rian smiled.

"If you truly knew me, you'd know my reputation is inconsequential to me." He released the knife from the elf, leaving his body to fall to the ground. Rian then dragged the body into the bushes next to the inn.

Rian entered the inn, meeting Zane at a table in the far corner to his right. Many took no notice of Rian, he was a local in their eyes, only brief glances before resuming their meals. Zane looked at Rian suspiciously. "What was the hold up, Rian?"

"A certain individual confronted me about the gemstone. He's taken a stab at hide and seek."

Zane smiled, shaking his head. "You found what we are looking for haven't you?"

"Very easily. Not that the other two will be that easy to retrieve." "Keep it hidden, Rian. Someone in the bar could be watching us."

"You don't have to tell me that. Believe me I have been known to keep secrets well, even this." Rian placed the gem in a small bag, leaving for the bar for a drink. Zane could see Rian trying to restrain violence when walking away. *Anger still burns in his heart against me. I cannot let him betray us. But how long are we going to pretend having this little friendship of ours?*

Rian peered out the corner of his eye back at Zane, though enough to make sure the young man couldn't see. *Fool. If he thinks I'll forgive him for letting my wife die, he's mistaken.*

Zane went outside the inn and saw Reika and Junayd resting on a bench behind a house, along with Tabitha and Melito. He decided to join them, sitting on the right side of the bench on the floor.

Tabitha leaned over to Zane. "The gem has been found, hasn't it?" She whispered.

"Yes, Rian has it."

Melito squinted his eyes. "He has it?" He then closed his eyes. "I wonder how he managed to retrieve the gem."

Berinon arrived after speaking with the couple. "Very nice they were. Pity they didn't have the answer we are looking for." The others filled him in. Berinon nodded. "Once Rian gets out of the bar, we'll head off to the United Peak." Zane smirked back at Berinon. "Waiting for Rian to leave the bar? Or are you wanting a drink?"

Berinon sniggered. "You know me too well, Zane."

I can wait, I am a patient man, Zane thought, as he leaned back against the wall of the house.

Berinon turned to Reika. "What is it?" She asked.

"Before I head for a drink, it's going to be very cold where we are going next. Zane has a cloak, you yourself will need to get one. That and some shoes will be beneficial."

Reika left with Berinon, the others waiting for them. A few minutes later, Reika was stood inside a clothes shop, wearing a very elegant dark blue cloak. It wasn't a conventional one for purely wearing on the shoulders, there were slits for the arms. The elf shopkeeper, a young, blond-haired, blue-eyed woman, examined Reika and was pleased.

"Suits you, young lady," she said, "Is there a different cloak you want or are you satisfied?"

"I'll buy it, it's lovely."

"Might I recommend some shoes for you?" the shopkeeper asked. "Yes, what is the selection you have, ma'am?"

"Well for one with such unusual attire as yourself... Try one of these." The shopkeeper showed Reika and Berinon two pairs of shoes. One pair was brown with a single strap. It would cover a few centimetres above the ankle of the wearer. The second pair was black but this time, only the ankles were covered with the top of the shoes open with a black strap across the top. "I'll go for the brown ones."

As soon as she tried them on, Reika found them very comfortable and at once purchased them.

It didn't take long to cross to the other island along the bridge and very soon, the group found themselves gazing at United Peak. It wasn't a mountain to scoff at and was much bigger than it had seemed when viewed from the hamlet.

They weren't quite there yet. The group were behind a different mountain, one they didn't know the name of, that was in the way. The two mountains were separated by a chasm with a long winding path that snaked its way round the perilous slopes. There was a small grassland at the entrance of United Peak.

"What lies inside United Peak anyway?" Melito asked.

"It's a mine," Berinon said. "The dwarves have been conducting an excavation for some time, mostly giving what they find to the elves in the village to sell it as jewellery. To get there, we must go along the trail on the mountain before us." He gestured towards the trail. "Once we leave United Peak, we need to go to the other two towns and retrieve the gem pieces." Berinon made his way over to the trail. "Don't dally here, we haven't got all day."

Reika surveyed the path ahead as she walked.

"Does Berinon know the way?" She asked curiously.

"I wouldn't worry at all. If anyone knows this terrain, it's him. He strode towards that trail as if to meet an old friend. I think we are in capable hands. Weren't you the one who wished he journeyed with us? After all, you were the one who spoke to him in the port."

"I agree, he is a valuable asset, perhaps I made the right call."

"Perhaps? You either did or you didn't, there is no shame if you admit the latter, I don't think you are naive or stupid at all."

Reika chuckled, "You are so sweet."

She then ran cheerily towards Berinon until she caught up with him, resuming a normal walking pace alongside him. The knight like a guardian patted Reika on the shoulder, then moved in front of her to lead the way along the trail. Junayd laughed. He then ran to Reika and Berinon, eventually walking beside the young woman again.

The others followed from behind. "I'm starting to see a connection between Reika and Junayd, don't you, Tabs?"

"I think you may be right. Makes sense she would find a possible mate outside Carthage."

Melito raised his right eyebrow. "But is he willing to cherish her? When I'm married, I want to be a leader of the family, a protector and guardian, but never a dictator."

"I'm sure you'll find someone," Tabs said. She started to walk backwards with her arms crossed behind the back of her head. "Maybe there is a sweet woman just waiting for you, you never know. Maybe there is a nice man for me too, though it's not the end of the world if we don't find one."

"Thanks Tabs. However, you are making me nervous walking like that, turn around."

"Oh, come on it's not that bad, the path will be just fine," she said with a playful smile. Tabitha faced in same direction as Berinon and Reika once again. Melito's composure was restored.

Zane and Rian walked side by side, though the atmosphere was somewhat strained.

"Almost like old times, Zane? The open road and dusty highways."

"Yes. I won't be throwing you down a cliff here if that's what you are thinking."

"I haven't forgotten you throwing me down a chasm in that temple. Don't forget it's the payment Junayd offered that prevents me from killing you right now."

"Noted."

It was a long trail, but the wind did not possess a bite thanks to the sun beaming down on the mountainside. Instead, the wind was a comforting embrace. They beheld many beautiful sights, including immense canyons dotted with towering green trees growing within. The sediment carried a diverse range of colours ranging through red, orange, pale yellow and white—it almost looked as if the rocks had been artistically decorated. The path ended halfway up the mountain, with a slope that led down to United Peak.

"Why is it called United Peak anyway?" Melito enquired.

"The reason it's called that is that the mountain itself is close to all three borders of Triterrain," Berinon explained. "It does rest on the grassy plain, technically, but just on the edge of the grassland and the frozen tundra. Other mountains separate it from the desert."

They got closer and closer to United Peak, halting at the entrance.

"That's one big mountain, it makes the one in Carthage look like a hill," Reika said in awe and wonder.

"You don't suppose we have to be in peak condition to climb up it?" Junayd asked in a deadpan manner. Zane sniggered to himself.

"Thanks, at least someone got it," Junayd said. "I am one for puns," Zane said.

"Time to mount up then?" Tabitha added.

Melito wasn't impressed. "Melito, what's wrong, you don't like puns?" Reika said.

Melito placed his right hand on his face, dragging it down slowly. He sighed heavily. "Let's just move."

With that, the marmoset journeyed into the cave. "Does he really have that much of a stone heart?" Junayd asked.

Junayd, Zane, and Tabitha entered the cave after Melito. Rian and Reika were left alone outside.

Rian sniggered a little. "That is funny actually... I admit to getting a chuckle out of that one, if not a lot of them." He went into the cave also, as did Reika.

The cavern itself had a decent amount of light within it courtesy of the torches. There were some stairs as well as some steep pits. The stairs themselves were neatly carved stone, kind on the feet as the group walked up the first set.

"We need to go through the middle stairs shortly, we haven't the time to explore this place," Zane said. He jumped off the edge, landing safely between a small area between the two cliffs. He proceeded to the northwest to another set of stairs, jumping off the small cliff to a relatively sandy floor, the others following him as best they could. Two wooden bridges connected to a rocky cliff. The staircase led to another section of the cavern. Close to that staircase was another one leading further up. Before going to that staircase, they saw more staircases and bridges.

"Another mine?" Reika asked. "More like a maze."

"Yes, though I don't think they have made progress outside of here," Zane replied. He made a light step towards the next staircase to their right. "See, up there, light... Time for us to get outside again. I stress we need to be careful, high gusts exist outside."

Sure enough, Zane's comments were correct, though the gusts were thankfully sporadic. The landscape was even more incredible from their high vantage. The young members, aside from Zane, were all awestruck at the sight of the massive landscape around them.

The forest and grassland they left behind in the east, with the desert in the northwest and the tundra in the southwest. In the distance to the north, tall mountains caked in snow and ice could be seen. Melito squinted. He noticed something unusual on the contours of the mountain tops. Snow on one side in the tundra, on the other side, scorched rock, with no sign of snow or ice.

"What is wrong with those mountains?" Melito asked.

"Triterrain gets its name from the unusual climates that all exist here," Berinon replied. "It is believed one of the caves houses ancient orbs that have the ability to change the weather and the landscape. Several exist in one of the caves on the far west of the island."

They headed around the mountain in an anti-clockwise direction. The wind picked up, forcing Junayd to dig the Draco Ferrum into the ground, holding him in place. He squinted his eyes with a grimace on his face, the wind pressing against him with crushing force as his robes violently thrashed about. Reika tried to summon a barrier, but ultimately, she collapsed on the floor, rolling across it and nearly colliding with the rock face.

She summoned her blade just in time, echoing what Junayd had done, only she was facing the rock itself. Melito and Tabitha barely stood their ground against the mighty wind. Melito summoned Entella's Bane, embedding it in the ground, with Tabitha holding onto him by the chest. Berinon held onto his lance that he lodged in the ground, requiring the least effort to stop himself crashing into the mountainside. He allowed Zane and Rian to hold onto the lance too.

"Hold fast friends!" He called as loudly as his lungs were allowed to in the ferocious wind. Soon the winds died down, allowing the group to recover. Reika, Melito, and Tabitha lay on the ground exhausted. Junayd slumped to his knees. Berinon and Rian were mostly fine. Zane had struggled a little bit. He too was on his knees.

Reika got up; her hair scuffed by the wind.

"Bad hair day?" Junayd remarked. Reika glared at him, straightening her hair as best she could. Her glare vanished as they both fell about laughing afterwards. The group headed off round the mountain path again, with Melito pulling Tabitha onto her feet.

Their fur was sticking up, worse than Reika's hair. "Better scruffy than dead, I'll say," Tabitha said.

"You said it," Melito replied.

Berinon walked past them, beckoning them without even giving eye contact. "Don't just stand there, we have to move before the next gust arrives."

So, they did.

On the other side, they faced the tundra and desert. A small mound revealed an entrance that allowed them to go down into the mountain once more. They headed down a set of stairs, finding themselves standing near a ladder made of vines, which proved stronger than it looked. Junayd was the first to head up. He could see the passage that led back upstairs. A faint light shone from the western side to the eastern side.

The blinding light of the setting sun shone into the cave exit. Junayd made it out first. Reika remained close to him. Berinon, along with the others, finally vacated the cave too. Zane reached into the right-hand front pocket of his trousers, producing a battered, old map. Some creases were present at the edges, although the drawing on the map was mostly unmarred. Zane beckoned the rest of the group to gather around him. "First, we need to go to Chilling Citadel to find the piece there, then we will head to Arezzo once the airship is obtained. That's where the final piece lies."

A short distance away to the west near the cave exit, the frozen tundra lay before the group as did a snowstorm. Reika summoned a fireball, chucking it at the tundra to see what would happen. The fireball landed on the snow, exploding, then fading away without a trace. The melted snow dip in the floor was filled up swiftly like a wound repairing itself at a quick pace.

"Not sure how long I can sustain a fireball to keep us warm, even a ten-foot ball may not be worth the risk," she surmised.

"Don't bother Reika, the citadel will think it's an attack and besides it's not worth travelling there right now. We'll head there in the morning," Berinon said. The knight then gestured to a smaller cave some twenty feet to their left in the mountainside.

The group gathered in the cave not venturing too deeply within. Berinon and Zane sat down, getting a small fire going. The others soon followed, sitting in a circle around it. Berinon spent time putting pottage soup together, with plenty of carrots, cabbage, parsnips and garlic mixed together. Its chartreuse green appearance was rather alluring. "All ingredients I picked up while back at the hamlet. The elves may not be miners like dwarves, but they certainly know how to grow vegetables and fruit." Rian couldn't help but nod in agreement.

All were satisfied by the taste of the pottage soup. "I will not get tired of your food, Berinon, it's so good," Reika said after she drank the dregs of soup in her dish.

"Thank you." Berinon wiped his beard. "I can give you some of my own recipes so you can try to make them yourself back at Carthage. Have you ever cooked yourself a meal before?"

Reika leaned back, using her arms to support her weight. She shut her eyes. "Occasionally... I mostly waited on people. Usually if the head chef was either ill or extremely tired, I would help the sous chef out. Mark did teach me to cook as a child, but I didn't utilise it much. I am quite rusty there."

"I can remedy that," Junayd said. "That or Berinon can show you the ropes throughout this journey. Why put off cultivating a vital skill?"

Reika merely nodded.

Tabitha had a grin on her face. "So warm, that soup, I almost don't need a blanket to sleep." She then lay on the floor, falling asleep instantly. Melito shook his head with a smile on his face.

"Thanks very much. I'd ought to get some rest now." "Yes," Berinon said. "It's time we all did."

Chapter 9

Cold Road

All were asleep, though Reika slept less soundly than the others, turning restlessly. Junayd awoke and saw Reika's face. He could see she was distressed. He went over to her to wake her up. He touched her arm gently and Reika opened her eyes swiftly, yelping, holding her heart, breathing heavily. Junayd let go of her arm and fell back on his posterior.

"Don't do that... I thought you were about to kill me." "You were worrying me. What was your nightmare?"

Reika sat with Junayd and told him. In her dream, she was running through darkness. Her friends could be seen right in front of her and no matter how much she ran or even flew; they were always out of reach. They vanished, leaving her alone to be consumed. Despite her efforts, Reika went further into darkness, her body mutating into the weredragon and back again, as the dragon separated from her, grabbing her on the arm. Then she awoke.

"It was just that Reika, a bad dream. It happens to all of us," Junayd said.

"I know. It's no less frightening," Reika replied. She laid back down. Junayd lay down near Reika just a few feet away.

"Why don't you and I talk about something else, let's get your mind off the dream."

Reika tapped her stomach, struggling to think about a different topic. She then remembered the Chilling Citadel that they would head towards the next day. "What do you think that citadel is like?"

"Not sure, probably colder than the cave, unless they have an inn."

"This would be my second time sleeping in a cave. The first was back home when I was eighteen. It was on the night I first transformed."

Junayd shifted his eyes towards Reika's face. She still stared at the top of the cave roof.

"The whole night like this?"

"Yes. Doesn't beat sleeping in a bed though. I had an open window where I could see the whole courtyard and the plains in the south. A lovely sight indeed." Junayd moved his eyes back to the cave roof. "I can imagine it. My father and I on peaceful evenings looked at the stars, trying to guess what shapes could be seen. I saw there was one shape that resembled a vase. He saw one shaped like a horse. Haven't done that since I was a lad." Junayd lay in his place. "You going to be ok this evening?"

"I think I will. Thanks for the talk." Reika then went to sleep, happier than she had been previously.

Later, Melito awoke and headed outside of the cave. He summoned Entella's Bane and began to twirl it around. Now he could take a closer look at the majestic weapon he held in his hands. *My people will be avenged.* He swung the weapon to his right, then to his left and followed it up with a twirl, slamming the axe head into the ground. He de-summoned the axe, leaving an imperfect gap in the ground of the mountain, a miniature crater with cracks reaching out like tendrils. Tabitha was watching from a distance.

"That's a cracking weapon isn't it, Melito?" He sighed at the pun.

"Yes, other weapons or a person with great strength could penetrate his hide, but this digs deep into it."

She didn't have to ask who he was talking about. Tabitha walked over to her friend. "I think you'll be ready for Welk. You defeated him once before, despite his escape, and you'll be able to deal with him again."

"I hope so. You heard what Zane said, he won't be easy like last time. Welk is a poltroon. I saw what he did to my father. The foul creature has neither honour nor shame."

Tabitha crossed her arms. "What will you do when Welk is dead?" "Rebuild Entella, that's next on the list. How I am going to rebuild it, I am not sure. Welk has to be killed first otherwise he could attack Entella again."

They sat down near the cliff. "I need you to do me a favour, Tabitha. If you can track down other metazoans from Entella, that would be helpful."

"Track them down? How am I going to do that?"

"As to how, I think it's worth asking King Tertullian if there were others left.

It should be easier than you think."

"They are mostly primates, aren't they?"

"Yes. There weren't that many other metazoan races. Some did come to Carthage. The question is will some of them be willing to leave? We'll give them a choice; same thing goes for anyone else who doesn't desire to return to Entella. It would not be a good idea to stab the king we serve in the back, eh?"

Tabitha grinned. "Aha... I see the making of a leader in you already. Grand plans for your kingdom sprouting from your mind."

Melito stopped for a moment, remembering what Zane had said to him. "There is a path to victory and restoration, you just need to find it... Looks like I'll be just fine."

"Who said that?"

"Zane did. Now I know I am up for the task."

Tabitha then got up and went back to the cave. "Get some rest, you'll need it."

Melito eventually left the cliff-face, leaving the cold air behind. *I'll make you proud, Father.*

~

The grey brickwork of the castle was layered with ice, including that of the bridge that went over a frozen moat.

"The Chilling Citadel, despite its name, it won't be scaring you," said Berinon.

Reika simpered awkwardly.

"Never mind." Berinon went across the bridge shaking his head in dismay. "Admirable attempt however," Rian said, heading along the bridge too.

As they all moved down the bridge, Reika shivered once again as she held the cloak tightly around her more. "Brr, it's cold!"

Berinon looked back. "It's good we got you a cloak and shoes."

"The advantage of having fur, no need for a cloak," Tabitha said with a smile on her face. Reika just glared at Tabitha.

Two guards were posted at the gate. They noticed the group walking towards them on the bridge.

"HALT! What do you want? State your business."

Junayd stepped forward. "My friends and I have travelled a long way. We need a place to stay."

The guard held his ground. "And yet you bring this cursed one here?" He said as he pointed to Reika. She instantly became vexed though found it very unusual they knew of her affliction. She didn't have time to find out.

"Don't worry, I take full responsibility for her. The clouds should keep us safe from the curse," Junayd said with assurance.

The guard finally relented. "Very well, you may enter here."

The citadel contained many wooden houses as well as what looked like a massive storage house. "Where is the inn?" Reika asked.

"At the northern end of the citadel," Zane replied. "We'll need to book a few rooms for the night. Stay sharp, any one of these villagers could be hiding another piece of the gem."

Later that night, Reika was fast asleep, only to be woken up by a strange sound. Her grogginess was very short-lived. Peering through the keyhole of her door, she saw an old man, a frail figure with clothing like Zane's, only with a more regal looking appearance, though she doubted he was a member of a royal family. The strange man had small pebble glasses that sat gently on the bridge of his nose. He sat down at a table at the far end of the room, where he went out of Reika's field of vision. Quietly she opened the door to leave, shutting it as silently so as to not wake the rest of the inn up.

The old man took out a gem from his pocket, staring at it with great delight. Reika silently made her way to Zane's room, inaudibly opening the door, slinking inside.

"Zane, wake up." She said in a harsh whisper. Zane opened his eyes. "What is it?" He asked quietly.

"The second gem piece is with the man out there. We need to get it from him.

He's the agent in the town."

Zane rose from his bed. "Oh, interesting you informed me first."

"These agents could be anyone as you said Zane. I am thinking of the best way to take the stone from the man. I thought it would be better to ask someone... more prudent in these matters."

Zane shook his head.

"I think he is going to let his guard down. I'll lead him downstairs, when it's clear, *you* take the gem piece."

Reika pondered this for a time. There was something unusual about the man outside. Reika then remembered the man had been at supper. She almost hadn't recognised him because he'd been so hunched over, and his hands had shaken as he ate. Not quite so here. He sat upright and his movements were robust.

"Being very healthy when old is one thing," Reika said. "Overpowering someone despite one's age is another. Antonius is in his mid-sixties, and he is no pushover. He'd give *you* a run for his money." Zane nodded at her as she continued. "He is a bit rusty however, he told me himself. In his youth he was lauded for his strength in battle and the many he trained."

Zane left his bed, nodding in agreement. "Indeed, he was. But back to the matter at hand, be very quiet when getting the gem. We don't want anyone out there to know you have it."

Zane left his room casually, closing the door behind him. The old man turned around to see what he was doing. The young man walked down the stairs, and without Zane even having to come up with a ruse, the old man followed behind him. Reika exited from the room quietly.

To her disbelief, the gem piece sat on the table. The old man had carelessly left it there. Reika edged her way to the table, snatching the gem from it. *Two down, one to go,* she thought, smiling that they were one step away from their goal. Some part of her felt a little guilty taking the gem away from an old man. At the same time, she knew there was something off about him, he could be one of the agents. Preventing the gem from falling into the wrong hands was worth it, whether her acts might be considered theft or not. Reika quietly made her way back to her own room.

Zane went downstairs into the lobby, sitting by the small smouldering ashy fireplace. The old man kept his distance, pretending he was not spying on Zane, keeping up his ruse.

"You can cut the act sir; I know what you are."

The old man stopped for a moment. His visage transformed from that of a frail old man into that of a crystalline red golem, bulkier in comparison to the other two Zane previously had seen.

"Ah, the Temporal Knight, what a pleasure to finally meet you face to face. Keahi Ruber is my name." The golem sat next to Zane on the couch. "What brings you and your companions to this cold place?"

Zane smirked. "Hmph, you are in quite a good mood."

"I have a chance to slay you! Not worth hiding it. Pity you and your friends won't live long enough to find the gem around here." Zane sucked in his cheeks subtly, trying not to burst out laughing. *A complete fool, Reika has already taken the gem away and he doesn't suspect a thing,* he thought.

"What's so funny, fleshie?" the golem asked.

Keahi got up from the chair, his red, piercing eyes focused on the young human, who casually remained sitting where he was. A small blade grew from the back of his wrist. He thrust the blade at Zane's head, who saw it, tilting his head out the way, causing the blade to lodge in the cushion behind him. As Keahi tore the knife out of the cushion, feathers burst out of it, falling to the seat and the floor.

Keahi attempted to hit Zane again, but this time he stood up at an incredible speed, evading the blade by inches. "Mock me, will you?" Keahi said in anger, grabbing Zane by the arm, throwing the young man across the room and crashing through the window. Zane lay on the ground, shards of glass sticking into his arms, he restrained his cries of pain. The golem crashed through the wall of the inn after his quarry. He made his way towards Zane, ready to bludgeon him with his mighty crystal hands. Zane anticipated this and began using Temporal Regeneration. The glass shards dropped out the wounds, allowing them to close. The Temporal Knight got to his feet swiftly, summoning Verwandeln in its basic sword form. Keahi formed a sword of his own with a mighty clap with his hands.

The two swung their blades, locking them together. The golem was caught off-guard by Zane's strength. "For such a scrawny man, you are very strong." The golem backed off for a moment, his downward strike missing Zane. The ground was not so lucky, and the golem hit it with such force that clumps of stone and dirt flew into the air as if a gunpowder barrel buried beneath the icy cobblestone had exploded.

Verwandeln transformed into a bludgeon, Zane smashing it against Keahi. The big golem staggered, managing to maintain his balance, attempting to bring down his crystal blade upon Zane, missing once again, the ground exploding from the force. Zane's weapon transformed into a spear, and he used it to keep the golem back, now fighting from a distance. Keahi grabbed the spear but didn't expect Verwandeln changing into a snaking rope that coiled around him, hardening into a strong steel structure. "This isn't going to hold me for long, boy!"

Keahi broke the structure around him. Zane called the pieces back to him, allowing them to reform the familiar sword shape. Keahi was ready to attack once again. He charged at Zane, grabbing the human, trying to crush him. Zane struggled to break free of Keahi's grasp. Eventually, Zane pushed his way out of the grip, a war cry emanating from his throat.

Guards took note of the fighting from the city walls.

"Wait!" said their commander, who wore a silver belt around his waist. "This is his fight."

Reika watched from the window; the moon thankfully obscured by the thick clouds.

"Come on Zane, you can do this."

Zane's speed had begun to pick up the pace in her eyes, every subsequent slash closing the gap between the previous one. Verwandeln shifted into brass knuckles and Zane threw a punch that was so fast, it caused Keahi to fly through the air, skidding along the icy pavement only a few feet away.

"It's over, you've lost, rocky," Zane said.

"Don't call me rocky, little boy!" Keahi got back to his feet, throwing the crystal blade at Zane. Zane dodged swiftly, letting the sword crash to the floor. Keahi paused for a moment. Seeing the sword lying there, glistening on the cobblestone, He realised he had made a mistake.

The gem! he thought, and hurried back towards the inn, leaping back through the hole he'd made in the wall. Reika opened the window, throwing the gem piece at Zane before leaping out of the window herself to join him. She landed gracefully.

Keahi stopped, spinning around and noticing the young woman stood next to Zane. He was frozen in place, seething with anger. "So, you are the one who took it, huh? You'll die as well!"

Reika stepped next to Zane. Keahi charged and without a moment to lose, Reika held up her right hand and began to channel energy through it. She slammed it on the ground, allowing the energy to ripple along it, causing the golem to lose his balance. He still continued in his path, unable to stop himself.

The moon emerged from the clouds as a gibbous and huge, though not quite at its fullest. In that moment, Reika felt her strength increase and she called upon a barrier around her right hand. The barrier collided with the side of the golem, throwing him across the ground.

Keahi saw the moon but dismissed its effects, and went for the pair again, not caring what manner of woman he faced, only desiring to kill her. He drew his arms behind him, throwing a double punch. Zane and Reika caught one fist of the creature each in their hands.

Keahi was not surprised by Zane; he knew the strength of the young man. Reika, on the other hand, was something he did not expect. Zane himself was taken aback, though didn't have the luxury of thinking on it. All that mattered was quelling the rage filled titan in front of him.

Zane sent a freezing sensation into the creature's arm, and Reika matched him with a boiling heat. Keahi recoiled. Zane saw the moon's shape, looking at Reika; her eyes were beginning to turn reptilian. Reika did not look back, she just powered her left hand with energy, throwing a wide punch into Keahi's stomach. He stumbled backwards, overawed by the power of the blow, then turned and fled, grabbing his sword, shrinking the blade and reuniting it with his body. Keahi climbed the wall, escaping from the town.

Zane and Reika watched him run. "It's not a full moon tonight, but still, I am amazed by your strength. Have you ever had this before?" Zane asked.

They headed back to the inn.

"Yes. There was a wicked thug named Magnus. He and his band of scoundrels came to the citadel I lived in. It was the full moon and my power was immense." She pointed to her arms. "Even with some muscle on me, could I push back a golem naturally? I don't think so."

"I had a struggle with releasing that grip on me earlier. In your case, there is only one group I can think of whose power increases due to the moon. Be wary for now considering the affliction that you have. Nevertheless, thanks for the assist."

Reika couldn't help but agree; she had to be more careful than ever. "Can we go back inside now? I'm shivering."

As they re-entered the inn, her eyes resumed their human form. It was just in time, as the innkeeper arrived downstairs, a stout gentleman in simple clothes like Zane. He wiped his small pebble glasses with a cloth found in the upper pocket of his white shirt.

"That hole in the wall wasn't caused by you, was it? Care to explain?"

Zane stepped forwards. "Just a mess from a golem. He threw me against your wall."

The innkeeper said nothing for a moment. "Where is this golem now?" "Gone. He won't be coming back, I don't think."

The innkeeper turned to leave. "Worry not about the mess. I'll have that cleaned in the morning and I'll have the builders here to fix the damage to the wall and window. You stopped that golem from causing further damage to the inn, you hold no blame in this matter."

"No please," Zane said. "Allow me to help."

Zane slammed his fist into the floor, a blue dome emerged from him, expanding over the rest of the room, causing the damage to be repaired in a flash. Reika and the innkeeper were awestruck.

"The amount of money you saved me from rebuilding this place, I am grateful for it. Have a pleasant evening."

The innkeeper headed off upstairs. They heard the gentle close of a door. "Where do you suppose the golem is going, Zane?" Reika asked.

"Back to his master is one possibility. He won't be pleased. He might not even be able to face him," Zane replied.

Reika looked like she was mentally elsewhere.

"He'll be even less happy if I get a taste of his blood. I wonder what golem blood tastes like? It might be rather delicious."

Zane looked round at Reika, disturbed by what she had said. "That's not like you." Her eyes were reptilian again.

"Perhaps you don't know me?" She replied. "How about I have your blood instead?" Reika pinned Zane near the wall, her left hand planted on it. She smiled nefariously. "Maybe I should go straight for the head?"

Reika giggled in a baleful manner. She placed her finger on his throat, simulating a knife cut. He showed no more sign of emotion. He simply waited for the moment to pass. She didn't scare Zane, but he was still troubled, nevertheless.

"Stop this madness Reika, this is not who you are."

Reika's diabolical grin transitioned to a horrified look, her eyes returning to normal. She stepped away from Zane and the wall. "What am I doing?" She said, visibly rattled. "Forgive me, Zane. Idiot I am, I wasn't careful. I... I need to go to sleep."

Reika went upstairs to her room in disgrace. Zane only watched her leave.

Reika closed the door behind her. She shut the curtains frantically and sat down in front of a mirror. For a time, she just stared into the mirror. In her mind's eye, her visage transformed into the monster's, then shifted back to her own face. Eventually, she hung her head in shame. The thought of drinking the blood of any creature, friend or foe, churned her stomach. Part of her wanted to scream in frustration, but she couldn't as someone might hear her, so all she could do was suffer in silence.

Two gem pieces down and one to go, Zane thought quietly after he had his breakfast. Fried eggs, bacon, and sausages. He'd left his plate remarkably clean. Reika came down the stairs to the reception where the innkeeper sat at his desk. "Thanks for the stay here. How much do my companions and I owe you, sir?"

The innkeeper smiled back at the young woman. "Only twenty-five pieces of gold. Glad to help my dear."

Junayd spotted Reika at the reception and went over to her immediately. He made sure not to embarrass her by mentioning the events of the previous night. The innkeeper took the money from Reika, placing it in a small box under his desk. Then he attended to a customer who'd appeared behind Reika.

Junayd took Reika aside to the once ruined but now restored feather chairs. "Did anyone see you with reptilian eyes?" He asked softly.

"No, they didn't. Not even the innkeeper saw them."

"Make sure it stays that way. We don't want anyone else

finding out what you are, it isn't worth it. If the reaction of my people to your transformation is anything to go by, what if it is worse here? Make sure the moon isn't full or is hidden before you venture out at night. Don't ever forget that."

Reika clutched her chest with her right hand, unsettled. "I don't think it works," she said quietly. "The moon wasn't full last night, but I still nearly transformed. A golem had the gem piece. Zane and I fought him. I said that the golem wouldn't be happy if I got a taste of his blood..."

"You didn't actually mean..." Reika cast her eyes down in shame.

"My eyes had changed in front of Zane. I wanted *his* blood too." Junayd tried his best to hide his disgust.

Reika nervously sat there. Junayd reached for her left hand, clasping it in his own gently. "We'll get the Anodyne Stone Reika, I guarantee it."

"What I would like to know is how one of the guards knew what I am."

"Must be a dragon himself, they can smell the curse in any person. That guard was deliberately vague, must have been for your protection. I could be wrong." Reika dropped the subject. Berinon quietly watched the two from afar. *Poor woman,* he thought. He sipped his drink gently, foam hanging from his beard, which he wiped promptly with a cloth on the counter.

"So where will we find the final piece of the gem in Arezzo?" Reika asked Junayd.

"In a dungeon. Then we should be able to access Welk's fortress and get that stone."

"But what about Arezzo? Is it far?"

Junayd reached for a book behind him on the bookshelf. Scrolling through swiftly, he found a posh-looking map of the world. "It is quite a trek. We need to go to the desert in Triterrain, north-west of the United Peak." Junayd pointed to the far western tip of the island. "It makes sense for us to go to the airship yard. We'll hire the crew to help us. It will allow us to get to Arezzo to get the final gem piece quickly and once we have it, we can then head on to Welk's fortress."

Reika nodded then Junayd continued, "Our first order of business is to get through the cave here. Despite increasing the strength of the Draco Ferrum, there's some special metal I need from that cave in order to make it more powerful."

They left the Chilling Citadel behind. Despite the cold air and snow, the blizzard had died down, leaving the sun shining on the untouched snow. Not a cloud was present, none of the snow was disappearing, and the cold air was not too bitter. Berinon led the group across the snowy plain to the west. It took three hours, with at least a fifteen-minute respite between each hour, until they had finally reached a cave. The group set up camp outside the entrance to the cave, staying there till the next morning to recuperate.

"The metal you spoke of is in here, isn't it?" Reika asked Junayd.

"Correct. This isn't just ordinary metal. Its properties have the power to enhance any weapon it comes into contact with, including that of the Ferrum."

"Let's hope none of it gets in the wrong hands."

"Unlikely," Berinon chimed in. "The metal you speak of, called Excandescite, is a very dangerous one, highly explosive. Just to correct you, only certain magical weapons can be imbued with it. Though that's not a worry for you two, with the Draco Ferrum and Luniram."

"Luniram too?"

"Indeed, Reika, even your blade. A trial awaits us."

"What about us? It's our job to escort and protect Reika," Melito said. "This was the mission Ignatius sent Tabitha and I on."

"Don't worry, I am sure he won't mind others taking over for a few minutes," Zane said.

"I'll stay out here, the monkeys as well," Rian said.

"Very well. Rian, make sure you and the others meet us at the other end."

Junayd remembered the cannons back in the ruined tower and Reika recalled that Magnus' ship cannons were alike in nature. They glanced at each other.

"Some weapons use Excandescite as well?" Junayd asked. "There are powerful cannons at an abandoned tower back in Caledonia."

"Yes," Berinon said. "Others have entered this cave in the past but the metal is never given to those who do evil. Unless it was stolen of course."

Melito pondered for a time. "Entella's Bane... my axe... Can Excandescite be fused with it?"

"I'm not sure," Berinon replied. "The Draco Ferrum and Luniram were both forged by a master blacksmith, a golem known to many as Caminus. The magical weapons he forges are robust enough to withstand the Excandescite's power. Entella's Bane may be incinerated by its explosive nature, as would you. Had it been built by Caminus, it would have a chance to work."

Melito sighed. "Oh well, if it kills Welk, it will have done its job."

As soon as Junayd, Reika, Zane, and Berinon entered, a yellowy, white cloud started to form in the air, seeping from the rocks like water breaking through. It fused together, creating an incredible face with white eyes. Junayd and Reika drew their blades.

"So, you've come for the Excandescite have you? Well, you will not obtain it that easily. I am willing, however, to see the mettle you possess. Now, if you be so good as to lower your weapons."

Berinon motioned to his comrades. "Do as he says, we don't want any trouble."

Junayd and Reika complied.

"Who are you?" Berinon enquired.

"Caeronvar is my name. I am a wraith. My duty is to guard the Excandescite. It is not for you to have, not unless you have been granted a powerful weapon of magical property. Survive this trial and the metal shall be given to you. Enter the cavern before you. The ones named Zane and Berinon, you will be spectators in this challenge. Junayd and Reika shall be the ones who proceed through it."

Caeronvar vanished in a shrinking light, leaving the entrance exactly as it was, relatively dark, with only the light outside revealing what lay beyond the threshold. They caught sight of an ancient door emblazoned with immaculate carvings of a battle, with a sculpture of a glowing chest in the middle of it.

A huge cavern lay before them. Junayd was in awe of the size if not by what dwelt within. "This is it? Where's the way out? Where is the Excandesite?"

Berinon pointed to the small mound shaped like a mountain in the room's centre. On top of the mound, there was a green orb, like an apple.

Berinon picked up a small rock from the mound, hurling it as hard as he could. The rock was about to hit the wall, but it instantly stopped short, making an unusual collision sound and falling down into the chasm below. Where the stone hit, there was a small surge of energy.

"No way of dispelling that, it looks like the terrain needs to be altered in order to get past this barrier. In fact, the orbs here were responsible for the unique look of this sub-continent."

"Unique?" Junayd said raising his right eyebrow. "If these orbs are responsible for how Triterrain looks, should we be messing around in here?"

"Worry not, they will not be used all at once, that is the only way to affect Triterrain in its entirety. The question is, which type of terrain should we change it to?" Berinon placed his hand on the green orb. In a moment's flash, with the noise of howling wind, the entire cavern was completely made of ice. Much of the floor was replaced with frozen water.

Junayd was amazed. "So, what's our means of getting out of here?"

"Guess we need to follow the path and see where it leads," Reika responded. She examined the pathway, walking on the perimeter of the mound. Something caught her attention: other green orbs had appeared around them on dwarfish islands surrounding the cavern. "Zane, do they look like they are making a path to you?"

Zane had a think. "This cave can be transformed by these orbs. If you go to each one, you can use them to make a pathway. If I'm right, the path behind you will be blocked as you alter the terrain. Good luck to the both of you."

Junayd hurried down the stairs, where he would be able to jump to the first island.

"Wait up!" Reika called, heading down the stairs after him. She halted for a moment. *I guess flying straight to the finish would be cheating then?* was the thought that crossed her mind. She stopped her train of thought. Junayd was almost at the first island with the orb.

"This way, Reika. Hurry!" Junayd called. She made her way to the islands, making a leap to her right. She slipped slightly, trying to regain her balance. Reika bounced to her right again, turning around to see Junayd still waiting at the island where the second orb lay.

"Don't stand there young one. Follow him." Berinon called very sternly. Reika finally made her way over to Junayd, trying her best to leap over every gap, taking one last leap to the right on the orb island.

"So freezing..." she said, shivering.

Junayd agreed with her. "I think it's time for a change." He placed his hand on the orb. This time, another flash ensued along with the sound of a fierce furnace. The terrain resembled the interior of a volcano, the freezing water replaced by lava.

∼

Melito and Tabitha waited outside the cave in anticipation. Rian scoured the horizon.

Caeronvar reappeared in front of them. Melito summoned his axe. Caeronvar said nothing.

"Are you... friendly?" Tabitha asked anxiously. "No need to fret. I am here to test your friend."

Melito pointed to his chest. "Me? I thought you wanted Reika and Junayd?" "True... but I am here to test you also, young prince. The Excandescite that your friends seek can never be fused with Entella's Bane with the same level of potency. If it had been built by Caminus the Forger, then it would. However," A small silver and cream coloured sphere appeared in front of all three of them.

"Show me your strength and I will imbue your axe with greater power." Melito nodded.

Caeronvar's form changed into a humanoid one. His eyes acquired pupils and green irises. His hair was a sharp platinum blonde. He wore what appeared to be black armour covered in a dark grey cloak. He summoned an ornate blade that was large, yet elegant.

Melito charged. He swiped Entella's Bane to Caeronvar's left. The entity quickly blocked. Caeronvar backed off and struck the axe, knocking Melito away. The marmoset flipped backwards with primate agility and landed on his feet. Caeronvar paused. "Hit me at least once with your axe and I will give you the Excandescite for your weapon."

Melito rolled the shaft of his axe in his hands in his eagerness to prove the guardian of the cave wrong.

Melito went for Caeronvar again. He tried to swing again from the right side. Caeronvar blocked the attack once again. Melito tried to change up the angle from where he would swing the axe. Caeronvar wasn't fazed, blocking every single slash from the axe. Then he began his assault, Melito edging his way backward away from the wraith, holding his axe in his right hand in front of him. Caeronvar leapt at the marmoset, bringing his sword down. Melito barely rolled out of the way. He held out the handle of his axe horizontally without much thought when the ornate blade came down on top. Melito strained to hold the blade at bay as Caeronvar pushed down.

"What choice will you make young one?" He asked. Melito held his ground, much to Caeronvar's surprise. The metazoan pushed back, then shoved the guardian and de-summoned his axe as he rolled away again. He called his axe to him to swing around at Caeronvar. The entity backed away sharply. With one swing of his mighty blade, he caused an immense gust of wind to fly towards Melito. Melito lodged his axe into the floor to keep his grounding, holding onto the handle tightly.

Tabitha could only watch the battle, hoping Melito would win. Rian was somewhat impressed by Melito's skill.

The wind finally ceased—in the nick of time, as Melito had been struggling to retain his grip on the axe. He raised Entella's Bane, running at Caeronvar. The wraith raised his hand in front of him, light projectiles firing at the marmoset, who dodged them as he ran. One final shot came toward the metazoan. Melito swung the axe, striking the projectile away. He flung the axe towards Caeronvar.

This distracted the wraith for a moment as the axe did not make contact with his own blade. Melito summoned the axe back to himself and struck. Caeronvar spun round just in time to block Melito's attack.

The marmoset began to get more aggressive in his swings, pushing the wraith further and further away from the cave entrance. Melito finally managed to knock the sword out of Caeronvar's hand and swiped the entity with his axe. As it passed through the guardian's body, the latter transformed into what looked like wisps of smoke or water. Once the blade emerged the other side, Caeronvar's body returned to normal. Melito wasn't sure what to make of it. Had he won or lost?

"Did I win?" He asked.

"I said to hit me," Caeronvar replied. He held out his hand and there it was, the sphere of Excandescite. Melito reached out. The

Excandescite began to shine with a bright light as if it were boiling lava. As it floated above his hand, the sphere began to transform into a cloud of sand, making its way into the axe's head. The weapon began to glow while the Excandescite vanished inside the axe head. At last, the axe returned to normal.

Melito twirled Entella's Bane high above his head and de-summoned it shortly afterwards. Tabitha gave Melito a big hug. "Nice work," she said with a beaming smile.

Caeronvar stood there, also smiling. "I'll send you all to the end of this cave.

You will meet your friends there. I must test them as well."

Caeronvar faded away in the shrinking light as before. Melito, Tabitha, and Rian soon also disappeared. They were not worried thanks to what Caeronvar had told them.

Junayd and Reika looked toward the west of the room, an upside-down T facing north pointed to another island. They traversed it, making sure to avoid the lava at all costs. Their next step was along a narrow island that spiralled around half of the mound to the east, leading to another slightly smaller one which turned back in the opposite direction towards the orb.

"Onwards we go, Reika," Junayd said.

Upon his contact with the orb, the fiery cavern was replaced with the freezing one from before, and the previous paths returned. Despite the size of the small island, it didn't take long to get to the next orb to the north. Contact made with the orb restored the fiery room.

"Urgh, I can't stand this extreme temperature," Reika said, wiping the melting snow from her head and shoulders. "We have to keep going, we are almost through to the other one."

The island they were on was even narrower than the previous islands. The couple pressed on along the meandering path. One final jump took them to an L- shape that connected to where the final orb in the room was. This time, the chasm possessed a small bridge to get across.

Junayd pressed down the orb, causing the lava and fire to disappear in a flash of light, leaving he and Reika standing next to it. The bridge they crossed had gone, the cavern was restored back to its original rocky self. The barrier previously cutting off the route to the next cavern had been removed. Zane and Berinon stayed where they were.

Caeronvar made his return. "Excellent work, the second trial shall begin, your fight against me. To the ones known as Zane and Berinon, I'll personally teleport you to the final chamber, you need not be here with your companions, they are the ones being tested."

Caeronvar allowed light to emanate from his brow, causing Zane and Berinon to vanish from sight.

Junayd and Reika entered the rectangular cavern. A burst of light appeared and there, standing in front of the door to the next room, was Caeronvar in his humanoid form, and sword in hand. "Prove your worth, let me see how strong you are, both of you."

He readied his defensive stance.

Junayd began his first attack. Reika followed suit. Both swiped furiously, with Caeronvar merely deflecting them with elegant precision. With a return swing of his blade into the ground, he ripped up a section of the floor, sending small rocks hurtling at the two humans. Reika pulled up a barrier just in time, this time encased in light, vaporising the boulders on impact, releasing her barrier quickly to allow Junayd a chance to counter. Caeronvar once again blocked the initial attacks quickly, but Junayd was fortunate that one strike got through, staggering the guardian. This was short-lived, as Caeronvar grabbed the Draco Ferrum, wrenching it from Junayd's grip, and then sending Junayd flying.

Reika held her hands up, stopping Junayd from hitting the wall and telekinetically landing him on the ground safely. She held her sword high in a defensive stance, a look of trepidation on her face. *Against this creature, both of us are crazy,* she thought.

She flew speedily and swung the blade at Caeronvar, who countered, forcing her to get back on the ground away from him. Reika countered herself, swinging the blade with both hands to the left, then to the right. She tried a final third swing but Caeronvar blocked the attack. Before a fourth strike came, Caeronvar swung his mighty sword upwards, throwing Reika off-balance. Junayd had recovered, striking at Caeronvar again. The guardian skidded along the floor from the impact, though he showed no signs of flinching.

Both humans went for a strike, but Caeronvar crossed his arms, a dark blue barrier appearing every time Reika and Junayd attacked with their swords. Junayd poured light into the blade, finally slashing the barrier itself. It shattered like glass. Reika made a cut of her own; it went straight through Caeronvar. Luniram phased right through him. The humans stepped away from Caeronvar, wondering why he'd stopped. Caeronvar de-summoned his weapon.

"I am impressed. You may now help yourself to the Excandescite."

Caeronvar stepped to the side, gesturing towards the passage behind him, as though he were showing them a work of art. The humans left Caeronvar behind, while he vanished, returning to his non-corporeal state.

Zane and Berinon were waiting by the ornate gem chest in the cavern. They saw Junayd and Reika enter the cavern from the south. Nothing was said, only smiles were exchanged. That is, until Reika looked around the room. "Will the others be brought here too?"

Melito, Tabitha and Rian appeared in the room in a blaze of light. "Caeronvar's work again," Junayd said.

"Yes," Melito replied. "He also tested me."

Tabitha scratched the back of her head puzzled. "Where is he now?"

"Not sure, he just wanted to test us to see if we are worthy of using the Excandescite," Reika replied.

Junayd walked over to the chest and opened it up. There, he saw a silvery and creamy powder within it. He stared at it in confusion as he knelt on the floor, peering deeper into the chest, picking up the powder in his hand. Reika didn't kneel, merely standing near the chest with her right hand on her hip.

"That's it?"

"Looks like it," Junayd summoned the Ferrum, and Reika called Luniram. The powder began to rise from the chest, resembling lava floating in the air, swirling with a great intensity. The temperature of the room continued to increase as well until the tornado split itself into two separate channels. The channels of energy fused with both magical blades, the wielders straining to hold onto their weapons against the immense pressure placed on them as the tornadoes poured into the blades. The superheated metals glowed as the tornadoes fused into them. Then, the blades returned to their original colours, smoking, before they finally cooled like a dying star.

"That was Excandescite? How strong are the blades now?" Reika asked. "Only one way to find out," Junayd said.

A boulder crashed through the ceiling, blocking their exit.

Junayd took hold of the Draco Ferrum and it glowed a shimmering cream and silver light. With a mighty lunge, he stabbed the stone, piercing it clean through. The stone had a crumpled look where Junayd had pierced it. Junayd then lifted the sword through the top of the boulder, cutting it in half. Both halves collapsed on their sides, and the exit now lay open again. The stone's interior resembled that of fine tan sponge cake crumbs. Junayd was very pleased. Reika stared at Luniram. It began to glow the same colour. She spun her blade and swiped the floor. The cut was smooth.

"Consider me impressed," she said.

Chapter 10

Flight to Fight

Seeing the massive airship yard near the coastline came as a relief to Reika. A cobblestone wall surrounded it. The group made their way through double doors set in the wall, entering a spacious corridor allowing crowds to move around easily; most people working there were building, repairing, or scrapping airships.

At last, they came to the hanger where a magnificent airship was being maintained, made of buloke wood. Its size from stern to bow was at least four hundred feet long and fifty feet wide from starboard to port. In gold letters on the bow were the words *COEPTUS*. They could see a few golems, humans, and metazoans working tirelessly on other ships, albeit smaller ones. The golems were not crystalline like other golems they'd seen. These ones were metallic, shiny, almost regal in many respects. They exhibited no roughness like the gemstone golems. They did have the same eyes, however.

An engineer left the ship via a single rope ladder, a bald and bushy bearded round man with a white vest and grey trousers. He noticed Junayd and the others with him.

"Can I help, mate? Lawrence is the name." The two shook each other's hands.

"Junayd, and as a matter of fact you can indeed, we would like to use one of the airships, we need to get to Arezzo swiftly. In fact, we're going to need the ship for a while." Lawrence wiped sweat from his brow with a small towel he held in his hand. "Would you like a tour of the *Coeptus*? Lovely accommodation as well as very good thrust from our engines, top notch speed. Guaranteed to work like a treat."

Lawrence beckoned the group to follow him up the ladder onto the deck above. It reminded Reika of the *Tetraspis*, which made her wonder whether this was where the *Tetraspis* had come from or if it had been stolen from its previous owner by Magnus.

"A ship with golem tech, just as Junayd said," Reika said.

Lawrence turned to her. "Indeed. The ship itself is actually a decommissioned sailing vessel that we bought in order to put it to use once again. We merely restored it and added the engines as well as the levi-panels from our golem friends to lift us into the air." Lawrence turned away from the party. "Come along with me down to your quarters."

Two small set of stairs in the middle of the deck led to the bedrooms. There were twelve, the carpets all different colours, though otherwise the rooms almost mirrored each other. The colours from the bow to the stern were pink, red, purple, chartreuse, olive and finally pickle. In the bow of the ship, they found an immaculate kitchen, one fit for royal guests. The captain's cabin in the stern had a seaweed carpet with golden trimming. The iron chair, despite its look, was actually very comfortable for the captain sitting at his mahogany desk, writing with a quill on a piece of parchment. The captain had short curly brown locks along with a thick, straight moustache. He wore long black robes with a grey cummerbund holding them together.

After Lawrence had taken the group to their bedrooms, he went past the deck stairs and walked down another set of stairs past the other bedrooms into the stern where the captain resided.

"Captain Tybalt, we'll be ready for flight soon." "Very good, proceed my friend to make flight."

Lawrence hurried back up to the deck, rushing to the stern to a small room on top. There, the pilot Ulric stood by the steering wheel, that still resembled a nautical one. He was dressed in an almost princely upper garb of navy blue, with black trousers and shiny boots. He had piercing blue eyes with short, neatly arranged red hair. "The captain has given all clear for flight. Ready, Ulric?"

The pilot nodded. A creaking noise could be heard over the sound of the roaring engines as the *Coeptus* rose into the air out of the hangar. It turned, leisurely, towards the east. Blue shimmering rims were located on the underside of the ship and around the sides, allowing the ship to float in the air. Once the ship was high above the airfield, the four engines at the stern roared to life. They propelled the ship forwards. After ten seconds, the ship moved faster, picking up speed with each passing second. Once it hit its pace, it moved faster than a regular sailing vessel, at least three times the speed.

"She is holding up quite well, I think. I knew that hard work would pay off." Lawrence remarked.

"Just make sure you keep her in working order. I can drive, but what good am I if you are not keeping this thing well-maintained?" Ulric said. Lawrence nodded. He left the pilot to his work and proceeded to get on with his own down below.

Reika stared out of her window in amazement at the view. It was not like the first time she'd flown over the forest; this was different. In her eyes, the fact this huge vessel could fly was more wondrous than her powers.

Junayd had goosebumps on his arms. *I never believed I would be in a transport like this,* he thought. Melito and Tabitha were just as enamoured with the sight just as Reika was; Berinon and Zane smiled at each other. Rian said nothing although he did admit it was impressive.

A further two hours had passed, and they shared a meal in the captain's cabin with Tybalt.

"Thank you for offering the services of this magnificent vessel, Captain," Berinon said.

"It is I who should be giving you the appreciation for allowing us to test the ship," Tybalt said as he raised a glass to his mouth, sipping an exquisite wine, and placing the glass back on the table with great precision. "A chance to show how we can cut travel time between countries. But we will assist you, Lord Berinon, as long as you are on this journey. No expense shall be spared, considering the trials you have been through on your journey, especially from what the young lady with you had said." He turned to Reika, smiling kindly. "I am still sorry to hear you have suffered such an affliction."

"I am almost beginning to get used to it," she said. "Though I do want to be rid of it."

"In the meantime, young one," Tybalt said. "Sit back, relax, and enjoy the trip. It will be a smooth flight for us all. We'll arrive in Arezzo within the hour, so we have all the time we need to prepare."

Lawrence entered the room, holding a brown bag. "The beacons are ready, sir."

"Ah, thank you. Show one of them please."

It was a small, round stone disc with a cap on it. Lawrence pressed it, and a small tone could be heard. "This will alert the airship and allow us to recover you. It tells us where you are. Each of you get one. There are more being made for when this becomes a passenger vessel in the future, but that will take some time. Keep it on you at all times if you want a swift recovery or you want to board the ship." Tybalt then turned to Lawrence. "How long till we make it to Arezzo Lawrence?"

"About half an hour, Captain."

"Resume your duties, make sure the engines are still functional."

Arezzo itself was a wealthy village. The buildings resembled those of Caledonia. There was no market present in the village, but in the middle, there was a main hall, with two garden plots on either side. A row of eight houses stood on the north and south sides of the village. There was a pool on the south side of the village along with five houses on a row each on the east and west sides. Near the west entrance of the village itself was a cobblestone square dominated by four dragon statues, all of them facing each other towards the centre of the square.

Once the group arrived in the village, Reika saw a familiar sight near the square.

"Cyprian!" Melito and Tabitha followed her. Reika and Cyprian gave each other a handshake. Cyprian did the same with the two monkeys.

"What are you doing here? Shouldn't you be at the castle?" Reika asked. "I've been given leave for a while, so I came back to my home."

Berinon walked over to Reika. "Sorry for the interruption. I'll pay for us to stay at the inn tonight."

"Thank you—no trouble at all."

Berinon, Rian, and Zane headed to the inn. Junayd, on the other hand, stayed near the square.

"That's a forge down there my feline friend," Junayd said. "How do we get in?"

Cyprian held his right paw in the air to halt Junayd's speech, causing the young man to look at him with a vacant expression on his face. Cyprian gestured with his thumb behind him. "It contains a dragon forge, as you have said. I give you permission to go down there but do shut the door when you have finished." He held up his paw with one finger pointing up. "However, there is a small riddle I want you to guess, tongues wag you see." Cyprian grinned.

Junayd and Reika just looked at Cyprian somewhat befuddled. "Oh...kay?" They said in unison.

Cyprian cleared his throat. *"Hard as stone though abandoned and a failure as an idea.* I expect you will come up with the answer."

Cyprian headed off to the nearest house on the northern section of the village, presumably belonging to him.

"What now?" Tabitha said. "Shall we head to the tavern?" Junayd nodded. "Agreed, tongues wag as Cyprian said."

Little did they know, Lief was hiding in one of the condemned buildings further down the street near the southern row of houses. He was watching from the windows in the shadows of the upper room. "The other gem pieces were easy for them to obtain, but not this one."

Ensconced in the tavern, the group discussed where they were to go. Melito and Tabitha agreed to help Junayd and Reika find the switch to open the forge. The latter two had to enter the forge, while Berinon, Rian, and Zane agreed they would find the final gem piece.

Melito spotted a condemned house, this time behind the village hall. He peered inside the house, seeing a dusty bust on a small pedestal. He beckoned Tabitha over and she came towards him swiftly, peering through the door too.

"A bust? Could that be the answer to the riddle?" She wondered. They both entered the house, with Melito carefully lifting the bust off the pedestal to reveal a switch underneath.

"This had better work."

Melito pulled the switch and they heard a loud creak, and the sound of giant wheels occurred afterwards.

"Success!" Tabitha squealed.

~

Meanwhile, Junayd and Reika, standing at the square, witnessed the stone flooring retract like a fortress door, revealing a secret passage. Without a moment to lose, they headed down the ladder.

Below, the room had dark green-grey cobblestone walls. They were immaculate in their look, with cleaner grey cobblestone floors. The passage in front was narrow, both of them proceeding with some trepidation. It was a winding passage with the occasional wide room along the way.

Eventually they found themselves in front of a large pit.

On the other side of the pit was a golden idol. To their left was a wall. To their right was a section of flooring devoid of the usual mortar and stonework.

"As if that pit is going to be a hinderance!" Reika remarked. She backed away from the edge, taking a run towards it. With a tele-kinetic push, Reika shot across the pit, landing safely on the other side. She turned round, grinning back at Junayd. He smirked. He leapt across the same way, performing a roll, and stood on his feet.

"Not a bad leap, Reika. I'd give it a seven. You're getting better."

"The first time I used my powers like that was on Magnus' boat, when my friends and I were held hostage."

Junayd held his chin, letting himself drift into his thoughts. "Now how do we get out?" Junayd approached the golden idol, examining it closely.

"Anything?" Reika asked.

"I think, there is a switch in the toes. If there is a trap, however, we shouldn't chance it... Unless..."

Reika eyed the toes of the idol. "The odd one out?"

Reika touched the idol on the right big toe. A noise sounded behind them to their right, at the blank segment of flooring. The blank slate had opened revealing another hole, leading further down into the catacombs. Aside from the forge, what awaited them inside was their guess.

~

Zane went into the village hall, trying to remain nonchalant as he eyed the citizens within its walls, all of which wore bright white hooded robes to protect themselves from the heat. The hall was impressive, with red and green tiles on the walls, framing priceless artefacts, weapons, armour, vases, and chests. The floor's surface had a mix of teal and emerald colours, sparkling depending on where a person stood.

The agent won't show themselves yet. We have to find a way to draw them out. Zane stood closer to the staircase, looking at the impressive architecture; the red and green exotic patterns wove together on the wall like a tapestry.

Without him knowing, someone was watching him from the higher level of the hall, a metazoan hyena called Bryce. She had a small knife at the ready, concealing it in the belt. Her fur was similar in colour to that of an ordinary leopard's. Her stature was only a head above Zane's but imposing enough for her prey. She wore white robes like the other inhabitants of Arezzo, her hood was up like the others.

Zane turned away from the stairs, where he got a glimpse of Bryce. He made his way over to an incredibly well-decorated chest of drawers that lay next to a dark eastern wing that had been closed off due to being refurbished.

Bryce walked down the staircase, appearing composed, just about containing her excitement. She pulled the knife slowly from the belt, preparing to stab Zane. As she raised the knife, Zane summoned Verwandeln to create a shield, blocking the descending knife which stuck into it. Bryce backed off. Zane made Verwandeln disappear, the knife dropping to the ground. The citizens turned around and likewise stepped away from the two.

"Foresight, it's not easy to trick me," Zane replied.

"All the more satisfying to kill you afterwards, Temporal Knight," Bryce gave a sly grin as she pulled a second knife from her belt.

A gunshot sounded and the knife was shattered instantly. The citizens panicked; screams added to the echo of the shot within the town hall. Every citizen inside the building fled through the entrance to the hall. Bryce swivelled around, catching sight of Rian and Berinon, who had been waiting in the shadows on the western upper level.

Rian blew the smoke from his gun-barrel away.

Melito and Tabitha heard the screams from the hall. Making haste, they left the switch behind.

Bryce removed her robes, revealing the armour she wore underneath, just like Rian's.

"A bounty hunter like you," Berinon said.

"Part of the same guild, but not like me." Rian leapt down, holding his gun his hand, keeping it aimed at Bryce. "Tell me who sent you, what job are you here for?"

Bryce scowled. "That gem piece is mine. I have been hired by Lief to stop you from getting it, he knows you are after it."

"Lief?"

"He works with Welk Seha, The Scorpion King." Rian lowered his firearm.

"What of you, Rian, weren't you hired to slay this pipsqueak behind me? What changed?"

"I was offered a much bigger sum. No client has matched it so far."

Bryce laughed. "Your little ally better count on the fact no one else has paid you a higher sum."

Zane smirked, making sure Bryce didn't see his face.

Melito and Tabitha made it just in time. Bryce glanced at them briefly, not caring in the slightest how outnumbered she was.

Berinon stepped forward, he had made his way down shortly after Rian. "That gem is not yours."

Bryce shrugged. "Be my guest to search for it. This piece won't be easy for you to obtain." She stepped away from Zane, and a figure could be seen in the darkness of the forbidden room.

It made itself known and Zane backed away, summoning Verwandeln to him.

Berinon and Rian kept their weapons at the ready.

The beast was a cockatrice. A slender yet muscular bipedal creature, it stood a little higher than Bryce. The face was like a dragon, but also a bird. Its faded green scaled body had feathers on the forearms, sharp ones, as if it were wearing spiked gauntlets. Its piercing eyes, with red irises, stared coldly and malevolently at Zane. It wore a belt with a tattered loin cloth hanging from it, the gemstone was fixed on the buckle.

"Make them suffer," Bryce said quietly to the cockatrice, who grinned at Bryce, acknowledging her order.

Rian drew up his gun out in front of him, ready to fire. The cockatrice was quicker, firing narrow light beams at him. Rian narrowly dodged the beams as he ducked.

Melito and Tabitha begun their assault on Bryce, Melito wielding Entella's Bane. Bryce grabbed an axe from one of the wall-mounted suits of armour. The clash of the axes echoed the room. Melito was not impressed by Bryce's skill. He managed to uppercut the axe out of Bryce's hands. It spun and imbedded itself into the floor. Tabitha shot an arrow. It scraped the bridge of Bryce's snout. The bounty hunter grabbed the axe from the floor, tearing part of the polished stone up, throwing it at Tabitha. She barely dodged out of the way, the axe leaving dents and scratches in the previously immaculate floor as it skidded to a halt.

Bryce began to flee up the stairs, heading to the upper western wing.

Rian growled. "Lily-liver! Using this beast for your work!" He quickly pulled himself up from the floor. "Zane, get after her!"

I haven't used this much, I hope it works, I may be quite rusty. Zane thought.

Clenching his hands, and using his chrono-magic, all slowed to a crawl and he dashed towards the upper west wing and with a mighty heave, he leapt into the air and landed in front of the fleeing assassin. He stopped in front of Bryce with Verwandeln in his hand as time went back to his original pace.

The hyena growled.

"I thought you had a payment to kill me," Zane said, in a mocking tone. Bryce let out a battle cry using her hyena howl, throwing a few punches at Zane, each one missing him as he used his foresight to predict her every move.

Melito swung his axe towards the cockatrice, with the creature blocking one attack with its tail, which was covered in a flexible metal coating. Tabitha shot an arrow directly at the head of the cockatrice. It caught the arrow, snapping it in two. Melito managed to strike the cockatrice despite its incredible speed, but it was only a glancing blow. Melito charged the axe with energy, courtesy of the Excandescite. Without warning, the cockatrice whipped Melito's hands with its tail, knocking the charged weapon out of his hands; the energy dissipated uselessly.

Melito launched a sharp kick at the beast in the chest. All that did was knock it away. The cockatrice scraped its feet along the floor, firing a beam of light towards Melito. He called his axe and held it in front of him, deflecting the beam. "Berinon, are you thinking what I am thinking?"

"I believe I am!" Berinon replied. He began to charge and used the metal of his lance to deflect the beams of the cockatrice as he drew nearer. He tried to hit the creature, but its reflexes were incredible, dodging attacks by Berinon while landing a few hits of its own. Berinon didn't give up, he continued his assault, finally smacking the creature's jaw with the back of his lance. He tried to impale the creature, but it swung his tail, blocking the attack with the armour. He tried again and this time impaled the creature, it let out a howl and pulled away from the weapon. It removed a golden cordial hidden in its belt. two of those same small vials remained and the beast drank from the one in its hand. To Berinon's horror, the wound inflicted on the cockatrice healed before his very eyes. It grinned back at Berinon.

"Gunshots would be nice, Rian!" the knight roared.

The elf raised his gun. "Return to me. Melito, you take over."

Berinon kicked the cockatrice in his stomach, running to Rian while it was distracted. Melito chimed in, though every strike he threw at the cockatrice was blocked.

"I'll deflect his beams back at it. The cockatrice will be turned to stone if I do," Berinon said in a quiet voice.

"How will you do that, Berinon?" "Make yourself a target, I have an idea."

Rian was indignant, though he begrudgingly accepted the idea in lieu of no alternative.

"Oi, scaly bird, you want a target, come get it!" Rian called.

The cockatrice grinned. Striking Melito's axe with its tail to knock the monkey off-balance, it moved towards Rian, preparing to fire the beams from his eyes. He unleashed multiple blasts, missing the elf with every shot, who grabbed an exotic wooden dish to shield from the beams. No damage was done to the wood, though Rian felt sharp knock-back from every blast. The elf finally slumped to his knees, dropping the wooden dish.

Meanwhile, Berinon had grabbed a mirror from the wall, roughly the same diameter as his chest. He ran as fast as he could to Rian and made it to the elf in time just as he dropped the dish before the final blast flashed. The mirror deflected the beam back at the cockatrice, turning the creature to stone instantly. "Fell beast!" Rian said as he steadied himself and got to his feet. He pointed his gun at the body, firing a shot. The cockatrice's body was reduced to dust. The gem piece fell from the ornate belt, buried in the dust when it hit the floor.

"You two get the gem out of here," the elf said to the metazoans, "Bryce is ours."

Melito rummaged through the dust, picking up the gem swiftly. He and Tabitha dashed right back to the tavern on the east of the town.

Zane was too busy to notice what had taken place, as was Bryce. They were still fighting each other, with Zane effortlessly dodging and countering, but unable to pin the hyena down. She threw valuable vases at him, priceless artefacts shattering as they hit the floor behind him. She pulled an ornate jade sword from one of the statues, ripping its arm clean off. The two fighters clashed, an unpleasant ringing every time Verwandeln struck the sword.

Zane ceased the use of his foresight, exhausted from the prolonged use. He hoped he had enough energy left to stand up to the deranged hyena.

"What's wrong, boy? Run out of time? What a waste!" She said, throwing another punch at Zane. Verwandeln changed into a shield, allowing Zane to block the attack. Bryce yelped in pain after hitting the shield, giving Zane enough time to change Verwandeln into a miniature reaper. Zane kicked Bryce into the wall and then he used the reaper to hold her against the wall by the neck. Rian made his way up to the walkway quickly, climbing one of the columns.

"When I get out of here..." snarled Bryce.

"Oh, shut up," Rian said, punching the hyena in the face, knocking her out.

Zane removed Verwandeln from her neck. Bryce's body slid gently to the floor, slumping forward as if she were asleep. Zane and Rian exchanged a nod, nothing more.

They both jumped down to the main hall bottom floor.

"Zane, some repair is needed," Berinon said. Zane allowed his right hand to glow with energy, he spun round, creating a spiral that fixed all the damage that had been done the hall upstairs and downstairs, repairing the artefacts. Bryce still lay where she was, unconscious.

Zane stood there for a moment. He turned to Rian. "Conflicting goals, eh?" He said.

"If it wasn't for the fee Junayd paid to me, I'd be fighting you right now.

Bryce wasn't wrong." Zane shrugged.

The group made their way out of the hall, with Rian exiting first. The mayor of the town rushed down from the upper eastern wing. He was a stout looking ocelot with ginger and tan fur as well as hazel eyes, wearing the white robes of his citizens with a black cummerbund. Zane and Berinon stopped.

"What is going on here? How *dare* you cause trouble!" The mayor froze, seeing that despite all the clattering he had heard, the hall looked untouched.

Zane turned and looked at the mayor in the eyes. "You'll find a bounty hunter on the upper western wing. If you have a dungeon, lock her up."

The mayor checked the wing, finding Bryce sitting there. "I'll have the guards remove her."

"There's a bit of dust that will need clearing too, Mayor."

"My servants will have that dealt with, young man." A guard, himself a hyena with a darker pallet, grabbed Bryce's unconscious body and slung it over his shoulder, hauling her away through the west wing.

Zane and Berinon began to leave with the latter picking up the belt and taking the cordials. "You didn't tell him about Rian?" Berinon observed.

"The last thing we need is to provide an explanation as to why he is here." Berinon then looked at the cordials.

"Elixirs?" He said. "Whatever the case maybe, we can't let these fall into the wrong hands. Only two left."

"Perhaps Bryce gave that cockatrice the cordials, she must have gotten them from Lief. But how did he escape?"

"Escape?" Berinon asked.

"That is my guess, wherever he is now, we must be vigilant."

Junayd and Reika found themselves in a large treasure trove, immense in scope. Reika could not contain her awe. "What is this place?"

"It's known as the Eternal Trove. It has the illusion of a cave that extends for eternity. We won't get lost, but we may get confused."

Junayd proceeded to walk along the pathway before him. "How small is this place—if the illusion didn't exist, that is?"

"It's not a large trove, it's just the gold and jewels here are very valuable, that's why it's locked up."

The path they traversed meandered and weaved around the cave. To any person observing the cave from a high height, there was the impression of multiple entrances and exits and even copies of the people in the trove. Individuals gifted enough in magic would know that if a person were to walk on a pathway through a wall, they would end up at another wall opposite from the position they started, a subtle and unnoticeable form of teleportation.

Junayd and Reika eventually found the exit. Reika observed the ceiling, seeing precise joints where the stalactites met. She caught sight of the entrance to the trove, the column an explicit indicator of the illusion.

"Did we... just end up back where we started or close to it?" Junayd was about to head into the exit when he stopped himself.

"I told you; it would be confusing. Now come on, we need to go to the forge."

Junayd swiftly climbed his way down the mirrored ladder. Reika rubbed her forehead, sighing, eventually following after him.

The small room housed a teleporter, coupled with the dragon forge entrance, its familiar layout giving Reika the feeling of re-entering a house after a long journey away. Junayd stood before it. He allowed the Draco Ferrum to glow thanks to the Excandescite. The forge's light clashed with the blade, flashing with an incredible brightness. Junayd shut his eyes. Reika remained outside the forge. She too had to look away despite her friend bearing the brunt of the light on him.

It subsided. Junayd emerged from the forge, the Draco Ferrum glowing for a few long seconds before resuming its original colour. "Almost there. Now let us return to the surface."

The teleporter that lay just outside the forge had swept the two humans away in a flurry of flames to the highest room. They climbed up the ladder out of the room back to the homely sight of Arezzo. Cyprian was there waiting at the top.

"Right then, you stay here for the moment. I'll close this trove off."

Before he departed, Reika began to speak. "How is everyone at the citadel?" Cyprian stared at the floor. "They are ok. The other guards, they miss you. Your father and mother miss you too." Reika became crestfallen and tight-lipped.

Junayd gaped at Cyprian but decided he better not wade in on this sensitive issue.

"We are still trying to track the Anodyne Stone. Now, we are trying to get into Welk Seha's fortress. We need the pieces of the gems to destroy the magical field around it. We're convinced the Anodyne Stone is actually in Welk's possession."

Cyprian listened to it all calmly.

"Well, good luck to you. We all hope Reika comes back to us."

"Thanks for letting me use the forge." Junayd didn't know what else to say; he turned to leave.

"It is no trouble at all. Just take care of yourself and the rest of your friends."

Junayd then began walking over to the inn on the eastern side of the village. Reika gave Cyprian a handshake. "Enjoy the rest of your leave, Cyprian." "Cheers. I will." With that, Cyprian departed.

Zane was examining the gem pieces within the confines of his room at the inn. He shared the room with Junayd, who sat at an old table. Zane was attempting to put them back together. After a few hours, he slumped back in his chair almost relieved. *A hassle,* he thought, *This gem is just tedious to put it back together.* He squinted as he placed the final piece back into its rightful place in the gem. Its glow was very strange. Colours of the rainbow spun slowly around each other within the gem's dark shading. "Finally."

Junayd left his seat and came over to the table to see the gem for himself. "It's more impressive than the picture you showed us. It's kind of eerie too," he remarked.

"Too right. It is powerful enough to dispel the barrier surrounding the castle."

Junayd didn't say a word for a few seconds. "I feel like I can practically reach out to touch the Anodyne Stone itself."

"The less allies, the better. Falk has already been dealt with. I just hope that stone is there."

Zane and Junayd both retired to their beds, drifting off into sleep.

Reika was wide awake in the room next door. The curtains were firmly shut on her window. She stared at the ceiling, not being able to shake the dream she had in the cave from her mind, it was still so vivid. She knew that she had to get some rest and tried her best. Despite finding no deep sleep, she could at least make sure was rested enough for the fight ahead.

Chapter 11

Anodyne Stone

The group waited until dusk and prepared for the trip, returning to the *Coeptus*, which continued its way east. They eventually drew close to the island that Welk Seha had taken for himself, turning to the south to avoid any possible detection. Melito gazed at the island, the lush fertile southlands and the ashen volcanic northlands he saw. He didn't care about the look of the island, all he wanted to do was to stop the tyrant that attacked his home.

The *Coeptus* then lowered to the water, using the engines to push its bulk along, and then finally edging its way towards a forest on the very southern point of the island. The group disembarked, leaving the captain and his crew with the ship.

Zane poked through a thicket, taking a look. "What can you see Zane?" Berinon enquired.

Zane stared intently, moving his eyes gradually from right to left. A vast open field lay before them. Then Zane noticed structures near the steep hills.

"There are some barracks to the northwest," Zane replied. "See if you and Rian can find the Anodyne Stone. The rest of us will go after Welk."

Berinon nodded. "Very well. We'll need to be as covert as possible. If Welk has the stone, we'll leave for the *Coeptus*. If we find it, Welk will still need to be killed and we'll help you if we can."

Rian turned to Berinon. "Let's remove our armour. We don't be detected as easily while we sneak around."

"A good idea." Both the men went back to the *Coeptus* to do just that. Rian had decided to leave his usual gun behind in the room and he decided to holster a small revolver on his shin. Berinon attached a knife in a sheath on his right leg. It was slightly longer than the one on Rian's gun. They strode out of the airship. The unlikely duo headed onwards to the barracks, venturing through a section of the forest to hide their presence.

The rest of the group moved for the castle, heading north-east across an open section of land, running quickly to reach another copse of trees. Soon, Zane spotted a cave, directing the others over to it, all entering safely. It wasn't vast by any means, and they swiftly emerged the other side, finally seeing the castle over the horizon.

"Who would ever want to live there? The fields behind us are more appealing," Junayd asked. He reached into his robe to pull out a scarf to wrap around his face. "Do any of you have any scarves for yourselves?"

"Already prepared!" Zane said as he wrapped a scarf around his mouth and nose, and handed three others to Reika, Melito, and Tabitha. "Courtesy of Captain Tybalt. We'll return them when we are finished. Hand them to me when you don't need them."

Berinon and Rian saw the open grounds where the barracks were situated. Rian could see one guard stationed at each side of the main gate of the compound. All of them scorpions, just like the ones who invaded Entella.

"I think this calls for real blending in," Berinon said as he knelt in front of a small pool of mud. He scooped up the mud, spreading it all over his face, his ears and his neck until his face was as black as his hair.

"Good thinking," Rian remarked, smearing the mud in like manner. They left the forest. If any scout could see them without any light, they would appear more like monkeys or a beast roaming the field. They moved swiftly across the open ground like cheetahs and inaudible as snakes.

Once they got very close, both men began to crawl toward the barracks, staying far from the entrance and heading around the corner to the guard's left. They edged their way to the wooden staked outer wall. They straightened up and clung to it. Both then climbed up the poles and once Rian got to the top first, he stared at the open grounds of the barracks. The inner walls were eighteen feet tall and built from obsidian with uninviting windows covered by bars.

They were evenly spread, and cube shaped and even the buildings that dotted the perimeter near the walls matched. The tallest tower, stationed in the middle of the barracks, was cylindrical and about double the height of the walls. The tower was closely guarded around the perimeter. At least thirty guards lay within the walls of the barracks.

"So many of them, and there may be more in the middle tower," Berinon said, joining Rian on the wall.

"If there is any building that might have the stone, it's that one." Rian pointed at the middle tower.

Berinon mused for a moment. The look on his face afterward confirmed his agreement. "Quite possibly. Now, how to get in?"

The two men climbed over the wall, making their way down to the ground, hiding close in the shadow of one of the buildings stood near the southern east corner of the outer wall. Removing their armour had helped them to sneak around but they now felt more vulnerable, especially to arrows. A direct confrontation was possible but ill advised. Berinon held off summoning his lance.

Rian assessed the surroundings. "Frustrating. There are too

many guards. If you can think of a way inside, I am open to suggestions."

"Look over there." Berinon pointed at an eight-foot pile of discarded equipment that was decaying or in need of repair. They approached and once they drew near, Rian stared at it in disbelief, scrunching his face and squinting his eyes.

"This... you cannot be serious. It's useless."

"Not so," Berinon said. "This rope has decayed in parts but most of it appears to be strong. I just need to lop that bit off and then see how long it is." Berinon found at least three feet of the rope was compromised. He grabbed hold of the rope's end. "You keep watch, I have a little work to do."

Rian shrugged. "Whatever you're planning, do it fast."

Rian glanced around the corner of the building he and Berinon were crouched behind, glancing to the west.

The guards around the tower either looked dead ahead or they gazed around the perimeter, ensuring there wasn't a possible gap for anyone to slip through. A young guard was patrolling nearby and turned his head to the alley that Rian watched. Rian withdrew but it was too late. The guard frowned and began to move towards them. "Berinon, there is a guard coming this way. Can you do what you are doing somewhere else?"

"Can do."

The young guard rounded the corner and found only a pile of rubbish. He looked around nervously. He could have sworn he spotted someone...

The two men stayed in the shadows, leaning against the building near the northern corner of the barracks as hard as they could. Berinon waited for a moment. Rian, glanced back around the corner. Eventually, the young guard moved on his way.

"Mind if I do the rest?" Rian asked. Berinon gave the rope and knife to the elf and let him continue. Rian kept on cutting the decayed section of the rope until at last, it was severed. He gave the knife to Berinon.

"We still have to get inside that tower. How long is the rope?" Berinon asked. "Not long enough, only ten metres."

"It will have to do." Berinon wrapped the rope around himself like a sash. He then noticed a small manhole cover that was back in the direction that they previously had come from. "Follow me Rian, if we can't go up, we'll be going down."

Rian kept watch to see if the guards were looking their way. Berinon cautiously pulled the manhole cover open, he moved it gently to the side. He examined the inside of the hole intently.

"We won't need the rope to climb down, take a look inside." Rian just marvelled at the tunnel that sloped down. He chuckled.

"I should have known; the barracks of the scorpions are not just above ground but below ground. Any more ideas locked within that cunning mind of yours?"

"I may have a few," Berinon said as he tapped his head with his finger. "Though I think we still need to be cautious," Berinon entered the tunnel and Rian followed, taking the manhole cover and making sure to slide it shut, as if it had remained untouched. They found themselves within the tunnels under the barracks, though not intricate as an ordinary burrow.

"I can barely see, I don't think it's a good idea to have a light down here," Berinon said, though he could just about see the outline of Rian standing in front of him.

"I can see better than you in the dark, so I'll lead the way." Rian was examining the contours of the cave. He moved slowly forward. Berinon edged his way down the tunnel. A small fork was in front of them. Rian and Berinon carried on straight ahead. The elf halted. He briefly saw a figure far in the tunnel pass along the opening. It turned away from them and never saw Rian and Berinon at all. Secretly Rian was relived the scorpion guard had not seen him. He saw the scorpion guard climb up another tunnel to the right. A small light was seen, and the guard appeared to climb up. The light vanished shortly after; a short clang was heard.

"There's our way into the tower," Rian said.

Zane held the completed gem in his hand loosely. It floated in the air, hovering. A ghastly sound emanated from the gem. Suddenly, a dark energy beam, filled with a menagerie of colours, darted at the castle with incredible speed. The beam collided with the barrier, piercing it with ease. The barrier, though magical, shattered and fell like glass, morphing into powder then phasing out of existence, leaving the castle exposed. The gem floated down, and Zane caught it, handing it to Junayd to place in the pocket of his robes.

The jagged giant door was a sight to see, not in a way that was inviting, its appearance was designed to throw off anyone who wanted to conduct a siege. Its jagged spikes were positioned in such a way that if anyone was to look at it straight on, it resembled a monstrous face, staring back at an opponent to instil terror. The illusion would eventually be lost should anyone get close to the door, which the group certainly did.

The two guards were stationed at the door. Melito swung his axe around with a flash of light firing from it. A massive scythe of energy flew past one of the soldiers, causing him to collapse on the floor fear. The other one who remained standing froze in fear, his legs quaking in a manner unbecoming of a warrior.

Melito was about to swing his axe but stopped for a moment, looking into the creature's eyes. Then he looked at the other cowering on the floor, wondering if they really deserved the brunt of his wrath. Judging by how they looked, they were no older than he. Melito lowered his axe, sharply shifting his head, indicating to the guards they should leave. They departed quickly.

Zane was astonished.

"They won't hurt us, and why should I slay them pointlessly? Let's take care of this fiend once and for all! He is the one who has earned my ire."

They all nodded.

Berinon and Rian exited the tunnels, climbing through the manhole as before and quietly sealing it off. Rian spied out the corridors to ensure they were alone. Once he indicated that all was clear, they then began to search the inner rooms of the tower. They found decorative, jewel crusted chests in one room, presumably the office of the head guard. It also had shelves filled with lengthy tomes, some food rations, and even colourful rubies, emeralds, and sapphires.

"Any idea what's inside the chests?" Rian asked.

"Only one way to find out," Berinon replied. The knight went to the desk and opened the right drawer. Three gold keys were lined up neatly inside the drawer. Berinon chucked a key to Rian.

"Now for the ultimate test, to see if the Anodyne Stone is here."

Rian nodded, maintaining a stoic disposition. Berinon unlocked the chest in front of him using the key and prying it open. He examined the contents: a sphere, white with black swirls.

"This is too easy," Berinon said, apprehensively. "Check the other one." Rian opened his chest, finding an identical sphere.

"Fakes, just as Zane said." Rian crushed the sphere in his hand. "If there are more of these fakes, we need to destroy them."

Berinon couldn't agree more.

The two could hear footsteps and hastily shut the chests, locked them, and placed the keys back in the drawer. They ducked behind the desk in the room. The same young guard that had been on patrol near the rubbish heap entered. He squinted, looking around the room. Eventually, his eye rested on the carpet, which was coated with the dust from the fake stone Rian destroyed.

As he was heading out of the room, intent on warning someone, he felt a terrible, warm grip around his neck and his mouth. Rian held the guard against the wall while Berinon shut the door with little noise.

"You alert the guards right now and I'll break your neck," the elf said, in a hushed threatening tone.

The guard was mortally afraid. "What is it that you want?" Rian let the young man go.

"First, your name," Berinon said. "Akins."

"These fakes stones, Akins, any idea where the real one is?"

Akins was quiet for a time. "Welk didn't tell us," he said at last. "All he did was make sure that these stones are shipped around. It's to throw the Temporal Knight off."

"I know that," Rian said. "I already crushed one, as you noticed. Are you certain you don't know where it is?"

"I told you already. What more do you want? I know nothing." Berinon nodded. "I think you are telling the truth young man." "I concur," Rian added. "I think we are done here."

Akins looked at the two men, wondering what they would do to him.

Berinon watched, surprised, as Rian slowly relinquished his hold on the guard.

"You're a decent lad," the elf said. "Why waste your time working for a tyrant?"

"He's our king," Akins replied. "I have to obey him."

"It won't be forever. A friend of ours will take him down. Then what?"

Akins was surprised. "Who will be taking him out? I heard that the king was once defeated by a marmoset with an axe, even though the siege of Entella was successful... You know him?"

"Oh yes."

Akins scratched his head. "Some are very loyal to Welk. But please understand, many of my people hate him, they don't want to live under him and are quite happy to see him killed, though they're too afraid to say it. It's treasonous to even talk with you about it."

"Nobody said anything about committing treason. Serve him while he's alive, keep your head down, and wait. I am not asking you to commit any sedition, that would cause you to lose your life."

Akins clenched his fists. "If I don't kill you, it will be my head on a spike.

I'm sorry, but this is for my master."

"You won't get the chance," Rian said.

Akins lunged at Rian. The elf dodged out of the way and bashed his head against the desk. The guard fell unconscious. Berinon looked at the young guard on the ground.

"What are you planning to do with the young one?" He enquired.

"Isn't it obvious?" Rian said. "Why don't we take him out of here onto the ship."

Berinon was somewhat alarmed. "And how are you going to explain this to the captain? Is this not kidnapping?"

"You heard what he said. I don't believe for a second, he's loyal to Welk. So why not get him away from here?"

"We still have to get past the guards with him, even going through the tunnels with him is a risk. Maybe he can lead us to the fake stones."

Akins awoke. "Urgh, that hurt." He gazed up at them. "Why are you staring at me?"

Meanwhile, the others entered through doors to Welk's castle. The throne room had the same obsidian lining as the exterior. Welk Seha sat upon his throne, looking down upon the five. He recognised their faces.

"Time travel..." he muttered. "I shouldn't be surprised. The Temporal Knight is among your ranks." The group finally stopped just short of the throne near the staircase. Welk Seha's attention was drawn to Reika for a moment. "The cursed one is here too, as I thought she would be." He reached behind his throne, producing a white and black sphere. A sharp dark spiral could be seen on it. "You want the Anodyne Stone, don't you? It's a shame really, this one is merely a fake."

Welk crushed it, reducing the sphere to powder. "Destrian hid it, and you'll never find it." Reika felt disheartened. Junayd was enraged. *Trying to break our spirits, are you?* Junayd thought. *Disgusting.*

Zane was frustrated. However, for him this was merely scar tissue for all the times he failed to retrieve the stone.

The creature heaved his massive limbs from the throne, walking down the stairs casually, opening his arms. "I am amazed you managed to get here. Very impressive. I feel tempted to congratulate you in a way." Silence fell after he finished speaking. Welk lowered his arms and finished his descent down the stairs. "What's wrong? Cat got your tongues?"

"Are you mocking us?" Melito asked.

"That's the general idea," Welk responded. He remained silent for a few minutes. He reached out his arms again, bending his elbows, and a huge gust of wind entered the room. Reika, Junayd, and Zane held their ground, managing to stay where they were, but Melito and Tabitha were blown to the back of the room, colliding with the door, knocking them out cold.

"NO!" Reika cried.

Zane summoned Verwandeln immediately into his hand. "You foul beast!" He growled. He also cursed himself. He'd known Welk would be more powerful than their last encounter but not so immense that he could blow Melito away like a feather in the wind.

Welk merely smirked. "They'll be fine, though not for long. I'll kill them too. But first, I'll face you myself."

He began his assault on the three, drawing his sword and smashing it into the ground, causing a tremor which made Reika, Junayd, and Zane fall to the ground momentarily. The three promptly stood, with their weapons in hand.

Reika for a time, kept her distance from the creature, then unleashed a small ball of lightning, stunning him. The effect was short-lived as he shrugged it off as one brushes dust from a coat.

Junayd and Zane both attacked, smashing their weapons down, with Welk blocking them both. Junayd's blade glowed with power, but the sword couldn't break Welk's blade.

"Excandescite, now that is interesting. It's a pity for you that this sword of mine has been made to combat close quarter weapons of that calibre," Welk crowed.

Reika quickly flew behind Welk to land a few quick cuts to his back, getting away quickly as Welk spun and attempted to hit her with the back of his hand. Welk winced in pain, though the damage done to him was superficial, a mere distraction from her. He pushed Junayd and Zane away from him, striking Reika with a lightning blast of his own. Reika speedily raised a magic barrier, however some of the forks of lightning slipped through the barrier swiftly and managed to singe part of her torso. She yelped and the barrier dissipated. She landed safely on the ground clutching the cauterised flesh.

Zane rushed over to Reika, rotating his hand just as he had done with Julius' wounds. Her once cauterised flesh returned to normal.

"Thank you."

"Anytime, just don't get injured too often, it takes a toll on me," Zane responded.

Junayd kept Welk in combat, their swords clashing with a booming echo each time.

"Look forward to an early grave!" Welk shouted.

"Don't count on it." Junayd rolled out of the way of the giant sword.

"Try me!" Welk said as he spun his blade, then, opening his hands, he sent the sword flying at Junayd like a thrown spear. Junayd swung his blade to knock Welk's sword away, but the sword spun in the air quickly, causing Junayd to bend backwards, the very tip of the sword and handle both narrowly missing him as the blade spun away from him onto the floor.

To the untrained eye, Zane seemed to disappear and reappear above Welk. Zane fired an icy blast upon Welk, freezing him in place. Zane was about to deliver a final cut when the ice instantly cracked, Welk breaking from his icy prison, much to Zane's shock. Zane disappeared before Welk's eyes. The arachnid's rapid swing failing to make contact. Junayd managed to get an easy cut to the chest before Welk could react.

"I am above you!" the creature yelled, recoiling from the wound.

Reika sneered. "Be silent, lest you humiliate yourself." She hurled a fiery ball at Welk from a safe thirty feet away, which he countered with a freezing spell, dissipating the fire.

"You'll die at my hands," he growled. Welk's blade flew through the air back into his hands and he used it knock Junayd away. He followed this up by punching Zane in the chest. Reika charged quickly at Welk, her sword in hand, dodging swiftly when Welk tried to bring his large blade down onto her. She stabbed in an instant, holding the blade there. Welk stood, looking in shock. He winced as he pulled the blade gently from his chest. He sent a current of heat with a spell into the blade, causing Reika to let go of it.

Reika de-summoned Luniram and backed away from the creature, who himself was still surprised the young woman had managed to penetrate his thick hide. Even she was taken aback by the damage done. Welk could feel the stabbing pain in his chest. He looked to the window of his castle and saw the moon. It wasn't a full one, though it was gibbous.

Curse or no curse, she is one of them. A pest, like her parents. he thought. Welk had no time to dwell on this. He knew he had to fight these young irritants and win. Junayd and Zane were approaching from behind.

He used a repulsing blast to knock Junayd and Zane away, granting a brief interval where he grabbed a small golden cordial from inside his sash. He drank it. Before their eyes, the stab from Reika sewed shut as did Junayd's cut from earlier.

Junayd recovered and landed a heavy energy-infused fist to

Welk's gut. Welk staggered backwards, falling to his knees, leaning on his sword.

"Such a pity," Welk said. "You would have been a great asset to me." "It's over now. Don't bother fighting anymore," Junayd said.

Welk smirked, pushing Junayd to the ground with a fiery blast before striking Zane to the floor with his foot. The limb impaled Zane at the hip, knocking him to the floor, shrieking in pain. Zane attempted to reverse the damage done to him as he did with Julius, but before he could, Welk smacked Zane with the back of his hand, knocking him unconscious.

Welk had had enough.

Junayd struggled to his feet, though this was short-lived as Welk punched him in the stomach before kicking him across the room. Reika watched in horror. She fired an icy blast at Welk, who used a barrier to deflect it back at her at a high speed. The young woman wasn't that lucky and was frozen solid by the spell.

"I think there is only one kind of death that is befitting of you," Welk said. Welk raised his left hand in the air and a small electrical storm encircled his hand. "To oblivion you go!" He fired the small storm at Junayd. The young man was struggling to get out of the way. Reika managed to break free of the ice, using fire to melt it, splitting the ice asunder.

"Junayd!" Reika called as she sped through the air toward Junayd, pushing him to safety. The stormy blast pushed Reika away from Junayd, knocking her to the floor and causing her to roll over and over. Junayd was in shock and unable to pull himself to his feet. Reika lay there, motionless.

"Hadn't counted on that, but still, a consolation prize for me..." Welk said.

The two monkeys pulled themselves to their feet. Melito saw Welk heading towards Reika's lifeless body.

Tabitha fired an arrow at Welk. The creature reacted, using his sword to deflect the arrow.

Melito summoned his axe, charging with unbridled rage. Its glow was as fiery as his temper. Tabitha fired more shots to distract

Welk, allowing Melito to get closer. The marmoset brought his axe down, only for Welk to counter with his blade just in time. The scorpion launched a kick at Melito, forcing the marmoset to the floor. "Perhaps you'll die like a dog, or maybe you should suffer like your father?"

Melito roared.

Zane awoke slowly. He stretched out his hand, causing the time around his body to reverse, healing the damage until he was fully recovered. His breathing was ragged; he spluttered as though his lungs were full of phlegm. In truth, it was merely exhaustion.

He got to his feet, forming an icicle of magical power, and he threw it at Welk. It plunged into the dark king's back, but still was not deep enough to kill him. The creature winced and disappeared in a dark vapour, leaving the group behind and the icicle shattered on the floor. Melito got up, his axe vanishing from view.

"WHERE IS HE! I'LL KILL HIM!"

"He's not coming back. Calm down," Zane said as he was trying to restrain Melito.

"Don't tell me to calm down. Look at her!" Melito said, pointing to Reika. "Killing him won't solve anything, Melito. Let me take a look."

Melito pulled Zane away from Reika. "You've done enough! I could have hounded him and slain him there and then but no, you tell me to go back to the future."

"Then consider what I'm doing as my amends to you..."

"Surely you, with your foresight, would know the future?" Melito said.

"I can't see that far. My foresight is limited. For that matter, I didn't realise Welk would be this powerful."

Tabitha sensed something was wrong and made her way over.

Zane crouched to feel Reika's head. Despite her eyes being open, it was as though she were dead. Zane could sense something strange. "She's... fine."

Melito shook his head. "Do her eyes look like the eyes of someone taking a nap?"

Zane glared at Melito in anger. "If you would let me finish, her *body* is fine. But her mind has completely gone to another realm." Melito's anger subsided, turning into confusion. "Her mind is gone?"

Tabitha then gasped. "Where has it disappeared to?" She asked. Zane stoop up. "I have seen that technique before, but not like this." "What is it?" Melito asked.

"It's a form of elf magic called Rasgar." "Rasgar?"

"Very dangerous spells." "You know how to use one?"

"One variant of it yes, Seele Rasgar. It is for exorcism of evil spirits, allowing me to tear the spirit out of the possessed."

"Well, that's something," Melito said. "What was used on Reika?" "Verstand Rasgar. It tears the *mind* of a person out of their body and places it in a realm known as Somnium Carcerum." Melito was shocked.

"So is her mind running around there?" Tabitha asked.

"Yes. I cannot reverse the damage done to Reika and retrieve her mind, not even with my magic."

Zane paced about, his expression increasingly puzzled and desperate. "It's strange. Rasgars are not something the elves would teach to anyone unless they deemed the person trustworthy. Krea must have taught Welk how to use them. In his hands, it's destructive."

Melito could only postulate why he had been spared such a fate. "Must have been recent, otherwise, he could have done the same to me if he wished. Even now he didn't as I was considered too weak... to him anyway."

"I should have known he would become this powerful. How foolish I was. I should apologise."

The marmoset then pressed on to the present matter at hand. "Can we restore Reika to normal, Zane?"

"It's possible, First, we must take her to Antonius. Then we'll plan how to get her back."

Melito picked up Reika in his arms. *I am glad we have an airship, or else how long would it take?* He turned his attention to

Zane. "If there is a way to get Reika back, consider yourself forgiven. But for now, what will you do?"

"I need to go back to Berinon and Rian. They may need my help. Get the *Coeptus* to us as soon as you can." "Take care, Zane."

The young man saw Junayd, lying on the ground in pain. Zane crouched and reversed the damage done to him. Junayd eventually rose to his feet.

"Where's Reika?" He asked. He saw her in Melito's arms, who was walking with Tabitha towards the doors.

"I'll explain later," Zane said. "I need you to come with me, Junayd. Let's see how Berinon and Rian are doing."

Berinon and Rian had made their way around the tower down into the basement. It resembled that of an old inn's cellar though no barrels were present. Akins was held in the used rope that Berinon stolen.

"Move it!" Rian said. Akins reluctantly made his way down the stairs. "You are making a serious mistake about this," he said, locking his eyes with Rian disdainfully. Rian responded by smacking Akins with the back of his left hand. "Just stand over there, you pipsqueak." The elf shoved him against the wall near the bottom of the steps.

There were several crates stacked up against the wall. Berinon opened one of the crates, finding only more copies of the Anodyne Stone lying inside like smooth pebbles on a beach.

"Will you help us destroy these or not?"

Akins refused to answer. Rian just scowled, leaving the scorpion sulking in the corner of the room. He kept his eyes on Akins to ensure he didn't try to run.

"Just burn the crates," Rian said. Berinon was about to reach for a torch on the wall when he could hear footsteps. "What's going on down there?" a voice called.

"Intruders!" Akins called. "They're trying to destroy the fake stones!"

The guards pounded down the stairs, eleven making it into the room, though Rian and Berinon could hear more upstairs; fifty-one men ready to kill. One led Akins away up the stairs.

The tallest guard grinned at Berinon and Rian, who were without armour. "Before you die, is there anything you like to say?"

No response came.

"Silent...? Then we won't say anything either." Berinon summoned his lance, facing the enemies in front of him. The guards fanned out from the stairs.

Berinon slashed at the stomach of the tall guard and performed an upwards cut towards another. Rian fired rapidly three bullets at three of the scorpions, one for each and killing them. Three guards closed in, more wary than the first wave.

Berinon and Rian drew side by side, pausing. They could hear some clashing upstairs.

Berinon smirked. "I know who that is."

The three guards in front of he and Rian dismissed the noise, charging suddenly. Rian fired on two of the guards, with Berinon swinging the lance and cutting down the third, leaving them all dead on the floor. Rian grabbed a torch from the wall and threw it onto the crates. The fire spread like a remorseless beast, consuming the fake stones, melting them and burning the crates. Before Berinon and Rian headed up the stairs, another guard tumbled down them, then leapt up, evidently surprised, and delighted that his neck had not been broken in the process. It was short-lived as an icy ball smashed into his skull, knocking him out. The two men fled from the inferno blazing behind them.

Berinon and Rian saw more guards were retreating down the corridor when an icy cloud appeared, freezing some of the scorpions in its proximity while knocking others off-balance.

The ice receded as a bending of space revealed Zane and Junayd. Berinon smiled. "Good timing, Zane."

"The airship is nearby, hurry. Some of the patrols are gone but more troops will arrive." As the four men were making their way down the corridor, they found Akins alone and unbound from the ropes. Rian and he exchanged a long look, then the elf turned and left him there. He had made his choice. Rian reloaded the revolver with break necked speed as he ran.

More guards arrived, barring their path. Rian hesitated for a moment before he began to fire upon the scorpions. "They never learn that bullets can penetrate their hide," he said in an exasperated tone.

Berinon charged, pushing the scorpions back with the lance, causing them to back off with his superior reach. They tried to encircle Berinon, an unsuccessful attempt, as he unleashed an orange shockwave at them, which burned their exoskeleton flesh, adding a vile odour of sulphur to the air, which lingered.

Zane soon found himself surrounded by another six, countering every punch and kick of the scorpions with unmatched precision, predicting the attacks from all sides. But he was tired from the fight with Welk, he slipped up for a moment and one of the scorpion's claws made a small tear in his left arm. Zane winced for a moment though he managed to heal the wound even as he lashed out in retaliation. A small glob of pus-like substance pushed its way out of the wound before it closed. Where the poison fell on the floor it hissed and sizzled.

"Don't let their stingers or claws get you, we'll be dead in minutes if we are not careful!" Zane called. Junayd took out two of the scorpions that encircled Zane, and Berinon killed two more. Zane got the upper hand, and the final two fell by his sword. The tower was clear and the only scorpions inside it were dead save for Akins who was now nowhere to be found.

"These creatures are persistent," Junayd said. The *Coeptus* flew over to the tower and Lawrence flung a ladder close to the window where Zane and the others were standing. Zane climbed up, followed by Berinon, Rian, and finally, Junayd. As soon as Junayd made it on board, Ulric piloted the *Coeptus* away from the barracks and Lawrence swiftly pulled up the ladder.

Akins watched the airship fly away from the barracks from outside, alongside his brethren.

～

On the airship, Melito and Junayd sat next to the bed Reika was lying on. "I'm sorry," Junayd said quietly. Melito turned his eyes upwards to look at Junayd.

"You serious? How is this your fault?" He blurted out.

"We all fought against Welk Seha and got overwhelmed. He has become stronger since last time. I have been defeated and because of my weakness, Reika is like this."

Melito stood up and shook Junayd. "Get a grip, listen to yourself. It wasn't your fault. If anything, *I* should have killed him back when we were in the past, but he escaped. I was angry with Zane, but he made an honest mistake." Melito let go of Junayd and backed away. "You held me and Tabitha to account and rightly so for not staying close to Reika. Why beat yourself up when you weren't able to help to begin with?"

"She pushed me out the way of a spell that Welk fired, and she got hit instead."

"Do you know why I am not as upset as you think I would be? Because there is a way to get her back, as Zane said."

Junayd said no more for the rest of the trip.

～

Antonius was inside his floating castle, when suddenly he heard the door burst open. Junayd entered carrying Reika in his arms. The group ran over to Antonius.

"Explain what has happened," he said. If he was bothered by them barging in, he didn't show it.

Melito, Tabitha, and Junayd made their way to the bedroom after bringing Antonius up to speed. Junayd placed Reika gently on the bed. Antonius entered the room briskly, striding with a look of determination on his face. He placed his hands gently on Reika's forehead.

"Are you able to tell us what she is up to?" Junayd asked. Antonius nodded.

"Yes. Any good news I'll give it to you. However, I must ask you to take that miserable look off your face."

A glow surrounded Antonius' hands. Tabitha watched, biting her bottom lip. Melito retained a calm demeanour as he watched what was happening in front of him.

Chapter 12

Somnium Carcerum

R eika awoke on a grassy plain. She sat up. Her eyes began to focus. She saw the grass perfectly but noticed something was wrong. She found herself on a floating rock, seeing many rocks floating around her as well, some completely stationary despite being suspended in air. The sky was a mixture dark, black, purple and grey colours. *Where am I?* she thought. *What is this weird place? Am I dead?*

Reika moved to the edge of the rock to see if there was another place she could get to, and lo and behold there was, many metres below. *Good thing I can fly, I'd hate to fall into that abyss below. Need to jump down to that platform.* Reika leapt off the edge, allowing herself to fall like at Antonius' Castle, bringing her descent to a halt to land safely.

"Junayd! Tabs, Melito, Zane! Anyone!" No answer came. "HEEEEEY!" Reika yelled at the top of her lungs. Her voice merely echoed in the abyss. "Where are you all? Is there a way out of here?"

She saw what appeared to be a stone panel. Stepping onto it, a dark orb surrounded her and she disappeared, only to reappear at another panel, further away. Despite some level of confusion, Reika ran to the east of the small rock, jumping to one that was close by, reaching the other teleporter which took her even further away to a small cluster of rocks. She leapt across them one by one, occasionally flying to the next one. "What place is this?"

She at last came across what appeared to be a shiny blue stone embedded in the ground. Voices could be heard coming from it and Reika investigated the stone.

"We can't leave her like this, I still feel it's my fault she is in a coma."

Reika looked bewildered. "Coma? Am I in one? But if so, what connection does this place have to that?"

Reika's head started to feel faint. "Ugh, what's happening to me. I have to get moving."

What felt like hours passed as Reika explored more floating rocks. Even with the ability to fly, she feared she might faint and fall endlessly, unable to return. She still pressed on, eventually finding an island that had a small tunnel enabling her to venture inside the rock. Reika felt exhausted, even after many respites from her flying. For the time being she felt safe but knew she had to find a way out and eventually jumped down the hole next to her to another island below.

A small structure caught her attention, and she made her way to the island where the structure was. She approached it with trepidation and found a red orb sitting on a podium. Reika touched the orb, hearing a cracking noise followed by a rumble. The floor gave way and Reika went down with the floor, landing on sand below.

She winced as she was feeling the side of her chest. She tried to levitate out of the hole but couldn't. Her powers were blocked. She saw a rune above her head inscribed with the word *nil*, exactly the same as the rune Heston held.

Down in the hole, there was another inert teleport panel. Reika wondered if she could find anything else that would enable her escape. She dug her hands into the sand, searching every nook and cranny meticulously.

A skeleton rose out of the sand behind her. Reika spun around, gasping. The skeleton was human sized, its robes tattered and torn. The skeleton roared at Reika, trying to grab her. Reika stumbled to her feet, then saw two more skeletons rise from the sand, also wearing tattered robes. Reika wasted no time trying to search for the means to escape. They continued their clumsy assault, trying to claw her with talon-like fingers. Reika panicked, frantically trying to find any kind of door handle or lock.

Her fingers brushed an ornate, round brick embedded in the floor. Reika brought her hand down hard on it, activating the teleporter. She ran towards the panel, but one of the skeletons grabbed her by the leg and pulled her away from it, pressing against her back with his foot. Reika attempted to pull herself along the ground, but the skeleton was too strong. A small light emanated from the teleporter, knocking the skeleton that was on Reika's back onto the dirt. Reika picked herself up again, dashing into the teleporter, finding herself outside the structure that she had investigated.

She watched a brief glass sheen like light disappear. It looked like a magic shield of some kind.

Reika spotted another island, this one containing a small tunnel. She leapt onto it and found herself in a small cavern. A dark blue portal was just lying there. Reika investigated the hole, approaching it with caution. She stepped into it and the room began to warp and bend around her. The environment changed as she found herself in her old room at Carthage's citadel, albeit unnaturally dark. She approached the window of her room, seeing the night sky and the familiar courtyard before her.

"Why am I back in my bedroom? I have to keep moving, but where is the exit? Unless...?" In the common room in Carthage, a teleporter stood at the edge of the room near a stack of crates, allowing one to leave the castle for an easy escape in an emergency. Did the one that Reika was thinking about exist here? Or was this a fabrication of this realm? Reika started to feel weak again, but knew she had no time to give up.

Searching her bedroom first, overturning everything, she found faint white balls of light, all floating. She headed to the common room to search for more, overturning more tables, removing pictures from the wall, opening a clock, looking under a chair and other places to find more lights. Their energy reacted with the teleporter in the room. Reika wondered if there was a place she hadn't looked and then she remembered, The Carthagian Citadel had a large swimming pool bordered by cobblestone. It was indeed a large and deep one, complete with bathing pools for one to wash in. Reika found herself in the room with the pool and without hesitation dived into it. She made her way through the water, looking for the light. She spotted it and touched it like the others.

Quickly she swam to the surface, exited the pool, and made her way back up the stairs, stepping onto the teleporter, finding herself back in the very place that took her to the room. Afterwards, the portal vanished. Reika's anger grew and bashed her fist against the floor. Another hole in the ground had caught her eye and without a thought, she leapt into the hole.

Reika landed her feet gracefully on the floor. She found herself in another room which had marble walls with silver stone flooring; the border of the stonework was golden. She spotted another stone exactly like the one she'd found earlier that enabled her to listen to a conversation between her friends.

"How is Reika?" Tabitha asked.

"She seems to be hanging in there. She must be trying to escape," Junayd responded.

"Antonius, will Reika get out?" Melito asked.

"Those inside the Somnium Carcerem are trapped there. The chances of escape are minimal," Antonius answered.

Reika paused. "Somnium Carcerem? What is he.... Wait, I know... Antonius told me about this place. It's where sorcerers are punished. It would explain how I briefly entered my bedroom. This place built a room based on my memories. Built... from me." Reika then remembered what'd happened to her: she was hit by an electrical blast from Welk Seha. "That spell? It wasn't a death spell, it banished me here."

"Can't Reika just teleport her way out if she had the power?" Junayd enquired.

"Even if she could teleport, she couldn't use it to get out," Antonius replied. "And her mind? What will become of it if she doesn't leave Somnium Carcerem?"

"Eventually, Reika if she lingers there for too long... her mind will fade away and disappear."

Reika's eyes widened and she started to tremble. *This is bad, I shouldn't be here.*

"...assuming she hasn't been killed first or hasn't found a place there where she can keep her mind from vanishing."

"What! We have to get her out of there. We can't just leave Reika to die."

Reika looked away from the voice-stone. She was about to leave the room when she heard Junayd talking to her. "Reika, I don't know if you can hear me. You saved me from going to Somnium Carcerem and it's just incredible that you would do that. We have only known each other for a while. But over our journey, I have come to realise one thing... I..." He choked. "It's hard for me to say..." Reika listened intently. "I..."

Unfortunately for Reika, Junayd's voice faded out. "I *what?* What were you going to say? Junayd?" She despaired in her soul. "Junayd, I am glad I stopped you from coming here, you don't want to feel what I am feeling right now."

Suddenly, Reika could a voice in her head, a gentle but deep one. "My child, what are you doing in this place?"

Reika stood up instantly. "Who said that?"

"A young one like you shouldn't be sent to Somnium Carcerem. It's a place for serious offenders."

"You... can hear me?" Reika asked, with an earnest hopeful tone.

"I sensed your presence when you arrived. My castle is not far from here. Come to it, but be swift about it, lest you be consumed," the voice's tone was kind yet commanding.

"Who are you if you don't mind me asking?" Reika asked. "We'll talk when you arrive. Make haste, little one."

Reika found herself alone again, but more at peace. *That voice, whoever it is, I sense he is close. Need to be cautious though.*

Reika made her way towards a hole in the ground, climbing down a ladder into a small cavern. She floated down gently onto another small island. She caught sight of a large castle in front of her, a grand-looking place. Its entire appearance shone with a navy blue finish.

She was ready to head for the door, but she collapsed onto the floor to her knees. Reika looked at her hands, the colour on her skin had started turning sooty, starting at her fingertips, spreading to the rest of her. Even worse, a few seconds after turning black, the skin evaporated, becoming like smoke, revealing her bones beneath. "No, I can't fade yet, not now."

She felt the left side of her face and instead of finding warm tissue, she felt bone that gradually grew cold. Reika was terrified. She couldn't say anything, nothing emanated from her throat. A man watching from one of the castle windows made a gesture to someone, telling them to go down to the dying woman.

Reika made her way to the door fast, each passing moment feeling more of herself slipping away, each moment getting weaker. She finally made it to the door. It opened to her but as she burst through it was as if she had stepped into absolute darkness; her sight had vanished along with her hearing. Finally, Reika collapsed once again, crawling, losing all strength.

A small dragon being, a drake, rushed to Reika's side as she lay there, lifeless. Though the drake was diminutive for one of his kind, his Aegean body was well built, with great muscle mass. Two horns on his head bent backwards on the top of his head. He shut the door to the castle without hesitation. He stood over Reika's skeletal form. "Come on young one, you cannot succumb to this." His right hand glowed a familiar colour, and he placed it on her ribcage.

Antonius knew something was wrong, though he said nothing to Junayd. Part of him felt guilty for not disclosing Reika's condition, the possibility of her mind being lost was something he knew Junayd couldn't bear.

Junayd tightened his fists, his heart beating rapidly, He'd never felt this way about someone he knew, let alone someone he had met so recently. He saw the concerns on Melito and Tabitha's faces respectively; they too were perturbed.

Floating in a dark void, Reika gradually woke up. She could see the weredragon coming towards her. She found herself in the grasp of the abomination; it was trying to wrestle the life out of her. Reika strained against the might of the creature. Over time, she started to feel weaker, the seconds dragged as her vision was on the verge of blurring.

An image of the moon appeared in front of her. Reika's strength grew, her vision returning along with it. She grabbed hold of the arms of the weredragon, pushing them off and threw a swift punch, causing the weredragon to be thrown far. Reika stared at her hands, amazed. Looking once again at the weredragon, she saw it had recovered, preparing to lunge at her.

Reika could respond to the speed of the weredragon. She spun around in a sideways twist, allowing it to pass her. She then summoned a lightning blast, firing it into the weredragon's spine. It shrieked in pain. Reika beheld a light that was shining above her, closing fast. She flew towards the light as fast as she could. The weredragon followed, grabbing Reika by the right leg, pulling her down. Now, the weredragon flew towards the light.

The young woman wouldn't give up, also reaching up and grabbing the creature's right leg, throwing it down to the void below, following it up with one final attack. A small electric surge flashed from her left hand and with a mighty crackle, the surge shot from the hand, crashing into the weredragon, knocking it out cold, leaving it to float into the void. Reika shot back to the light before it vanished. After only ten seconds, she contacted the light and was consumed.

Reika's body began to regenerate in the same way it had disappeared, only in reverse. As soon as Reika was fully restored, she breathed a huge lungful of air, coughing heavily. She got to her feet, her strength returning. She looked at the strange dragon-beast next to her.

"Who are you?"

"Galeru, at your service," the drake said in a calm voice. "Strange you do not seem shocked my presence."

"I figured you wouldn't hurt me. A voice beckoned me here to safety. You must serve him, right?" Reika said.

"True," replied Galeru, "You're far too trusting. Nevertheless, your conclusion is correct."

The dragon set off and Reika followed. She noticed the interior was very similar to that of Antonius' Castle. The halls here, however, lacked light, except for dim refractions. She caught sight of a teleporter in front of her. *I can't use it to leave here, can I?* Reika thought. *Maybe due to the fact my mind is here.* Galeru knew why she arrived in this world, but remained silent.

"That stone panel isn't the way out anyway, so it will not help you in that regard," the voice said again.

Reika looked up. "Where are you?"

"Go the panel, it will take you upstairs. I shall meet you."

"Do as he says," Galeru said. "My master will not hurt you; he is very kind." Reika stepped onto the teleporter, a similar dark orb from earlier enclosed her and when it subsided, she found herself in a much small room.

Reika could see a man by the window of his room. She ambled towards the man but halted a few feet away, overtaken by a sudden feeling of uncertainty. Galeru's words went round in her mind: *You're far too trusting.*

"So, you have been sent to Somnium Carcerem?" He said.

Reika was uncertain what to think about the man standing in front of her and gently replied "Who are you?"

The man turned, revealing his face. He was human, with short brown hair, though flecks of grey were present. He had a broad chin, decent muscle mass, and wore long robes, like Antonius' robes though with dark and light blues. His blue eyes, however, were reptilian.

"You're a dragon as well?" Reika said.

"Correct. My name is Gorvenal. I am the guardian of this place. Sorcerers of all stripes who commit serious violations are banished here, to essentially fade and never return. It was built as a prison by the gods and is the common place to send a sorcerer's mind as punishment for their misdeeds—if there is no repentance or amends made."

He approached Reika gently. The old man respected her space as to not intimidate her, and to reassure her he had no wicked intention. "Since you became a sorceress the only offences you have committed mostly boiled down to rather rude conduct toward an elder and a prophetess. Both of which you promptly apologised for. You shouldn't be here unless you refused to acknowledge your bad decorum."

Reika at once felt at ease. "Is there a way for me to leave this place? I am unconscious, my body is back at Antonius' Castle. My mind is trapped here, and I don't know the way out."

"No one leaves except on my authority and at my discretion," Gorvenal replied. "In light of your innocence, I am willing to carry your mind to the exit."

Reika beamed. Her smile was short-lived as she noticed Gorvenal clearly was perturbed. "What's wrong?"

Gorvenal faced away from Reika, crossing his arms behind his back. "If I can save you from desolation, unlike the rest who were sent here over the years, that will grant me ease."

"Others?"

"Other innocents, they were afflicted with the curse that you have."

Reika's eyebrows rose. Gorvenal directed his gaze back to Reika once again. "This curse has existed for nine hundred and fifty-eight years. It was halted for six hundred and forty-nine years. It has claimed many victims. Many sent here were afflicted by it, mostly individuals your age. Luckily, you were sent close to my castle. Verstand Rasgar was used on you. It's a judicial spell designed to send an individual's mind to here to be consumed. But..." Gorvenal then looked intensely into Reika's own eyes. "You are aware the weredragon has a mind of its own. If one such as you were to fade from existence, the weredragon will take your place."

"As in?"

"When you disappear, the weredragon doesn't. This realm has a terrible fate for the minds who venture here without the proper means: a dwelling such as this."

He lifted his hands up, then simulated a ripping motion. "Rip the human mind from their body, it ceases to exist in this realm and the weredragon remains. It's that simple."

"What of those horrid skeletons? Is that what I would have become?" Reika asked.

Galeru entered the room. "That would have been the case. Your mind would have transformed into a foul entity known as a Tentorian. Mindless and soulless creatures that can neither live nor die. They have no identity to speak of, and care only about adding to their number. Had you not entered the castle when you did, in a few minutes you would have become like them." Reika felt sick to her stomach. Her usually charming face was screwed up as if she had been fed bile. "The problem is..." Gorvenal continued. "Though those who make it through those doors can be restored by Galeru, I cannot get to the other innocents to rescue them. Both Galeru and I are imprisoned here thanks to the efforts of Destrian. We cannot venture outside of a mile of this place. His victims are far away from me. I compelled you to come here where you would be safe." Reika felt like the situation was quite hopeless, but Gorvenal was not done. "Stay put,

I'll have the one who wields the Draco Ferrum come here to help you. *He* shall help you escape."

Reika was pleased by the news. However, she couldn't shake off a nagging thought. "Won't he fade away?"

"No. He will not suffer the effects when his mind and body are in this realm together. If only his mind was sent here, then he would be in trouble. The stones of this castle provide that protection to the mind."

Reika smiled again. "I didn't say this before but thank you for saving me. Both of you."

Gorvenal inclined his head, his eyes looking as if he were reminiscing. "Thank you... That's something no one has said to me for a while." He then went back to peer outside the window as he did before. "Stay here until Junayd arrives."

"Ok..." said Reika in an anxious manner. "But if he takes too long, won't I die?"

"While you remain in this castle, your mind will stay intact. Your body will not age at all. All things are in stasis, no decay will befall it while you are still here."

"Is there any way to set you both free?"

"The Anodyne Stone," Gorvenal said, smiling. "It will set us free by breaking the seal that has only been placed on us two."

Junayd waited on the other side. *Hang in there, Reika.*

Antonius recoiled away from Reika's head, as if some energy had forced him back. "Aha, she's safe at Gorvenal's Castle."

Junayd was ecstatic. He tried to contain himself. "He's in charge of Somnium Carcerem right?"

"Correct. Reika is residing there. I can't teleport you inside the building, but I can send you there."

"Just my mind or me?"

"Better to send you wholesale. I can send you to the specific region where Gorvenal is. Hurry and get Reika back."

Junayd gave a thumbs up. "I understand, I shall return."

Antonius opened a small black hole, a dark whirlpool. As Junayd jumped in, it whisked him away to Somnium Carcerem itself.

The black hole reappeared in quite another realm, then shrank to nothingness, leaving Junayd near a pair of castle gates. He entered the castle as fast as he could, rushing to the teleporter, sending himself into Gorvenal's room. He made his way over to where Reika was, but restrained himself from hugging her; instead, he kept his composure as he advanced.

"Lord Gorvenal?" He then asked.

Reika was happy to see Junayd as well. Gorvenal walked to where Reika was and stood next to her. "Junayd, my dear boy, you have arrived even sooner than I thought."

Before Junayd could speak, they heard bellows and roars echoing outside the castle. Each of the roars were different. Junayd summoned his blade ready to fight.

"What was that?" Reika asked, trying to stay calm.

"Weredragons. They are on their way here, they sense the Ferrum. You must retreat from here now. Junayd, there is an exit for the both of you. I'll accompany you to it."

Junayd was confused. "I got here both in body and mind, what happens if Reika goes through the door?"

"Her mind will return to her body," Gorvenal spoke while he quickly strode to the teleporter. The other two followed. "We must leave now before it's too late," Gorvenal turned to his servant. "Galeru, defend the castle. I'll return after I have escorted these two."

Galeru accepted his master's command, cracking his knuckles. "Time for these abominations to face a real dragon." Reika and Junayd promptly followed Gorvenal out of the castle.

The three were transported to a large rock half a mile away from the castle. It looked just like the others Reika had seen, but ahead was a door that glowed brightly like the sun. Junayd turned to look behind him and caught sight of the weredragons in the distance.

Gorvenal's body glowed and changed into his dragon form, a sight to behold it was. His form was roughly eighteen feet long, had a robust musculature, a broad tail, grey scales and sharp blue eyes. His wings were folded away on his back, it was a hard to gauge how large the wings were. Reika was awestruck and trembled at the sight.

"Head for the portal both of you!" Gorvenal commanded them. "I'll hold them off."

Reika and Junayd had no time to spare. Junayd grabbed her hand, feeling no resistance to his touch, and the two pelted for the portal. Junayd soon lifted off the ground, flying faster to the portal, and with that, he and Reika dived into the light. There was a blinding flash and Junayd found himself on the floor of bedroom in Antonius' Castle.

Melito and Tabitha were there, smiling.

"You made it back. Well done!" Antonius said.

"Thanks," Junayd said. He eyed the room, somewhat puzzled. "Where's Reika? We both went through the portal together."

"That was Reika's *mind* you were speaking to. Gorvenal told you that already, didn't he? It's back in her body now. She needs rest," Antonius replied. Reika, lying on the bed, strained to open her eyes. She attempted to move, but her limbs did not obey her.

"Whe... mm I?" She slurred. "Can't... move..."

"You are exhausted. Please rest," Antonius said to her. "If you'll excuse me for a while, I'll get an elixir to speed her recovery. Don't talk to her too much."

The wizard left them.

Junayd approached the bed, kneeling to Reika's eye level on the bed. She feebly turned her head towards Junayd. Though it was faint, he could tell she was smiling back at him.

"You ok...? I am so sorry; I was too weak to fight him. If it wasn't for me, you wouldn't be like this," Junayd uttered, holding back tears in shame.

"You... saved me..." Reika said. "I could hear... your voice."
"Thanks... I don't want this to happen again. You rest up, ok?"
"Yep..." She smiled back weakly at the two metazoans.

Junayd moved from the bed to the door.

"I think I know what you were going to say now..." Reika said.
"Say what?" Junayd asked.

No answer was forthcoming, as Reika had fallen asleep.

I'd better leave her for now, Junayd thought, leaving the
bedroom. He caught sight of Antonius, who was in a low stance,
preparing to fight someone.

"Who is out there?" Melito asked.

"It's an elf. Stay where you are, he's dangerous!"

They agreed and stayed with Reika. Junayd ran over to Antonius. He instantly knew it was the same man Reika had talked to
him about in Caledonia, Lief.

"Of all the places to hide Reika, how interesting," the elf said.

"*You...* What are you doing here?" Antonius asked.

"Reika, that witch you have here, is your pupil? An airship was
reported to have headed away from the Entellan Islands. Their
barracks suffered from a terrible fire. It was quite easy to follow if
you know how. Besides, Welk told me what he did to her. A pity his
work has been undone. Perhaps I should try to re- do it myself."
The elf smiled nastily.

I should have known, Junayd thought.

"So, are you going to hand her to me, or should I remove her by
force?" the elf went on.

"I will not hand Reika to you!" Antonius snapped. Lief smirked
back at the wizard.

"Suit yourself, dotard." Lief summoned a hefty icicle-shaped
blade. He leapt toward Antonius, slashing the old man across the
chest. Antonius collapsed on his knees.

"ANTONIUS!" Junayd shouted.

"I'll be fine... Just a scratch," Antonius said, slightly grimacing.
"I underestimated him."

Junayd stepped between Antonius and Lief. "Reika told me

about you. I thought Visiert captured you after you turned Reika into the weredragon in my hometown?" Junayd bared his teeth in anger.

"Ooh, somebody give you a full reward!" Lief said mockingly. "Visiert should have killed me when he had the chance. It is silly not to take precautions when locking a sorcerer in his cell. It was helpful being able to escape under a veil of illusion."

Junayd was a little puzzled, but he continued speaking anyway. "If you are after Reika, you can forget it. She is staying with me," Junayd said, as he drew the Ferrum.

"She has no choice. All I need is the moonlight and that's enough for me to control her." Lief seemed unfazed by what the mighty youth had said.

Bright grey energy flowed from the elf's fingertips once again, snaking into the bedroom. Melito and Tabitha saw Reika wake up from her sleep with reptilian eyes and a dark wispy cloud surrounding her. Her transformation into the weredragon was underway. Junayd heard a roar emanate from behind the room's door and Reika burst through into the hallway.

"Don't waste your time talking to her, she is under my control now," Lief uttered.

How many times must I fight with this creature? Junayd thought. The dragon charged towards Junayd, attempting to slash him with razor-sharp claws. Junayd dodged and parried the attacks with his blade. He swung his leg under Reika's, tripping her up and knocking her to the ground. Reika bounced back, grabbing Junayd by the neck, forcing him to the ground in return. Junayd didn't stay down long. He managed to wrench her off him, pushing her hands away from his throat. However, like a stubborn stain, she didn't go away, promptly pinning him to the ground again.

Reika's jaws widened ready to bite off his head. Junayd quickly pushed against her mouth with his hands. With all his strength, he finally threw Reika off, standing to his feet. He launched a final uppercut to her jaw. Reika somersaulted into the air, before landing on her spine. The weredragon form peeled away with Reika finally back to normal as the moonlight left her body.

She staggered to her feet. "You ok?" Junayd asked.

"Urgh, my head... What happened?" Reika asked, rubbing her head. "The moon? It's not even fully out." She then remembered the spell that had been used on her in Caledonia.

Lief's smile had faltered. He'd hoped Reika's transformation would cause more chaos. *I can't use the spell again, the weredragon will be unconscious for twenty-four hours.*

Junayd looked concernedly at Reika. "Reika, you're exhausted, step down." "Agreed."

"She's safe for now," the elf conceded. "But what of your friends back on the ship?" With that, and one final smirk, he disappeared. Antonius finally rose but had to lean against a nearby pillar for support. Junayd and Reika walked to the old man.

"He hits hard," the wizard said, grimacing. "Your friends on the ship, they need your help."

"What about you?" Junayd asked.

"I'll be fine. The armour I'm wearing stopped the blow from being deadly," Antonius replied. "You must get back to the ship."

Antonius gave Reika a small, gold bottle. "Drink it," he said.

Reika did, and felt her strength return instantly. She and Junayd ran outside to the *Coeptus*. Antonius went to his bed to rest.

A familiar face materialised from the shadows. "Visiert," Antonius said.

"I'll get you to the council, you'll recover there where it's safe." "But your rune, it's energy is running low..."

"It's got enough to last for a while," Visiert said.

Gorvenal still had his own problems with the weredragons. Some he had slain but others overwhelmed his defences. *Too many, I must retreat.*

Gorvenal flew quickly back to his palace with the weredragons chasing him. He transformed back into his humanoid form, flew through the door, and landed on his feet with a thud. Galeru shut the door in haste and bound it shut with a spell. A weredragon snarled at door. It slammed its fist against the door in frustration and then left. They would abandon their mission for now, leaving the dragon sorcerer alone.

"If only the others could be saved!" He said to Galeru, gritting his teeth in frustration.

The drake did not know what to say. "Doubtful, master. How could they possibly escape from this grisly fate while we are stuck here and can't go beyond the surrounding mile?"

"If the stone is found, then we can destroy the seal."

Chapter 13

Illumination

Junayd and Reika, ignoring the brightness of the morning sun, arrived at the ship which was parked near Antonius' citadel. They soared up onto the deck and saw Zane, Berinon, and Rian standing ready to fight. Lief stood in opposition, confident despite being outnumbered. Zane held his sword ready to defend himself.

Reika squinted. The elf looked familiar. Putting this together with the spell that'd had been worked on her previously, it all came together in her head. "You! The elf from the inn in Bahaduro!" Reika yelled.

"Oh, so you finally remembered me? Well at least I will not bother with an introduction," Lief said.

"You gave the vials of elixirs to that cockatrice, didn't you?" Berinon said. "I admire your deduction," Lief said. "A pity that your fighting prowess

doesn't match that in my mind."

Rian raised his gun high, firing a scattershot of bullets at Lief. The elf merely deflected the bullets with a barrier.

"Krea taught you well, didn't she?" Rian remarked.

"She did. Unfortunately, you will not live to see her show her full strength, especially after your betrayal."

"I have my reasons for turning against her. None of which is your concern boy," Rian said, making no attempt to cover up who hired him. The others were impressed by his honesty.

Lief pointed at Reika. "Now, if you would be so kind as hand Reika over, I'll be on my way."

Junayd stepped in front of Reika. "You'll do no such thing."

"Fine then... Oh, about your airship, your engines were made by the golems of Budúcnosť, quite powerful engines in addition to the potent fuel in them. Should I fire on them, this ship will be completely incinerated and you all with it." Lief looked directly at Reika. "Should you or others escape, your master will die."

Reika scowled back at him. *I would never want to see Antonius get hurt.*

Lief produced a small rune in his palm that housed the image of a cloud, holding it high in the air. Zane's suddenly felt a sharp pain in his head. Visions flooded his mind, confusing him. He knelt on the ground clutching his head, overwhelmed. A moment later the young man unconscious. *That little rune of mine should keep you from meddling,* Lief thought, *as long as it is within a twenty-foot radius, it will mess with your foresight.*

As he turned to look away and continue his address, Lief felt a fiery blast at his back. It did very little damage, washing over his magical defences. When he turned, he saw it was Reika who had attacked him. He grew irritated. As she tried to fire a ray of light at him, Lief held up his hand to absorb the ray. Reika froze in place, alarmed.

"Pick a fight with me, will you?" Lief spat. "Pity, you are not a challenge like Visiert." He sneered at Reika. Lief fired a lightning blast towards Reika, who summoned a barrier to deflect it, she and the others contained within it. Lief arched his eyebrows. *Heh, this will be easy. That barrier cannot stand against my spell for long.*

A portal opened and Visiert shot through, punching Lief away from Reika. The elf leapt out of Visiert's grasp and kicked the knight to the deck, winding him. The elf dropped the rune he used on Zane. Reika's barrier was removed shortly after. Berinon grabbed hold of the rune Lief had used and with energy in his hand, ground the rune to a fine dust.

Junayd stared at Visiert. "Who is that?" Lief growled. "You dare impede me?"

From the floor, Visiert used a rune to open a sangria-coloured portal. Lief closed it with his magic. "I'm not going through there again, Visiert. You caught me unawares before. Not so lucky this time!"

Before Lief could strike Visiert, Reika hit the elf with an electrical blast, stunning him.

For a brief moment, Lief looked disturbed, unable to regain movement and control. Reika stared at the elf.

I thought she wasn't powerful enough. How can this be? Lief thought, wincing from the pain.

Reika was somewhat surprised herself.

Lief threw off the paralysing effects with a roar. "If you want a fight, I'll give you one! Show me what you can do. How will you stand against an elf sorcerer?" Reika held her hands out in front of her. *I'm about to find out,* she thought apprehensively.

Lief shoved Reika off the *Coeptus* with a telekinetic push, and she fell toward the hard rock of the island. Reika managed to land her on her feet, only just slowing her descent enough to prevent injury. Lief leapt from the Coeptus and before Reika on the ground.

Visiert got to his feet but before he could join the fight, Lief summoned a transparent barrier around him and Reika. It shone for a moment before fading from sight. Visiert stepped forward and the barrier flashed into existence, stinging him with deep pain, intensifying the more he tried to push through. Junayd and the others likewise tried the barrier, but they could not get through. All of them exchanged dark glances. Junayd pulled the Kaleidogem from his pocket, but it was dragged by an unknown force out of his hands into Lief's, he crushed it in his hand.

"There is no escape, Reika. Give it up!" Lief cried.

The elf shot two balls of light at Reika. She called up her own barrier around her right arm, pushing it forward. The balls of light exploded across her shield. She reeled from the force of the magical attack.

Before she could recover, Lief landed a spinning kick, Reika collapsing to the floor beneath the power of the blow. Lief leapt, intending to crush her, but Reika called on a barrier for protection and retaliated with a telekinetic shove into Lief's chest that sent him sailing backwards.

Reika got to her feet. Lief was already on her. She barely dodged Lief's punches.

Visiert watched from the *Coeptus*. *She won't win, and not even with the strength I have could I conquer him this time. She needs an extra edge.*

"I want to know the truth, Lief," Reika said, dodging Lief's relentless attacks. "I turn into that monster every time the full moon is out. Welk Seha locked me in Somnium Carcerem to unleash it. All those people whose lives were destroyed just to enslave them." They stopped fighting quickly. "I want the truth!"

"The weredragons, when rightly made, can be useful slaves," Lief replied. "All it takes is dumping their hosts into Somnium Carcerum and stripping their minds away. Then the weredragon replaces the empty husk, no longer imprisoned within the individual. Placing them under a spell so they serve Krea and Destrian will be an easy task with only one mind present in the body. An army of weredragons could subdue the Consortium itself, and that is what they fear most."

Reika recoiled, finally kicked Lief backwards. The two stood opposite each other, tensed, ready for the next flurry.

"You are ok with this?"

Lief shook his head in amazement at her seeming naivety. "Years before you and I existed, weredragons were the creation of

Tahpenes. A faction of dragons and elves loyal to her used human, metazoan, and elf test subjects, turning them into monsters. Eventually, the Dragelve Consortium learnt of this and banned the practice. They banished Krea for wanting to continue creating the weredragons along with Destrian."

Reika's composure finally broke. The whole idea disgusted her. She snapped and she fired a blast of light at Lief, who countered with a dark energy beam. The two beams collided, coalescing into a mass that resembled a sun's light blinking in and out, the dark and the light melting into each other in a contest of strength. Lief was much stronger, and Reika was struck to the floor by the black beam, landing with a thud. *He's not a pushover at all. He is very dangerous, But I can't give up.* Reika thought.

She quickly bounced back, flying through the air at Lief. Her attacks came in rapid succession with Lief backing off, parrying every single one with ease.

Lief let his guard down, perhaps complacent, and Reika managed to land one solid blow, Lief stepping back quickly to avoid any more attacks. The two were at a standstill once more.

"They stopped Krea for a reason," Reika said. "They knew it was unethical and she persisted in creating them despite the practice being outlawed. Don't you see that what you are doing is evil and wrong by even associating with them?"

Lief turned his back on Reika. "What good is a soldier with a will of their own? The only downside for the myriad of hosts is that they must be old enough to be transformed. The curse couldn't manifest until you turned eighteen. It would have been better to have you from when you were a small child." Reika reeled. Lief knew her heritage. Lief had known all along. "Unfortunately, my comrades were not able to find you and one of the golems Krea hired disappeared after being given his mission. You were hidden well. But I found you eventually, chasing down a mere rumour, and now I will return you to my master Destrian."

"But why me? Why bring me into this?"

"They need you, young one. With the powers you have, once

you are a weredragon, you'll lead Destrian's armies on his behalf. You'll be the strongest of them."

Reika shook her head. "My life was ruined so I could be used? I don't even know who my parents are. The ones who raised me loved me dearly, that does not excuse what was done to me. I am an outcast with no home. I cannot serve in the citadel. I can't even have children; they would be tainted by my curse. Can you live with that, knowing you are aiding such despicable people?"

Lief was silent for a moment. His expression was hard to read. Perhaps he *was* a little troubled. Oceans seemed to churn beneath the surface of his face. "Well?" Reika said.

The elf regained his composure. "Enough of this prattle. You are going to help us whether you want to or not, even if I have to take you in."

Visiert summoned a small ball of white light. *I hope this is strong enough to go through the barrier.* He shot a ball of white light at Reika, which collided with her. Reika sensed something strange within her and felt her power rise. Lief saw what Visiert had done but was too late to react. Cursing, he attacked Reika with another kick from the right. She reacted and grabbed it. He also noticed something strange about her then.

Reika's appearance had changed, much like Visiert's. Her hair was much longer with the silvery sheen, and her pupils and irises had turned different shades of grey. Reika glared at Lief coldly. She shoved his kick away. Lief stepped away from her. "This changes nothing, you are not well trained as Visiert."

Reika examined her hands. *This power? What did Visiert do to me?* As Lief flew toward her, Reika moved away, amazed at her own speed. Lief launched a punch once again, it struck and pushed Reika back. Unlike the pain of his previous strikes, this was more like a light pain that one would be irritated by, all the while pressing on, never letting it bother them. *Whatever has happened, it's not enough. Lief can still kill me. Maybe I have a fighting chance?*

Lief launched his next assault. Reika avoided the swift attacks.

She did counter with a punch of her own, which fazed Lief briefly. It was short-lived as he pressed his attack even harder.

Reika couldn't keep up her defence for any longer. She managed to land another kick. Reika summoned Luniram, but Lief effortlessly knocked it from her hand. She backed off a few metres away, planning what to do next. Lief shot several small lightning balls at Reika. She somersaulted backwards on her hands and dodged the balls one by one. As she landed on her feet for the final time, a lightning ball she didn't anticipate collided with her left side.

The first pain was brief but intense, giving way to an ache half the initial intensity but still so agonising it robbed her of focus and strength. Reika could barely stand. She stooped over, clutching her left side with her right hand and her left arm dangling uselessly. Her hair and eyes reverted to their natural state. After a few seconds, she dropped on her knees, weak and weary.

His magic... Are elves really this powerful? They really do rival dragons in strength. Yet Zane could go toe to toe with Krea... Reika's thoughts were wild and crazed.

Visiert dropped to the floor, his mask hiding his despair. *I've failed.*

Lief raised his hand to deliver the final blow. Reika didn't move an inch, too weak to struggle.

Lief stopped in his tracks, staring Reika straight in the eye. He smirked, and for the first time his smile wasn't a malicious one. Instead, it seemed like he had just had much fun. "You are persistent, but you have a long way to go young witch."

The elf pulled a small golden cordial and handed it to the young woman. Reika pulled her right hand away from her damaged side and drank it. The burns on her healed instantly, her body functional again, no longer fatigued or wounded. Reika got to her feet slowly, backing away from Lief with a bewildered expression.

"Why?" Reika asked.

Lief's face beamed, which further puzzled Reika. "I'm in a good mood. There is potential in you yet." Lief walked past Reika, not even giving her eye contact anymore, and disappeared through a portal from view. Reika's mind went blank, and she fell to her knees. She didn't notice the barrier had disappeared, nor Visiert approaching her along with Junayd and the others.

Zane re-awoke and felt a terrible feeling in his stomach. "Can you move, Zane?" Berinon asked.

"I think so, I should be alright."

Reika sat down on the floor. Her friends all approached her. "Are you ok?" Visiert asked.

"Yes, I'm alright. Lief wasn't a pushover but it's strange, he healed me." "Indeed, but why didn't he end it there and take you away?"

"Your guess is as good as mine."

Visiert didn't respond right away. "A very odd thing for him to do, I'll admit. Still, his escape from prison I did not anticipate. I went to the cell to check on him and discovered he wasn't there. The guards didn't know it but I knew he wasn't there; it was only an illusion. Whoever helped him escape, he was able cover his tracks."

"What about Master Antonius?" Reika asked. "Where is he now?" "He's safe, I've taken him away to recover."

Reika was relieved. All was quiet, except for the winds blowing that howled past the *Coeptus*, and against the castle's stone walls.

Junayd did not understand what had taken place. He knelt and brought his eye level with Reika's own. "What happened? I have never seen you use that power before. What was it like?"

Reika's expression was odd mixture of wonder and perplexity. "Strong, immensely so. Thinking about it, I am almost terrified of myself." She stood up and stared back at Visiert. "What... what was that strange transformation? Did you do this?"

"The moon has an effect on your magic, as it does mine," Visiert said. "We come from a line of sorcerers and sorceresses who absorb moonlight to make themselves stronger."

"Lunarmancers, right?" Junayd asked.

"Correct," said Visiert. "Centuries ago, a nation of humans from the southern archipelago discovered they could harness the moon of Maromago, to bolster their power. They caught the attention of the dragons. The Lunarmancer Elite were asked to serve as bodyguards for the Dragelve Consortium and some were brought here. Your parents were part of that line."

"Then that means..."

"Yes... You are a Lunarmancer, Reika."

Reika could not believe it. It seemed her destiny was linked with the moon in more ways than one.

"What does this mean?"

Visiert sighed. "You'll see," he said. He shot another ball of white light at Reika which collided with her. *Moonlight?* she thought, as the same light engulfed her once again, transforming her.

Visiert changed too, his hair matching her hair colour. Melito and Tabitha were mesmerised and at the same time fearful, even though one of the Lunarmancers standing before them was their friend. "You can resume this transformation at any time as long as there is enough energy from the moon's light to sustain it," Visiert explained. Reika's transformation faded, rendering her normal once again.

"What matters is you are safe," Berinon said. "Zane has fought against elves; he knows how powerful they can be. Lief is no exception."

"Yes," Zane said. "I know from experience, back when I fought Krea. Remember the incident in Valoa?" Zane crossed his arms with grim countenance. "I sparred with her when she was young when I went back in time before the incident in Valoa. I believe her power has grown since then. Considering Lief's own strength against Visiert now, we may not have an easy victory."

Junayd nodded.

"Where Lief has gone is anyone's guess," Melito said.

Reika knew Zane was right, but there was something else at play. "Lief isn't as on board with the weredragons as he would like to let on," she said, at last. "I think that is why he spared me and didn't kidnap me there and then. Do you think we can persuade Lief to help us and turn from what he is doing?"

Junayd gawped at Reika. "You're joking right? I think he hit you too hard." "No, I'm serious," Reika said.

Junayd was furious. "After what he's done, why?" He asked.

Zane stepped between Junayd and Reika. "Hear her out. Janshai, whom I faced, was driven by an evil spirit, he was the leader of the very group Krea was a part of. But I freed him from that spirit and he sought to put things right. If Lief has been led down a dark path, we should try to bring him back, make him come to his senses."

Junayd had calmed somewhat but was still frustrated. "It didn't stop Lief from fighting Reika. How do we know it is actual remorse or merely appeasing his conscience?"

"I have dealt with renegade elves longer than you have. I have had higher- ups of the Dragelve Consortium elves teach me their magic and I was chosen to be the elves' hero," Zane said. "Reika has a point."

"You used a Rasgar to set Janshai free from an evil spirit, right? Lief isn't driven by such a spirit, it won't be that simple."

"It doesn't matter, as long as we bring Lief to his senses. Once we bring him in, it will be up to the Consortium to decide whether he should be granted amnesty for his past actions. Or put him to death if he refuses to make amends for his deeds. If they see fit to do so, they can put him to death either way. Any decision of theirs cannot be overturned in a case like this, so what they go with will be law, life or death." Zane turned his gaze to Reika. "I say we give Reika's plan a try."

Reika smiled. "If he has to die, I will not stand in the way, Zane. It is an outcome I am willing to accept. I don't think I could make that decision, it's too hard for me. Leave it to the judges."

"Junayd," Berinon said, "Zane may sometimes be an easy-going man, but when the situation is dire, he can think things through with a level head. It will be worth trusting him in this matter."

"Fine, we'll try to rescue Lief, but if he doesn't comply, I'll kill him."

Zane nodded. "Very well. But know this, Lief could have been holding back from using his full power. The Draco Ferrum must be strengthened so we have a chance to defeat him, saying nothing of Krea and Destrian himself."

Junayd and Reika did not speak to each other for three days on the *Coeptus*, even when they and the crew had their meals. There was food on board to last a few weeks, which would give them time to figure out where they were going to next. No one knew where Lief had gone, and the next Draco Ferrum forge had to be found.

The night sky was a sight to behold, not a cloud present, just the small twinkling stars on the dark canvas. The full moon wasn't out that night, granting Reika solace that she could stare at the stars. She lay on the bow of the *Coeptus* alone.

Junayd awoke, restless, climbing up the stairs, making his way over to Reika. He didn't say anything, he instead sat gently beside her, also gazing at the stars. "I... have a reason to be angry, but it wasn't fair of me to snap at you like that, and I am sorry," he said quietly to her.

Reika sat up, placing her left hand on the floor, allowing Junayd to place his right hand gently on it, indicating she had forgiven him. "It's just...If I had my way, Lief would be dead. He is aiding Destrian in building the weredragon army and one of his associates cursed you to become a weredragon at night. Why would you want to help Lief?" This time, he had managed to ask in a calm voice. Reika said nothing for a moment, just continued gazing upward.

"I know he may not deserve a second chance, but isn't it worth trying? Besides, he may not turn a corner, and the judges may condemn him forever," she said. "The Consortium are going to be the ones to decide. I have no problem with either, but if he is willing to patch things up... Shouldn't we allow that? You had a choice to kill me multiple times and yet you spared me, even when I was a weredragon. I was poised to kill you."

Junayd held Reika's hands gently. "Reika, I get where you are coming from, but a mindless beast isn't the same as one who is consciously doing evil. You couldn't help attacking me." He sighed. "I just need time to think. I am glad you see two sides of this."

Reika decided to move onto a different subject. "When I was in Somnium Carcerum, I could hear your voice, but a statement of yours, I didn't hear the whole thing, it was muffled, but I think I know what you were saying to me."

Junayd knew where this was going. He grew embarrassed and his throat tightened, rendering him unable to say anything. "I..."

Reika just waited, staring at him. "I said... I love you," he managed.

"I knew it... I knew that's what you were trying to say. I think for some time I have felt the same way about you."

Junayd smiled back. "Well at least I don't feel awkward now." Reika chuckled.

"What if..." Junayd asked, "What if we after this journey has finished, when we find the Anodyne Stone and cure you... How would you feel?"

Reika knew what Junayd was asking. "Marriage?" "Of course," Junayd replied, "Is it too soon to do so?"

"No, no... It's fine," Reika said. "Good thing you said after, I don't think I want our children running around with a curse, so we can reserve it for after the journey is done."

The two leaned on each other, just listening to the sea and drinking in the night sky. "Do you think Destrian really has the stone?"

"Probably. If he does, he must have hidden it well and it will be difficult to retrieve. Assuming we take Welk at his word. Either he is obfuscating, or he is an idiot for even telling us Destrian has it."

Reika's face dropped. "I have been away for too long."

～

Zane and Berinon watched from a distance. *Sweet,* Zane thought. "Reminds you of Emeline, doesn't it?" Berinon asked.

"Certainly does. Time will tell, Berinon." The knight chuckled silently to himself.

～

Reika was struck by a thought. "There is a place in Carthage, I am uncertain of what is down there."

"That's vague, Reika, what sort of place?"

"A passage used to help citizens of Carthage move between the citadel and the village. There was a turning that was blocked by a boulder. I am wondering if a forge could be there."

"Why don't we go there and check? It doesn't hurt to do so. I'll talk with Captain Tybalt and ask for him to take us over to there."

～

Lief returned to Mt Carthage in deep contemplation. He didn't feel the same after speaking with Reika. "What does she know about me? Nothing," he said. He had been talking to himself for a while now. He wondered if it was a healthy habit.

A tall figure emerged from darkness wearing brown robes with orange trimming. He had dark boots and grey trousers. His eyes were a dark blue and reptilian. His skin was tan, and grey hair hung from his head, along with a small beard.

Lief spun round in surprise. "Master Destrian, what are you doing here?" "I see you still haven't retrieved Reika. You haven't been reporting in."

"She is still weak, but I won't discount her. Her Lunarmancy has been unlocked unfortunately and..."

Destrian took hold of Lief by the neck. "So, I can't even rely on you? She was in your hands, and you let her go free," Destrian snarled.

"Wait... I was only trying." Lief choked as Destrian gripped his neck tighter than before.

"Krea gave you instructions to subdue Reika and turn her into a weredragon. Welk has already failed us, I don't need the same from you," Destrian finally released his grasp. Lief gasped and coughed. "For many years I intended to carry out Tahpenes' instructions. Then, the world will be under our heels. That won't happen if you can't even follow simple orders."

Lief didn't respond.

"Am I detecting a soft spot? You had one job: bring her into the fold. Krea has done much for me in that regard. Surely one simple servant girl is easy for you? Should she become a fully trained Lunarmancer, she will become dangerous much like Visiert, the Temporal Knight, and the Ferrum Champion are. Not even the power you so crave will help if that happens," Destrian said.

"Master..."

"Just get the job done! Do I make myself clear? The prophecy against the weredragons must not come to pass."

"Understood," Lief said, this time with a stern expression.

"Good. Meet me in Caromago soon," Destrian faded into the shadows. Lief picked up a stone off the ground and hurled it in frustration into the forest below. His yell echoed across that same forest. "Stupid brat, pricking at my conscience like that!" He calmed down rather quickly but his mind housed an uncomfortable feeling. "But what if she is right?" The elf began to push away the conflicting feelings. "She will be a weredragon, just like the rest." Lief journeyed down the mountain steps.

Chapter 14

Home Again

A t dawn, the *Coeptus* drew near to Reika's home village of Reme. Berinon was with Ulric. "Where do you think the best place to land is?" he asked.

"There, just outside the north entrance of the village. Your lady friend claims there is a forge here, but she wants to check to be sure, so that's where we need to be."

The airship landed safely. Both Junayd and Reika departed, heading towards the village. Reika beheld the village before her, just as it was when she left. There were guards present, including Ignatius. Reika was hesitant to go into the village; she remembered her banishment until they found a cure.

"If you are worried about your exile Reika, don't," Junayd said. "You are with me, and I take full responsibility for this. Perhaps it may be good to see them again after all this time?"

She saw Mark in the distance, along with Andrea. Reika welled up with joy, speeding over to them without a thought of what Ignatius would do. Mark saw her in the distance. He walked gently over to her, patting her on the head when she arrived.

"I missed you, Father, both you and Mother."

Mark smiled back, a tear rolling down his fur. "So have we, I am glad you are back."

Junayd was scratching his head. *She was raised by dogs. Huh,* he thought. "Who's your friend?" Andrea asked.

"Junayd, the wielder of the Draco Ferrum."

Mark patted Junayd's shoulder. "Thanks for taking care of her." Junayd smiled, "Happy to assist."

Ignatius strode over. Some of the guards, Basil, Augustine, and Vips had arrived. Reika was mortally afraid. Ignatius stared at Reika, eventually his face gave way to a smile.

"You are here because of the forge, and to reunite with your loved ones, I have nothing against that." Reika's fear subsided, a warm deep feeling of relief washing over her.

"We still haven't found the stone. I am not sure where it is." Ignatius placed his arms behind his back.

"Keep looking. The curse must be fully lifted before you can return. Nevertheless, I am granting this visit." Reika gave a nod of the head, and the other guards hugged her, relieved to see her again. King Tertullian arrived.

"Pray tell, where are Melito and Tabitha?" He asked Reika. "Inside the ship."

"Bring them here."

Reika flew back to the ship quickly. Basil, Mark, and Andrea weren't too surprised although the other animals were shocked by her powers. Their mouths were left gaping open.

"Did... she just... fly?" "I think so."

Tertullian then examined Junayd. "Strong man, you are. Champion of Dragons, The Messiah of the Draco Ferrum, you are the key to saving our world."

"I am honoured, your majesty. I'll do my best."

Reika walked with Melito and Tabitha back to the village. Tertullian turned to address them once they stopped near him. "I made the right call when I brought you both into the royal guard, but especially you Melito, son of Julius. Your father would have been proud of you for saving the kingdom. I realised as you grew that one day, you would travel to the past and stop Welk Seha."

Ignatius' eyes widened. "What? You never told me that? *I* trained him." "Indeed," Tertullian said with a grin on his face. "There was no need for me to disclose to Melito his mission when he was being trained. If I had told him, it would not have happened, or he would have lost."

Melito gulped. "Your majesty, I'm sorry, but I failed to stop Welk Seha: he destroyed Entella. But I will regather its people and rebuild Entella when this is over."

"I was charged by King Julius, your father, to raise you as my own son and prepare you for this day. Welk believes Entella is an empty ruin, he will not know what hit him." Melito stared at the birthmark on his hand, clenching his fist tightly.

Junayd turned his head this way and that. Tertullian turned to Reika. "Would you be so kind as to show Junayd to the forge? It's in the emergency passage." *As I thought.* Reika nodded, beckoning to Junayd to follow her.

Junayd proceeded down the stairs with Reika and they arrived at the same underground space. The boulder had been moved. Beyond it, they found a lone statue.

Light emerged from the statue, colliding with the Draco Ferrum once more. A metal band formed along the back of the sword, leaving the blade intact. Junayd felt his power grow immensely. Once the light finally had gone out, all was silent for a while.

Both the humans left the forge, heading back up the stairs. Junayd stood in front of the small crowd that had surrounded the emergency tunnel. He raised the Draco Ferrum into the air, the crowd cheered at the top of their voices. Junayd stopped for a moment; he could see something in the distance. Reika also looked to the horizon.

"Oh no, Magnus."

"Him again? What's he doing here?"

The caiman made a theatrical entrance, approaching the

guards and king without fear, clapping mockingly. Vera, Felix, Barzillai, Darius and Marcion all followed behind him.

"The cursed one returns to her home," Magnus said.

Reika seethed with anger. "Don't you ever give up? How did you survive?" "You are not the only ones familiar with Budúcnosť you know," Magnus replied. "I had stolen some of their technology for myself. An easy escape for us. Though not so easy to put together, a lot of hours put in. Such a pity that civilisation fell all those centuries ago, it would have made it easier for me to prepare my ship for what you and the *Hikari* did."

Ignatius stepped forward; his teeth bared. "Vera, how dare you show yourself after your betrayal," he growled.

Vera jeered back at him. "Aww, is that how you speak to an old friend after all these years?"

Ignatius pointed at Vera. "Don't toy with me."

Vera merely winked back. "Heh, still an old stiff as usual, aren't you? Such a shame. Don't think your friends, either new or old, can save you. We will kill them."

Ignatius drew his fist away. He remembered the last time that Vera had defeated him, leaving him on the throne room floor as she walked with Magnus out of the citadel. It had taken him a few days to rest up and recover from his wounds.

"It's the death sentence for your betrayal of the king. Especially after you assisted that two-bit thug Magnus who also dares to show his evil face around here."

Vera yawned.

"What difference will it make if you can't back up your own words? Amazing how you utter such empty threats. Reika and her friends are going to suffer, then we will kill them before the eyes of your king."

Ignatius looked at Reika and the others. "All of you, stand back. I will take care of Vera myself." He turned to Vera again. "I will take you down just like that, you will not win this time you filthy snake. Prepare to defend yourself from me because of the treacherous road you have taken!" Ignatius strode to Vera, his pace quickening until he was running.

Vera began to charge too. "Tough luck arrogant fool, I'll come out on top in this fight."

The two swung their paws viscerally, not bothering to defend themselves, each blow colliding with shocking force. Ignatius struck Vera on the right side of her face, staggering her a little. She retaliated with a punch to the right side of his face. Ignatius took two steps back. He interlaced his fingers to make a double punch, smashing his fists into the jaws of Vera in an uppercut.

Reika watched. *You can do this Captain!* Melito cheered Ignatius on as the Rottweiler successfully landed more blows on Vera. The leopard growled when she hit the floor, tripping Ignatius over with her legs. Ignatius hit the sandy floor hard, getting kicked in the face. He spun along the floor, getting to his feet, slightly wobbly. Vera struggled too.

"You've gotten better, my canine friend," Vera said. "You haven't seen anything yet!" Ignatius replied.

Reika nudged Junayd. "We need to lead Magnus' goons away from here, I don't want my home destroyed."

"Agreed, Reika."

"Let us fight with you, my human friends!" Augustine said, with Vips, and Basil standing beside him.

Magnus growled. "What are you buffoons standing there for? Get the others!"

Darius went for Melito, lunging as his ancestors once had to catch their prey. He missed Melito by a thread, leaving the marmoset's heart beating incredibly fast. *Come on, Melito. You fought against Welk; you can take on Darius too.* Darius stepped away from Melito. "Been a long time since I held you in my grasp. Looks like you beefed up a little," Darius said smirking.

"You won't get the chance. This time, I'll defeat you," Melito said firmly.

The lion squinted. "I am better off seeing a weed breaking through a fortress wall."

Darius swung a few punches at Melito, though as fast as he was, the marmoset managed to dodge out of the way in time. He threw a flying kick at the lion, knocking him down to the floor.

"Where did you get your strength?" Darius said, winded.

"Training and plenty of good food," Melito quipped. "I've faced worse than you." Melito called Entella's Bane to himself before making it disappear, showing just enough to intimidate Darius. "I think it's safe to say for me I won't need it for this fight."

The lion roared, both he and Melito continued their struggle as Marcion went for Tabitha. She was very nimble, keeping her distance, firing arrows at the bear.

"Run like the dog that you are!" Marcion yelled.

Tabitha ran through part of the village with Marcion tailing her. Tabitha, with as much strength as she could, backflipped over the mighty bear. Holding her bow in front of her, she fired an arrow at Marcion's right leg, grazing it. Marcion slumped to the floor, dropping his sword onto the ground. Tabitha ran over, kicking the bear in the right side of the face before he could get up. He pulled Tabitha to the ground by the left leg. When Tabitha smacked her bow onto Marcion's head, he let go of her leg. The tamarin was relieved she had managed to escape. She then decided to go to Melito to help him.

Meanwhile, Reika drew her sword, seeing Felix menacingly advancing towards her. "No light of the moon to help you little one. I would love to see a brat like you try to defeat me properly. Especially after your shoddy performance on the boat when fighting Captain Magnus. Heh, I hope you are not going to resort to some pathetic tactic of wearing me down."

Reika stood there, ready to fight. *Little does he know of Caeronvar. Junayd and I faced him and he wasn't using his full strength. This beast will go all out.*

Felix drew his sword, bringing it down to crush Reika, who dodged quickly with a short burst of speed.

"Junayd, take care of Barzillai. Felix is mine!" Reika said. She whizzed back towards Felix, slashing swiftly. Felix parried the attacks, following up with an upward swipe that knocked Reika back, leaving her wide open to attack. A barrier appeared as Felix attempted to stab the young human. Reika strained against the mighty tiger due to his strength, though certainly the effort courtesy of her training was less strenuous. Though she knew she was a Lunarmancer and thus could overcome Felix, Reika wasn't sure how long the transformation would last and decided not to risk it. She also wondered if she would be sensed by Lief or anyone who wanted to come after her.

She then used a telekinetic projectile to shove him back. His boots scraped the ground, leaving blackened furrows in the dirt. Reika spun her blade around, letting it glow with the energy from the Excandescite, then performed one right slash followed by a downward slash, creating scythes of light that shot through the air at the tiger. Felix dodged out the way, though he now couldn't see Reika anywhere.

He smelled the air and performed a one-handed backwards parry of Reika's attack.

"Wow, quick reflexes I must say. Let's see what you are made of, but how long will you last? Feel free to come at me any time, little one. Unless you are afraid?" Felix said in an attempt to bait Reika. She said nothing, withdrawing her sword as she hovered back to the floor.

"Vips, now!" Reika called. Vips sank her fangs into Felix's right arm. The tiger roared in pain but before he could grab the cobra, Vips leapt away from him.

"Disgusting snake!" Felix said.

"Be glad I chose not to pump you full of venom, just enough to disorient you for a time," said Vips. Felix growled. He brought his sword to bear, but it was a failed endeavour, her reflexes were incredible by virtue of her cobra heritage.

"If I were a mongoose, I would have clawed you to shreds!" Felix shouted, every slash missing as Vips dodged the attacks. The venom was starting to make the tiger's head fuzzy. Unfortunately, Vips was careless in her footing, tripping over. Felix saw his chance for his strike, Reika held her sword in front of Vips just in time, nearly buckling under the strain. Even with her training from Antonius and her enhanced strength, she was just about on equal footing with the beast. She once again didn't risk transforming.

"Vips, get up!" Reika said in a strained voice. She complied and Reika flew a few feet away, causing Felix to strike the dirt. Vips came to Reika's side.

"You fight well, Reika." "Thanks."

Barzillai cracked his knuckles as he made his way to Junayd.

"Grab this, Junayd!" Basil yelled. The young man caught the rope Basil had flung to him, then waited for Barzillai to get closer. Suddenly, Junayd grabbed the horn of Barzillai, swinging round onto the beast's back. Barzillai opened his mouth in amazement, which was a mistake as Junayd pulled the rope into the creature's mouth.

I have heard about mankind reigning over us years ago, but this is absolutely absurd and ridiculous. Barzillai thought as he flailed about in his attempt to remove Junayd from his back.

Barzillai was forced to his knees. He lifted his arms high, grabbing Junayd on the legs and started to swing him round. Barzillai spun like a top. He opened his mouth, then his hands, letting go of Junayd, causing the human to fly, almost colliding with one of the buildings. Junayd stopped himself just in time, floating in front of the house safely onto the ground. "Don't bother trying that again, you great brute!" Junayd said.

"I won't," Barzillai said. "I think I'll just focus on splitting you in half next time."

Darius shoved Melito to the dirt. He grabbed the marmoset's

arms and pinned him down. "I think I'll put you on the menu today, even if there is too much fur on you," Darius said, allowing his tongue to glide along his rows of teeth.

"I don't think so," Melito said. He kicked Darius in the crotch. The lion rolled away onto the floor, howling in pain. Melito leapt to his feet. Tabitha drew nearer. Darius was distracted by the pain and couldn't concentrate on the fight, allowing Melito to land a few punches and a kick to the chest. The lion merely staggered but didn't fall. Melito backed off and as he did, Tabitha arrived, standing to his right.

"You were quick, Tabs!"

"A little blow to the head for Marcion." "Whatever the case, I need your help now."

"What about help from me, my friend!" Augustine said. Darius looked up to see the young elephant ready to fight.

"Come at me if you dare, tusky!" Darius said, derisively, as he got to his feet with a grin on his face.

Augustine brushed his armour then banged the right his chest with his right fist. "Time to give you a world of pain."

Junayd and Basil were still facing off against Barzillai. The rhino charged at Junayd with intense ferocity, ready to throw a punch with his right hand. Junayd caught the punch. The rhino struck with the force of a toppling tree. Junayd baulked under the momentum, which was enough to drag his boots through the dirt. He was unhurt, though no less angry. Junayd went in with a charge of his own, a punch to the left of the creature's face. Barzillai rolled along the floor, coming to a grinding halt.

"Not bad, skinbag. Were it not for that blade and magic you possess; you would be dead."

Junayd wiped his chin. "You won't get the chance to kill me."

Reika and Vips' fight with Felix was still going. "Why can't I hit you?" Felix yelled in pure frustration. "You're just a human!"

Reika steadied herself. "Go help the others, Vips! I've got this!" She said. Vips nodded, heading for Barzillai.

Marcion woke up. He picked up his sword, and instead of heading for Tabitha, he went after Reika. She saw him just before it was too late. *Stupid me sending Vips away.* Felix swung his sword with a high right cut and Marcion with a low left cut. Reika jumped and spun in the air, narrowly avoiding the blades and landing on the ground on her front bending her arms to cushion the blow.

Reika turned onto her back and summoned a barrier before the beasts' swords collided with her. *There is no question that these guys are not pushovers. But it certainly doesn't mean that they can't be beaten.* She burst the barrier into shards which caused Felix and Marcion to recoil away.

"I won't rest until you get the justice you rightly deserve. You murderous beasts will terrorise the innocent no more!"

Reika her fists glowed with bright light. She struck Felix swiftly on the left cheek, sending him spinning into the floor; such light also appeared around her foot. She swung around in the air, shoving Marcion with a telekinetic projectile, he was sent spinning through the air and landed on the floor. He steadied himself. Reika touched the ground with her feet once again, reopening her eyes.

"How dare you!" Marcion yelled.

"I wouldn't fret, your friend is unconscious. Still breathing. If I'd hit harder with the energy in my hands, he would be dead." Reika stood upright. "You won't win against me so back down. Your master is next and my friends will take care of the others. You murder, you lie, and you steal. All of you. Yet you show anger because I knocked Felix out cold? I'll give you one more chance, take your friends with you or be brought to justice."

Marcion didn't listen, drawing his blade to his side. "Who made you my judge and jury? I shall turn you into a blood smear you furless wretch." He charged at Reika with full force.

"You senseless beast," she said. She threw an energy-infused punch right into the left side of Marcion's face. The force knocked the bear out, sending him skidding along the floor. He lay unconscious on his front. *Two down, three to go,* Reika thought.

~

Junayd wrestled with Barzillai. The Draco Ferrum empowered Junayd's strength when he used it and even when de-summoned. His strength grew as he enhanced the Ferrum, allowing him to take on creatures that would otherwise tear him to shreds, If Junayd was able to face Welk again, it would be a different outcome. Junayd was able to push Barzillai back slowly, as one would push a

boulder up a steep hill. He threw a punch to Bazillai's stomach; a wad of spit the size of a round stone left the rhino's mouth.

Barzillai clutched his stomach, being forced to let go to block more of Junayd's punches. This didn't faze the man, as he landed an uppercut on the rhino's chin. Barzillai fell to his knees in what resembled an exhausted bow. He charged at Junayd, successfully colliding with him and bashed him into one of the houses. Junayd yelped in pain, then Barzillai pulled him from the ruin of the wall, leaving a hole with some of stonework crumbling onto the ground.

Junayd broke free from the creature's grasp and straightened himself, brushing the stone off his robes. He did have some cuts and bruises on his body and his skin was coated in dust. Barzillai threw a right-handed punch at Junayd, with the young man catching the fist in his hand. Junayd kicked the beast in the chest. This sent Barzillai hard to the dirt once again. Basil tried to jump in with a spear, attempting to leap onto the rhino and impale him with it. Barzillai managed to roll away and got to his feet, punching Basil hard into the collapsed house. Basil rose to his feet, wincing as he went.

"Nice place you have," Barzillai said. "I wonder if you'll miss any of this—"

Junayd had swiftly grabbed Barzillai by his trouser belt, raising him into the air and with all his might throwing the rhino to the floor; the rhino hit the ground like boulder hitting the bottom of a crevasse. Barzillai staggered to his feet, rubbing his back.

"Just give up," Junayd said. "You can't win."

The rhino charged once again with a slight stagger to his steps. Junayd rolled out of the way. He telekinetically pulled the rope to himself and made a loop. Barzillai, who was still staggering, managed to slow himself down and raced for Junayd once again. Junayd lassoed the rope, smirking while he did it. The rope went around Barzillai's neck, allowing Junayd to start to pull on the rope. Barzillai was pulled to the ground, completely worn out.

"No... fair," Barzillai said.

"Reika told me about what you and your comrades did to her friends. You want to talk about fairness? Give it a rest."

Darius and Augustine traded blows. The elephant was quite sturdy, and Darius' attacks couldn't topple him.

"You can't keep this up forever!" Darius said. "True, but can you take on all three of us?"

Augustine dodged a straight jab from Darius, successfully catching him in a grapple.

"Now!" Augustine said.

Teeth bared, Melito and Tabitha attacked from both sides, throwing flying punches at the sides of Darius' head. The lion wobbled about after Augustine let go of him.

"That's for my back in the forest fleabag," Melito said contemptuously. Darius snarled at him. Little did he know, Vips was heading for him. She scratched Darius' legs with her claws, causing him to fall. He didn't get back up. "All right! I give up, just stop, no more!" Darius said. He lay there humiliated and defeated. Melito and Tabitha high-fived, returning the favour to Augustine and Vips respectively.

Vera still was engaged with Ignatius. The two grabbed each other by their necks, each one trying to overpower the other. Ignatius could hear Vera's ghastly growl as she leaned further against him.

"Give it up you worthless mutt, I have you in my grasp!" She snarled. "Never!" He barked. He shoved Vera away from him, quickly throwing punches at her. Vera reeled from the punches, a look of dismay crossing her face as Ignatius managed to gain the upper hand. The dog gave the leopard a backhanded smack into the left side of her face that left her spinning. Vera doubled over. She eyed Ignatius with contempt, wiping blood from her torn cheek.

"You don't deserve to wear that uniform, Ignatius."

The dog nodded. "Perhaps I don't. The king I serve is one who grants second chances. But not to a traitor such as you. Maybe you should look in the mirror."

Vera bared her teeth, screaming at Ignatius as she scrambled to her feet and sprinted at him. "I'll kill you!"

Ignatius seized Vera as she leapt through the air, slamming her into the dirt. Her eyes were still filled with rage. Ignatius grabbed hold of Vera's neck and began choking her. She vainly reached for his face, she was severely weakened and finally blacked out. Ignatius arose, wounded but triumphant.

"Be grateful. Every breath you take from now on is my gift to you." All saw Ignatius victorious and cheered. He smiled back at them all.

Magnus drew his sword angrily and charged at Ignatius. Reika darted in front of the Rottweiler with anger in her eyes and blocked the caiman's attack with a barrier, stopping it from hitting Ignatius just in the nick of time. She shoved Magnus away from the group with a telekinetic push, flying after him.

Magnus landed on his feet, Reika summoned Luniram and her attack was blocked by the caiman.

"I am disappointed," Reika said, baiting the caiman. "You are still causing trouble? I would have thought someone like you would have learnt your lesson after what was done to your boat."

She backed away, their two blades clashing.

"I am going to enjoy lacerating you," Magnus whispered.

Reika threw a punch into the left side of Magnus' jaw, causing him to drop his sword on the ground. He felt the brunt of the attack. "A good hit, but not good enough!" He remarked. Magnus slashed Reika across the right cheek. She screeched and dropped Luniram.

Reika winced in pain. "How did that sting of my hand feel? Care to tell me?"

Reika felt agony spreading across her cheek. "It hurts, but what's your point?"

The caiman grinned. "If you bleed, you can die."

"I am so sick of you, sick of your arrogance, sick of your selfishness!" Reika said. "How did you become so detestable?"

Magnus didn't care, rushing Reika. She swiftly floated away from him and clapped her palms together. A wave of telekinetic energy, with the force of a bullet, hit Magnus in the chest, knocking him to the ground. It wasn't deadly, just enough to render him unconscious. He was the last to fall. The defenders had won.

All the unconscious *Tetraspis* crew were brought back to the village. Tertullian was very pleased with what had transpired. "Well done, all of you.

This is truly a momentous day for all." He pointed to two of the Carthagian guards. "You two, load them in the carriage and haul them to jail. Get them out of my sight."

Vera and the rest of the crew were placed inside the carriage. They were fully conscious, all felt defeated and too weak to struggle.

Junayd went over to Reika. "Are you ok? Get Zane to heal you, those scratches look nasty."

"I'm fine and you're right, they do hurt. We'll get back soon. Although... You look worse than me."

Junayd wiped some of the dust off his forehead.

Magnus reawakened as he was being loaded into the carriage.

He saw Reika with Junayd. He leapt from the carriage before it was shut.

"You worthless brat!" He said as he charged towards her. Reika fired a sphere of light as Magnus. It hit him with enough force to send him flying back into the carriage. Slamming into the back of it, he fell to the floor. The bars of the carriage were shut by Augustine and Basil tightly. Magnus rushed to the barred window in the carriage door. He and Reika kept each other within their sights.

Vera stared at Ignatius. She said nothing, only glaring at him with hatred before she faced away from the bars, sitting in utter silence as she and the others were hauled away.

Reika and the others watched the carriage as it trundled along the road. *Good riddance to bad rubbish,* she thought. Basil and the other guards all gazed at the carriage too.

"I'm beginning to think we should have killed them," Basil said aloud. "It will be for the king to decide their fate," Augustine answered.

Ignatius bowed before the king. Tertullian inclined his head, with Ignatius rising to his feet. A smile appeared on his face, one that Reika nor the guards had not seen in years. The remaining villagers all cheered at the top of their voices.

"Who is the true captain of the guard? Long live Ignatius!" They said in unison. Mark grabbed Ignatius round the neck with his left hand, giving him a noogie on the head with his right knuckles. Ignatius was indignant for a second, changing his mind quickly, giving Mark a pat on the back and a partial hug.

"Thanks for the assistance," he said to Reika. She nodded back in silence. "It's time we beg your leave," Junayd said.

Reika went to speak to her guardians. "I'll see you soon, there is a curse to be broken."

Mark nodded. "You be careful now."

Andrea gave Reika a pat on the head. "Take care little one."

Reika beamed at them, then walked back to the *Coeptus*. Mark and Andrea didn't see the look on her face afterward of sadness.

Junayd headed to the ship as well, saying nothing aloud, only in his mind. *Soon Reika, you'll be free of the curse.*

As soon as Zane met them at the *Coeptus*, he reversed the damage to Reika's cheek, the scratches shutting like a zip on a boot, as well as Junayd's own robes being repaired along with his body.

Both of them noticed Zane's breathing was out of sync, stertorous, as if he had come back from a run.

"Will that kill you, Zane?" Junayd asked. "Helpful as your power is, I don't want you to die as a result."

"It is possible," Zane said. "Time is onerous to control. It's not to be done lightly."

Chapter 15

Snared

As Junayd was sitting alone in his room. Visiert reappeared on the ship. "Am I interrupting anything?"

"No, no. It's fine, what can I help you with?"

"Junayd, there's a forge at a lone tower, The Order of the Ferrum reside there.

You need to strengthen the Draco Ferrum one final time." Junayd rose to his feet. "What? Where's the tower?"

"It's to the southeast of the Entellan Islands. I'll take you there personally through a portal. Be warned, I only have a few trips left before I need to charge my rune."

"Rune?" Junayd asked.

"Yes, it gets me around but again, it's only a few limited trips. It needs recharging at Aerouant Citadel where dragons reside, and I still need energy for the return trip." Visiert checked Junayd was ready. "I'll take you back here when we are done."

The portal opened, and Visiert and Junayd entered. On the other side, Junayd looked out into the horizon. All he could see was desert sand stretching out into the distance until it touched a beautiful sea on the vista. Lifting his head, he beheld a large stone tower made of reddish bricks, clashing with the desert sand around it.

"This is a forge as well?" Junayd asked.

"It houses one would be more accurate. It is a place of worship. The forge was built here centuries ago and is currently guarded by the monks who reside with these walls." Visiert knocked on the door and a tall, bald black man with a cleanly cut beard emerged from the door. His sandy robes had a purple cummerbund around the waist. The robes themselves looked heavy but the man was able to move around with ease.

"The wielder of the Ferrum stands before me. An honour to meet you," the man said with an authoritative yet benign tone. He and Junayd shook hands. "I am Reuben. Head monk of the Order of the Ferrum."

Reuben led Visiert and Junayd inside the large hall. Monks were lighting candles, others prayed silently before altars. The sandy interior of the hall was well carved, the arches all smoothed out with scarcely a fault or crack.

"Our predecessors built the forges all over Perusia in order restore the weapon you bear. It is our hope you will kill Destrian," Reuben said. "You will find the forge behind a block of marble stone. I trust, Junayd, that you have ventured to the other forges?"

"Of course," Junayd replied. "There is only one left I believe."

"Very good, now if you will follow me this way." Reuben led Junayd to the marble block.

"Behind this?"

"Yes, the forge is down there."

Junayd summoned the Draco Ferrum, slashing the marble several times. The stone split, revealing a walkway to the dragon statue. Junayd approached the statue. The same light began to grow, flickering, then colliding with the Ferrum. At first it glowed, then the Ferrum formed a tough shell around it that hardened, enclosing the light as it formed.

Junayd felt power like he had never known.

It was worth the effort, Junayd thought. *This is just... incredible!*

He returned to the tower, where Reuben and Visiert waited.

Junayd smiled at them. Visiert sent Junayd through the sangria portal back to the *Coeptus*. "Take care of yourself, Junayd."

"You too, Visiert, stay safe."

⁓

The portal closed, revealing Reika standing a few feet away at the door of his room. "All done with the forges, Junayd?"

"Yes. Visiert took me to where the monks of the Order of the Ferrum were waiting. I should be ready to defeat Destrian now." Junayd sat down. "Let me ask you something, Reika. You've met Visiert before, haven't you?"

Reika nodded. "I first met him in the mining town in Caledonia." "Do you know who he is?"

She shook her head. Junayd grinned.

"No, I didn't think so. I wouldn't mind knowing who he *really* is and why he brought on that transformation of yours."

⁓

Zane did not sleep soundly. He was troubled by a terrible dream, one he never disclosed to the others. Would Rian forgive him and what of the girl he rescued? Despite his conversation with Visiert in Entella, he still was conflicted inside. He finally awoke in groggy manner after he began to hear a voice in his head. "Young temporal warrior," the voice called. "Direct your ship to the Moon Tower. I must speak with you all."

Zane pondered on the voice. "I know who that is, I'd better see Tybalt about going to the Moon Tower."

Zane spoke with Tybalt, explaining to him where to go next. While overall accepting of the idea, he was somewhat concerned.

"It's risky, but I'm sure Ulric is up to the task," he said to Zane. Once informed of the next plan of action, Ulric turned the ship gently, keeping it from shaking the crew about.

A few hours later, the group was approaching the Moon Tower.

It stood upon a small lone island in a green field, surrounded by large grey walls of impressive stone. The Moon Tower rose high over the walls, an awesome structure with four huge clocks made of quartz on each of the four sides, reflecting the sun's rays.

"Who lives there?" Junayd asked Zane, as they drew near the tower. "Zaius is the guardian of that tower. He knows where Lief is."

The *Coeptus* landed close to the south side of the tower, with the seven all disembarking from the ship, approaching the birch doors that were held together by massive steel columns, entering as the doors opened by themselves.

The large hall had golden wooden flooring, with ancient— though well- maintained—brown stone walls. Two sizeable bookshelves stood against the walls, housing colourful, lengthy tomes. The group could see a spiral wooden staircase leading them upstairs to a similar hall, though this one had a floor covered in a gold trimmed purple carpet. Four statues stood in each corner of the room, surrounded by pools of water.

At the northern end of the room, an elf man with brown eyes, mid-length brown hair and pale skin waited, sitting on an oak chair behind an oak desk. His robes were simple, black with dark blue trimming on the edges of the sleeves and the chest. They all approached the man to speak with him, the one called Zaius.

"Sir, are you the one in charge of this tower?" Junayd asked.

"Correct, dear boy. I own this place," Zaius replied. "What you are inside is an ancient tower, designed as a means of getting sailing ships from here, Perusia, to the one of our moons, Caromago, and vice versa. Maromago itself is barren, but Caromago houses and contains life. Some of the life up there is as old as the life down here."

Zane stepped forward and knelt before Zaius. "Where is Lief now, has he gone there?"

"Indeed, dear boy. Lief is on that moon. His Master's fortress is up there, a desolate land claimed by a dark hand. From that moon,

Destrian will be able to rule the entire planet. That's why we are putting an end to this conflict."

Tabitha was scratching her ear, thinking to herself. "Hmm... Could we use the airship to get to the moon?" She asked.

Zaius nodded his head. "Why yes, you can, but only via the portal which I will be happy to open up."

"Why help us out?" Tabitha enquired.

Zaius didn't say anything for a few seconds. "Lief was led astray. He was my pupil and because... Krea is my daughter..."

All but Zane and Berinon were in shock. "A few years ago, Lief was promised more power by Krea, provided he bring Reika into the ranks of the weredragons. I tried to bring him back, but he refused and cast me aside."

"We'll bring him to justice," Junayd said.

"Whatever the Consortium, decide to do with Lief, it is their decision. I will not stand in the way, the law is the law," Zaius said. "Krea... I am not so sure what happened. When she was a young woman, she was kidnapped. Somehow, she was changed from the gracious woman she once had been. She is now a pernicious tyrant," Zaius fixed his eyes on Zane. "Perhaps you can look into what happened?"

Zane nodded. "If I can, I may look into it."

Zaius got up from the oak chair. "I will open the portal for you to Caromago.

You'll be free to come and go to the moon as you please."

Reika turned over the thought of Lief's fate in her mind. The old man's words regarding his final judgement echoed inside her head. *Will Lief change and help us defeat Destrian? I could be wrong; it is better to trust one wiser than me.*

Tabitha had been looking at the four statues, and suddenly she let out a cry of surprise. They were of Zane, Rian, Krea and a fourth whom she didn't recognise. She pointed this out to the others.

Rian stood by the statue of himself. "Why do you have a statue, Rian?" Reika asked.

"For a job I did many years ago, in my youth. I was given this as a reward for it. A conflict between golems and elves had arisen over land possession in the Crystal Fjords and I was hired to quell it. They agreed to share the land, in the end, and anyone caught violating the treaty would be executed on the spot."

The reward is all you care about, Melito said in his mind, cynically. The marmoset turned his attention to the statue of Zane.

"I didn't expect to have this built for me, I'm just a simple country man," Zane remarked.

"Nice of them to do so." A question then ran through Melito's mind. "If you were allowed to change the past, would you?"

Zane chuckled. "I would, but the problem is I wouldn't have the restraint to ensure that I didn't change the past for ulterior motives. I have a strict code that I must be continually bound to while I am the Temporal Knight. I cannot change the past for myself."

Junayd was standing before Krea's statue. She looked more youthful to how she had looked in person.

"So pretty," he said.

"She was very young, then, only one hundred and ninety years old at the time," Berinon said. "Zane met her when he travelled through time. Even at her age, she was kind though very assertive. A tremendous shame she chose the dark path she is on."

Junayd looked at the fourth statue. He examined the face. It was a man. He was sure the face was one he was acquainted with. He looked at Reika, thinking as he looked back at the statue. *Who is he?*

Zaius made his way to the top of the Moon Tower. There was a rune on the edge of the northern balcony. Placing his right hand on it while simultaneously holding his left hand in the air. Ripples started to appear in the sky, causing it to warp. Blue and purple lightning tore open a huge hole until it grew large enough to allow an airship to pass through.

"Safe travel, friends," Zaius said.

The others had returned to their ship. Zaius remained on the balcony, watching the *Coeptus* take off in flight.

"Steady," Berinon said to Ulric. "Fly straight and don't veer off course." "I've been doing this for a while, I know what I am doing! My mentor was a golem and a direct descendant of the golems from Budúcnosť. He taught me everything I know."

"Have you ever flown through a portal? If not, heed my advice." "I would not be too concerned about this portal."

The *Coeptus'* engines began to fire up, blue flames emerging then bursting into intense white furious fires, pushing it through the air into the heart of the portal.

It closed behind them.

A portal reopened elsewhere for a few seconds allowing the *Coeptus* to emerge safely. Junayd, Melito, and Tabitha left the interior of the ship to see the view that lay before them. To their amazement, they could see the planet from a distance, along with that of the other moon.

The airship drifted to one of the continents below; four could be seen. To the west, a forest stretched over a narrow looking continent. To the south, a pale desert continent that sprawled to from west to east. To the northeast, the largest of the continents had a citadel visible even from their great height rising from its middle. These three continents encircled a small continent of obsidian. They could see a castle surrounded by a moat of lava, a foreboding structure that to ordinary folk would be a place only fools dared to tread. The airship shortly made its touchdown on the north of the western continent, close to the sea adjoining a barren desert.

Berinon stepped out of the interior of the ship onto the deck, followed by Reika after him, who was amazed.

"Welcome to the moon, Caromago," Berinon said. "Did we just land in the desert?" Reika asked.

"A small one, I wouldn't worry too much. The heat of this particular desert is also quite low."

"What an odd climate." Reika made her way to the port-side of the airship. Shielding her eyes, Reika saw grass plains in the middle distance. A little further on, a forest could be seen, a lush one in stark contrast to the dusty desert.

"How many miles do you think that forest is away from us, Melito?"

"A good twenty miles. It's going to take a while." Melito faced away from the edge of the port-side, leaning back casually. Zane also made his way to the port-side.

"It would be unwise to head straight to Destrian. We'll keep out of his way and go take the long way round. Through the forest, we can have food along the way. Luentinum is next, there is a rebel army to deal with and finally, Aerouant Citadel, where we shall meet with the Dragelve Consortium's council. Visiert maybe there too."

Melito leapt off the side of the boat. Reika gasped for a moment. Tabitha panicked and ran to the railing, peering over the edge. They both breathed a sigh of relief when they saw Melito walking away from the *Coeptus*, a grin on his face. "You are going to accompany me, right?" He said.

Ulric approached Berinon. "Are we waiting here?"

"No, get the *Coeptus* into the sea, sail near the coast slowly. You'll be our means of heading to the next island. We'll meet you on the south side of this one. Let the captain make up his mind."

With that, Berinon left the *Coeptus*. Ulric went below deck to the captain, who approved what Berinon suggested. As Berinon and the last of the seven made their way away from the airship, it lifted slightly off the ground, turning slowly in the air. Gently it set down in the sea, a safe distance from the land, while remaining close to it. Its speed matched that of the group. Two of the lookouts on the *Coeptus* kept the group in their sights as much as they could up until the seven made it to the forest successfully. The group disappeared from view, leaving the *Coeptus* to sail to the south of the island at a moderate pace.

There was hardly any sweat on their bodies even after traversing the desert for five hours; the moon was unnaturally cold. They reached the end of the desert and went to sleep and the next day, they began their journey to the forest. As they entered after a few hours, Reika could not stop examining the curious landscape as she walked behind the rest of the group. "This is weird, I find it hard to believe that this moon looks so similar to our world."

"Is it so hard to believe?" Berinon asked. Though it could not be seen, Reika knew that somewhere in the dark of the sky above them was a second moon, dark and lifeless; it was this second moon that was responsible for her transformation, for her curse.

"As a child I was always confused. I thought it was another planet that was close to us. I didn't even know it was a moon until Father mentioned it to me."

Berinon chuckled and shook his head. "Caromago has always been like that.

It's really a remarkable place, home of the dragons themselves."
"The dragons live here?"

"To the east," Junayd added. "The dragons live in a citadel on the other side of the moon. We saw it on the northeastern continent as the *Coeptus* made its way down to the surface. The dragons emigrated there and found a continent that was empty and took it for themselves."

Tabitha scratched her cheek. "Hmm, I bet they chose a really nice place to live right? I can't picture them living in a mudhole."

"Everyone has got to start somewhere," Zane added. "Prosperity doesn't come out of the blue. My great grandfather had to build his farm up after many failures before he could make it thrive."

Tabitha then started to be a little anxious. "Who lives in this forest?" "Araneans," Melito said. "Or as they are known as, Arachnoids. I asked my father about other species when he and I were at the banquet table, my younger self probably wouldn't remember that. Welk Seha himself comes from the scorpion line. But the ones here... they are spiders."

Reika visibly looked terrified. "Giant... spiders...?" She said timidly. "Really? You're afraid of spiders?" Junayd said, raising his left eyebrow in the process.

"An Arachnoid attacked me when I was little," Reika said, clutching her chest nervously. "He and two others webbed me against a tree in the Carthagian forest. I couldn't break out and it took Chip an hour to find and rescue me."

Berinon placed both his hands on Reika's shoulders, then looked her in the eyes. "I wouldn't let that fear arise again. You are much stronger now." Berinon then let go of Reika's shoulders then proceeded to go east to a turning to the south. "Let us keep moving on to the south of the forest."

They stayed together closely to make sure they were not taken by surprise. The forest path they traversed was devoid of twigs yet had plenty of grass to walk on. The path taken was in the shape of a large S that meandered through the forest. Reika grew uneasy, it was almost too quiet. She listened carefully to the trees, rustling. Melito kept his axe in his hands, ready to swiftly cut into a predator if it crossed their path.

Rian didn't care. He was used to living in dangerous places. To him, it was like walking with an old friend. He held his gun in his right hand casually. A twig snapped. Reika reacted with a brief yelp, covering her mouth swiftly. Rian snapped.

"Reika! What did Berinon say earlier? We'll be ready... Is that clear?"

Reika nodded, taking her hand away from her mouth. They went a little farther and could see a clear fork in the path. One route led straight on, deeper into the forest; the other went to the south, leading them to a path out of the forest.

Without warning, a white, rope-like structure fired from the shadow of the trees towards Reika. It crashed into her, sending her flying into a tree. It pinned her to the tree as the rope formed into a netting. Other ropes hit the other rest of them, covering them in netted structures too.

"What is this rope?" Junayd said. "It's sticky!" "Not rope!" Melito cried. "Web!"

Reika's mouth had been covered by the web. She screamed as loudly as the net would allow her, a tear rolling down her right cheek. Though possible for her break loose, Reika was too terrified to try. She looked in horror as a large, humanoid arachnid jumped from the trees, landing on its feet with a thud. It was a large behemoth of a creature, covered in light brown hair. It had two big toes on its feet with four fingers on its hands. Parts of his hair were of a lighter shade on his body, resembling tribal markings. The beast turned to stare at Reika. Her eyes widened in alarm. Six eyes stared at her. Two of them were roughly the size of apples, with two pairs of smaller eyes in the middle of the face. A tarantula.

"Well, we caught quite a catch today," it said. "What are people like you doing here in this territory of ours?"

Two more arachnids emerged, one the same height as the first. The other was smaller.

"Prepare to..." the beast began. He stopped for a moment to examine Reika.

He recognised her scent. "You... I remember you." Reika squinted in confusion.

"Release the others," said the tarantula. The small one was surprised.

"Why Tarquin?"

"Do as I say and release them."

The two tarantulas complied, releasing the group from their webbing. Tarquin, who was close to Reika, split the web that encased her, gently helping her to the ground. She backed off, breathing somewhat heavily, though she fought to remain calm.

"Why did you release me?" Reika asked.

Tarquin bowed to the floor; his head hung in shame. "I... I was the one who pinned you to a tree in the Carthagian forest. My friends and I taunted you and left you stuck to the tree until one of your guardians found you. When your adoptive father Mark found out, he rebuked me and my friends, later meeting with my father near Carthage. I was punished for what I did to you. In the end, however, I never apologised to you. I am sorry. I should never have done that to you. All I did was cement a hatred of my people in you."

Reika realised she couldn't be angry with the creature anymore. She offered her hand. The tarantula accepted the gesture of good-will. "I forgive you," she said. She was shaking somewhat, the fear still existed with her and Tarquin knew.

"Bring them back to the village. Feed them," he said to his friends.

Junayd observed the village that they had arrived at. There was a diverse range of spiders that were getting on with various tasks. Some of the children, a black widow, a money spider, a menardi, and a redback were playing in a small lake, splashing each other with water, laughing amongst themselves while their mothers were fetching water from the lake. Three strong male tarantulas were toasting food around a campfire. One elderly black widow spider, clothed in simple robes of beige along with a headdress with a symbol on top, held a spiked white trident in his hand. He was sat on a throne of felled trees, held together by strong rope. He rose and approached the group.

"Humans, metazoans, and an elf? What were they doing?" "Roaming through the forest. We mistook them for a threat." "A careless mistake, give them something to eat here."

The elder, introducing himself as Arjan, turned around to the square where a large fire was burning. Reika was a little uncomfortable, keeping silent. A small child tarantula approached her, holding her hand. Reika swivelled around instantly, saying nothing to the creature. It chattered to Reika, lightly pulling on her arm.

Tarquin smiled. "Celeste wants you to go with her." "I wish I could understand her speech," Reika replied.

"She knows what you are saying. The young one is learning the Consortium Standard so don't be concerned that she mostly resorts to our tongue."

Reika walked with Celeste over to the other children. They crowded around her. Eventually, Reika's unease vanished, she remained with the children, observing them play once more. The rest of the group went to the fire at the heart of the town square, sitting comfortably on logs that had been placed in a circle around it.

A few hours had passed. Most of the spiders headed to their nests to sleep. "Thanks for allowing us to stay for a while," Berinon said.

"Anytime," Arjan responded "You'll need all the strength for the journey that lies ahead. My apologies for the misunderstanding. We receive many 'visitors' in the woods, and few are friendly."

"No offence taken, elder. We were just passing through and had no intent to trespass."

Arjan removed his headdress, scratching his head. "Itchy headdress... It's customary to wear one as an elder, but that doesn't change how uncomfortable it is. Don't tell that to my subjects." The two shared a brief laugh with each other. Meanwhile, Reika sat inside one of the nests. Celeste was snuggled up to her asleep like a puppy. Reika rested her hand on top of Celeste's head.

She left the spider to rest as she climbed up to the web hammock next to her. Falling asleep was very easy despite where she was staying. Junayd and Zane were asleep on the other hammocks next to her with Melito and Tabitha resting on futons on the floor. Rian wasn't asleep. He sat in the chair, his right leg crossed, leaning on his left hand.

"Long night sir?" It was one of the small tarantulas who was with Tarquin when they'd attacked in the forest.

"Hard to sleep," Rian said. "Sometimes I can get a good night's rest. But most nights thoughts of my wife enter my mind, ruining it. The thoughts of her death are like a parasite, they just won't go away. I failed her."

The tarantula known as Bengt sat on the chair opposite Rian. "It's not something that will leave easily. Mourn her, yes, but never stop living your life because of what happened. What's in the past is done."

Sunrise arrived eight hours later. Junayd got up from his hammock. "Best night's sleep I've had, despite being a little nervous sleeping on a hammock of web."

Leaving the nest, he noticed a thicket of nettles in the distance. He already knew what needed to be done.

Tarquin arrived shortly after to get a fire going outside his nest. He planted himself neatly on a stump that he had carried with him, placing it on the ground. He rubbed the sticks ferociously on a dry section of the earth where some old ashes resided. The fire appeared just as planned, a gentle flame with light smoke rising into the open air. Tarquin grabbed a copper pot from next to him along with a rod and two holders, allowing him to hang the pot over the fire. *Some boiled rats will do me just fine for breakfast, maybe lizard tail for lunch,* he thought, rubbing his hands together in delight.

Reika finally awoke to the smell of the fire. "Morning," she said as she removed the dust from her eyes with her right thumb.

"Sleep well?"

"Yes, where's Junayd?"

"He has gone to relieve himself. He'll be back for breakfast. I am thinking a nice fruit bowl will do you some good. You look like you are in need of some nourishment."

"Well, when I was serving in a citadel, I was well provided food-wise. On this excursion, I have had some lovely food, but the fruit has been quite minimal..."

Tarquin chucked an apple at Reika, who caught it in her right hand, thanking Tarquin. Without a second to spare she bit into it. Melito and Tabitha awoke from their sleep. Tarquin handed fruit to both monkeys, with Melito taking an orange, tearing a hole in the rind then sticking the orange in his mouth. "Incredible taste! Haven't had one for a while."

Tabitha stuck a cluster of grapes in her mouth, pulling the branches out as she plucked each grape from its stem. "These grapes are so sweet, thank you."

"You're welcome," Tarquin replied. "Eat all the fruit you want."

Junayd arrived back, sitting down near the fire. "I'm starving." Junayd reached for a small stick on the ground, taking some of the fruit that had been given to him, consisting of orange and apple slices. He roasted them on the fire for a while, breathing on them to cool them down, and then bit. All but Tarquin looked at Junayd in disbelief. "Haven't you ever roasted fruit over an open fire before? I recommend it, good taste. Just make sure you don't destroy too much of the sugar."

"If you say so, we'll consider it," Reika said.

Zane also awoke from his slumber. "Everyone alright?"

The others nodded their heads. Rian arrived on the scene. He didn't say anything to Zane.

"Breakfast time, Rian, want anything?" Bengt asked. "What you all are having right now."

～

Berinon was alone with a young, grey tarantula named Merek in front of another nest, managing the fire.

"There are some lizard legs stored away in the nest. If you can bring them out, I'll get started on cooking them, Merek."

A few seconds later Merek brought out four lizard legs, handing them over to Berinon. He began to place them on a grill, turning them at the right time so that the heat made its way all the way through. Once finished, Berinon gave two of the legs to Merek, ready for consumption. He took his first bite into the leg. *Marvelous, haven't had this for a while,* he thought.

Merek spun his head round at the sound of a snapping twig. "Merek, what is it?"

"I heard something come from that thicket. It's watching us."

Berinon rose to his feet, summoning his lance in his hand, walking slowly to the bush with a defensive posture. "Merek, go to the others and warn them. I'll handle this."

Merek shot a web from his abdomen, pulling himself high into the trees, leaping through the trees across the village away from the nest while Berinon stayed to investigate.

"Out of the shadows wretch, I know you are there."

The figure paid no attention to Berinon; he instantly vanished from view Berinon gripped his lance, heading to Tarquin's house at breakneck speed.

Before Berinon and Merek had a chance to get there, the same figure appeared in the trees behind Tarquin's house, watching. Obscured by the thick thistles he stood behind, he clenched his left hand, blackened with a ghastly purple cloud.

Reika had no idea what was happening: her mind began to fill with hatred towards Tarquin, her eyes turning into the all-too-familiar reptilian orbs. Junayd could see something wrong with her. She raised her left hand and with the force of a small battering ram, used a telekinetic projectile, shoving Tarquin away from the camp-fire, lying on his back.

Before Berinon and Merek had a chance to get there, the same figure appeared in the trees behind Tarquin's house, watching. Obscured by the thick thistles he stood behind, he clenched his left hand, blackened with a ghastly purple cloud.

Reika had no idea what was happening: her mind began to fill with hatred towards Tarquin, her eyes turning into the all-too-familiar reptilian orbs. Junayd could see something wrong with her. She raised her left hand and with the force of a small battering ram, used a telekinetic projectile, shoving Tarquin away from the campfire, lying on his back.

"What are you doing? I thought all was forgiven?" Tarquin said, trembling. The young woman didn't listen. She raised her blade against Tarquin, ready to cut into the tarantula. Junayd grabbed Reika by the arm, preventing her from bringing her sword down on Tarquin.

"Snap out of it, that's enough."

Reika's head eerily twisted round. She said nothing, only giving him a cold stare. A few seconds later, the anger receded, a perturbed expression replaced it and the eyes shifting back into their normal state. She looked back at Tarquin, a look of shock on her face.

"I... don't know what came over me, I'm sorry."

Bengt arrived. He saw Reika standing in front of the prostrate Tarquin with her sword in her hand. Luniram disappeared from view.

Bengt flexed his fingers on his right hand. A small stinger shot out into Reika. She felt a slight pain in her side and blanked out, falling asleep on the grass next to the fire.

"A novice witch, an apprentice. Strong, no doubt. A human with a small structure could not by mere strength alone shove Tarquin to the ground, unless I am mistaken?" Bengt remarked. Tarquin rose to his feet. He grabbed Reika's unconscious body, slumping it over his shoulder.

"Elder Arjan must be informed what happened."

Junayd strode over to Tarquin. "Wait. Don't take her away, it wasn't her fault," he begged.

"We offer you hospitality and I begged for your friend to forgive me for what I did to her as a foolish boy. Is this how we are to be repaid? Be grateful Bengt didn't snap her neck. Back off or we shall carry out this execution here and now."

Junayd reluctantly stepped away. "Shouldn't we at least try to determine what happened?"

"You'll get your chance soon."

"Wait!" A young voice called from the distance. It was Merek, with Berinon only a few seconds behind. Merek began to speak frantically, "There was a sorcerer in the woods. He was hiding in the bushes; we have to warn..."

"What's the meaning of this?" Tarquin cut in, irritably.

Celeste had awakened due to the noise. "Daddy... What's wrong?" She asked, her grasp of the Consortium Standard not quite up to scratch like her father's.

"Go play sweetie, have some breakfast too, your daddy has some business to take care of."

Celeste could see Reika slumped over the shoulders of her father Tarquin.

She quietly went back inside the nest, saying nothing.

In the middle of the village square was a passage that led to a cavern whose borders matched the perimeter of the village itself. A small cell was there in a place dug out in the northwestern side of the cave; Reika sat in it, alone and miserable. The floor of the cave was very uncomfortable, and no natural light could be seen, only that of the torches that lit the passageways beyond her cell.

Junayd was allowed to visit her. They sat in silence.

Zane spoke with Berinon in private in the nest the latter had stayed in overnight. "I know you saw something within the trees," Zane said. "Reika fell under its influence; the fault doesn't lie with her. What was it?"

Berinon scratched his hair. "The figure, I am certain I may have seen that man before, but I could not quite make out who it was. A sorcerer of high calibre, an illusionist. He disappeared, going to another thicket near Tarquin's house. Reika then fell under his sway. I cannot even prove that to the Arachnoids."

Zane sighed. "It isn't your fault, if it is an illusionist, he has the potential to send anyone false visions of the future, so it will be difficult to determine where he has run off to or who he is. Even in a battle against him, my foresight can be blocked."

"I also believe this illusionist maybe the one who enabled Lief to escape," Berinon said. "As Visiert said, he noticed the cell was empty, but the guards did not notice this until it was too late. That and when I confronted the figure, he paid me no heed and vanished, likely getting to Reika quickly via teleportation. It does not bode well for us should he decide to lure us into a trap with his trickery."

Zane kicked a small stick into the fireplace of the nest. "If this true then this whole mess just keeps getting worse."

One of the guards, a money spider, entered the nest. Bengt accompanied him. "The Ferrum Champion, is he still with the human girl?"

Zane looked the guard in the eye. "Yes, he is."

A few minutes later, Junayd entered the nest and Bengt turned to face him. "Elder Arjan has made an offer that allows you to keep your friend and go free, if you can defeat a champion of ours in a fight, that is."

"And what if I lose?"

"Then I have an execution to carry out." "It wasn't Reika's fault."

"The young man speaks the truth Bengt," Berinon said. "I saw someone in the trees."

"You have no proof of that, you thought you saw something and that does not absolve the young sorceress of her actions."

Junayd clenched his fists in anger. "Alright, direct me to the champion and let me fight him."

Within the cavern echoed the sound of cheering crowds. At its heart was an arena where combat was practiced. The arena was floored with incredibly smooth sand, fine as sugar. Elder Arjan sat upon his throne, signalling silence to the crowds.

"Tonight, the young human, Junayd, will face off against our champion. His prize, the woman who attacked one of our own."

Junayd stepped out into the arena wearing scratched bronze armour that covered his body like Berinon's own battle-plates. He didn't hold the Draco Ferrum in his hand. Instead, he held a medium-sized blade of iron with serrated edges along it. Melito and Tabitha watched from the crowd, incredibly anxious. Bengt, who had escorted Junayd to the arena, spoke to him very quietly. "I hope you are prepared for this battle. Interesting you opted not to use that magic blade for this..."

Junayd didn't give Bengt eye contact. "I agreed to a fair fight. If I do win, will you not give us a chance to explain what happened?"

Bengt snorted. "Very well. But we'll worry about that if you survive."

At the sound of the gong, Junayd made his way over the arena grounds. He held his sword in the defensive stance, a look of determination on his face. The armour however did bother him, he was convinced that it hadn't been maintained to hold together properly. Any concerns he had were too late to rectify.

Out of the cave to the west, thundering footsteps echoed across the cavern. A humanoid hornet, roughly three heads taller than Junayd, emerged from the shadows. His markings were a blood red. His head was that of a hornet, plated with natural armour, his antennae bending backwards. The mandible-like structure on his face opened, revealing his mouth. He grinned at Junayd, who was staring at the insect in awe.

"So... You're the little man who is going to fight me. Name's Viggo. Doubt you'll live long to remember it."

"Don't be so arrogant. You might lose." Junayd did not sound convincing even to himself.

"Unlikely, little man." They arranged themselves so they were two paces from each other. Junayd resumed his defensive stance.

Viggo reached for his abdomen with his right hand, removing the sting from it gently. The sting began to grow until it grew to a size that was slightly longer than the iron blade Junayd was holding in his right hand.

"Let the match begin!" Arjan yelled, the gong once again clashing behind him, signalling the combatants to start fighting.

They charged full pelt at each other, their swords clashing, locking together. Junayd stared at the sting blade, perturbed. Viggo smirked at him. He shoved Junayd back, making his advance on the human, trying to cut him at every turn. Viggo eventually made contact with Junayd, slashing him across the chest with the stinger. It broke off the armour and cut into him. Junayd winced in pain but held in his scream. *He wasn't jesting, he certainly doesn't waste time.*

Junayd didn't loosen the grip of the serrated sword. He wiped the sweat of his face, beginning his attack as Viggo began to parry. They traded blows, their clashes reverberating inside the cavern, the sound of the swords bouncing off the walls before degrading into nothing. Each clash layered over the one before it, turning it into an elongated tune.

From her cell, Reika could hear the sound of their swords. "Be careful, Junayd," she said silently.

Junayd yelled at the top of his lungs as he swung the serrated blade from the right. Viggo blocked the attack, though the blow staggered him, causing a pain in his ankle, though it would not be enough to impede the giant hornet.

"You've got spirit, boy. I'll give you that!" Viggo allowed his wings to unfold. For a split second they flapped, propelling him into a jump, positioning his sting in a downward stab. Junayd flew out the way just in time, skidding along the floor. He wasted no time in advancing towards the hornet. Viggo caught sight of the space warping around the serrated blade as Junayd swung it. The hornet blocked again but a shockwave was released when the blades clashed, flinging Viggo across the room like a kicked pebble. His wings managed to slow down his flight, preventing himself from crashing into the cave wall.

"Big mistake, skinbag!"

Viggo started to zip around the room, attempting to slash Junayd with the sting. Junayd had difficulty dodging and parrying the attacks, they seemed to come from every angle at once. He felt a stab of pain in his right shoulder first, then his left thigh, and finally along the right of chest third, the armour was broken where Viggo had struck. Junayd collapsed to the floor, holding up his left hand, a fiery burst emanating from his hand towards Viggo, who let himself drop down just in time, using his wings to safely land on the floor just a few feet from the ground.

Junayd steadied himself up to his feet, using the sword as a crutch. *This armour is useless, I should have known something was wrong.* The venom coursing in his veins was an agony, to the point where the young man wanted to die. However, if he allowed himself to succumb, he knew Reika would lose her life. He ignored the pain and continued to fight. He knew that Viggo was also weakening. He simply had to hope Viggo fell first.

Junayd stood his ground once again, preparing to parry the next attack from Viggo. The hornet flew across the arena, causing the sand to be lifted by the immense sweep of his wings. He darted around Junayd swiftly, raising a large sand cloud around the young man. Junayd choked, closing his eyes tightly. He couldn't see where Viggo was in the cloud; all he could hear were wings, then the sound of the dust flowing around.

Junayd listened carefully to find out where Viggo was, the dust clearing. A silhouette appeared in front of him. Junayd held up the serrated sword, blocking the blow just in time, deflecting it up into the air, following it up with a kick to the stomach of Viggo, who fell to the ground in a thud.

Junayd then stabbed the serrated sword right into the middle of Viggo's stomach.

Arjan stood up in amazement. For a time, the caverns were devoid of a single sound. Then the crowd began to cheer, chanting Junayd's name in the process. Arjan sank back into his throne.

"Release the girl. She may leave with them," he said quietly to the guard on his right. "And send a healer to remove the poison from his blood, he'll die otherwise." Junayd's breathing was laboured. He collapsed onto the sandy floor. Before he fell into a dreamless sleep, the last thing he saw was Zane running towards him.

"You, like your friend, profess that a sorcerer was the one controlled Reika's mind and compelled her to attempt killing one of my own?" Arjan asked, his tone etched with disbelief. "Despite the fact we are letting her go free, you are wasting our time with your lack of proof."

"Proof? Reika would never attack someone like that, it's not who she is!" Melito cried.

Arjan scowled. "What of rumours of a weredragon sighted in Carthage and Caledonia in particular? Wouldn't it be more logical to assume that she was giving into her most base nature?"

"Evil comes in various forms; some are more susceptible to certain sins than others."

Arjan sat in his throne, thinking. Tarquin also was steeped in thought. He leaned over to Berinon. "The feeling of regret on her face. I didn't think of it at the time. Her eyes should have been the first sign to me that she wasn't herself. Perhaps you were telling the truth."

"You acted rashly," Berinon said, unable to hide his frustration with the way things had turned out. "You should've held back your aggression. This trial and fight wouldn't have happened."

Tarquin looked indignant. "What of Reika? A cursed one brought through *our* grounds?"

"We are trying to retrieve the Anodyne Stone! Once we have that, she'll never be a threat to you again."

"If you insist. I'll believe that when I see it." They ceased their conversation.

※

Bengt spoke to Reika in private after the trial. "I begin to wonder if you were yourself. What if the illusionist actually brought out your true feelings? You hate Tarquin for what he did as a child."

"Perhaps I do, I don't know what came over me, but rage grew within. I was filled with shame when I came to my senses. I wouldn't want to do that. Maybe some part of me is finding it hard to forgive, but that's something I need to work on... I thought when I first granted forgiveness, it was genuine, now I am not so sure. I hope I can come here again and make things right with him," Reika said, clutching her hand over her heart.

Bengt looked at Reika, his face changed to that of commiseration. "I don't know how to sort that out. When you get that curse lifted, maybe you can return here and talk it over. Elder Arjan has spared you from death thanks to the intervention of friends. Junayd was willing even to risk his life for you. The bond I see in you and him is a great one."

Bengt held out his hand. "If we meet again, may it be on good terms. Give Tarquin time to calm down."

Reika shook Bengt's hand, smiling back. "It's a deal."

Junayd was brought out by Zane. The poison had been removed from his body by a healer, and Zane had sealed his wounds.

Chapter 16

Luentinum

U ric was waiting rather impatiently on the *Coeptus*, when he caught sight of the group in the distance. He brought the airship close to the land and threw down the ladder. Berinon made his way up, followed by Zane

and the two monkeys. Junayd clambered onto the deck, then pulled Reika up after. Reika sat to the right of Junayd on the port-side, leaning against the deck wall. The *Coeptus* began to sail across gently away, all were safely onboard, and the ladder was brought back up.

Junayd felt absolutely exhausted mentally. He was, however, happy that Reika had been allowed to leave. Reika said nothing to Junayd, only smiling back at him. Junayd held his left hand out and Reika took it with her right hand. They rested against the deck wall. He could change into his desert robes later.

Tabitha was sitting near the stairs below deck, quietly consuming some berries that had been given to her by the spiders. Melito sat to her right.

"How much further until we get to Aerouant Citadel, Melito?" Tabitha enquired.

"We have to pass through Luentinum. The citadel is on the

other side of the moon. We should be there soon," Melito replied. Tabitha passed Melito a few berries. "They'll know what the next course of action to take is."

Melito shoved at least three berries into his mouth. "Quite delicious, thanks." "No problem. Can't be expected to eat all of them."

Melito scratched the wooden decking with his right hand, losing himself in his own thoughts. "That man Berinon warned us about. Where is he now? We need to stop him before he causes any more trouble for us. If he gets a hold of Reika again, there's no telling what he might do. Especially with Lief now free."

They docked near a set of ruins made of tan-coloured stone, lying abandoned in the desert along with a temple structure. The stone was cracked and split, reduced to rubble by an unknown force.

"Was this a town?" Reika asked.

"Yes, dragons once worshipped here," Junayd replied. "I wonder if Destrian attacked it."

The rest of the group gazed upon the ruins. Tabitha went over to one of the houses, picking up a small piece of broken pottery. She examined it intently. A small figure could be seen on the side, the image of a woman with bolts of lightning sparking from her. Another piece Tabitha immediately recognised: it was the man with the sword fighting the dark dragon; the bottom half of their bodies were again missing.

"I saw this in Caledonia," she said. Melito arrived next to her. She handed the piece with the woman to him. He examined it.

"Any other pieces?"

Tabitha picked up a third shard of pottery. This one had several dragon-like creatures on it. Melito knew instantly what they were.

"I have seen these before... What could these images mean?" Tabitha pondered.

"Only one way to find out Tabs. The temple might have some answers."

They rushed towards the temple, heading up the stone stairs. The others saw them and hurried along. The massive hall's roof had cracks and large holes, the light of the sun shining through. To their astonishment, Melito and Tabitha saw an incredible mural in front of them. The two stared at the pieces of pottery one by one, they realised the images on the pottery matched what was engraved on the mural.

"Just as the potters said," Tabitha remarked. "Potters?" Reika asked. "When?"

"We spoke to some potters in Bahaduro, they believe in a prophecy pertaining to the weredragons," Melito replied.

"May I look?" Reika asked. Melito and Tabita held the pieces up. She looked between them and the mural to her left. The full picture of the mural showed the man with his sword, engaging in combat with the beast, itself holding a blade. The other dragons could be seen on the left side of the mural, their teeth bared and their claws ready for battle. On the right side was the woman, the lightning flashing from her body and colliding with a few dragons above her. The lightning struck the beasts and ran right through them. Junayd and Reika were completely mesmerised by the mural, as was Berinon. Rian also looked at it, scanning the image with his eyes.

"This mural... Is this a prophetic one?" Rian asked. "In all my travels, I have heard of a prophecy regarding weredragons but never gave much thought to it."

Reika stared at the woman; she saw swirls below her. *I have seen this image before, it was incomplete. Antonius had a piece of broken pottery in his palace, only half of the picture. Those markings below her I have also seen.* She thought.

Her eyes widened and she remembered the stone that Welk held and crushed in front of her eyes. "Could that be the Anodyne Stone under the figure's feet?" Reika said, not realising she'd spoken aloud.

Junayd looked at the man in the mural. "It is. The woman is you; the man is me. Is this what is going to happen?" He was trembling. "The dragons never told me this."

Reika then remembered Ysellian. "Ysellian has the answer. If she is at the citadel, I need to ask her about this mural."

Twenty minutes after the group left the temple, they found themselves outside a pure orange stone fortress. It towered over the desert sands.

"The Luentinum Fortress, a place where dissidents gather," Berinon said. "What kind of dissidents are we talking about?" Junayd asked.

Berinon cleared his throat, almost hesitant to speak. "Soldiers from all over Perusia, many of them have left their respective armies or were exiled for bad conduct." He eyed the fortress more. "The sad thing is this fortress stands as a testament to their defiance. Fools like this give soldiers such as me a bad name."

Melito scowled at the tower. "I think I know who we are going to be taking care of. Time to put down these rebels."

Reika crossed her arms, shutting her eyes. "What is wrong with these soldiers? Why would they rebel against their respective nations, nations they once protected?"

No one had an answer for her.

The high wooden door opened, revealing the narrow hall. The interior was surprisingly well-maintained. The hallway pillars were composed of ornate hickory-coloured brick. The walls were orange stone with white, chalk-coloured flooring.

The group entered the hall, weapons on hand as they made their way to a door at the end. Two small corridors led away from the central hall. Before the group had even made it a third of the way of the hall, six soldiers wearing grey armour emerged from the corridors.

A disgrace to knights, guards, and soldiers, Berinon thought as he gripped the hilt of his lance tighter. The six strode towards the group, their swords in their hands, standard blades but with sharp tips and gleaming edges. Rian did not draw his gun, thinking it would be too antagonistic.

"Something about these soldiers is off," Rian said. "They don't appear to be themselves. Just knock them out!"

"They are bewitched?" Junayd said. "How can one sorcerer do this to so many?"

Rian dodged one of the guards, who had mindlessly attacked with a downward cut against him. The elf landed a sharp blow to the back of the guard's head. The man hit the floor with force, though not dead.

Melito parried two of the guards. "Tabitha, fire the arrows at their shoulders when I say!" He called. Tabitha readied her bow. She was caught off-guard by another soldier who had circled around to attack from behind. Tabitha launched a punch swiftly to the guard's face, knocking him to the ground. "Now!" Melito called.

Tabitha fired two arrows in a quick succession, and they hurtled right into the shoulders of the guards in front of Melito. They yelled in pain. Taking advantage of their distraction, Melito swung the handle of his axe into the chin of the guard on his right, following it up with a sharp jab in the stomach of the guard on the left.

Berinon had no problems parrying the attacks of the guard who was attacking him. He spun his lance around like a windmill. The guard cocked his head indicating he was trying to plan where to strike. He didn't have time to attack, however, as Berinon instantly struck him in the chin with the butt of the spear. *Disappointing,* Berinon thought.

A seventh soldier leapt from the ceiling, attempting to attack Reika. She saw the attack just in time, swinging her sword at the guard who blocked her attack. He advanced on her, striking with ferocity, pushing Reika further back as she parried. Reika swiftly slid backwards to give herself enough distance. Luniram began to shimmer, then Reika threw it like a boomerang toward the guard. The energy emanated from the blade creating a small explosion as the blade struck the chest of the guard. He collapsed on the ground.

Reika pulled her sword back to herself. It vanished from sight.

Junayd and Zane held their own against two of the guards exceedingly well. "Is this the best they can do?" Junayd asked. "They are going down easily, no reason to even try."

Zane threw a punch at the head of the guard he was fighting. The man fell and didn't get up again.

"Merely a test," Zane said. "They should be better than this, they are being treated as expendable."

Junayd de-summoned the Draco Ferrum. The guard looked at him with surprise, throwing his sword on the floor, readying himself in a boxing pose. The two clashed in a bare-knuckle brawl, throwing hooks and jabs, their fists becoming calloused with each collision. Junayd smirked at the guard, throwing a punch, his right fist smacking into the guard's jaw. He was careful to make sure it only rendered the guard unconscious. "He's going to feel that in the morning."

The group left the unconscious guards where they were on the ground as they headed for the door. Beyond it, they found themselves in another corridor. At the far end was a treasure room, with deep pits surrounding their right side. Two bulky guards were present on the other side of the pits; a small platform floated in the middle of the pit. The guards cracked their knuckles, along with their necks.

Berinon summoned his lance, slamming the end of it onto the stone floor. He leapt onto the small platform then over to the other side where the two guards were.

"Foolish little man!" one yelled. The two punches they threw at Berinon were in vain as he dodged effortlessly out of the way. The guard's punches instead collided with the face of their ally, knocking themselves out. All but Zane looked on in amazement.

"Still a crazy fool," Rian said shaking his head.

Berinon turned around, de-summoning his lance. "Running into an ambush is one thing. Going against these hulking beasts? It's something else..." He remarked. Berinon didn't stay for long and continued on his way, leaving the unconscious guards behind. He vaulted across another pit to a small platform and found a little winding bridge pathway.

Tabitha snuck her head round the northern door to the treasure room. She could only gape at the piles of gold, silver, and bronze. Gold bars were stacked up against the walls. Crates contained glittering coins. *The money that we could make from all this... The possibilities are endless.* A big grin stretched across her face.

Melito also stepped inside the room. "It's Luentinum's own vault. Sadly, it's not ours, I suggest we move on."

Tabitha spun round. Melito looked serious. She sighed. "Very well."

Tabitha walked away from the room. Melito clenched his fists, restraining himself from attempting to grab any of the gold bars.

Reika was waiting by the pit for her friends. "You took your time; we need to get moving."

"Treasure Reika, it's very alluring."

"For a place like this, I am astounded it's still here."

~

Junayd explored an open area of the castle. He had his sights focused higher.

Berinon caught up with him.

"It's unwise to go on ahead, young man. We need to stay close." Junayd nodded. "You're right. How are the others?"

"They'll be along shortly. Since we are both here, let's take a quick look at what is through that doorway."

Junayd ventured to the door. He was cautious not to go through. Peering his head round the doorway, he saw a guard there patrolling a stone structure. Berinon came over to Junayd.

"There's something odd about that one, I'm going to take a closer look." "Guard yourself, Junayd. Appearances can be deceiving."

The young man entered. The guard didn't see Junayd at first, but he smelled a change in the air. Junayd ceased moving.

"He has picked up my scent. How?" He pondered. The guard turned around to look at Junayd. He removed his helmet to reveal a pale skinned face with ginger hair. His physique was that of a man in his prime who had endured hard labour.

Chucking his helmet on the ground, the guard opened his eyes to reveal blue reptilian orbs. He smirked then transformed before Junayd's eyes in a cloud of vast dark energy. The guard revealed his true form, that of a wyvern roughly twenty feet tall. His wing-claws raked the ground before slamming it. The wyvern let out an ear-piercing shriek.

The Draco Ferrum appeared in Junayd's hands in a moment. Four more guards emerged, one with an axe, another a sword, one with a spiked mace, and another with knuckle dusters on his gloves.

"Quite a crowd," Junayd said.

Berinon entered the room with his lance in hand.

"So not even wyverns are safe from an illusionist?" Junayd asked.

"This one was weak willed," Berinon said. "The elders in the Aerouant Citadel will not be easily tricked or swayed."

The rest of the team arrived. Reika drew her blade. She looked at the wyvern towering over them. *Unease fails to describe the sight of the dragons in their true form.* she thought.

All brought their arms to bear. Junayd gripped the hilt of the Ferrum tighter. "Rian, Berinon, you're with me to fight the wyvern. The rest of you, go after the guards," he said with a fervent command.

The wyvern began a mighty charge, shrieking as it moved. The dragon's legs causing tremors in the ground.

Junayd, Berinon, and Rian yelled as they ran too. Junayd swung his blade to the right. The wyvern successfully caught the Ferrum between its jaws. The dragon's breath began to heat up the blade, turning the metal extremely hot. Junayd didn't let go of the Ferrum, pulling with all his might. It released the Ferrum, then began snapping his jaws at Junayd, pushing the young man away. He kept his distance from the wyvern, using the Ferrum to ward the creature off.

Berinon threw a punch straight into the wyvern's chest. The beast recoiled from the pain. It hissed, ready to hit again.

Rian stood at least twelve feet away, firing rounds at the chest of the wyvern. "I thought it was agreed we don't kill them?" Berinon said crossly.

"These bullets won't kill him... just annoy him," Rian said with a smug look on his face.

Meanwhile, the others had their hands full with the guards. Reika was fighting against the swordsman with Zane by her side. Melito struggled against the ones with the axe and spiked mace, and Tabitha fought against the one with the knuckle duster.

Melito parried the axe and mace effectively, swinging Entella's Bane in retaliation with such force that it made both the guards stagger. The guard with the mace recovered quickly, however, smacking his weapon squarely against Melito's armour, sending him flying a few feet back, sliding on his posterior with Entella's Bane dropping to the floor. The two guards ignored the axe and closed on Melito. The marmoset was undeterred. If anything, his resolve to win only grew. With a smile on his face, he repositioned his fists, still lying on his back. *Crazy monkey,* the guards thought, racing towards the marmoset. Seeing the attack, Melito slid under the mace-wielding guard, whose weapon embedded in the stone floor. Melito instantly stood up, slapping both his hands against the guard's ears.

"Aaaah!"

Melito kicked the other guard in the stomach, causing the axe to fall from his hand. Melito forcibly grabbed the guard's head and bashed it against the head of his comrade. The two collapsed. Melito summoned his axe back to him.

Tabitha was cautious not to let the knuckle dusters touch her. She unleashed a few punches of her own against the guard, who dodged them easily. Confidence made him careless, allowing Tabitha to strike the guard in the face. He reeled so much from the blow his knuckle dusters flew off his hands and dropped on the floor.

"Not so tough without that, are you?" Tabitha said.

The guard smirked. "I don't need those knuckle dusters to kill you."

The two traded blows. Tabitha evaded a straight jab, following it up with a backhanded swing with her left fist against the guard's helmet. Tabitha shook her hand, wincing slightly from the pain of connecting with steel. The guard cracked his knuckles.

"I'm going to enjoy this." He launched three punches in rapid succession, Tabitha evading them all. A fourth blow was landed on her chin. Tabitha growled as she backed away, rubbing her chin. She grabbed the soldier's head, smacking it on the wall, causing him to fall unconscious.

The swordsman who faced Reika and Zane was rather proficient. The two humans were effortlessly parried. Reika's sword hit the guard's armour, leaving only a scratch.

"Any further and you would have killed me," the swordsman remarked.

Reika said nothing. She and Zane merely carried on with the

fight. The flurry of blades from all three combatants created to a tuneless melody.

Zane had an intense look of concern on his face. *I can't waste foresight on this man, he's not worth it, though his skill is impeccable.*

Reika raised her blade to defend herself from the next swipe of the guard's sword. The recoil caused Reika to take a few steps back. Swiftly she brought her sword back in front of her while slashing at the guard again. She nodded to Zane who in turn responded with a swipe of his own. The guard's right arm was cut by Verwandeln. The guard winced, still holding the sword in his left hand. He tried to hit Zane with his sword although it was to no avail. Zane changed Verwandeln into a small club and with a mighty swipe, slammed the club into his chest, The guard fell down silently and remained still.

Now, only the shriek of the wyvern echoed, reverberating to the sky. Junayd, Rian, and Berinon were still in close combat with the dangerous beast.

Junayd defensively held the Draco Ferrum. "Hold the wyvern off, I need some time!" He called to his comrades. Rian fired a few bullets at the left of the wyvern's head, directing the creature's attention at him. Sticking the Draco Ferrum into the floor, Junayd kept his right hand holding the blade handle, holding out his left hand to the side, bending his arm. His hand glowed with an intense light before the light shrank in on itself. He thrust his arm and hand forward, firing a burst of light at the wyvern's head. It shrieked loudly, stamping around wildly in pain. Its swipes at Rian failed to touch him; it was dazed and confused, thrashing about like one in a drunken stupor trying to reach for a door. The creature stopped, shaking its head, shrugging off the pain.

Rian and Berinon paused, wondering what the creature would do next, priming their weapons for combat. The wyvern transformed back into a human form, red-bearded and pale faced, and summoned a sword to himself as he flew towards Junayd at breakneck speed. His sword slammed into the Draco Ferrum causing a shockwave that created immense splits on the side of the wall as well as a small crater where Junayd was standing.

Why has he resumed his human form? Junayd wondered as he strained against the might of the wyvern. "What do they call you?" He asked.

"Joonas, young human, and this is where you lose."

The wyvern-man leapt out of the pit away from Junayd, leaving the young human to float magically out of the crater. Junayd resumed his defensive stance. "If I remain in my true form, I'd be an easy target," Joonas went on. "I'm not going to let what you did happen again. That, and I like a little competition. Let's fight against each other as equals, boy."

All except Junayd kept their distance from Joonas. The battle commenced, their swords thundering against each other. Joonas was swifter in human form, his aggression channelled into every single strike. Junayd had no problem countering the attacks, however. He slid away from one slash which almost cut into his nose. Junayd stood there holding the Ferrum in his right hand, hunched over, legs apart and a look of determination on his face.

"Don't forget whom you are facing, Joonas," he said.

"I haven't, but you have yet to live up to your reputation." Joonas said snidely.

Junayd shook his head in amazement. *Tell that to the deceased hornet in Aranae.* The two charged towards each other and locked their blades. With neither able to gain advantage, they backed away from each other.

Junayd was impressed by Joonas's strength. One final clash commenced. Both warriors brought their full power to bear, turning, flipping, striking, a continual clash of blades which would have echoed for miles had it not been for the desert wind that brushed the exterior of the castle.

Joonas threw a punch into Junayd's left cheek, making him reel back three steps. Junayd dropped the Draco Ferrum onto the ground, slightly disoriented. Joonas slashed from the right, Junayd just about managed to catch the sword in his hands, his vision making him see double. He didn't hold the blade long lest Joonas twist it in his hands and ruin him. Relinquishing the blade, Junayd kept his distance so his vision could readjust.

At last, it did and he struck Joonas's right hand to make him drop his sword; the two began trading blows with their fists, elbows, and kicks. Reika could only watch with awe and concern. At last, Junayd threw a final punch, colliding with Joonas's left cheek. The wyvern's legs wobbled. His punches failed to hit Junayd, leaving the young human to dodge. For every punch thrown and missed by Joonas, one followed from Junayd. Eventually, Joonas collapsed in exhaustion, falling to the ground, sitting there, slumped. His right foot rested on its sole and his left leg lay straight on the ground, as though he were relaxing in a summery meadow.

Joonas and Junayd both breathed heavily.

"A worthy fight, young man. Your strength is impressive. I can see why you were chosen to be the Ferrum's wielder."

Junayd was confused. "Why the high praise?" "You released me from the grasp of Montanus." "What do you mean?"

"Simple," Joonas said. "Montanus, the illusionist. He brainwashed us. We attacked our homes; we were banished for our transgressions. Montanus claimed that he would give us a home but all he did was put us under his spell, keeping us in his thrall. An army fit for Destrian to use as he saw fit, soldiers for his cause. Forgive me, young man, for the trouble I have caused you. I wish I could take back what I did to my home."

Junayd knelt down. "It's not your fault, Joonas. Get some rest. We'll stop Montanus." The others approached. It was time to head on. Junayd rose. "Hey, when this is over Joonas, what do you say to a friendly sparing match?"

Joonas smiled. "May it be so one day." The group proceeded on their way.

❧

A cylindrical room was next, with an open pit surrounding an inner platform. Beautiful gold trimming augmented the purple, orchid, and crimson-coloured carpets.

"Be careful," Zane said. "This room is not what it seems, we are in the dwelling of an illusionist."

As they ventured into the room, the group reached the middle of the platform. The room terraformed before their eyes. First, it transitioned into a lava-filled cavern, then transitioning into a comfortable forest, next to a sandy oasis surrounded by water, and finally a version of the room where the pit had completely vanished.

The transition happened in a loop with no end. Fire, forest, sand, and a copy of the room without the pit. They all felt disoriented as colours whirled around them, unceasingly blending together like a messy soup.

"How do we make this stop?" Reika called, grasping her head in pain. "There is only one way!" Zane replied. He lifted his right hand into the air, waiting for the room without a pit to reappear. Time wound down to a crawl around the group once Zane slammed his hand down, causing a powder-blue dome to encircle them.

"Move in ten seconds or we'll be trapped again!" Zane called as he dashed to the northern side of the room. The others swiftly followed. With only two seconds left, they made it to the next staircase that led downwards to the ground floor. Time picked up its pace once again, and the room didn't change.

"Thanks Zane," Reika said. "You're welcome."

Zane dropped the floor, his energy depleted.

"Whoa..." Melito said. "Easy... are you going to be alright?"

"I'll be fine, just give me a moment's rest," Zane replied. The young man straightened himself and arose. He headed down the stairs and bade the others to follow him. Berinon and Rian went down after Zane, followed by Junayd and Reika, then finally Melito and Tabitha.

After getting to the bottom of the stairs, they found a desert garden with palm trees and small desert flowers growing together on light grass, all surrounded by a wooden fence. *Some part of me wishes I could admire the scenery, there's no time though,* Reika thought, as she took in the sigh of the little oasis.

They made it to the door to the Luentinum Throne room. The room was sealed off, with no way to enter. It looked on the surface like an ordinary castle door with wood and golden metal rims, a regal door in surprisingly good condition.

"Be careful with this one, he is dangerous. We need to move fast. We cannot let him continue in his work," Rian said.

Zane kicked the door in. The remaining group members rushed into the massive throne room. The illusionist sat on a dark throne at the top of a raised stepped dais. His flowing cream-milk-coloured robes featured a cummerbund holding them together and a large hood covered his face in shadow. His physique though ancient was muscular. The sleeves were long though not very wide. Bulky black boots were worn by the illusionist.

"So, you're the ones who have been attacking my fortress? The name is Montanus." The man's voice was monotone. He saw Rian in the room and instantly fired a small but powerful blast of energy right through the elf's shoulder. Rian lay on the floor in agony.

Zane ran to Rian's body, placing his hand on the elf's wound, reversing the damage done, helping Rian to his feet. "Blaggard!" Zane yelled.

"That's for the fool's treachery. I could have done far worse if I wanted to."

Berinon was incensed. "The Luentinum Fortress doesn't belong to you. How dare you defile these hallowed halls."

Montanus merely smirked. "Oh really?" He jumped from the throne, landing in front of them. He made his slow advance to the group. "How typical, all of these men thrown out like yesterday's detritus. That's nothing new. I have given these soldiers a home. Soldiers left to die, unwanted and uncared for."

Melito himself was furious too. "That's a lie!" He roared. "Many soldiers defected. Some were pronounced dead and some openly attacked their own homes and were thrown out. Joonas revealed to us he and the others were under *your* control. You caused them to be banished so you could have an army of your own for Destrian to use."

"Sure, let us run with that narrative," Montanus said in a sarcastic tone. "Are you the one who one who helped Lief escape?" Berinon asked.

Montanus grinned. "It was a simple task, by the time the king realised what was going on, both of us had already departed."

He turned his eyes on Reika. "Well, well, well, the weredragon has arrived." Montanus moved closer to Reika, who backed off.

"It appears to me that my little test paid off. Your friend managed to stay your hand." Montanus removed his hood, revealing a white face and bald head, with piercing green reptilian eyes, and a scar running down his face.

"I think it's time I showed you the truth, why you shouldn't be placing your trust in the Ferrum Champion," Montanus said.

A skylight in the ceiling opened at a sluggish pace, revealing the moon. Reika looked up into its baleful light. "That's it? I haven't turned into a weredragon since I got here?"

"Oh child, do you remember how you lost control in the forest? The transformation may be blocked here, but it doesn't change the fact that you used your *full* power, your true power. Your lack of control was all *my* doing. Now, you are mine again."

A dark aura begun to emanate from Reika's body. She clasped her head with her hands, shrieking loudly as she fell to the floor.

"Leave her alone!" Junayd yelled. Reika turned to Junayd; her face contorted in pain.

"Leave now! Please, I beg you."

"No way, I am not leaving you." Junayd turned to everyone else. "You go!

I'll help Reika. Leave this room now."

Tabitha and Melito nodded. "Don't you die on us Junayd!" Tabitha said.

All the group except Junayd left. The aura around Reika didn't stop, it only grew, engulfing her. When she was fully enveloped it dissipated, leaving Reika as she was when she fought Lief, the difference being her hair had retained its natural colour.

"Reika?" Junayd asked. Her head hung down with her eyes closed. As she lifted her head, a look of anger crossed her face.

"Am I ok you ask?" She looked up and opened her eyes, darkly reptilian. "You lied to me."

Junayd's eyes widened. "Lied? What are you talking about?"

"You weren't trying to protect me, were you? You and everyone, you were planning to kill me rather than find a cure."

"Of course not, I want to help you. I want to get rid of the were-dragon's curse."

"But you are carrying the Draco Ferrum, right? You powered it up at the forges, intending to bring me to Destrian, and allow him to turn me into a weredragon and kill me."

Junayd for the first time shed a tear in front of Reika. "That hurts me. I don't want you to die. How could you say that?"

"Montanus opened my eyes. He can see right through you." "He is the one deceiving you."

"No, he isn't, he's helping me."

Reika was silent for a second. "I have seen where my parents are held in the vision he bequeathed to me, they are captive in Destrian's Castle, I'll set them free." Junayd shook his head. "What are talking about? Your parents are dead! You said so yourself. Don't you think it's weird that this sorcerer is telling you these things? Why now would you accept the words of this teller of untruths?"

Montanus stepped forward in anger. He spoke softly into Reika's left ear. "Forget his lies Reika, don't you have a task to accomplish? Slay him, then you can rescue your parents."

"Reika, you have stop listening to him, if you don't, you'll die!" Reika's disposition changed from rage to confusion.

"Huh? I'll die? Junayd?" Reika recoiled again in pain. "UNGH!"

"Come on, Reika! Fight it!" Reika released her hands from her forehead, staring at Junayd once again.

"No." Reika drew Luniram.

"You draw your sword at me, Reika?"

"To think I trusted you. I will not die at your hand. You on the other hand will perish at mine." Junayd summoned the Draco Ferrum at its full strength, empowered by the forges, holding the sword in a defensive stance. His body began to glow with a pure white aura. "You won't be able to defeat me, as long as I hold this blade."

"Oh really? Try your hand against me!" Reika began her first attack, flying towards Junayd at full pelt. Junayd was caught off-guard, only just managing to parry her lunge. Reika had demonstrated her real strength while under the moon's light, though not quite like this. She was almost as strong as him. He saw the moon above was full. *Her strength, her magic, her speed, it's amplified by the moon's light, just like the fight with Magnus' thugs, that golem and Welk Seha. The more moonlight there is, the more powerful she becomes. There was a full moon on the day she used her powers for the first time, Tabitha and Melito told me this after I defeated her as a weredragon back in Bahaduro.* Reika swiftly moved back, planting her feet firmly on the ground.

"Reika! Stop this! I don't want to fight you!"

"Silence!" Junayd clutched the handle of the sword tighter. *I have to defeat her. It's the only way to break control over her. Hang in there, Reika, I'll help you.* The two warriors leapt high in the air, each beginning their assault with quick powerful strikes. Montanus observed the battle smirking, impressed by their strength.

The two soon locked blades, looking each other in the eye. "You have to listen to me Reika!"

"Why should I?"

"Because I want to help cure you, let me do so!"

"Just perish." Reika kicked Junayd in the stomach, pushing him away from her, following it up with another attack in which she held her hands out, shooting a tornado spiral. Junayd span a while in the air. He managed to summon a kinetic wave around himself to knock the wind away.

Reika summoned dark magical shards, sending them flying towards Junayd like speeding arrows. Junayd wasn't impressed. The Draco Ferrum glowed with pure light and with a mighty slash, he sent a crescent of light towards the shards, vaporising them completely. "Reika, fight it. Don't let him control you!"

Reika was hesitant to attack this time. "I'm... trying..."

Montanus' face contorted into a scowl. "You will obey me, you worthless brat!" He raised his hand. The young girl gripped her sword tightly once again, her worried face now changing to a stern one.

"You don't deserve that blade, Junayd!" She yelled. Desummoning Luniram and lifting her curled hands high, fire, ice and lighting snaked around Reika's arms, coalescing into a ball of triple-coloured light above her, the three elements encircling it like moons orbiting a planet. Junayd raised his blade for his own defence, shocked at the power in front of him. Reika lowered her palms and the energy spun towards Junayd in a dazzling display of clashing elements. Junayd didn't want to risk striking the energy ball with his hands and swung his blade into it. It exploded, sending the three elements violently crashing around the room. The water pools in the room heated to scalding levels.

Junayd was struck down to the floor by the explosion, the Draco Ferrum slamming to the floor beside him, embedding itself in the stone floor.

Reika also wasn't lucky. An electrical surge crashed into her, knocking her straight to the floor at high speed.

The two managed to clamber to their feet, groaning in pain. They both hobbled forwards, stopping opposite one another. Both shook, immense pain coursing through their bodies from the explosive surge. Reika called on her blade and held it high feebly, exhausted. She attempted to fire another burst of energy at Junayd, but her arms trembled, barely able to hold her sword in her hand.

"What's wrong? You're not fighting fully, are you?" Montanus watched with a look of glee on his face. "Now, Reika, finish him off! Kill your conniving friend!" Montanus commanded.

Reika's anger subsided, her hair returned to its normal length, and her eyes returned to human form. She dropped Luniram on the ground in defiance, not that she could hold it anymore, she was too weak. The sword vanished.

"I... I can't. I won't kill him."

Montanus eyed Junayd. "Maybe perhaps you can give the killing blow?" This of course Montanus didn't want as he had to bring Reika to Destrian alive. This was purely to see what Junayd was willing to do.

Junayd straightened, using his sword as a crutch. Instead of drawing the weapon up, he let go of it, banishing it away in glowing light. "Reika, look at me." He strained to hold his hand out as a supplication gesture. "I don't have the sword in my hand, I am not going to hurt you. I promise you that."

The young woman listened to Junayd. She croaked his name. Suddenly, she limped to Junayd and threw her arms around his neck to embrace him. Reika couldn't contain herself anymore, she sobbed uncontrollably.

"I'm so sorry. Please forgive me," she said in a quavering voice.

Junayd held Reika, shedding a tear as well. "It's alright. Everything is going to be ok." Junayd then laughed. "Now look what you've done, you've made me tear up again."

Reika chuckled as well. The two of them let go. The fight was over, and Reika was back in control.

Montanus saw how weak the two were and prepared to wound both of them with one blast. "I think I'm going to puke," he muttered quietly. Without a second thought, he released the energy blast. Neither had time to react, except to look at the blast, when suddenly a purple glass barrier blocked the energy. The shield dissipated and a figure stepped between them and Montanus. There, standing between them all, was Visiert, holding his hand in the air. He lowered his arm. Behind him, Reika and Junayd's wounds had been healed.

"Why? You dare interfere?" Montanus uttered in a rage.

"Why indeed?" Visiert retorted. "How gutless you are, pitting them against each other in the hopes of weakening them, it's unconscionable." Visiert walked away from the throne, then turned to address the two. "He's all yours."

Junayd focused his attention back to Montanus. The two young humans called upon their blades once again. They stood facing the wizard.

"Are you that heartless?" Reika asked.

Montanus cocked his head. "How *did* you break my spell?" "Junayd opened my eyes."

"I figured out your scheme," Junayd said.

"Scheme?" the sorcerer said, deviously. "I just merely showed Reika the truth, she doesn't want to face it."

"No, *Junayd* was telling me the truth."

"You were planning to send Reika to her death. You wanted her to go to your master's fortress alone. You knew Reika would lose and would be banished, thus Destrian would have the weredragon under his control."

"Banish her?"

"To Somnium Carcerum. You kill Reika by leaving her there to disappear forever, reducing her to being a Tentorian, and in her place the weredragon alone

exists. It's not the first time and the sad thing is one who you would consider beneath you very nearly succeeded."

Monatanus sneered at Junayd in disgust. He knew Welk had succeeded in banishing Reika to Somnium Carcerum once before. It galled him to have failed.

"Fine... You saw through my spell, boy. But your death is certain."

With a roar, Montanus transformed into his true dragon form.

It was a creature of hideous muscle mass, the contours of its limbs were like that of a chiselled statue but exaggerated beyond sense. His scales were a cream colour.

Reika and Junayd stood their ground ready to fight, the full moon regenerating Reika's power.

The two begun their attack on Montanus, who swept aside their attacks with invisible barriers, revealing themselves only when struck. Montanus countered, pushing the two away. From his maw burst two spheres of light and dark particles. Reika summoned a barrier to surround Junayd and herself, the spheres bounced off the barriers onto the floor, rolling like marbles until they were visible no more. Reika dispelled the barrier and Junayd unleashing a crescent of light at Montanus.

Montanus staggered, transforming back into his humanoid form, collapsing on the floor kneeling with his right hand holding tightly to the left side of his chest. "You miserable brats," he snarled. Junayd flew across the room, grabbing Montanus by the scruff of his robe.

"You owe Reika the truth, after the lies you fed to her. Tell her now!"

Montanus growled. "I have looked into your heart, Junayd. You are protecting Reika."

Reika stepped closer to the old dragon. "Where are my parents? Did they die?"

"Yes, they are dead, that is the truth. They fought valiantly against my master and lost their lives."

Visiert continued to observe from afar. He remained reticent. Junayd closed the grip on the sorcerer's robe tighter. "Run back to your master."

Montanus was indignant. "We'll meet again. Destrian will destroy you and he will rule Perusia from this moon."

Junayd pointed his blade squarely at Montanus' face. "We are coming for him. Tell him I'll be the one to kill him. Cross me again and you'll be next."

Then Montanus started to laugh. "If I recall, Welk made a joke of you, boy. Though I admit my information needs an update, I like to see how that sword

can fare against *him*." With that, Montanus vanished from view, leaving the two humans with Visiert.

~

Zane and the others re-entered the throne room. They saw Reika and Junayd holding hands.

"I am so sorry, Junayd."

"It's ok. You were under his spell." "I know. But it keeps happening."

"You are safe and no longer under his control."

Reika started to bite her top lip gently. "What held you back? You had me at your mercy. You could have ended my curse then and there with one blow."

Junayd placed the back of his hand on Reika's cheek, stroking her face gently. "I told you. It's because I want to help cure you."

"We all do," Tabitha said, striding forward.

"What if Lief helps us get the stone from Destrian?" Melito added. "That's a big *if*," Zane said.

"In any case, we journey on," Junayd said. "We must head to the Aerouant Citadel. Once there, we can formulate an assault on Destrian's Castle."

Reika said nothing. She pondered what she had been told. She didn't look upset, instead, she looked disappointed. *Montanus... He was lying... I wish they were still alive...Worse that I've never met them.*

"Let us depart from this place. Hopefully the other soldiers have been released from the spell they were under, much like Joonas was," Berinon said.

Melito clenched his fists, reopening them once he brought them up in line with his eyes when he looked partly towards the floor. "I am so foolish; I can't believe I used to think they were traitors. I don't know what to say."

Berinon patted Melito on the shoulder. "Fear not, you made an honest mistake, we all did. Let us leave and go onwards to the citadel."

Reika went to speak with Visiert. "Thanks for saving us."

Visiert nodded. "Anytime. I apologise I didn't get here sooner; I have a lot of business to attend to of my own." Reika wasn't sure, but he sounded dejected.

"Please stop apologising," Reika said. "You're not all powerful, you can't be everywhere. I am just pleased you have rescued us. You do a good job as a

saviour so keep doing it."

Visiert nodded, giving Reika a handshake. Junayd approached the two. "I suppose I should offer you my gratitude as well."

"It is the least I can do. It's said that Montanus isn't that much of a fighter anyway, he'd rather have underlings to do his dirty work." Visiert began to leave.

"Why don't you stay with us?" Junayd asked.

"I am needed back at the citadel now. We'll meet again short-ly." Visiert strode through the door.

Chapter 17

Avowed Secrets

A s opposed to sailing the sea, the *Coeptus* took off into the sky, allowing the group and the crew of the ship to reach the citadel faster. Ulric turned the wheel of the ship gently to steer it in the right direction, turning it slightly to the north-east, ensuring it flew in a straight path to the citadel found on the northern side of the eastern continent.

"Land to the south Ulric," Tybalt said.

"Aye Captain, bringing her down now," Ulric said. After a gentle landing, the group departed.

This is it, Reika thought, as she stared at the citadel. The dusty highway in front of them snaked along the grassy plains north of the ship, stopping at the ocean blue mosaic gate on the south side. Walls of alabaster stone reflected the sunlight with great intensity, so much so that it heated the grass.

The citadel belonging to the dragons was a sight to behold. Many of the buildings were beautiful, and the cobbled streets running between them were a soft, light-yellow sandstone. Even the colours of the tiles were pleasant to the eyes.

The group approached a large castle in the middle of the citadel which towered over the rest of the buildings. A hatch opened and a figure, hidden in shadow, stared out at them. "State your business!" He called.

Junayd stepped forward. "It's me, Junayd. I and my friends have travelled far across Perusia. Our journey has led us to this moon, Caromago. So can you..."

"Stop right there, I know who you are: The Ferrum Champion. Come inside. Visiert, you, and your friend need to talk," said the figure. With that, he shut his window. The doors opened to allow the group in.

Inside, they found themselves in a stone hall with a pleasing green carpet. Four small pools, each overlooked by the skilfully crafted statue of a dragon, formed a cross shape.

The living dragons, all in human form, various shades of skin tone, were conversing at the table with each other, including the king, who noticed the group walk into the hall. The king, Nestor, was an impressive figure. Old yet healthy, his physique was that of a man who had been in battle for his whole life and was in peak condition. He had pale skin, a long beard that covered his broad chin and dull brown eyes. He wore a crown around his head that was regal, with gems stationed evenly around the band. His robes matched that of the dragon elders who had paid Reika and Antonius a visit at the latter's castle, only with shining gold and silver trimming.

"Good day. The two known as Junayd and Reika, go upstairs to the very top and speak with Visiert. We shall discuss our plight later. The others shall rest in the rooms that have been prepared."

A servant, a young blonde woman with sharp blue eyes led them to the next room, an odd-looking chamber, too small for anything useless to occupy it. "Where are the stairs?" Reika asked.

"There are no stairs here. This device is called a lift," Berinon replied.

They all entered the room and the doors closed behind them. A loud whirring could be heard, and Reika felt a weird sensation as though her stomach were dropping out through her feet.

The lift went up, horizontal cogs below the chamber turning, the teeth of these cogs gently sliding into holes in the stone supports that ran vertically up through the tower. As the cogs turned, their teeth pulled them up the stone supports. All but Junayd and Reika exited on the first floor to their rooms.

The two proceeded to the second floor, entering a room like the hall on the ground floor. A small chair stood in front of a gigantic window.

"Hello?" Reika said.

"It's good to hear your voice again. Now you get to see my true face," said a familiar voice from the chair. The man stood and turned. He wore robes like Antonius, only with dark navy blue with light blue trimming. He had taken off his mask. His face was similar to Reika's own, though with a wider jaw. "Do you recognise me now?"

Reika couldn't believe her eyes. "You... your eyes... You were Visiert? Are you my..."

"Surprised? My name is Kenzuo. I am your brother."

"Brother?"

"Reika was the name your adoptive parents gave you. Your real name is Hana."

"Hana... That's the name I had?" Reika beamed at her real name.

"Yes. But I'm not adverse to calling you Reika or Hana, whatever you like, I'm an easy-going man," said Kenzuo.

"Thanks... I..." Reika halted. "Our parents... They're dead. Montanus... He was telling the truth...?"

Kenzuo sighed. "What else can I say?"

She moved closer to Kenzuo. There were so many things she wanted to discuss, but they were all bubbling up at once. "Montanus claimed they were slain by Destrian?"

Kenzuo hesitated briefly. "That is true... As far as I have been told, they fought him off and died protecting the citadel. I was kept here and adopted into the dragons' royal family. You yourself were given to the metazoans."

"I was found as a baby in the Carthagian forest."

Kenzuo nodded. "I wish our parents were still alive, to see how we have grown. What matters is you are here now."

Kenzuo headed back to his chair and sat down. "There's much to do, both of you need a rest I should think." Reika approached Kenzuo, bowing next his chair. She summoned Luniram. Kenzuo examined the blade. "Our father's blade, where did you get this?"

"Antonius gave it to me. It has served me well. What do you say to using it yourself?"

Kenzuo sat there silently thinking, clearly a little amazed. "Yes, I don't see why I cannot relieve the burden, but why pass it on to me? You are the one who fought your way here."

"I insist, Kenzuo. Perhaps another day I could take it up again, but that may be a while. A waste to keep hold of it where I am planning to go."

The young man argued no more. "Very well, give it to me when you are ready to do so."

"A fair warning," Reika continued. "It has been powered up with Excandescite, so be careful when unleashing its energy."

He laughed. "Thank you for the tip, Reika."

Fourteen council members gathered around the table in the morning with the king in his main chair. The king motioned for silence among the council members.

"The weredragons have already been harvested within Somnium Carcerum. They are set to be unleashed shortly. We're almost out of time. Destrian must be stopped before they come through and the Anodyne Stone must be found," Nestor said forcefully. "The foul beasts cannot be allowed to escape."

"Your majesty," Ysellian said. "If I maybe so bold, the weredragons will escape by other means, not necessarily from the castle itself."

"A good point to be sure. Our goal is still the same."

Junayd and the group were present in the crowd, listening to the debate that was going on. Reika contemplated the points being made, wondering if Destrian possessed the Anodyne Stone. It had been stolen and was the only artefact in the world that could vanquish the weredragon's curse once and for all; Destrian was therefore unlikely to allow it to fall into the wrong hands easily.

After the meeting was adjourned, Reika went to Nestor. She approached him with caution, then bowed before him, as she had done with Tertullian. Nestor took notice. "You wish to speak, child? I am aware of your affliction. Part of me wishes to apologise to you for the pain you have had to endure as of late."

"It isn't your fault, your majesty. You were not responsible for the spread of the curse," Reika said.

Nestor smiled, closing his eyes. "True, Tahpenes left a lot of damage for us to clear, even this. I regret not being able to get rid of it sooner. The creators of the Anodyne Stone should have listened," Nestor said. "Be careful on this final step. May the gods have mercy on you and your companions."

Reika bowed her head to the king and returned to her friends.

Melito surveyed the room. There were many different types of people there, including Arachnoids, metazoans, and even some of the soldiers who had been enslaved by Montanus back at Luentinum Castle. He recognised an elderly marmoset couple and went over to investigate. Tabitha then followed suit, wondering where he was going.

"Excuse me," Melito said to the couple. "Don't I know you from somewhere?"

The old male marmoset turned round. It was Julius, the king of Entella. "Melito, my boy!" The old king gave a cry of joy. Julius threw a big hug around his son. "It's been years, so good to see you again."

Laria, the old female marmoset also gave a hug. "Young man, Tertullian did a great job taking care of you."

"I am glad you're safe. After I got back to my own time, I could not stop worrying about you."

His father became serious. "Son, the castle is in ruins is it not?"

"Yes, Father. When shall I rebuild it? After the death of Welk? King Tertullian spoke with me about this."

"I agree with him. You must get rid of Welk first. He was at the Caromago Castle last I heard. I understand you and your friends fought with him again."

"He's stronger than before. I might not win, even now. Even with Entella's Bane."

"Whatever tricks he has picked up; you are still prepared for him." Julius then noticed Tabitha standing next to Melito. "Sorry my dear, I didn't mean to ignore you just now. It's been a long time you understand, nice arrow work back at the castle all those years ago."

Tabitha smiled back. "Thanks. No hard feelings at all. I'm just happy you get to see your son again."

Junayd saw Joonas talking with one of the dragon elders. They patted him on the shoulders, comforting him. Junayd walked over to them. Joonas turned to the young man. "I see you made it back safely, the other guards too?"

Joonas nodded. "It will take some time to make full restoration and restitution for what has happened. In any case, I and my comrades are in your debt."

"It wasn't easy. Reika and I had a little trouble, if it wasn't for Visiert, we wouldn't be here." Junayd suddenly grinned. "I'm still up for that little rematch if you are?"

"Still on the table, although I think it's better to get rid of Destrian first.

Afterwards, we'll fight to our heart's content." The two locked their hands in a fierce grip. "Consider it a deal!" Junayd replied.

Reika spotted Antonius with Ysellian. She was ecstatic, dashing over to her old master. "You're alright!" She said with a beaming smile on her face.

"Still a little achy, but don't count me out just yet!" Antonius said, returning her smile. A shadow passed over Reika's face. She crossed her arms, closing her eyes.

"What it is child?" Ysellian asked.

"My journey is almost at an end, and we haven't found the stone. Welk crushed a fake in front of me to taunt me. He said Destrian had it. Do you... know where it is?"

Ysellian frowned. "Where he has hidden it escapes my sight. Montanus' magic has blocked my vision. I'm sorry."

Reika was disappointed. "I understand. Zane has had the same trouble. If I do find it, what happens next?"

"Hold the stone, unleash its power, and destroy the weredragons," Ysellian said.

"Is there a price to pay?"

Ysellian's expression was grave. "It may eliminate the curse, but to unleash the stone at full power while the curse is still inside you is a great risk. Should you survive, it will be a draining experience."

Reika remained unperturbed outwardly. Part of her didn't care whether she died using the stone. Either way, the curse would be lifted, and she would no longer be capable of hurting the ones she loved.

"That mural I saw back in the temple. Melito and Tabitha found various murals on our travels, but none of the images gave us the full picture."

Antonius' eyes widened. "You saw the mural in Luentinum?" He asked. "Why yes. Junayd and I reckon it's a prophecy, is it regarding us? Forgive my presumptuousness if I should not ask."

Ysellian nodded. "The mural speaks of two people, the Ferrum Champion and an anointed one whose appearance will hail the destruction of the weredragons. It was a vision that came to me many years ago. That is why I paid you a visit. You are the one in the mural and I had to be sure it was the truth. It was confirmed to me when you asked me about the pottery piece back in Antonius' Castle."

"What of Destrian, is that who Junayd is fighting?"

"Yes, that task is not yours. That's where he will fit in all this. Destrian's downfall will come from him. However, I do not know where this battle will take place, only the smallest glimpse has been accorded to me."

Reika fell silent once more. "Why only tell me of this now?"

"Delusions of grandeur are dangerous," Ysellian said. "Had I told you your destiny, and that of Junayd's, the arrogance you would have displayed would have caused the prophecy to suffer delay, or worse, turn out to be false. Arrogance and pride make fools of us."

A look of satisfaction crossed Reika's face.

"Now then," Antonius said. "It is time that you the rest of your group prepare for the final battle. This will be tougher than anything you have faced so far; be very careful. Destrian is incredibly powerful."

Reika returned to her bedroom in the Aerouant Citadel, staring out of her window at the darkened horizon where Caromago Castle lay rising atop an obsidian island.

Zane entered the room. "You alright?"

Reika faced in Zane. "Yes, I have been thinking. The prophecy, I understand, but what if it goes wrong?"

"Then it will be a false one we have wrongly pinned our hopes on and Ysellian will be in serious trouble, possibly even face death for giving us a fallacious prediction."

Reika gulped. "Then this is an enormous risk." "It is. But it's too late to turn back now."

The young woman said nothing and then dropped the subject. She moved on. "How was it Krea was never able to find me?"

"I can answer that. I travelled back in time, and I was charged by your parents, Ryo and Kaiya, to safely hide you away. The first place Destrian would look to find you is here."

"You?" Reika asked. "When were you sent back?"

"A year ago. I travelled to the time when you were a baby to protect you from Destrian and Krea. I left false trails for them to follow." His right hand glowed blue and he placed his hand over Reika's head.

"Maybe this will make it easier for you," Zane said. A flash went through her mind, and she found herself in the forest where the Time Gate was located. Reika was curious to see what was going on. Zane ran past her, holding a baby swaddled in cloth in his hands. Reika followed swiftly, trying to keep up. Eventually she stopped once Zane reached a clearing. Zane sharply turned his head this way and that, wondering where to go. Reika eyed the baby carefully, realising she was seeing herself cradled in the hands of this young man.

Krea appeared, standing there in front of Zane, clad in full armour. "Where are you taking her?" Krea demanded.

"I will not tell you that, you will never get a hold of the child."

Zane drew his familiar sword; Krea drew her own blade. Time ground to a halt, the sounds of the air winding down in pitch till nothing was heard and the leaves hung still like a painting. Another version of Zane appeared next to Reika. "What happens next?" She asked. "Where are Krea's troops? This would have been easier for her."

"You'll see, Reika." Zane snapped his fingers and time resumed its normal pace again. Zane placed the baby on the ground, leaving her by a tree.

Reika and Zane watched as the memory-battle began to play out. Krea went to slash Zane with her sword. This proved unfruitful as Zane swiftly dodged, changing his sword into a spear, plunging it deep into her back. Krea gasped and slumped to the floor. Zane stopped for a moment. Krea's arm twitched slightly. Zane left his weapon embedded in the elf, not removing it. Flexing his right wrist, he bent the spear around her chest, holding the elf down. She reached for white powder in a bag, placing it on her wound. It healed up around the weapon.

Zane backed away in awe at what he was watching. Krea's appearance changed to that of a golem. The golem's armour was bright white and had bulk to it. His red eyes, for it now was a he, shone from his helmet, one that had two sharp horns. His full height was nine foot tall.

"Zane, who is that?" Reika asked with a croak in her voice.

Zane remained calm as he spoke. "Falk Corundum. His team was responsible for stealing the amulet, the one that the eupithecia had. He is a gun for hire."

Falk yanked Verwandeln out of the wound, which allowed it to close shut, and then snapped the ancient weapon in two. Zane re-summoned Verwandeln to himself, it took what was to Reika the recognisable sword form. Falk lunged at Zane, then lodged his knee into the stomach of the young man. Zane clutched his stomach. He staggered then collapsed. Reika wondered how he was able to survive such a crushing blow from a being made of crystal.

While Zane writhed, Falk pulled a small potion out of the bag he'd reached into earlier. He picked up the crying child, poured the red liquid inside her mouth, causing her to splutter. "I will be taking this child to Krea now. Pitiful weakling you are, you can't save her."

Zane said nothing, but energy flowed around him. His stomach's pain subsided, and he swiftly got onto his feet, punching Falk squarely in the jaw. The child didn't drop to the floor. Zane's speed was so swift, all the child felt was a change of hands, from cold gemstone to warm flesh. Zane tried to comfort the child as best he could. Reika's eyes under the moonlight were dragon-esque for a second before returning to a human form.

"Forgive me, I failed," he whispered.

Reika kept her eyes on the bottle. "That potion... what was that?"

"The weredragon's curse. There are various methods of administering it, that is one of them. It's the blood of the ancient dragon, Tahpenes, she who created the curse. She was in charge of a powerful and dangerous empire. Destrian was one of her clan leaders. He must be carrying out one of her final orders before she was sealed away years ago in the underworld, building an army of weredragons for her. Despite Tahpenes being out of the picture, Destrian is using them to further her plans, even trying to use you."

Falk recovered from the attack and gave a right hook. Zane

placed the child on the ground again and stopped Falk's attack just in time, shoving the golem away. "I still won't let you take her away."

Zane thrust out his hand, telekinetically shoving Falk into the trees. He picked the baby again and made his dash further into the forest. Falk soon followed. "You won't escape me, Temporal Knight!"

Reika chased after the past version of Zane with the present-day Zane accompanying her. The past Zane touched a strange band on his wrist. It appeared for use then would vanish shortly afterwards. A portal opened up to the Time Gate. He jumped in, allowing Falk to follow him. The present versions of Zane and Reika also leapt through the portal.

"Keep following me, Reika." "I am."

"Not me, the other me!"

The past Zane readied his sword to fight Falk.

"Give the child to me, boy," Falk said. "Before I break your bones."

Falk drew a blade from his body. He leapt forward. Zane, despite keeping one hand on Verwandeln and one arm holding the baby Reika, kept Falk away as best he could. He assumed a fencing stance, continuing to block Falk's attacks with great effort. Zane flew quickly to the time machine, avoiding a downward slash from the golem. Falk's sword went back into his body as he chased Zane up the stairs, but was too late as the door opened, allowing the young man to pass through it. The door sealed in front of the golem. Falk began smashing the door, trying to break through. Reika kept her eyes fixed on where the past Zane went.

"Wait and see what I did next," Zane said with a smirk on his face as the two went up the stairs, phasing through the door. They both entered the room where the past Zane was fiddling around with the dial of the Time Gate, the machine whirring, ready to transport anything through time, leaving Reika safely on the ground nearby. He opened a small compartment that was big enough fit a treasure chest and out of it, he produced a loaf of bread. Quickly, he swapped the baby

Reika with the loaf of bread, wrapping it in a swaddling cloth. He then placed the baby inside.

"What?" Reika said.

"As I said, wait and see."

Falk finally broke through the door. He saw the swaddling clothes. The past Zane expressed what looked like genuine shock as Falk approached.

"That child is going nowhere with you fool." Falk grabbed Zane by the back of his neck, the hold wasn't there for long as Zane gripped tightly and reversed Falk's grip. Despite the pain he felt, cutting himself on the gemstone body, Zane's strength was immense. Falk howled in agony as he dropped the young man. Zane healed his sliced hands with chrono-magic. He planted a swift brutal kick into Falk's chest. Zane turned Verwandeln into brass knuckles. He struck, grazing the golem's chest, and cracking his helm.

Falk took more powder from his bag, regenerating his wounded stone body. He shoved Zane into the left wall, grabbing the swaddling clothes. "At last, this chase has come to an end."

Falk opened the cloths, finding a loaf of bread wrapped up. "Bread?" He yelled, outraged.

The past Zane got to his feet and subtly twisted the dial as best he could. Falk spun round in horror. He was caught within the energy dome. "Catch you another time," Zane said, grinning at the golem. Falk roared as the lightning clashed with the dome, transporting him and the loaf away.

Reika was still mesmerised by what was going on as the past

Zane reopened the compartment, holding the baby Reika in his arms. He bobbed the baby up and down to relax her and she smiled, laughing. He then placed the baby on the ground, holding his hand above her head. He twisted his hand in order to reverse the curse. A small purple bolt shocked his hand. He tried again, this time twisting his hand further. He yelped as another small bolt singed his skin. He used his other hand, twisting it the same way, causing the wounded hand to be healed of the damage. He picked Reika up and departed from the room.

"Where did you send Falk?" Reika enquired, still in awe.

Zane shut his eyes, smirking. "Heh, I sent him to about... two years from our present time. At least he won't be punished for his failure. Can't happen if you are missing for twenty-four years."

Reika chuckled. Zane did the same. "In all seriousness, I arranged for golem soldiers to assemble at the Time Gate to arrest him upon his arrival. We shouldn't get any trouble from him for a while. Their training should be enough to bring him in."

He clicked his fingers, causing time to rush forwards with he and Reika teleported to Antonius' Castle. She saw Zane approaching the sorcerer, who was younger, with short brown hair, though his beard was unchanged in style, though not in colour. Antonius placed his hand on the baby's forehead.

"He sealed my magic away?" Reika said, realisation dawning.

"To help hide you away, awakening it when the time was right."

"It briefly appeared before then, when Barzillai attacked me. It allowed me to survive a fall down the cliff into the lake below."

"But you couldn't control it, it was instinctive in that moment."

Zane clicked his fingers again, bringing him and Reika to a small stream. They watched up close, seeing the past Zane lay Reika on the ground. He grabbed some mud, smearing it on the spare swaddling clothes. The baby didn't care as she was falling asleep, tired from the ordeal. The past Zane's eyes glowed.

"Foresight?"

"Yes. I was seeing when Chip would come."

"You took a risk didn't you, leaving me there like that." "No, I made sure the surrounding area was safe."

Zane left the child by the stream, hiding in a bush. Chip arrived moments later. He walked slowly alongside the stream. He saw baby Reika and began wading across the stream to the other side. He scooped up the baby, who awoke instantly.

"What a cute little baby you are! Where did you come from?" Chip said as he tickled the baby's face. She giggled. He then took the young baby away, continuing on his way along the stream. Zane snapped his fingers and Reika found herself back in the Aerouant Citadel in her bedroom.

"I just wish I'd stopped Falk sooner. Even as you saw, I tried to remove the curse by turning back time around you. You saw it didn't work. Later I realised... I wasn't meant to stop you from being cursed, only to keep you hidden. It had to happen. The prophecy of Ysellian *required* it to happen."

Reika was somewhat conflicted; she didn't know how to feel. Angry? Sad? Insulted? She kept Zane waiting with a look of shame on his face. Reika finally understood how Rian felt. A burgeoning question was on her mind that she had to share.

"I wonder... What if we recover the Anodyne Stone from the past or prevent it being stolen in the first place? You have the power to travel through time, why not go back and stop it?"

"By that logic, why not go into the future where the curse has already been cured?"

Reika felt like her head might explode.

"It's the same answer: I can't, as much as I want to," Zane said. "I went back to the Anodyne Stone's creation, warning the people who forged it that it would be stolen. They laughed at me and scorned me. It is fruitless to take the stone, even temporarily." Zane sat on a small chair in the room, his face now glum.

"As a consequence of not heeding my warning, Tahpenes came along and stole the Anodyne Stone, killing the forgers. She destroyed its physical form, trapping its energy in a container. No matter how many times I went back, I thought I had found it, and it always turned out to be a fruitless search. She had knowledge of me and prepared for me accordingly." Reika remembered all too well the fake Anodyne Stone that Welk Seha crushed in front of her eyes.

"I have to be frank; she was one of the few who has actually defeated me. Trying to prevent her takeover was just impossible. All I could do was lessen her grasp." Zane's calm was eroding once again. "It wasn't relevant to me who would defeat Tahpenes at the time. Just that someone got rid of her."

He sighed, trying to keep himself calm. "The theft is going to happen, whatever we do. The weredragons will inevitably exist no matter what. The question is where the stone is being kept now; over time it regenerates its original shape." He brushed a tear away from his eyes. He composed himself swiftly as he stood. Reika gave Zane a hug of thanks.

"I don't understand," he said. Reika relinquished her hold. She placed her right hand on Zane's left shoulder. "You saved me from Krea, you gave me a loving family, friends and a home. For that, I am grateful to you, and grateful to them for the care they have given."

Zane smiled back. "Count me grateful as well." Reika removed her hand from Zane's shoulder.

"No one would suspect you would be hidden away in the Carthagian Citadel," Zane said. "Especially with Antonius sealing your magic away. That is why you couldn't be tracked by Krea."

Reika crossed her arms. "All this just to keep me safe, you being so calm and collected."

"Calm and collected? Sometimes but not all the time." Reika smiled.

"I'll leave you to rest now," Zane said, departing from the room, shutting the door behind him quietly. Reika continued to stare out the window.

As Zane walked down the crimson corridor with paintings, candles, and tables, he had time to think by himself. He pondered on Somnium Carcerum, its link to Reika, and what Welk tried to do. He knew Reika had been rescued from that grisly fate, where no one else had been. Yet, he also was aware of many rumours that had arisen about the weredragons when he was working at the farm. Sightings of them occurred over the years before his first journey and after the restoration of the timeline. Unusually, they always mysteriously vanished afterwards. The prophecy dictated their gathering for an invasion had to happen.

He was hit with inspiration and headed away down the corridor in silence.

Rian checked in on Reika a quarter of an hour after Zane had left. "You really need to get your sleep, young one," he said.

"I know," Reika replied. She directed her eyes to the elf man. "Can we talk?" "Of course."

"Why did you take a job to kill, Zane? Will you do it if it comes to that?

Also, why did you become a bounty hunter?"

Rian sat down on a gold sofa with hunter green cushions. He beckoned Reika to sit down with him, so she did. The look in his eyes was like that of a father trying to explain something to a child. From his perspective, Reika was young enough to be an elven child.

"I have been around for three hundred years. Half of that lifetime ago, I was married, I had a wife named Etheldreda, along with a son, Kyrilu, and a daughter, Melisende. I lost them to robbers. I fought with the robbers, thinking my family had escaped via horse and cart. But without me knowing, a rocket had been fired at her cart as she escaped. Etheldreda died instantly, as did my children. It broke my heart, nothing but anger consumed me, hence I became a bounty hunter." Rian contorted his face slightly, trying to keep his composure as the image of his dead family before him entered his mind. "I tracked the murderers who killed my family and I slew them. It brought me no satisfaction."

"And Zane didn't stop it, did he?" Reika asked. "He wanted to preserve the timeline. He cannot just change history like that, who knows what disruption could have been caused? He couldn't risk it. I noticed you were furious when talking to him back in Entella."

"He could have changed it," Rian snapped, only just restraining himself from shouting, remembering who his anger was to be directed at. "Zane has the power to time travel and he *refused* to help me."

"That is not true," she blurted out. "It's not about you, He just cannot deal with personal problems, only the events that affect many, otherwise where does it end? He nearly lost his composure after talking with me. He tried to stop the Anodyne Stone from being stolen and failed."

"A prophecy by Ysellian, Reika, that's what stopped him. Granted there is a possibility of one being conditional but what happened to my family was not. There was no prophecy for them to die."

"He wanted to stop this curse. He warned the forgers of its theft, but they would not listen and thus matters have been made worse."

Rian hung his head, seemingly tired by their exchange. "I didn't choose the life of a bounty hunter because I wanted to, even if it pays well." He met her gaze. "The ones who murdered my wife needed to be destroyed."

"There are other jobs to choose from," Reika responded. "Even if you became a soldier legitimately, it's no use carrying grudges, they will never be satisfied."

"What can I say? I let my anger get the better of me." "Do you... hate me, regarding Zane?"

"No," Rian replied. "I don't like you agreeing with him on the timeline, but nevertheless, I don't hate you, if anything, I respect you for sticking to your principles. I tend to prefer someone who is upfront and sticks to their guns rather than someone who is a coward: saying one thing and thinking another."

Reika kept her eyes locked on Rian's face. He was left in contemplation. Nothing but the calm wind brushing the window and the sea waves shifting in and out in the distance could be heard.

"You say it is useless to carry grudges. My question to you, do you hold one against Montanus?"

Reika was hesitant to respond. "Yes. I hate him for what he did."

"It would be wise to heed what you have said to me should you face Montanus again. Will your revenge bring you satisfaction? It's easy to preach, harder to practice. Justice and vengeance will never be interchangeable with revenge." Rian stood. "I leave you to your rest, young one. Kenzuo will train you for the next few days." He ventured to the door and shut it behind him. Reika sat there still on the chair, eventually heading to bed long after. Beforehand, she wondered how powerful Visiert, or rather Kenzuo, really was.

Zane made his way to his own bedroom for the night, when suddenly he heard Rian call to him. The young man faced Rian.

"Let us talk, right now," Rian said in a tone that surprised Zane, polite and earnest.

"I'm listening," Zane said.

"All this time, I have been bitter towards you for not helping Etheldreda. Not anymore, I realise you cannot interfere with personal affairs when travelling through time. Though I have come to accept that, I still am upset. What's the point baring resentment towards you for something you cannot control. I only wish I'd accepted that fact when you spoke with me back in Entella."

Zane smiled back. "What changed your mind?"

Rian explained what he said to Reika. Zane remained attentive and nodded his head. "I have a plan, for the battle to come. Why don't you and I discuss it? I could use your help Rian, my friend."

Rian and Zane both locked their hands in agreement. "What's the plan then?" Rian asked.

~

Reika entered a large dome under the citadel grounds. It bore a resemblance to an underground coliseum that she had seen underneath the Carthagian Citadel as a little girl. The coliseum was about eighty feet tall and of equal diameter. When not working, she had sometimes watched Melito, Tabitha, and the other guards training, be it combat, endurance tests, or other tests of skill, such as a small game of tag between two people. There were two such coliseums found in Carthage, one various shades of brown and the other a metallic silver. This coliseum was about the same size, it had bricks of light sand colour and the same type of sand that had spread across the arena in the Arachnoid village.

The siblings approached each other, standing in front of each other about two metres apart. "You have a simple task. You need to try to best me," Kenzuo said. "You need to be stronger for the fight ahead. It's time you learnt what a Lunarmancer can really do. That, and with Lief being much stronger, I think I need to build my own strength up."

"Understood," Reika said. "Ready when you are."

The two backed away until they were a further ten metres. Kenzuo then transformed into the familiar moon-gifted warrior Reika had seen. She too followed, a little wary. She was about to find out what "Visiert" was truly capable of.

Kenzuo flew at high speed toward Reika. She caught his punch. She strained against his might. *He's holding back,* Reika thought, as she released his hand, moving out of the way. Kenzuo spun round and threw a small flurry of punches with Reika blocking them with a magical barrier. She removed the barrier and leapt back two metres, casting an energy scythe from her right hand. She flung it at Kenzuo. Despite the close range, he held his hand in the air and the scythe collided with his hand, which showed an invisible barrier surrounded him.

Reika was gobsmacked. Her brother's power was immense, if not frightening. Even with the training Antonius gave her, Reika knew never to be cocky in a fight, especially with a more experienced warrior than she. Lief had already fought and defeated her.

"Take that!" Kenzuo finally cried as he made his advance. Reika was able to block most of the punches thrown before she threw one of her own. Kenzuo backed off after being hit in the chest. Reika took a leaf out of Antonius' own book and fired bullets of energy from her hands at Kenzuo. He briskly backed away. He floated a foot in the air and summoned a barrier of light. All the bullets crashed into the barrier, they fused with it. He then concentrated the energy from the barrier along with that of the bullets, firing a beam towards Reika. Alarmed, Reika moved out of the way barely in time as the beam struck the ground. The shock from the explosion knocked her to the floor. She tried to stand up but felt a sharp point on her neck. Reika dared not move another step lest the blade draw blood.

"On your feet," Kenzuo said sternly. Reika complied. She then turned to see that Kenzuo was holding Luniram in his hand. "How are you holding that? It

isn't time to hand it to you yet." She asked. "We share this weapon. I had no use for it as Visiert. Only one of us can use it at a time. You didn't use it in this case hence why I was able to snatch it from you."

Reika brushed some of the sand from her hair and clothing. Kenzuo also brushed his robes while de-summoning Luniram.

"Again."

Reika launched at him, punching rapidly, but each punch turned aside.

The young man formed an x with his arms, forming a barrier that Reika struck. She let out a squeal. She shook her hand and backed away as Kenzuo narrowly missed with a punch of his own. Reika staggered a little as she landed. With a swipe of her left hand, a smooth wave of light zipped away from it. It crashed into Kenzuo, knocking him through the air. He stopped himself in the air and quickly turned around, landing on his feet. He fired a beam of energy at Reika. The young woman also made an x shape with her arms. The beam pushed her back ten feet while shattering her barrier, rendering it as floating dust. Long furrows in the sand could be seen where her feet dragged. Reika dispersed the dust.

Kenzuo was nowhere to be seen.

She turned her head this way and that, even turning around to look behind her. A hand gripped her shoulder. She turned around to see her brother behind her. He sharply shoved Reika and she was knocked to the ground.

"You are no pushover, are you?" She said, propping herself up on her elbows. "That was just a gentle push, as it were. You are my sister, after all. Keep in mind, the enemy will not be so kind, and I will not pull punches again the further we go in this fight and neither should you."

He helped her stand, and they resumed their training.

After ten days, the training got harder and harder. Reika and Kenzuo gave everything they had, their strength rising day by day. On the final day, Reika was dead on her feet, and didn't have enough fight to keep her going. She tried to punch Kenzuo, but Kenzuo dodged and threw her to the floor. He pinned her there with his foot. Reika could just about push Kenzuo off her.

Rising, Reika fired small lights at Kenzuo's eyes, not to maim him but only temporarily blind him. He staggered away. Before Reika thought of her next move, his sight returned. He moved quickly, delivering a punch to Reika in the chest. She gasped and staggered back. The two both stood, completely exhausted, their Lunarmancer states finally receding, returning them to normal. "I think that's enough," Kenzuo said. "At least now you can keep up with me."

Reika was pleased. "A bit stronger now."

"An understatement! There is a difference in physical prowess, nevertheless, I reckon your magic is equal to mine."

She paused for a moment. "Will this be enough for both of us?"

"I am not so sure. It should, however, be easier for you now to take down other foes. Never give way to arrogance, though, it will be your end."

"There was a golem I faced with Zane... I didn't even think about my own strength at the time. I thought it was a bit strange. And then with Welk Seha, I was able to penetrate his hide with Luniram. Neither time was there a full moon." "It depends on the exposure of the moon. Your power will be either slightly or *immensely* increased. All your transformation does is unleash that stored energy, bringing it to its fullest, even if it is temporary."

"Kenzuo... Are there people who use sunlight to bolster their magic?" "Solismancers exist. They live in the southwest on the continent Karanog, an

island some twenty miles from Perusia. They don't have much business with the dragons or with us."

"Do they hate Lunarmancers?"

"No quarrel with us at all. I have only met a few in my time. Some of their elite, like the Lunarmancers, do work with the dragons."

The two stood up and went to the coliseum exit. "I believe, it is time to get some rest."

Chapter 18

Battle of Caromago

A day later, the group made their way to Destrian's Castle. Kenzuo was to follow afterwards. The foreboding castle, with its jagged towers, appeared to merge with the obsidian floor of the moonscape. The castle was ravaged by corruption, the vile stench of sulphur permeating the air. The group took one look at the fortification and felt their confidence waver. They faced the tower, beginning their ascent.

They found themselves in the first of a series of halls, built from grey marble stone with paved tiles on the floor arranged in a pattern that could only be described as crazed. The stone columns of rose high, strong, and stable. Crates like the ones found in the Moon Tower armoury were piled at the end of the hall.

Standing at the entrance to the next room, was Lief himself.

"You go no further young one," Lief said, pointing to Reika especially. "Don't hinder us Lief, Begone!" Reika said in an angry tone.

The elf just laughed at the top of his voice. "That isn't going happen. You are all going to die."

"Junayd," Reika spoke as she drew her blade. "You go with the others; I'll take care of Lief."

"Be careful, Reika," Junayd replied. He led the rest of the group upstairs while Reika faced Lief. Her anger left her.

"It's not too late, come with us," Reika said, staying as calm as possible.

Lief arched his eyebrows. "You still harping on that? It's too late now. The weredragons will soon be unleashed."

No other sound filled the room. The two only locking their eyes with each other. Lief conjured a dark shadowy blade into his right hand, holding it in a reverse grip in front of him. The elf then closed his eyes, as though in pain; the young human looked puzzled. *Reika, forgive me.*

He charged suddenly. Reika transformed and charged toward him.

The others made their way to a long corridor like the hall, heading up the stairs with ferocious speed, and found themselves on a walkway overlooking the floor below. The path was too narrow for more than one person.

"Make your own way across, we need to hurry, not too many at once however," Zane said.

Rian ran across the side of the wall, skipping a small section of the pathway and heading the rest of the way properly. Berinon traversed the path, he jumped to cut corners on each section of the pathway. Zane, Melito, and Tabitha ran along the path to the other side of the room, all of them heading up the stairs to another room.

They found a small arena there with a deep, wide pit surrounding it. Melito stopped near the entrance, he smelled the air. "I have a feeling who may be behind that door."

"Who is it?" Tabitha asked.

"Welk Seha. I need to take care of him." "What? You can't fight him alone."

"You're right, you'll provide cover fire. I'll fight him head on. We need to watch out for his magic; we cannot let him win again."

The door opened, revealing Welk. He stomped into the room with his sword in hand. He removed his headscarf, revealing his mouth. He grinned at Melito, as though he had eagerly awaited their third encounter for a long time.

"Our final battle is at hand. Such a pity regarding Reika, she could have joined us. But... it's time I ended your bloodline once and for all young Melito... I should have done it when you were a soppy little boy, but it will be more satisfying to kill you now."

"Reika is not going to lose sleep over it and you'll pay for what you did, Welk."

"Fine, then sleep... Forever." Welk leapt at Melito, bringing his sword down.

Melito blocked it with his axe. "Junayd, go! We'll take this foul beast!"

Melito started his assault after pushing Welk away, with Tabitha firing her arrows from a distance.

Junayd led the rest of the group into the next room, leaving Melito and Tabitha alone to face the Scorpion King. The group proceeded down the next corridor and found themselves in a smart, carpeted tower, with ten scorpion soldiers ready to kill them. The four prepared their weapons for combat as the scorpions began their assault.

Reika and Lief were almost on an even playing field. She fired an electrical shard at Lief's dark blade, causing him to drop it to the floor. Lief yelped in pain clutching his hand, allowing Reika to land a few blows with her sword, though Lief's magical barriers defended him even when unarmed. Lief felt the strength of her blows, realising he was facing a more dangerous and powerful enemy than before. He finally countered, smacking Reika into one of the stone pillars to the ground. She dropped Luniram. Reika rubbed her back, straightening. She felt only a little pain, smirking at the elf. Lief snorted in anger. "You shouldn't have this strength," he growled.

"Training helps. If you don't turn from what you are doing, I'll have to use it," Reika said sternly.

The elf charged again, with Reika holding him back with her telekinetic power. She blasted Lief to the floor.

Melito and Welk traded blows with axe and sword, clashing like never before. Welk summoned a fiery gauntlet, trying to smash Melito but the marmoset dodged out the way, jumping close to the pit behind him, steadying himself from falling below. Tabitha continued to fire her arrows at every opportunity to distract Welk. He soon grew tired of her distraction and fired a concussive projectile against her. Tabitha barely avoided the attack, her right arm rendered numb and paralysed from the pain, her bow dropping the floor.

"When I am done with you, it won't be just your arm that's numb!" Welk snarled.

Junayd and the others fought valiantly but more scorpion soldiers entered the room. Rian shot them from a distance. Berinon swiped with broad powerful strokes of his lance, knocking many to the ground. Zane propelled himself into the air in a giant leap, landing next to Junayd. They functioned like a tag team, slashing their weapons, cutting their enemies down like weak bamboo shoots.

"Child's play, hey Junayd?" Zane said with a smile on his face. "Certainly is. Easy fodder!" Junayd replied.

Zane slowed down time briefly, taking down five enemies at once, giving each one a deadly blow. Junayd lit the Draco Ferrum, shooting a long beam which cut through the scorpion soldiers.

~

Reika allowed Luniram to float back into her left hand.

"Little pest aren't you, human? Time I end this." Lief went to strike Reika but every hit failed to connect with her. Reika's speed was immense. Finally, she shot a sphere of light at his stomach, sending him flying into the wall. Lief hit it with a bone-crunching thud.

Reika flew from the pillar with her sword in hand, letting out a battle shriek, pushing Lief into the wall, plunging the sword into him. She floated away from him back to the floor then at the snap of her fingers, the blade exited from Lief's belly, flying back to her hand. The elf slid slowly down the wall, finally slumping on the floor. Reika stared at Lief with sorrow in her eyes. He looked at Reika, smirking.

"Heh... Should have known... I underestimated you... Powerful... like Visiert... You have great resolve... But it won't end here." Lief blasted Reika with incredible telekinetic power; it was like getting slammed by a battering ram. Reika screamed as she slammed against the opposite wall. She rose, in pain but not debilitated. Still, it had given Lief enough time to reach into his pocket for a cordial like the one he used on Reika. Death would not claim him on this occasion. Lief knew it was his last elixir a fact he didn't disclose to Reika.

Reika got to her feet, lunar power shining from her.

Before considering another attack, she saw something had changed in Lief, the man was smiling without malice. She desummoned Luniram ventured over to Lief, though still keeping her distance; she knew what the elven man could do.

Lief looked up. He was still smiling, still very different from the man only a few moments ago trying to kill her. "I know where the Anodyne Stone is."

Reika's eyes widened. "Don't lie to me... I have been tricked before." Part of her was curious. Part of her wanted to believe.

She looked to her left and saw Kenzuo emerging from the corridor. He looked at the two in confusion. "Reika?"

Lief saw the young man. He said nothing. "What's going on here?" Kenzuo said.

Reika strode over to Kenzuo, transforming back to her normal state. Lief remained where he was, which left Kenzuo rather puzzled. "Lief knows where the stone is. He just told me himself. I am sceptical of his claim, but..."

Kenzuo raised his eyebrows suspiciously. "A wise policy. Perhaps it is worth investigating the claim."

The twins directed their eyes to the elven man who approached them. "I think you don't need to be told what will happen if you play any tricks on us."

"Indeed, I'll lead the way," Lief stopped. "Wait, aren't you Visiert?"

"You are correct, Lief." The elf laughed to himself. "I must say, both of you impress me. Reika, you've come quite a way since I defeated you. The progress you made astounds me."

Reika blushed. "Thanks. Kenzuo really helped in that regard."

"Good. Now we need to get that stone for you."

Melito found himself weak from the struggle; he knew Welk was also losing strength. Melito couldn't give up, it was not an option.

"When I kill you, boy, I will have finally had my revenge for that embarrassing defeat at Entella. Then I will kill your friend, nice and slow."

Melito flew into a rage, throwing Entella's Bane with all his might, the Excandescite charging the blade of the axe, catching Welk off-guard. The axe smashed with such force into Welk's own weapon that it sprang out of Welk's hand, falling down into the pit below. The force pushed Welk off the edge of the arena; he started to fall but managed to grab the edge just in time. He was too weak to pull himself up. The axe rebounded, landing next to Melito embedded in the stone. He ignored it and went to the ledge Welk was holding.

"Urngh! It cannot end this way... It can't!" Welk yelled in anger.

Melito stepped onto Welk's fingers, glaring at the monstrous angry fiend, whose countenance had changed to one of fear. "For Entella, for my father, my mother, my family name!" Melito said.

He summoned his axe which began to glow with a fiery light and slammed it into Welk's back. The arachnid let out a hoarse gasp, letting go of the ledge. Melito dislodged the axe. It left a light glowing from the wound as the creature fell into the pit below, his body colliding with the walls on the way down. The light from the wound vapourised the body just before it hit the floor below.

Melito stepped away from the edge, weary, wounded yet triumphant. Tabitha walked over to him, smiling at her friend. Melito returned the smile. He then turned to the door opposite the one Welk had entered from, seeing Reika and Kenzuo standing there.

Kenzuo waved his hand, and the two monkeys felt their wounds soldering. "I hope your other friends aren't hurt," Kenzuo said. "Healing power is pretty taxing."

Lief stepped through the door after them.

"Hey... What are you playing at?" Melito said, pointing a finger at the elf. Kenzuo held his hand up. "He's helping us. The Anodyne Stone, he claims, is currently held within a treasure room. Its entrance is just in the next corridor." Melito's anger subsided, although he still gave Lief a wary look. "The elf I don't trust, but you, something about you is familiar..." He and Tabitha approached Reika and Kenzuo.

Tabitha shifted her head left then right, first looking at Reika then at Kenzuo and back to Reika. "You're Reika's brother?" She asked.

"Yes, we'll have a long chat later. Right now, let's get rid of Reika's curse."

~

"So where is the treasure room?" Melito asked, as they entered the next corridor.

"Be patient my simian friend... well, I guess friend isn't quite the expression I'd use..." Lief replied. They stood in the middle of the open corridor, facing the left wall. Lief eyed the floor carefully. He made his way to the wall, placing his hands on it. A blue glow emanated from the wall, and a clicking sound was heard as the glow disappeared. Lief pushed against the brickwork, shifting its weight as a heavy door. There, sure enough, was the Anodyne Stone, resting on a pedestal in the centre of the room. They all paused on the threshold, fearing traps.

Lief went inside the room, taking the Stone from the pedestal and giving it to Reika.

She stared at the stone with glee. This was it, the final cure, what she had been searching for, for so long...

Before she could activate it, Krea appeared and fired a lightning blast at her. Reika turned her head to see the blast soar towards her. It was too fast. An explosion encircled her, pushing the others around her back. Reika was flung backwards with the stone as it left her hands. She landed with a thud on the ground. The stone thudded on the floor beside her. Melito and Tabitha stood there speechless.

"I am disappointed with you, Lief," Krea said. "Why? Why suddenly play the righteous card?"

"I was promised power but at what cost? An innocent girl who never wronged me. What of the others you and your friends cursed before I was recruited? It's wrong what we are doing. I don't care what happens to me, you will not get to her."

Krea remained composed. "You will do as you are told. I'll give you a chance to recant your decision. Bring Reika in or I will."

Lief closed his eyes. All waited in anticipation. He shot a fiery blast at Krea. "Now Kenzuo, get them out of here."

Kenzuo activated his rune, and a portal opened below him,

with Melito, Tabitha, Lief, the stone and the unconscious Reika falling through. The portal closed like ripples as a stone collided in water. Krea looked to where the party had previously stood.

"I knew Destrian couldn't rely on him. Soppy weakling."

~

Kenzuo floated in the void. Melito, Tabitha, and Lief were there with him. "A little help would be nice. We can't fly like you," Tabitha said.

"I'm glad I'm not airsick," Melito put in.

"You'll be fine. I'll be over there shortly," Kenzuo replied as he went to recover Reika and the stone.

"Allow me," Lief said in response. Melito was still wary but said nothing and allowed the elf to grab him around the waist. Tabitha was just grateful to have escaped the castle.

Using the rune, Kenzuo opened a second portal near the other three, allowing them to pass through.

~

Gorvenal saw space open outside of his castle and he saw Lief, who planted the monkeys firmly on the ground after he arrived through the portal. Another opened with Kenzuo carrying Reika.

"Open the doors," Gorvenal called.

They came through. Kenzuo propped Reika against one of the pillars. She awoke, very weak. Kenzuo held Reika's head carefully. Green energy flowed from him, and the wounds closed shut. Reika leaned against the pillar to help get herself up, as her vision was still a little blurry. Slowly, she regained confidence.

Kenzuo was starting to show how tired he was. "Thank you... Kenzuo."

"Happy to help, Reika."

She then remembered the Anodyne Stone. Kenzuo handed the stone to her. As Reika held it, the stone crumbled to dust, its light fizzled out. She was silent, a tear rolling down her face. She slumped on the floor once again, distraught. She stared at the ground in a dejected manner. Lief solemnly looked on. If Reika's words hadn't convinced him of his evil, this event certainly punched him in the gut. Kenzuo could only feel sorry for her. Gorvenal eyed Lief.

"No time to stay for any of you. Reika, I'll send you back to the Aerouant Citadel," Reika nodded.

"Kenzuo, you need to go help Junayd, Zane, and Berinon. Even Zane will not be able to handle them all," Gorvenal said. "His chrono-magic is too dangerous for him to use constantly. As for the Stone, do not despair over it."

"The stone has crumbled to dust. I still have this vile corruption. It's over," Reika said. "I needed it to be free and destroy the weredragons."

Kenzuo led Reika away and through the portal. "What about us?" Melito asked Gorvenal.

"I would suggest you both head back to the citadel with the twins. Kenzuo will rejoin with the others in Caromago once Reika is safe."

Lief held up his hand. "Allow me to help, I brought this misery on Reika, It's my responsibility."

Gorvenal was hesitant. He relented. "If what you say is true, you'll accompany Kenzuo in this fight. We'll discuss your punishment upon your return."

"I wouldn't have it any other way."

Junayd, Zane, Berinon, and Rian had made it to the throne room entrance. The door opened, creaking loudly, echoing in the vast chamber beyond. The throne room was built from the same dark stone as the rest of the fortress. There was a vast door, matching that of the entrance, in front of them.

There, before the door, Destrian stood. Krea reappeared out of shadowy vapour.

The four men advanced. "Nowhere to run, Destrian," Junayd said.

Swiftly he, Zane and Berinon summoned their weapons into their hands. "It's over."

All Destrian did was smirk. "You came all this way? I am impressed you made it here. It's over, but not for me."

Krea walked down the staircase, smiling. She nodded at Rian. "Rian, you have certainly paid a high price when you took money from your comrades to face me instead. The real measure of a bounty hunter."

Rian shrugged. "What can I say? If Destrian and you are in charge, there won't be any clients left."

Zane chuckled. "Junayd, let us handle Krea, you go after Destrian," Zane said.

"Right," Junayd said.

"If I were you, I should be concerned for your friend," Krea said, gleefully. Junayd stood there speechless. "What have you done to her?"

Her smile only widened. "Answer me!"

Destrian turned to leave and almost in an instant, Junayd charged toward him through the air, chasing the dragon through the double doors at the top of the stairs. Zane, Berinon, and Rian gripped their weapons tightly. Krea gave a simper as she raised her hand in the air, summoning a dark purple blade which appeared like glass repairing itself. Despite the blade looking like a sword in shape, the material was a strange crystal structure that glistened if exposed to sunlight or any light source: in this case, the fires lighting the room.

Zane was the first to clash against Krea, power coursing through their blades, releasing charges of energy that danced along the floor, jolting the stones, making the gaps between the stones flash with energy both dark and light. Zane, with a large swing of Verwandeln, smashed Krea's shadow blade, though in vain, as the blade had reconstituted itself. Krea summoned a second blade, cutting and narrowly missing Zane's shoulder. Rian attempted to attack from behind, using the bayonet. The elf, however, moved her arm behind her back in a flash. The arm was surrounded in a ball of light.

Rian stabbed the light by accident, the blade bounced off it as if his attack had been countered by someone of equal strength. Krea switched the sword in her right hand to a backhanded grip, turning and trying to cut Rian. The bounty hunter managed to stop the blade in time, holding it in place with his bayonet. As Berinon charged, Krea turned to face him, pushing Rian away. Berinon slammed the bottom of the lance into Krea's chin. The elf recovered almost instantly. Berinon kicked Krea in the stomach, then slashed her across the chest though not enough to make a deep gouge. The elf winced. Krea felt something white hot scrape her right arm. She saw Rian holding his gun, the smoke leaving the barrel. He was smirking back at Krea.

She had underestimated her foes.

Junayd stepped through the door after Destrian and found himself, to his surprise, in the Somnium Carcerum. The place he stood was an open area with walls and floors much like the interior of Gorvenal's Castle, though rather like an amphitheatre rather than a closed room and the stone was a dull grey rather than navy blue. The Draco Ferrum emitted a light, allowing him to see in this dark realm.

Destrian stood at the edge of a cliff-face, seemingly waiting for him to arrive. "Destrian. Turn and face me!" Junayd yelled at the top of his voice.

Destrian complied. "My boy, I see your strength has grown. Once again, I am impressed that you made it here to face me. The Temporal Knight made it too and my best lieutenants have been defeated," Destrian then laughed when he saw the rage in Junayd's face. "What's wrong, Junayd? Aren't you angry about what Krea did to Reika?"

"You wretch!" Junayd growled.

Destrian smirked. "She'll live. When I find her, I'll be able to retrieve the weredragon from her. The pity is, it's her life for its life. Or, if I send her helpless into the aether of this dark realm, the weredragon will take her place upon her destruction. The question is, what shall I do? Make it painful or not?"

Junayd darted at Destrian enraged. His anger was so overpowering it was unfocused. He wasted his attacks, utilising no strategy, swinging the Ferrum like a blindfolded child trying to hit a piñata. Destrian swung his leg into Junayd's hip, knocking him along the floor with the sheer force of the attack.

Destrian continued to taunt him. "She will not get the chance to obliterate the weredragons. You will lose, boy."

Junayd stopped for a moment. He stepped away, banishing the Draco Ferrum. Destrian was befuddled. "What, given up already? I expected a little more fight..."

Junayd didn't reply as he pulled himself to his feet. He was worried about Reika, and he knew he couldn't keep fighting with her in his mind. With a conscious effort, he pushed all thought of her out of his mind.

The man was doing his best to compose himself. He stared at Destrian with a stoic expression.

"All I know," Junayd said, his temper how under control. "...is that when we use the Anodyne Stone, the curse will be gone. I'll start by killing you."

"On the contrary, I shall strike you down and unleash the weredragons. My mistress' vision will be fulfilled."

Krea wielded two shadow blades to counter the three opponents, her right arm in searing pain that made it difficult for her to concentrate. Zane and Berinon both swung downward strikes with their weapons, Krea blocked the attacks. Zane had had enough, flying towards Krea with Verwandeln in his hands, slashing aggressively at her. Krea could barely parry the attacks from Zane, with the two blades both knocked out of her hands.

Eventually he overpowered the elf, striking her with a ball of light, knocking her into the air. Then, using his chrono-magic, he hovered above her in the air slowing time to a crawl. Allowing his hands to be covered by light, Zane blasted Krea into the floor with an energy wave. The power of his attack snapped Krea's headband and hair-tie. The attack ceased and Zane touched back down on the floor safely, slightly exhausted. Krea pulled herself to her feet. "I'll enjoy watching you die, Temporal Knight."

Kenzuo reappeared, with Lief by his side, to assist. Krea was incensed. "Lief!"

The young elf was quiet, sending a beam of light from his right hand at Krea in answer. She blocked the attack, holding a barrier in front of her until it shattered due to the sheer force of the blast. She screamed as the light burned her.

Krea summoned six more dark blades like the ones she had held. They flew at the party. A few of the swords landed, with Lief barely parrying one, others managing to bloody him. Kenzuo intervened and summoned a barrier of blue energy around Lief that halted the dark blades' assault. It pulsed and the shadow blades were broken in many pieces. Krea controlled the flying shards with magical finesse, redirecting them at Kenzuo, where they dug into his flesh. Kenzuo yelled in pain and used a large fiery blast to incinerate the shards.

Lief was astonished at what Kenzuo had done for him. He couldn't believe it was out of friendship for him, he just needed to keep an ally in fight.

As Krea charged at Kenzuo, Lief stepped in and fended off Krea's sword attacks with his own. He struck the sword out of her hand, but she didn't care and tried to strike him with her fists. Lief threw his own sword away. Kenzuo was astonished. Some of her attacks landed on Lief but he still managed to fend her off.

"Big mistake to train me after my capture, Krea!" Lief said as he grabbed Krea's wrist in his right hand. His opponent was silent.

Lief summoned his power. He had to kill her. Had to... Then suddenly Lief let Krea's wrist go. "Disappointing..." Krea said. "First you failed to get Reika to us and now you won't even kill me. All the more satisfying when I kill you."

Lief shook his head. "It's not my job Krea."

Zane reappeared in front of Krea, slicing her chest with Verwandeln. Krea gasped. She fell on her knees.

"You weren't the elf I knew all those years ago," Zane said. "It's a shame it had to end like this."

Krea staggered, a vomiting sound issuing from her mouth. "You're right about one thing, I am not the elf you knew." Zane was speechless. "But why worry about that... you have *already* lost foolish boy..." She winced due to the pain, her eyesight wandering to darkness. "Soon the weredragons will be unleashed... You have no hope... The Anodyne Stone has been... Destroyed..." Krea's body faded into the dark vapour one final time. Lief clenched his fists.

"She's right. The weredragons will come soon, we have to stop as many as we can."

"We'll start behind the door then," Zane said. "Junayd was adamant to handle Destrian on his own, and I'll honour his request, but that doesn't mean he can take on all the weredragons."

All four of the men entered through the door.

Junayd fought Destrian. The dragon seemed to be toying with him whereas, Zane observed, Junayd himself appeared to be using his full power. "Is he holding back?" Lief asked.

"I don't know," Zane answered, truthfully.

"If he is, why? He has been going to the forges to restore the Draco Ferrum..."

"Hey!" Rian said, tapping the back of his knuckles against Lief's chest. "If you two have time to stand there talking, you have time to fight."

It was in that moment, tumultuous roars sounded from the deep.

The weredragons arrived. At least twenty-five, though more were on the way, and could be heard roaring in the distance.

Junayd and Destrian paused for a moment, with the former looking at the charging monsters. Black fire spewed from their lips. Their flesh and manes varied in pallet, indicating the many humans, metazoans and elves who had been captured and transformed over the years. Their eyes glowed with reptilian malice. The weredragons were close to beginning their assault.

Junayd tore his attention away from Destrian to help his comrades. He leapt forward, managing to parry the attacks from three weredragons with his blade. He landed a cut on one across the stomach, but one of the dragons slashed him on the shoulder. Junayd yelled in pain, though he got his revenge, stabbing the weredragon with his blade.

Lief shot a sphere of ice into one weredragon, launching swift punches that the naked eye found tough to perceive, heavily bruising the chest of another. His defence was potent, but eventually he had more to contend with than he could handle. Lief was surrounded by five of them, resorting to a blast of light that vapourised the creatures on contact. The attack wore him out a bit though, and the others stepped in to give him some reprieve from the battle.

Zane had little problem with the weredragons, making use of the chrono- field around his body to evade enemy attacks with ease. However, he knew continued usage of his time magic would be taxing, so he tried to keep his usage minimal and swift.

Rian also had his fair share of problems. His bullets were damaging to the thick hide of the weredragons, but they didn't seem to stop them fully, only throw them back. He knew it was dangerous to engage the creatures head on.

One of the weredragons grabbed him, pinning him against a sheer face of rock. It didn't concentrate on the gun, thus Rian took the opportunity to stab the creature in the side. The creature roared in pain, Rian followed up by pulling the trigger, firing a bullet in the wound.

Berinon fought two of them. He rolled out of the way of one claw-swipe and slashed the legs of the beast on his right. The weredragon howled and Berinon then impaled it with his spear. The other weredragon tried to attack him from behind. Berinon dislodged his spear from the dead creature, then performed an upward slash on the other creature. It fell to the floor with a groan.

Kenzuo activated his Lunarmancer state. Fighting the weredragons was a walk in the forest to him. His punches were swift, striking with much force behind them.

As Junayd broke away from two weredragons attempting to bite him, Destrian fired an intense lightning blast at the young man. Junayd moved forward at a slow pace, his blade cutting into the lightning, splitting it. Everyone ducked, and the weredragons flew upwards into the air to avoid the lightning that dug into the floor, singeing the stone. Junayd pressed on, keeping the blade upright, splitting the lightning currents. Small tendrils of the lightning sprayed around the weapon into Junayd, partially burning his skin. He continued before stopping a few paces from Destrian. Light emanated from the Ferrum, which then began to push against the lightning blast with an incredible strain. Zane was about to go to Junayd.

"No! Save your strength!" Junayd yelled. Zane backed off and pressed on with killing the weredragons. Junayd charged the Draco Ferrum and with a mighty swing, he sent out a giant scythe-shaped wave of light towards Destrian which pushed back against the lightning blast and collided with the mad dragon. There was a shriek, then a large explosion. Destrian simply absorbed the explosive energies however, sucking the power back into himself like an implosion.

The old dragon charged his fists with energy, one with light and one with darkness. Junayd de-summoned his blade, channelling energy into his hands. The two exchanged blows, Destrian stuck on his right cheek, Junayd on his left shoulder. Destrian moved so fast it seemed as if he teleported. He swiftly went for Junayd, catching the young man off-guard with a punch. Junayd rolled along the floor, crashing into one of the walls. He rose quickly, drawing the Draco Ferrum again, standing his ground.

Only a few weredragons were left. Destrian was watching the others fight the remnants of the first weredragon assault.

Lief managed to stab a weredragon backwards, his arm encased in a dagger of light for a brief few seconds. Rian shot one and stabbed another with his bayonet. Berinon lobbed the head off a fourth. All four were fatigued. Kenzuo powered himself down after firing a shot of light into the chest of the final weredragon. For now, the tide had been turned.

"A minor setback," Destrian said confidently, grinning from ear to ear. Destrian leapt into the void. A burst of dark energy swirled around him, engulfing him. The sphere of energy expanded considerably above the group, eventually falling away. Destrian's appearance had changed into that of an eight- foot dragon with a bipedal shape. Two sharp horns curled from his head. His flesh was the colour of soot. His feet made contact with the ground with a thud. He smacked his fists together, taking up a fighting stance afterwards.

Junayd went to attack Destrian, who in turn summoned a thick dark blade like the one Krea used. Destrian held his ground against the young man, who strained against his might. Junayd's strength was enough to match the dragon's own but only just. They broke off their assault with Destrian retreating to another floating rock nearby. The others only watched. Little did they know Montanus had kept himself hidden from view within the throne room, edging his way upstairs. "I sense my master is in danger."

Destrian made one final sweep with his sword against Junayd's own, the two locking their blades. "Impressive strength from you, young man. But even now, I have toyed with you."

"I'm not surprised by that. I've been holding back as well." Junayd struck Destrian on the side of the face. The dragon spun in the air, scraping the floor with his feet. Junayd flew towards him the Draco Ferrum glowing with ferocious light. Destrian retaliated with his blade, swinging it at Junayd. Their swords crashed together, releasing a boom of sound. Destrian held Junayd's attack back while the young man continued to push against him, the ground underneath Destrian cracking more and more until the platform below them was split asunder.

Dark energy seeped through the door from the throne room. No noise was heard, even as it formed into the shape of Montanus.

He moved cautiously behind the group. Zane sensed Montanus' presence almost at once.

"The Temporal Knight..." Montanus cursed. "Fool that I am!"

Zane went to strike him. Montanus blocked the attack. Blows were traded at once in quick succession. Zane did not have the upper hand. He was driven to exhaustion thanks to the gruelling battle against the weredragons. Montanus was able to overpower the young man, thrashing him against the wall. Lief pulled Montanus off him and teleported him away along with himself. Rian and Berinon were left alone with Zane, who was drained of all strength.

"Rest for now, there's nothing more you can do," Rian said sternly. He turned back to Junayd and Destrian. "We must let these two battle it out."

Junayd and Destrian clashed, their swords meeting with sparks, their swings causing minor shockwaves to split the rock. The two de-summoned their blades, flying towards each other at high speed, a massive wave of energy bursting when their fists crashed, obliterating the cliffs and stones around them, leaving them floating in the void. The two combatants were flung in opposite directions, managing to stop themselves from hurtling too far away. There, they floated. Junayd held out both of his fists. Determination etched on his face. He felt a little weary and wounded but he had to keep on fighting.

Destrian remained facing Junayd, a grin on his face. Was he tiring? Junayd couldn't be sure. Destrian flew swiftly at Junayd, landing a blow on Junayd's cheek, sending him flying back. The beast followed the young man, eager to land a second blow, but this time Junayd blocked the creature's fist with his arms shaped like an x. Junayd halted, letting Destrian crash into him. He glowed with a bright light, grabbing Destrian's right hand, then grabbed his neck.

Junayd caught sight of a floating boulder above him. He dragged Destrian, encasing him in a bright light and with a mighty heave, Junayd threw Destrian into the rock. He disappeared and reappeared in front of Destrian, pulling the dragon away from the rock of him and smashing him into it a second time it exploded upon contact. The rock was reduced to molten slag. Junayd gave one final flying punch into Destrian, sending the dragon hurtling through the void. He crashed through another floating boulder, crashing into to terra firma in a hail of stone debris. Junayd speedily returned and landed on the ground. Destrian lay limp before the others.

"Rian, Berinon, take Zane and leave here. Kenzuo, go to Reika, check up on her," Junayd said.

Rian grabbed Zane and pulled his arm over his shoulder. "You have my word." Rian ran while holding Zane out of the mysterious door. Junayd shut the door telekinetically.

Destrian got to his feet, he launched himself, catching Junayd off-balance, bringing him to the ground. The young warrior's arms were pinned on the floor by the terrible beast. Junayd pulled his feet from under Destrian, kicking the beast in the stomach. He did it over and over in rapid succession. Destrian eventually let go of Junayd, clutching his stomach in pain. Destrian opened a portal to try to escape from Somnium Carcerum. But before he had the chance to close the portal behind him, Junayd followed him.

All was silent.

Berinon and Rian, along with Kenzuo fled from Caromago Castle through one of the portals of the rune, arriving back at Aerouant Citadel. The elf reached into a pouch on his belt and pulled out the airship beacon.

"The airship beacon?" Kenzuo asked.

"Captain Tybalt needs to get back here safely," Rian replied. "I hope we are not too late."

"We have got a lot of trouble on our hands now," Berinon added.

Chapter 19

Hope

Reika was still distressed about her plight. All that remained of her hope had been dashed. Kenzuo knew that there was nothing he could say that would comfort her. Even he wondered whether they would be able to stop Destrian. He was stood outside her bedroom when Ysellian arrived.

"She hasn't left since we got back," Kenzuo informed her. "The stone is gone. If it does regenerate, it's going to be a long time before it returns. She might pass away before then."

"I don't think it is the end. This must be a delay in the prophecy accorded to me by the gods. I will talk to her." Ysellian entered the room. Reika was by the window on the sofa. She stood up, looking down at the floor, her hair hiding her face.

"Let me see your face, Reika," Ysellian said calmly. Reika lifted her head.

Despite the lack of tears, as it was pointless to cry, Reika's misery was plain. "We've been stabbed in the back," she replied morosely. "All the long nights, all the battles, all the time spent away from my home, and it has to end like this." Ysellian sat next to Reika on the sofa. "This is not the end. Everything is happening as I have foreseen; I am convinced of that. Junayd and Destrian are in a long fight, the weredragons are rising. It's all happening." "But what of the stone? It's absolutely gone," Reika said.

"The stone is merely a shell, Reika. Did you not have a conversation with Zane about it?"

Reika began to think hard, then it then hit her. "Its original form was destroyed. That shell I held was its current vessel, wasn't it? One built by Tahpenes?"

"The energy of the stone *cannot* be destroyed; it will simply transfer to another vessel. Where did you last have it?"

Reika thought about it. "Krea wounded me. I thought I was going to die. I had it in my hands. Kenzuo healed me and..." Reika gasped. "It's me, I'm the vessel now? But the curse is still within me. It hasn't been expunged."

"The stone's effects haven't been activated yet. All that I can sense is that the creature is suppressed. Once the stone's power is unleashed, then the weredragon will be gone for good, as with the others," Ysellian said.

"It's as Ysellian said Reika," Kenzuo added. "Her track record for prediction has been on point."

Reika stood up. A look of determination on her face. "Time to end this, then," she said.

They all saw a small shadow appear in the sky. It peeled away to reveal Lief and Montanus hurtling through the air. The two crashed into the courtyard far below Reika's window, rolling like a stone flung from a catapult.

"Lief... What is he doing?" Ysellian asked, confused. "Giving us a hand!" Reika said as her face lit up.

Before Lief was able to connect a strike with the sorcerer, using a dark blade he'd called forth, Montanus grabbed it, yanking it from his hand. The sorcerer pushed the elf to the floor, stabbing him in the left shoulder to pin him to the grassy plain. Lief shrieked.

"You should have remained with us, traitor."

Lief lifted his hand. He dislodged the blade, placing his right hand on his bleeding shoulder.

"It will take you some time to heal from that. You should have

left it there. It's a shame you don't have those elixirs anymore."
Montanus sensed Reika's presence nearby and teleported away. He
reappeared inside her bedroom.

"You monster!" She hissed.

"What is a monster? That useless stone did not grant you
peace. The prophecy you so believe you are fulfilling is nothing but
a fallacy." His eyes shifted to Ysellian and Kenzuo, then back to
Reika. "Even if, somehow, you contain the essence of the stone, it
won't help. It gives me even more reason to kill you. I'll extract the
stone's energy from your corpse."

Reika eyes burned with rage.

Kenzuo stepped forward. "Finally, an illusionist such as you
has some mettle."

Montanus merely smirked. "Which of you is first?" Both
Kenzuo and Reika swiftly transformed into their Lunarmancer
states. Ysellian opened the window

behind Montanus and both the Lunarmancers charged at
Montanus, pushing him out of the open window.

Montanus slowed his descent and landed safely, the wide plain
now the battleground. The Lunarmancer siblings touched down.
Montanus roared aloud and tried to hit Reika with his bare hand.
The young woman was amazed how easily she avoided Montanus's
assault. Every attack Montanus tried to land missed. One final
punch landed on Reika's chest. This only caused Reika to recoil
back two steps. She felt no sharp pain, it was like a fly had landed
on skin and promptly departed. He threw another and then Reika
grabbed his arm, holding it effortlessly.

Montanus was rattled. "Powerful. How did you obtain this
strength?" He asked.

"Training with Kenzuo," Reika said as she smiled at the beast.
"Care to do the honours, brother?" She released Montanus' arm,
allowing Kenzuo to suplex the dragon. Montanus rose a little
bruised, more humiliated than hurt. He danced away.

"Reel it in a bit," Kenzuo said to his sister. "What do you
mean?"

"You're getting too sure of yourself."

Reika beamed back at Kenzuo. "Maybe..." she replied.

They resumed a fighting stance as Montanus rallied for a second attack. "If you had joined us, Reika, we could have been great. You, our personal messiah."

"I don't care. When this has finished. I'll have my life back and never have to put up with your ilk again." Reika instantly called on and swung Luniram, releasing a blast of energy from it.

Montanus leapt to his right, narrowly avoiding it. Reika de-summoned Luniram. "I want you and the curse gone!" Reika added, displaying an anger Kenzuo had never witnessed before. She held out her palms and shot a continuous lightning blast at Montanus who barely held the blast back. Kenzuo backed off in amazement. Montanus collapsed onto his knees.

"Still salty about what I did, I see," the wizard taunted. "That doesn't even come close."

Before Montanus could recover, Kenzuo swiftly flew towards him at high speed, blasting him to the grassy field, furrowing the dirt. Montanus slammed against the floor with his fists only to push himself to his feet. He swung at Kenzuo, landing a few hits. Kenzuo brushed them off.

Montanus grabbed Kenzuo's throat. "Finally, a chance to kill a Lunarmancer.

After you die, Reika is next."

Kenzuo smirked. "At least you are man enough to go after me," he croaked. The young man gripped onto the dragon's arms, easing them away from his neck, taking a lungful of air. Kenzuo levitated a foot into the air and swung Montanus away from him with a mighty heave towards Reika, who launched a sharp air- borne kick into the dragon's spine. Montanus howled in pain, much to Reika's amazement as her kick knocked him down to the floor once again. She looked towards Kenzuo as she floated like him. "You let him hit you?"

"He's not going to hurt you or me. He needs to be stronger to do that." Montanus struggled to his feet. "Oooh, I hate you both."

The siblings touched down on the ground once again. Reika scowled. "I am not fond of you either."

Montanus roared, his power starting to rise, a dark aura surrounding him. Kenzuo went towards Montanus. The dragon turned around fast; his left arm hit Kenzuo's right arm. Kenzuo backed off. He shook his arm.

"Stronger than I thought. Be careful."

Reika nodded. Montanus once again made his assault on Reika. She dodged the attacks quickly until Montanus scratched her left shoulder. Reika winced, clutching her shoulder with her right hand. Kenzuo shot a mighty blast of lightning into Montanus' back.

Kenzuo healed Reika and himself. "You know I can't keep doing that. Let's keep the healing to a minimum. It's tiring."

"Sorry. I was careless."

Montanus stepped away from them. He went for the two again; they blocked the attacks. Little did they know another Montanus was creeping toward them from behind. Kenzuo kicked the one in front of him away. A fiery blast shot from his palm at another. There was no collision with either attack, the images of Montanus being nothing more than illusions. Reika also saw another Montanus and sent a small lightning ball from her hand, but it also simply phased through the fake.

More copies of Montanus appeared. Both Lunarmancers punched the illusions in front of them. All the Montanus' illusions vanished, and they saw Montanus floating in the air. He brought his hands together to make a dark glowing sphere. He crushed it and many dark orbs shot away towards the Lunarmancers. Reika raised a barrier in time, each of the orbs crashing into the barrier.

"He never did this the first time, Kenzuo."

"He is a reluctant fighter. He believed you and Junayd were beneath him. It's only because you have shown how strong you are that he is willing to go all out."

Reika enlarged her barrier; the orbs show no signs of stopping. Kenzuo looked up. He saw Montanus firing a long beam of light at them.

"Move Reika!" Kenzuo yelled. Reika dropped the barrier, allowing them both to swiftly dodge the beam. A thirty-foot explosion erupted from the ground. Kenzuo and Reika glanced towards the sky where Montanus had been. He had mysteriously vanished.

The two kept their distance from each other just in case they could be manipulated into fighting as foes. Reika examined the landscape in front of her. She noticed Kenzuo behind her. Immediately she knew something was up.

"Kenzuo, I thought we were not to stay together like this? Montanus could pose as one of us."

"Are you certain of that?" "Positive."

"You're not strong enough to fight on your own, Reika?"

"It's not like that. We agreed to be alone for now. You can't be him."

Kenzuo grew angry. He grabbed Reika by the throat, hauling her up above him with his right hand. "How wrong I was and how Father was to think you could stand with us!"

Suddenly, a sharp pain burst in Kenzuo's elbow and all feeling up to the hand vanished without a trace. Reika dropped onto the ground. The Kenzuo standing in front of her was Montanus.

She saw the real Kenzuo on her left, holding Luniram in his hand. "It's not over yet," he said.

Montanus clutched the stump where his arm had been. "I'll break you both!" He snarled. He breathed fire and they were driven back, forced to block with magical barriers that eventually were broken through.. Montanus threw a punch but Reika caught it with her right hand before it hit her face. She then used her left hand to fire a telekinetic projectile into Montanus. Kenzuo struck Montanus with his fist, as the dragon was unable to block the attack without his right arm. Montanus flew through the air, slowing his speed at the last moment. He hung in the air upside down, firing a flurry of energy projectiles with a wave of his left hand. Reika summoned a barrier to protect her and Kenzuo.

"Now you are learning, Reika. You are not invincible like this, just powerful, there is a difference," Kenzuo said.

"Indeed," Reika replied. "Why say that in front of him though?" "He already knows. We need to hurry up."

Montanus righted himself. "You can't keep this up forever. You'll both eventually lose your energy."

Reika and Kenzuo braced, powered their punches with light, their flight swift as a cannonball. Montanus barely held the two back, keeping his arms—or what was left of one and his good arm—spread out, pushing against them with a barrier. His predicament was akin to a man caught in a dungeon trap with closing walls. The energy from the Lunarmancers began to spike; Montanus couldn't hold on any longer. Both humans ceased the attack, giving Montanus a false relief before firing a blast of light each into him. The dragon yelled in pain, cursing them as he was vapourised by the dual blast. Reika and Kenzuo gently floated down to the ground towards each other, their transformations reverting, and with that, the two showed their true exhaustion. Some of the moonlight from the other moon could recharge them but they had no time to stay for long.

Reika saw Lief walking towards them both. "As always, a fine display from the both of you, but Destrian will begin bringing the weredragons through."

Kenzuo looked at Lief's shoulder, the wound inflicted by Montanus was gone. *Zane's handiwork?*

The two Lunarmancers knew what was going to happen next. "Where should I go?" Reika asked.

"Don't worry about that," Lief replied. "Just get to Antonius. You can unleash the power of the Anodyne Stone from his castle, it's a good vantage point."

"Agreed," Kenzuo said.

"Allow me to assist." Rian arrived on the grass plain. "Where's Zane?" Reika asked.

"He needs time to recover, his chrono-magic in the battle against the weredragons has taken a toll on him. His one last favour was healing Lief over here."

Kenzuo headed back swiftly to the citadel to retrieve the rune.

403

Rian looked into Reika's eyes. Her conversation with Rian on revenge echoed in her mind. Although Montanus was dead and there was the knowledge no one else would succumb to his illusions, there was no satisfaction in her grudge. She was right he had to be stopped but her motive was hypocritical.

"It's easy to preach, harder to practice," she finally said. Rian nodded his head. "Remember that well."

Reika nodded back.

Junayd and Destrian fought still on the Order of the Ferrum's Island. The monks, including Reuben, couldn't quite make out what was happening in the distance, only see flashes of light, metal, and cloud, and dismal shapes moving between.

"The prophecy of Ysellian looks like it's about to come to pass brothers," Reuben said. "Prepare yourselves for the weredragons' arrival."

The blows of the combatant's swords never ceased, echoing, carried far by the winds.

Destrian's downward strike missed Junayd, the human countering with his fist into the left side of the dragon. Destrian dropped his blade, clutching his side with his right hand.

"Enough of this," Destrian growled. "It is time for your world to come under my dominion." The dragon regained his posture, his power beginning to rise with a dark aura surrounding him. Junayd felt himself pushed backward by the force of the tempest.

Destrian sent out purple lightning into the sky. It coalesced into a ball, then scattered into several bolts across Perusia, including to where he and Junayd were located. Portals opened close to them, allowing weredragons to pass through out of Somnium Carcerum. *Just as the mural depicted. I hope the rest of it will follow.* Junayd thought.

The creatures, all with one accord, began to leave the portals, making their way to the inhabitants of nearby cities and towns.

~

The weredragons poured across the island. Reuben grabbed his barbed spear.

A younger man like Reuben drew near to assist. "Brother, how many more are coming through?"

"We have to hope not too many Dalmar. If Junayd succeeds, then the next step is to wait for the Anodyne Stone to be utilised. Until then, we have no choice but to fight."

Reuben slashed the first weredragon across the chest, a clean cut. Taking heart, the other monks rallied behind him, following Reuben like he was a military general. A few of the monks fell before the weredragons to his dismay but he felt duty bound to fight on.

Dalmar plunged his barbed spear into the stomach into one of them, Reuben slashing the neck of another. The monks closed in on the weredragons and hoped to push the army back, despite more losses to their party.

~

Junayd continued his assault on Destrian. He was too late to stop the portals from opening up but he could at least keep Destrian from commanding the weredragons effectively.

"Why do you still fight? Your girlfriend failed to destroy my minions," Destrian said mockingly. Junayd felt his cool slipping, his attacks growing more violent.

"Your plans will fail."

Destrian said nothing. He knew secretly the stone's outer shell had been destroyed. "People are going to die and there is nothing you can do to stop it boy!"

~

Gorvenal and Galeru made their way back to the castle, seeing weredragons trying to escape from their confines in the Somnium Carcerum. They went after the weredragons and tried to wrench them away from the portal. The monsters turned their attention on the two and began to fight.

Antonius watched the portals from his castle. The look of horror on his face was a rare sight. A portal opened as Antonius summoned his sword. Reika and Kenzuo arrived through the portal a split second later, along with Lief and Rian. "Have you come to turn against me?" He asked, confused as to why Lief was with the two Lunarmancers.

"I have turned against Destrian, these two are innocent," Lief said. Antonius de-summoned his sword. "Is that so?"

"Lief can be trusted, Master," said Reika, "Hold me responsible is he does betray us."

Antonius nodded back. "Did you retrieve the Anodyne Stone?"

"Sort of, the vessel is gone but the energy of the stone is within me. I just need to unleash it." Antonius placed his hands on her shoulders. "You must be very cautious. That much energy released from your body could tear you apart... Unless..." He pondered for a moment. "Unless something else is used as the conduit." Portals opened up above them, weredragons spiralling down from Somnium Carcerum.

"Reika, we'll take care of the weredragons here. You use the stone's power!" Kenzuo said. He, Lief, Rian and Antonius began their fight.

Reika stood equally distanced from the edge of the stone cliff and the castle. She closed her eyes, white electrical bands curling around her with rapid speed. The symbol of the Anodyne Stone formed on the rock around her and under her feet. The moon could be seen above in all its fulness. She entered her Lunarmancer state. A white glow surrounded her.

Something else as a conduit? What did he mean? Reika pondered. It was in that moment she realised where the energy could be channelled.

Reika didn't yell in pain, no matter how much she wanted to. She stayed connected to the symbol and held on with all her might; electrical bursts zagged out of her hands. Reika then yelled at the top of her voice; it was almost an unbearable pain. The nearest weredragons started to roar as their bodies disintegrated into dust beneath the power of the surge, floating away and fading into smoke, phasing out completely. Other bursts spread through the portals around Perusia and into Somnium Carcerum, all the were-dragons were dying.

~

Reuben was about to impale a weredragon when the surge cut through the monster, vaporising it. Reuben stood gobsmacked. A few seconds later, he and the other monks raised their weapons high in the air, and cheering echoed far and wide on the island.

Dalmar was completely gobsmacked. "I never dreamed that this would happen. Yet here we are."

Reuben smiled. "Yes. The end of the weredragons."

~

Gorvenal stopped where he was for a time, as did Galeru. Through the portals he could see bursts of lightning tearing through the weredragons. Eventually, one blast shot into the weredragons he was fighting. Some of the energy forked off, colliding with him and Galeru. Instead of destroying them, it passed over them harmlessly.

Gorvenal could tell something was different. "The seal that bound us here is gone."

Galeru cheered and jumped for joy. They both re-entered the castle. "Perhaps we can help..." a voice said. Gorvenal turned around to see who it was hiding in the shadows. He knew the voice though he couldn't see their visage. "I'll lend you my ears."

~

A dark cloud emerged from Reika's body. It was surrounded by the same energy that surged around Reika; both she and it were connected by a beam. In vain the dark cloud tried to form a body for itself, but to no avail, the energy functioning like a spiked cage. Finally, the soul of the weredragon inside her suffered the same fate as its brethren, fading out of existence as the energy dispersed. All grew to silence as the energy frittered away.

While the energy swept the lands, Junayd and Destrian halted their battle.

The dragon shrieked as he saw the weredragons dying and felt the presence of the others who were not near him vanish.

Junayd smiled, laughing to himself. *Reika, you did it.* he thought. Destrian roared, "She spoiled my plans! I'll kill her for this."

Destrian swept in a flurry of dark wings through a portal.

Junayd gave chase after the raging beast, but Destrian shut the portal, preventing Junayd from following. Junayd felt ice in his blood. *I won't make it in time.*

Reika dropped to her knees, shrinking, returning to her normal form. She then began to stare at her hands in delight. The curse was banished from her, the Anodyne Stone's energy had worked. She was ecstatic. Clumsily, she got to her feet, still drained from the ordeal. She wobbled a little as Kenzuo ran over. He held her steady.

"Easy, you can rest now."

Reika waited a few seconds. "Much obliged."

Kenzuo let her go and Reika managed to remain standing, now a little sturdier. A portal opened behind Reika. She lurched out of the way in the nick of time and Destrian missed his attack. Reika stumbled to her feet again. Destrian glared at the young woman with seething anger and teeth bared.

"Weak from the stone's power, eh? Nothing will save you now."

Reika transformed again. Destrian swung in vain with his attacks as

Reika dodged them over and over before she launched a magical projectile into him. It knocked the dragon away. Reika noticed Kenzuo had disappeared.

He must be trying to retrieve Junayd. Come on brother, hurry it up. she thought. Destrian fired a beam from his mouth. Reika placed her right hand in front of her; the beam crashed into an invisible barrier. The beam vanished and the barrier shattered to pieces. Reika dropped her arm down. She knew deep down she was not strong enough at this present time, The Anodyne Stone's energy had taken its toll. The dragon fighting her had been weakened too, thanks to Junayd, but not enough that she and Destrian were equals.

Before Destrian could fire another blast, Junayd and Kenzuo reappeared behind him, with the latter striking the weredragon to the ground and the former pouring energy into his blade which glowed with increasing intensity. All backed away, including Reika.

"It's over!" Junayd cried as he brought his blade down in a mighty downward swing, causing a gigantic light beam to emanate from it. Destrian could only watch as he was struck by the blast. Incredible brightness flashed.

The air soon cleared. The noise of the beam echoed into the distance until it had no more resonance.

Destrian stood there, too injured to go on fighting. "Lady Tahpenes... forgive me..." he said weakly. Destrian collapsed onto his back. His body changed into a dark cloud, fading completely from view. Reika returned to normal shortly after.

"Destrian's plans, are brought to naught," Lief said with a faint smile, emerging from Antonius's castle with Rian. Junayd stood triumphant where Destrian had fallen. Lief called him over. "Junayd, bring me in. The elders can decide my fate."

"Are you sure?" Junayd asked.

"It has to end this way. Life or death, my crimes are to be dealt with. But how can I face my former master?"

"He wants to reconcile, if possible."

"Hate to break up the regret fest..." Rian said, holding up a money sack. He chucked it to Junayd who in turn caught it and looked inside. "Your money," Rian went on. "It's all yours, keep it."

"Er... Thanks," Junayd said bewildered.

"See you around," Rian said. Patting Junayd on the shoulder in a friendly manner, he left quietly.

"Just like that," Reika said.

All turned to see Gorvenal approaching them. "Lief, your trial is soon to begin. Come with me."

Lief complied. Junayd watched as Lief and Gorvenal vanished. Junayd, Reika and Kenzuo remained where they were.

Reika stared at her right hand, examining it intently. "Junayd, you go on ahead. Kenzuo and I need to talk."

"As you wish," Junayd replied.

She then held her sword in her hand, approaching Kenzuo. The young man looked at her. "What are you doing?" He asked, as he noticed the young woman kneeling before him, presenting the Luniram to him. "This is *your* blade," Reika said. Kenzuo gently took the blade from Reika's hand.

"Oh yes, you wanted to return it. You sure?"

"Yes, I think that you should be the one to have it. It will stagnate where I am going. It served me well, but you are out more on missions."

Kenzuo finally took the blade in his hands. "Just remember we share this blade. If I can take it from you, it's logical to assume you can take it from me." He de-summoned the blade.

"Come with me back to the citadel, we'll talk there," Kenzuo held the rune in his hand to open a portal.

"Junayd, I'll be back to heal you later," he said.

Kenzuo entered the portal first. Reika accompanied him.

Chapter 20

Aftermath

Junayd sat on the mountain side, the very one where Reika exited the cave as a weredragon for the first time. He was tired, had no sleep and just sat there the whole night, staring off in the distance at the remarkable landscape. Dawn approached, the sun climbing the skyline, its heat gradually reaching Junayd. A fiery pillar appeared behind him, disappearing into smoke, revealing Antonius himself.

"Antonius? What brings you here?" Junayd asked. "Lief's trial is going to begin. Your presence is required."

"I see." Junayd went with Antonius down the mountain. "I wonder what the verdict will be?"

Carthagian metazoans, Humans, Elves and Dragons alike took their place in the court, a grand room with a wooden floors and panels overlaying alabaster stone. The court magistrate was a dragon, sporting a long grey beard, blue eyes, and white skin, with magnificent robes like those of King Nestor.

"Here, I shall call this court to order." He cleared his throat as he pulled parchment from a nearby drawer. "Lief, you stand here on the following charges: assisting in, despite the laws against them, the profane creations of the weredragons. Although not guilty of assisting Destrian in collecting victims, you are accused of this attempting to kidnap one Lunarmancer, an apprentice of Antonius and assaulting Antonius which had it not been for his armour, would have died. How do you plead?"

"Guilty, I have no excuse," Lief said firmly.

The magistrate's grave face showed his surprise. "You will not say anything to defend your actions?"

"No, I have nothing to say. The charges are accurate."

The magistrate could barely give summation, such was his shock. There was a murmuring in the hall as the dragon elders discussed Lief's fate. Finally, the magistrate cleared his throat.

"Because of your confession and your willingness to assist the efforts against Destrian's vile creations, we are willing to spare your life. However, due to your previous escape and your attempted abduction of Reika, you will be sentenced to prison for five years in Aerouant Citadel. On good behaviour, and with no further attempt to escape, we will lower that sentence to one year. I suggest you behave."

After the magistrate brought his stone gavel down onto his table, Lief left the dock, escorted by Ignatius and Gorvenal from it.

Junayd spotted a woman with robes on the other side of the court. Her robes were dark navy blue in colour, the cuffs and rims a light blue with a simple pretty flower pattern, held together by a small belt, The long skirt of the robe came down just above her ankles. She wore shoes, her toes hidden, the tops of her feet covered with straps holding the shoes together. He couldn't make out her face. All the woman did was look at Lief as he was escorted from the room.

As everyone was leaving, the woman promptly left the room first, as if to catch up with Lief. *What is that woman doing?* he pondered.

Antonius gave him a nudge. "Stop staring and get moving lad, come on." "Sorry, there is a woman trying to follow Lief," Junayd said as he departed his seat.

"She won't change a thing, Lief's fate is decided," Antonius responded.

Beyond the courtroom was a long corridor with many doors, black and white marble flooring, and engraved wooden supports in the walls. Junayd kept his distance, but watched the robed woman speaking with Lief, though he couldn't make out what they were saying.

Gorvenal and Ignatius, flanking Lief, said nothing. The robed woman nodded. She walked alongside them. Junayd was left standing there, wondering who she was.

Zaius met with the group in the corridor. He looked at Lief in dismay despite his relief at his change of heart. "I don't know what to think or why you pursued this course of life."

"Nothing I can say excuse what I have done, Master. It was cruel what I did," Lief said.

To Lief's surprise, the man smiled.

"The only thing, Lief, is having you back," Zaius gave Lief a handshake. "I trust I'll see you after you are released from custody."

Lief nodded. The robed woman standing there held her hand near her heart, a small smile could be seen under her hood.

"You may go," Ignatius said. "Any further conversation with the prisoner must be approved." The woman departed back the way she'd come. She passed Junayd, not saying anything to him. He got a closer look of her mouth and chin, a youthful face undoubtedly, but the eyes eluded him thanks to the shadow of the hood.

Antonius tapped him on the shoulder. "Time to leave, come along."

~

Junayd met with all but Reika and Zane at Antonius' Castle for a celebration. The banquet table was immense and housed many plates, with many courses of meat, fruit, and vegetables, all the aromas blending together complementing the sumptuous sight. When the feast came to an end, the guests returned to their own parts of the world.

"I think we'd better get moving. It was an honour to fight with you all," Berinon said to Junayd and the Carthagians. "Junayd, Tabitha, Melito, feel free to visit us anytime."

"Sure, you're welcome at Entella when you may," Melito replied.

With that, Rian and Berinon made their way to the teleporter. Junayd turned to look at Melito and Tabitha. "Where do you go from here?"

"We're going to rebuild Entella," Melito said. "After the death of Welk, we shouldn't have trouble from his troops anymore. See you soon, Junayd." Melito and Tabitha made their way to the castle door, departing with a smile and a wave. Antonius and Junayd made their way to the entrance, talking softly. At the door, Antonius turned to face Junayd. "Until next time, young man. Though we'll see how long that is..." Antonius closed the door. Junayd walked to the edge of the cliff-face of the floating island. He sat down, staring at his home for a while.

Lief remained in his prison cell. He remained stoic, sitting on a wooden chair, staring at the iron bars.

The hooded woman who had spoken to him after the trial arrived. The guard allowed her to enter the cell. She pulled up a chair and sat down in front of Lief, removing her hood. Reika smiled; her hair arranged in the ponytail she had always worn when working in Carthage.

"How are you holding up?" She asked.

"I haven't been here long enough to tell you yet," Lief said. "But if you were to force me an answer, I am alright considering where I am."

Reika crossed her arms and her legs, sitting back in the chair.

"What is your plan once you leave prison? Still more training under Zaius?"

Lief casually sat back, letting his head hang comfortably back. "Yes, that plan hasn't changed. Is that all you came for?"

"No, I want to thank you for helping us."

Lief straightened. "You are very welcome." They continued to chat for a few minutes before Reika had to depart.

Two days later, Junayd awoke once again to a beautiful morning. His parents were already awake, going about their usual business. Junayd decided to start on his work early too. "Another day. Nice to be back at work again." He made his way over to the small field to tend to the fruit and vegetables.

At least an hour into his work, he heard footsteps approaching.

"Good morning, young man..." a voice said. Gorvenal approached, a small, hooded figure with him. It was the same woman from the court room. She did not speak, at first. Junayd had been confused by her appearance at the court, but with the light now falling on her skin, he knew it was Reika.

"I am just going to the market for moment," Gorvenal said to Reika. "Enjoy the rest of your day." The woman, who still had her hood, nodded. Gorvenal left the town. Junayd just stared at the woman. "So... how long have you been an apprentice to Gorvenal?"

"I'm not. He brought me here to have a chat," the woman answered. Reika's voice sounded *older*. He paused, concealed his smile, Reika was laying on the performance thick, the pitch was contrived. "Hehe. You are sure your voice is that deep? Some your age might have a voice like that but not you. You can remove your hood. There's no need to hide."

"Perhaps I just have a deep voice for my age?"

"True, but not yours, I can tell it isn't your natural one, Reika." The young woman sighed, then pulled her hood away.

"The next time you intend to disguise yourself, it might behove

415

you to wear different coloured robes to your brother," Junayd said critically. "At least you are wearing shoes still." She merely smiled back at him.

"Nice to see you again," Junayd continued. "The last I saw you was in the court room corridor."

Reika scratched her head. She resumed her regular pitch of voice. "The curse has been destroyed, once and for all. I couldn't have found the Anodyne Stone if it were not for you and our friends. I needed a little time away, to discuss my... arrangements."

Junayd crossed his arms. "Which would be?"

"Kenzuo will continue his work as Visiert. He is wielding Luniram right now."

"What about you?"

"Back to a normal life now. At least I'll have a home again. Although, we need to be prepared for another threat, should it arise."

"Well let's hope that won't be too soon."

Reika then turned to observe Naomi, Junayd's mother, working in the field. Her husband, Avi, was returning from his travels. The two embraced each other in the distance. Junayd also looked in the same direction as Reika and suddenly was struck by an old thought.

"Reika, I didn't have this chance before. But our quest is done so... Marriage still on the table?"

Reika grinned. "Yes."

Ignatius arrived with Mark, Andrea, Melito, and Tabitha accompanying him. Ignatius stopped once he drew close. "I thought I'd find you here, Reika. It's been a while. You really need to stop disappearing when I need to speak to you," Reika blushed, laughing awkwardly.

"King Tertullian has provided you with the choice to return to his service or live elsewhere. You are free, the choice is yours alone."

Reika didn't say a word. Junayd held out his hand and Reika clutched it.

Ignatius hadn't seen this coming. Mark raised his eyebrows.

"Oh, so that's what you want? Young man, Junayd, is it? You'd better take care of her, but I give you, my blessing."

"I thank you, Mark. I'll try to." The husky gave Junayd a pat on the head. "Smart lad."

Ignatius also smiled. "Get married in the castle, I say. Why not let your friends have the chance to see it? It's a solemn occasion and not to be taken lightly."

Reika saw the villagers gathering behind Ignatius. Some children were eyeing her from a distance, their parents also watching her. She remembered how she'd transformed into a weredragon the first night she slept in Caledonia. Shame filled her instantly. Jaser approached Reika and held out his hand, the mother watching in anticipation. Reika locked her eyes with his. She realised it was the same boy she'd nearly killed.

"I remember you," he said, "You transformed into that monster. Is it coming back?"

"I was that creature but not anymore." She gave the boy a gentle hug, reassuring him that she did not intend to harm him, a tear forming in her eye. The parents came to her.

"Sorry for the horrors I wreaked upon your village," Reika said. "I wasn't myself, but that does not excuse what I did." The villagers, with one accord, all walked over, murmuring a warm welcome. One of them named Sayid who was a gruff and middle-aged man with a beard and no hair, approached.

"A young man told us you were safe to approach," he said. "Now we've witnessed your change, we know his words to be true."

Reika saw Zane behind the crowd. "Did he?" Reika said curiously. The crowd parted, allowing her through to talk to Zane. Junayd followed after her. The three exchanged friendly hugs, returning to Junayd's tent.

~

"You're alright... Rian told us you were recovering," Reika said.

"He did and I was, the price one pays for being able to bend time. I'm glad you both are still alive." There was a brief interval where nothing was said. They had been through too much for easy words.

"What did you say to them?" Reika said, now that the three were away from prying eyes.

"Nothing, except to alert them your return. They were very nervous, especially the mothers. I told them they would be perfectly fine and to trust me." Zane sat on the floor. "I also had a little business to take care of."

"What would that be?" Junayd asked.

Zane smiled. "Well, I knew I couldn't prevent the Anodyne Stone from being stolen. Reika and I had a conversation regarding this. Afterwards, I thought about the weredragons. They went missing yet reappeared in Somnium Carcerum. There is a reason for this. All the individuals who became weredragons, they have been recovered. Their minds have been restored. All by me."

"I thought their minds were gone forever. They became tentorians..." Reika said.

"Galeru has the ability to restore a person's mind in Somnium Carcerum and reverse their transformation, the problem is that..."

"They were sealed away where Gorvenal and Galeru couldn't get to them!" Reika said, cottoning on.

"I could not," Gorvenal said, striding into the tent. "That is still true. Zane visited me, requesting that Galeru restored the people who had become weredragons."

"I and Rian went back in time after the final battle, once I had recovered. The reason the weredragons 'disappeared' was they were banished to Somnium Carcerum physically by us. They would eventually try to escape when Destrian summoned them to himself so their invasion could start."

Reika thought for a few minutes. "The weredragons you took care of but what of the people."

"Rescued them with Galeru's assistance," Zane replied. "He travelled with us. The minds of the people who vanished and became tentorians we managed to track. Galeru reversed the effects, and he sealed their minds safely away inside Verwandeln, leaving me to bring them back to their own times. Their bodies thanks to the effect of the Stone were regenerated in the present, at the very places where the Rasgar was performed on them. Even the ones slain by us, their human host's bodies were restored by the Stone. That is why the curse was treated as a myth or the sightings were rare; it's as if it never happened to those families."

"I'm glad they are ok," Reika said. "I have to thank you and Junayd for helping me be rid of the curse."

Junayd beamed back at Reika in silence.

"I am happy to assist you, Reika. Now, I must return to the farm, it's time to resume my duties there," Zane said.

"Before you do Zane, would you be willing to attend our wedding?" Junayd asked.

Zane stopped in his tracks. "I think I can spare some time," he said. "In fact, I think I have all the time in the world to spare."

Preparations were made for the wedding at Carthage, and many in the country gathered to the wedding hosted in the courtyard of the citadel. Mark was watching from the reception along with Andrea as Junayd and Reika stood in front of each other, holding each other's hands.

Reika had let her hair down with her bangs pulled back, wearing a white gown embroidered with flowery patterns. Her arms were covered by bell curve sleeves. Her soon-to-be husband wore rather dark regal robes that held blue and red stripes, held by a white cummerbund. His hair, in a rare turn of events, had been well combed, leaving a parting on the left top of the head.

At the right moment, he initiated the kiss and she reciprocated. It was very gentle but no less impactful, as many clapped and cheered. The two walked down the aisle, both stepping inside the carriage that was waiting for them. Ignatius smiled at Reika as she stared out of the carriage window, indicating that Reika was welcome to return any time she pleased.

~

Melito and Tabitha began the plan to rebuild Entella. Tabitha herself went to find out if any metazoans had spread across Perusia. She started in Carthage, asking Tertullian if there were any inhabitants from Entella that had settled in his kingdom.

"Obviously me, but I have already got a kingdom here. My son will be set to rule when the time comes. Aside from Reme, there were also towns folk on the northern coastline who settled in Iridum. Unfortunately, they were raided ten years ago a while back, so I am afraid that some of the Entellans maybe lost."

Tabitha was a little disheartened. "Will the few remaining be willing to go home?"

"That is up to them, I trust Melito will never betray me. Let me gather them here and I will talk with them. Go to Caledonia. Irenaeus will point you in the right direction."

Tabitha obeyed. She boarded the *Coeptus* and made her way to Caledonia. She spoke with Irenaeus, and he directed her to the library. A book caught her eye and she stared at the title in gold writing: "Chronicle of the Lost Nation". It began with the destruction of Entella and the diaspora of the people that occurred. It wasn't clear on the locations of the Entellans, except for one vague comment on those known to the people as "Dwellers of the Mountain Valley" who came into Caledonia two weeks after the attack.

The metazoans that came to Caledonia were in the mountainous region near the very castle that Tabitha had passed through previously on their journey. Soon after, Tabitha made her way to the citadel. She explained her purpose to the Sultan, and shortly after, he sent her away with a company of five guards to the mountains. They found nothing on the mountains themselves, but there was a small mountain pass.

The company finally made it through the pass to the village, finding an open valley. Unless one was to examine it from the air, it was well hidden by the heights of the mountains surrounding it. The village had stone buildings that matched the colour of the mountains, making it difficult to make them out from among the various rock formations that lay scattered around the area.

Tabitha and the soldiers made their way down to the village safely along a narrow path that had been worn by countless footsteps over the years. Once in the village, they had a chance to examine it up close. The buildings were decently maintained. As they approached, some of the inhabitants left their houses; all of them were metazoans. There were various species of primates, some squirrels, and a few rabbits.

Tabitha stepped forward; the other guards remained where they were. "Hi there."

A rotund orangutan with grey hair on his head stepped out of his hut. She recognised Juste. "Hi indeed, but who might you be?" He stared closely at the young tamarin. His eyes widened. "You! Good to see you, poppet." He went over to her, and they both hugged each other. "How are those arrows holding out my dear?"

"They work like a treat."

Tabitha went through the village, telling all that Welk was now dead and it was safe to return to Entella. Some of the villagers were a little apprehensive about returning.

"Melito felled the Scorpion King. He is, as we speak, at the ruins of the castle already. He needs many great men to help rebuild it. He wants to bring this diaspora to an end. Who wants to go home?"

Juste scratched his chin. "I think we shall consider your point. You heard the lady, let's follow her..." He paused for a moment. "Are you escorting us? How are we getting there?"

One of guards approached and took off his helmet, revealing himself to be a lemur. Unbeknownst to Tabitha, this lemur was Cyril. He had climbed onto Reika's back when he was just a young boy. Now, he was a man.

"There is an airship back at the citadel ready to go. It will take us straight to Entella. I am prepared for the trip if it means being home again on our little island. Who is with Tabitha on this?"

The primates murmured amongst themselves. "We are prepared to go from here. If the king has truly returned, we shall follow him."

Tabitha grinned and fist pumped the air. "What are we waiting for? Onwards!"

Melito was still at the Entellan ruins along with two guards from Carthage. One was a mandrill named Soren and one a baboon named Liam. They journeyed inside the ruin and passed the desolate throne room to a far-off corridor.

"What of the builders, your majesty?" Soren asked.

"They are on their way," Melito said. "Tabitha is getting them along with the other subjects."

"My mother said this day would come, your majesty. She would have loved to have seen this place being restored!" Liam added.

A small chamber had been sealed. Melito saw a small marking resembling a red banana cluster. Placing his hand on it, a crack appeared in the wall and like a door, a stone section that was four feet higher than him opened. He discovered a small room with chests that hadn't been opened for years, filthy and coated in dust and cobwebs.

Soren examined one of the chests in the corner of the room. He lifted the lid carefully and looked inside. The chest was loaded with coins, rubies, emeralds, and diamonds. "There is a lot of treasure here. Welk didn't take the spoils, I see." Melito came over to the chest. "Some of this may have to go. We need much stone and wood to rebuild the castle. The vault here is enough to cover the cost."

Liam picked up some of the coins in his hands, letting them slip back into the treasure chest. "Was this tribute to King Julius and the others before him? To the many kings of old?" He said.

"Yes, sealed off. Only kings and their heirs can access this vault." Melito then sighed. "If it is necessary to spend this to restore the kingdom, then so be it."

Liam and Soren both closed the chest, lifting it together. Melito was about to help when the other two kindly spoke. "Allow us, your majesty, we'll bring it up." Melito backed away. "Be careful with it."

Melito led the two servants into the throne room. He heard the sound of an airship in the distance. He went through the corridor to the west of the throne room, the same corridor where Junayd and Reika had helped the people of Entella to the boats. This time, The *Coeptus could* be seen. it landed in the water near the dock gracefully.

Tabitha waved from the *Coeptus'* bow, grinning. "Hey your majesty! I brought a present!" She called playfully. Freshly made boarding planks were lowered onto the deck, courtesy of Triterrain Airyard. The villagers made their way off the vessel gently.

Tabitha leapt off the bow, landing on the dock. "There's more to come, Melito, a few more trips. Here's your first lot for now."

"Any builders among them?"

"Yep, they are just gathering their supplies, hopefully they won't take too long."

Sure enough, some of the bigger apes climbed off the ship, one gorilla named Ambrose who was accompanied by chimpanzees, orangutans, and bonobos, five of each, all carrying their own bags, presumably their own tools for construction.

"Awaiting your orders, sir," Ambrose said in a gruff voice.

"For now, get yourselves settled," Melito said. "Some of the vault's treasure will need to be sold off so we can rebuild."

"Righto, your majesty." They all set off to the citadel. Many villagers looked back at the *Coeptus*. The young adults shed tears, some happy to return, others upset by the state their home was in.

There was some glimmer of hope in their minds that Melito would pave the way for Entella to return to its former glory.

Outside of Bahaduro, there was a stone house like the ones seen in Carthage's southern villages, though bigger in scale. This house was for newlywed couples as temporary accommodation. Junayd and Reika were sitting in their wedding clothes by the fireplace. Junayd poked the coals with a fire iron just to make sure the wood kept burning as Reika rested. She was happy, although something was on her mind as she stared at the window to her left. Junayd took notice.

"Something wrong?"

"No, I am thinking I am going to miss being at the citadel, my friends mostly.

Still, I'm happy here with you."

Junayd rested the fire iron next to the right of the fireplace, ensuring he kept it away from the flames so that he wouldn't burn himself the next time he held it. "You can visit them if you like, Reika. Even the kids could come along. Also..." Junayd continued. "It would be nice to introduce me to some of your other friends, the ones who I haven't been on a journey with."

"Sure, I'll be happy to."

"Here's to a new life," Junayd said as he and Reika each raised a chalice filled with wine. Both of them took a sip from the chalices and placed them on the oak tables. They remained sober throughout the night as they retired to their quarters.

710 A.E.B

A few months after their wedding, Junayd and Reika sat once again on Mt Carthage, Reika holding Junayd in a warm embrace. Melito and Tabitha had taken a break from rebuilding Entella to attend the wedding, as well as at this time. Zane and the others were there too. Rian had a faint smile on his face. Zane looked to his left, catching Rian's smile from the corner of his eye.

"Reminds you of her, Rian?" He asked.

"Yes, we watched the sunset often. I wish them a long happy life, same with you and your spouse. I hope you continue to cherish Emeline as well."

Zane nodded back. "You bet I will."

Berinon said nothing, but his expression matched Rian's.

Reika leaned her head on Junayd's shoulder. Her ponytail tickled him. Her eyes were closed, content and happy. She placed her hand on her belly, with Junayd looking at it. He beamed at the sight, knowing a child was on the way, his own child. Whether the child would be a boy or a girl, he would have to wait to find out. He didn't care which it is, so long as he and Reika raised the kid well. Reika reopened her eyes and stared off into the distance at the beautiful sunset. It wasn't the sunset that was most beautiful to Reika, however. It was the moon in the night sky. She could finally bask in its light without fear.

The curse was gone, she was free.

About the Author

A self-proclaimed movie and video game buff, Jake can often be found diving into immersive virtual worlds and sometimes listening to a book on Audible or reading it.

When he's not glued to a screen, Jake enjoys exploring the outdoors and taking long walks by the sea. A fan of Star Trek and Tolkien's works. Jake's love for science fiction and fantasy is also evident in his writing and storytelling.

When writing, you can find Jake in his room at home or in the hotel room with the noise of the sea, watching the passing waves and boats. When not writing, his two other passions are watching ice hockey and eating.

Printed in Dunstable, United Kingdom